# The Distant Light Within

## Jeff Bagby

Cover Design: Caleb Bagby
Cover Illustration: Jeff Bagby

Copyright © 2017 Jeffrey K. Bagby
All rights reserved.
ISBN: 978-0-9985717-0-6

To love the one

The solitary sheep lost in the wilderness,
The stone cast aside in the builder's trade,
The single penny missing in the home,
The lone ship on the sea,
indistinguishable from the twin safe at home.
The one is the delight of His heart.

Strength we could never endure.
Love we could never return.
Zeal we could never express.
The relentless love of a savior.

*excerpt from "Relentless"*
*by Veronica Bagby*

# Chapter 1

## The AD Isaacson Galleries, Atlanta

"Fifteen."

Stella motioned to Andrew on her way across the room. The night's goal was twenty-three, but they were on pace to sell thirty-one paintings. The mental spreadsheet displayed a net profit of $645,000, thirteen percent higher than the last show even with the higher commission rate for her. Now Stella had her sights set on the buyer from Orion Industries and closed in on the prey. Orion had a generous art budget and the buyer had the reputation for paying market price or better for works by favored artists. His presence here was proof to Stella that the last seven months attempting to garner the owner's interest in AD Isaacson had been a decided success. It wasn't enough to squeeze the price of a painting out of him now. She wanted him to embrace the artist. Develop an affection for the person behind the art, and become a collector. The buyer's preoccupation with the roast pig distracted him from noticing the confident gait of the approaching hunter.

Andrew's eyes trailed after Stella as she closed in. Watching her work was always more enjoyable than enduring the conversations with the endless stream of elite persona drunk on style. The majority came to these shows to strike a pose and make culturally appropriate comments concerning the art on display and the patrons in attendance. The threesome that wore identical clothes and makeup was the unexpected curiosity at this show. Their light green hair weirdly worked with the blue suits. It was clever how they said everything in sync. That must have taken some practice.

Andrew spent most of the evening fabricating comments when asked by prospective buyers about the art for sale. He tried to be consistent, but it was hard to keep track. The 36"x48" oil on canvas "Man Sipping Coffee", for example, could not have been executed simply because the model was willing and had an earthy look to him. For Andrew, the meanings grew more outlandish as the evening wore on. He thought he had crossed the line when he ventured that the woman in "Pier 17" was actually his mother.

Eventually, he escaped to his office and read email to occupy his time. Stella, on the other hand, knew who the buyers were and she worked them systematically for three hours. To the collectors, Stella lived to fulfill their every desire. He wondered if the art aficionados realized they could say no to her.

Andrew strolled back into the great room and stood near his largest piece, "Economies of Scale". The show had been very well attended. A good number of the money people here were, in fact, leaders of industry or the stewards of large estates. How Stella was able to make connections with so many incredibly rich people consistently baffled Andrew.

One key to that success was Dianne Hoestedtler. The deep, nicotine-enhanced voice came from across the room and wafted into everyone's conversation. The crowd of loitering people parted as the diva moved toward Andrew. He braced himself for the female many regarded as the foremost socialite in the Eastern United States. Ms. Hoestedtler sparkled as she walked. She liked to wear as much of her diamond collection as possible to each social function. This occasion was no different, but her black dress was elegant and simple for a change.

She was old money from Germany and subsequently Boston. It was sketchy how the family's fortune had been made, but Madam Dianne was committed to spending and flaunting it. The spending part was what Stella liked best. Of all the patrons and collectors Stella enlisted, Ms. Hoestedtler bought more and encouraged her friends to purchase more art than any other person. When Stella pulled her in, the company's profits took off to heights they had scarcely dreamed about. This was the first show Dianne had attended in several months. Things were looking up for AD Isaacson.

"Andrew, you have outdone yourself this time," she effused loudly for those nearby to hear.

"Madam Hoestedtler, you flatter me once again."

Andrew took her gloved hand and kissed it.

"I'm not one for flattery. Your work is the best I've seen. It explodes with emotion and energy. The use of color is more daring than all your previous work."

He could tell by the things she said that Stella had gotten to her first. Madam Dianne was one of the most influential persons in the fine art world, but she still needed coaching to understand why she liked an artist's paintings. Stella had perceived this early in their relationship and it became a secret ritual at every show Dianne attended to find the socialite and let her know what to focus on.

"Thank you Madam, you are insightful as always about my work. Will you be staying?"

"No, dear, I must run. There is a charity event for which I am already late, but I couldn't leave without saying hello to my favorite artist."

"I'm so glad you did. Thank you for coming tonight."

"Goodnight dear. Keep up the lovely work. I'm building a new house in the south of France that will have a lot of bare walls, so you need to get busy."

"You have my word. Goodnight."

He smiled and bowed slightly as she flowed through the room toward the door. Andrew almost cringed to think how good he had become at sucking up. He had improved dramatically over the first time Miss Dianne had cornered him without Stella. Andrew had been cocky, but still a bit naive. When he learned enough to pass the Dianne test, he realized he could handle most anything. Stella stepped in to save him that first time, but since then Andrew had flown solo. Stella caught his eye as he turned away and she gave him an approving look.

After another hour of mixing with guests and manufacturing conversation, Andrew noticed the crowd had thinned. He was anxious to leave, but not necessarily looking forward to retiring to a large empty house. The end of the art show was simply the beginning of the night for most of the attendees. As a rule, the parties would jump from club to club and last until dawn. The folks who remained at the gallery were the older set destined to simply go home after the show. The caterers cleaned up the serving table and the beverages were almost gone. Andrew motioned to Stella that he was headed home and he would call her tomorrow. How she gathered all of that from his sign language only they knew. Andrew slipped out the door to the office wing and walked down the dimly lit corridor to the executive elevator. Two floors below was the parking garage.

Andrew popped the door locks and eased into the front seat. He enjoyed driving, even in this city. Andrew pulled out onto Marietta Street and headed east, turning on the radio to the sports station to catch the end of the Braves game. As long has he stayed north of Midtown, he would miss all the club traffic. He breathed deeply and loosened his tie as he sped up the entrance ramp of Interstate 85.

The twenty-minute drive gave him a chance to reset his mind. It took almost the entire trip anymore. Andrew felt a growing void in his life that even the money couldn't fill. His wife and son had left him years ago, and his current girlfriend knew her limited place in his life. She busied herself by spending as much of his money as she could get her hands on. At least she won't be home when he gets there, he thought to himself. It's about time to move her out.

His career and the people he associated with had not made much room for many deep personal relationships. Until recently, he didn't fight it very hard. Even the tired line about how others would kill to have his life didn't help anymore. Unfortunately, the positives were easy to see. He lived the famous life and made so much money he couldn't think of enough ways to spend it all. No one was going to pity him. He was sure of that.

He had attracted fame in a faddish sort of way. Andrew was the young, up and coming artist and Stella managed his business and marketed his image. He sincerely believed she was devoted to him and his work, but as the business grew, their relationship devolved into a professional arrangement totally centered on money. Stella informed Andrew that he was truly brilliant as an artist, but he was too slow. His output was weak and she was constantly on his back, trying to step up his production. After several shouting matches and a fair amount of broken furniture, Stella and Andrew devised a plan. She would continue to market AD Isaacson as an American treasure and Andrew would find and disciple a number of artists to enhance production in the name of AD Isaacson. The 50-50 partnership would make them both rich, Andrew was sure. Stella had a priceless gift in modern-day America; the ability to market a product no matter how good, bad or mediocre.

The stable of artists was up to seven. Andrew was certain seven was the limit. There is a fine line between cranking out as much art as possible and providing so much product that the market becomes saturated. He found a desirable balance and the business grew by leaps and bounds.

Unfortunately, Andrew finally had to admit he was simply a prostitute. There was no heart to what the company produced for "Stella, Inc." It was only for the money, and he was sure he'd leave it when something better came along. On the bright side, at least this type of prostitution didn't result in sexually transmitted diseases.

As he neared his upscale community, Andrew slowed down hoping an idea other than going home would pop into his head. The only thing that came to him, the only thing that ever came to him, was to go to his regular dive in the middle of Overlook. Typical trendy, young, rich clientele in the heart of the trendy, young, rich part of town, etc. Andrew liked how Fanny mixed the drinks though. He liked her too. She did not fit in to the young, rich, pretty thing that gripped this area of town. How she kept a job at Trudy's he would never know. Fanny was a holdover from a bygone era when bartenders and hairdressers went into the business because interacting and listening to customers was part of the job. Middle-aged and sarcastic, she always made him laugh. As he pulled into the parking lot, he told himself it would only be for one drink.

The restaurant was full even at this hour. Andrew headed for the bar. He motioned for Benny and sat at the end.
"Hi, Benny. Same ole. Hey, is Fanny here?"
"Yes and no. She is here, but she is not happy," Benny said in his thick Slavic accent.
"Could you tell her I'm here?"
"Sure. Here you go." Benny handed him a Bourbon whiskey with ice.
The bar had begun serving TexMex a few months ago and the smell of fajitas was strong. Not quite strong enough to make him want to order anything though. One drink turned into three. A couple of acquaintances noticed him and sat for small talk. They were headed north to a new dance club. No thanks. That old basketball injury has been acting up.
Thirty minutes went by and Fanny didn't come out. Oh well, must be an off night, he thought. He pulled a few bills out to pay his tab and got up to leave.
"Where you goin', pretty boy?"
He looked up to see Fanny gliding his way, her hips made the ankle length skirt on them sway to the background music.
"I'm leaving. Tired of waiting."
"Sit down, you're not going anywhere."
"But I've already paid my bill."
"Next one's on the house. It's your reward for waiting so long."
"Hey, now you're onto something." Andrew sat back down.
Fanny began waiting on other customers as she talked with Andrew. She could carry on a conversation with someone at the other end of the bar without raising her voice. Andrew considered that a peculiar talent. It required that everyone hear your business, however.
"What are you doing here? I thought you had one of your artsy fartsy's tonight."
"I did. Went pretty well, too. When are you going to come? It's good art, cheap." Andrew smiled and winked.

"I'll buy one if it's me you're painting."

"You're on. When can you come over to model?"

"Paint me here at Trudy's. The real me. I can lie out on the bar. Just make sure you use a big canvas to get all of me." She slid her hands down her curves for emphasis.

Andrew tipped his glass to her.

"So, were you back there counting the money?"

Fanny bristled a bit. She enjoyed talking about herself, to a point.

"I wish. Had a phone call. Those heavy breathers are wearing me out."

"Hobbies are good."

Fanny rewiped a glass that was already clean.

Short silence. "I came in here so you could cheer ME up."

Fanny stole a quick look at Andrew. Not the happiest of looks. "Sorry, pal. Wrong night. What? Poor little rich boy doesn't like his life?" Her smile had the bite of a cracking whip.

"That hurts a sensitive artist like myself. I'll remind you, it's not easy being me…. Need a listening ear?"

"No, it'll pass. It always does." Fanny heaved a sigh. "Would it be too much to wish all men dead?"

"That's a pretty tall order. I'm nice aren't I?"

"Occasionally, but you're all the same."

"Man trouble?"

"Ex-man trouble actually."

"And to think that I didn't even know you were married. I would have gotten you a nice wedding gift."

"Something in a size .357 please."

"How could somebody up and leave you like that?"

"Scumbag didn't want to leave; I kicked him to the curb because he was good for nothing. I never met a more worthless lump of flesh in all my days."

"What? Was he an artist?"

"Worse. A preacher."

Andrew burst out laughing. "That's great! A bartender married to a preacher! Isn't that an automatic bolt of lightning? The blue hairs must have been keeling over in the center aisle."

"I didn't take up 'tending until well after I ran him off. Had to pay the rent somehow. The church sure wasn't going to support me. Believe it or not, I was a good religious wife, then I found him laying hands on one of the secretaries. I thought the whole ordeal would ruin him, but he's at it again somewhere in Arkansas."

"You decided against hunting him down?"

Fanny enjoyed the thought for a moment, but embraced reality. "Naw.
He's not worth it. I can't complain, really. I'm better off without him, and I
kinda like what I do now. You'd laugh, but bartending is a lot like working
in a church. Some people come in just to socialize and others come in to
find a solution to their problems. The hours are a little more convenient for
folks, too."
"You're not going to start wearing a funky collar, are you?"
"No, but I will expect an offering before you leave."
"I thought this one was on the house," he demanded.
Andrew checked his watch. The alcohol was starting to wear on him.
"I'd better go. I've got a heavy schedule tomorrow. Sleep late, then lay
around all day."
"Go easy son. You're burning the candle at both ends."
"Point taken. Thanks for the good word, Pastor."
Andrew got up, but he was weaving. He knew driving would be risky.
Fanny watched him and decided he was not fit to drive.
"Andrew, sit down. I'll call you a cab."
"Absolutely not. I'm not leaving my car in this parking lot all night."
"Well you aren't driving."
"What? I'll be fine. I own the road."
"I get off pretty soon. Just wait twenty more minutes and I'll drive you
home myself."
Andrew shot her a look. "You serious?"
Although they had been friendly for nearly two years, he couldn't recall
Fanny making a gesture like that before.
"Sure. Are you afraid I'll wreck that piece of junk you drive?"
"Never. That's very sweet and thoughtful of you, but I don't know if I'll
last twenty more minutes. The day is catching up to me."
"Okay. Let me tell Benny I'm leaving." Fanny walked toward the kitchen.
Andrew was pleasantly surprised. He secretly allowed that part of his good
feeling was due to the idea that someone showed friendly concern for him.
"Can you walk?"
"No, carry me."
"Get up and shut up."
"If I didn't have alcohol on my breath, I'd kiss you."
When they got to the car, Andrew popped the locks and gave the keys to
Fanny.
"How do I get to your house?"
"Turn right and look for the search lights in the sky."
"Typically understated. Is your house chrome plated also? Be serious. I
don't want to drive around all night."
"GPS will get us there. Just turn on the key and hit that button."

He pointed to a 13cm screen in the center of the dashboard. When Fanny touched the power button, it illuminated and a woman's voice beckoned for commands from the user.

"It's voice activated. Tell it to give you directions home."

Fanny looked at Andrew for a minute. "You rich boys kill me. I shouldn't be giving you a ride home. You probably have a wad of servants who can come get you."

"That's just it. I don't have servants or any employees that will stay more than six months. Gadgets fill the void left by fleeing personal assistants."

Fanny leaned over to the device as if it was hard of hearing.

"Give me directions to Andrew's house."

"A little louder please, the couple on the other side of the parking lot didn't hear you."

The computer interrupted with a specific list of directions from their present location.

"Wait. How did it know we are at Trudy's?"

"Satellite. We're being watched."

"Does it drive itself, too?"

"Yes, but how would I explain that to a police officer?"

The car eased out on to the avenue. One positive about the middle of the night was that traffic was relatively light.

Andrew emptied the mailbox as Fanny drove through the gates to his home and parked in the circle drive. It was supposed to be mild overnight so Andrew left the car outside. The timer on the exterior and interior lights made the 6,500 square foot house seem inviting, but there was nobody home. Each time Andrew arrived home after dark, he reminded himself that he needed to find a replacement for Doris the housekeeper. She was the third one in the past year to leave abruptly. The first two left due to Andrew's girlfriends. His money was a drug to his lovers and one of the side effects was it made them unnaturally abusive to hired help. Andrew wasn't around often enough to defend the employees and he didn't pay them wages commiserate with the combative environment. Doris, however, had fared surprisingly well, but a family matter drew her away to another state.

"Fanny, can you stay a while?"

"Yeah, sure. Actually, I'm not sure how I would get anywhere without taking your car."

"Are you hungry? There are a few things in the fridge."

Andrew threw his briefcase on the center island in the kitchen and pulled out some prepared food and fresh fruit he had bought for himself. As Fanny busied herself with that, he leafed through the sizable stack of marketing ploys and clothing catalogs. One item was a handwritten card from the International Orphan and Refugee Relief Fund thanking him for his willingness to participate in their annual auction. He'd check on that later.

"Feel free to look around. If you want to kick back, the media room is through there." He pointed toward a doorway across the dining area.

"Don't you want to hit the rack? You seemed pretty beat at the bar."

"I guess I got my second wind."

"So show me around," Fanny said as she crunched an apple. "I like nosing around people's houses." Fanny hesitated for a minute. "Do you live alone or are we going to surprise someone?"

"Well… technically, I live alone now."

Fanny decided to take that at face value and let it drop.

Andrew took her down the hall to the great room, the media room and the upstairs. He pointed out the artwork hanging on the walls and sculpture all through the house. Most were pieces by Andrew's friends he acquired by bartering his own paintings as payment.

At last, he led her out the back door and across the yard to the studio. The studio was almost a scaled down version of the main house. All the exterior details were the same style, but when they went inside, it was mostly a large open space. The walls were sheer with transom windows near the 17 foot ceiling. Andrew said it was to accommodate his work on large format paintings. An elaborate pulley system was in place for the same reason. It smelled like paint thinner and oil paint. The walls were relatively clean, but the concrete floor was forever stained with colors from a myriad of past works in progress.

"I like this. Do you spend much time out here?"

"As much as I can. You'd think my job wouldn't get in the way of spending time here, but somehow it does."

"You're an artist, but you don't paint?"

"Crazy, huh?"

"So paint."

"Paint what?"

"Me."

"Sounds great. When do you want to do it?"

Fanny turned back toward him from her review of a long forgotten unfinished canvas leaning against the wall.

"How 'bout now?"

Andrew looked at her to see if she was kidding.

"Really?"

"Yeah. I think I'm stuck here for the night so the least you could do is paint me."

Andrew wondered if he had the stamina to stay up the rest of the night.

"Why not. I've wanted to do it for some time." Andrew knew an opportunity like this would probably not happen again soon.

"Great. I'll go get something to drink while you get ready. Find me something to wear, too."

Fanny went back toward the house and Andrew walked over to the stacks of prepared canvases. He stretched his own and made a habit of having ten to fifteen ready at any one time. They ranged from three feet by five feet up to ten feet square. He didn't like doing miniatures and he typically only prepared for mural size works when he received a specific commission. He hoisted a 40"x72" canvas onto his primary easel. Andrew pulled out his acrylic colors because he imagined that the session would be a one-time shot. He left the studio and went into the house. His costumes were stored in one of the bedrooms upstairs. All the stories Andrew heard about artists' studios burning down made him want to put his extensive costume collection in as safe a place as possible. He met Fanny on the way.

"Ready?"

"Just about. Come upstairs with me and try some clothes on."

"Awesome."

"I'd like to do something along the lines of what we talked about this evening. I keep seeing you covered in gold and pouring a glass of wine over the head of a seeker. That would tie the past to your present - although in a little different way."

"Gold paint or gold coveralls? I get cold really easy you know."

"No, we'll drape you with some gold fabric, and I have a gold body suit in here somewhere also. Do you have to work tomorrow?"

"Not until 8 p.m."

"Perfect. Let's do it."

The next six hours were filled with prepping Fanny, getting the right props, positioning Fanny and applying paint to canvas. Andrew didn't have a bar for Fanny to lie on, but there was a grand piano in the great room. Perfect. Andrew himself modeled for the seeking soul receiving the splash of wine from Fanny's glass. Although he would spend considerable time painting her live, Andrew took numerous photos with his digital camera. The immediate acquisition of images made it possible to adjust lighting and props to perfect his composition, not to mention allowing him to be in the scene via a timer and a tripod. He would be able to refer to the photos long after the session this night.

Fanny proved to be an energetic model. Hours spent sitting still could be tiring even for veteran subjects. He got tired before she did though.

Andrew put his brushes down.

"Take a break?"

"Sure. How much longer do you want to go?" Fanny put the wine glass down and got off the piano.

"How about one more hour."

"Okay, but probably not much more than that. It's been fun, but I don't think I could do it every day. Bartending is looking better and better." Fanny walked over to the canvas and sized up the painting. Decent.

Fanny pulled the curtains back. "Sun's coming up. This is my first all-nighter in fifteen years. What should I tell Benny when he asks me if I spent the night with you?"

"Tell him the truth."

"Right. Yeah, Benny. I spent the night with him. Wine, paint, costumes, pretty boring stuff."

"Sounds about right."

"So what are you going to do with the painting?"

"I usually sell them through my friend's gallery."

"Do you make reproductions? I'd like a copy."

"I do if my friend thinks he can sell them. I can make a few special copies without too much trouble."

"Good. I'll take a dozen."

"Does that mean you like it?"

"I love it. Even if I didn't, how often does a person like me have their portrait painted? I'm going to put one up at the club."

"People will talk."

"That's how I make a living," Fanny said with a smile. "I'll be back in a minute." She went back to the house.

Andrew began cleaning up unnecessary props and equipment. He was going straight to bed after the final hour's work. Andrew was satisfied with the night's effort. This was one of the more intensive sessions he'd had in several years. He'd have to use Fanny again. Andrew wondered if she would accept money for her labors.

Fanny came into the studio with her things ready to go.

"Well, if you don't mind too much, I need to leave."

Andrew was almost relieved. "Is everything all right?"

"Yeah. It's fine. I called my daughter while I was inside the house and she needs me to come home."

"No problem. I'll be ready in just a few minutes."


"Where to, Miss?" Andrew had coffee and bagels waiting in the car.

"Can you drive?"

Andrew nodded. "I'm fine."

Fanny leaned over to the on-board computer. "1202 East Evans Road, please."

"Here, turn it on first." Andrew hit the buttons. "Now do it."

Fanny repeated herself and buckled in. "Let's go driver."

"It will be my pleasure." Andrew looked at the computer's response.

"Wow. You have quite a drive to work every evening."

"That's a fact. I can't afford to live in Fantasy Island near Trudy's."

As they pulled out into traffic, Andrew got nosier.

"How did you start working at Trudy's?"

"I worked for the former owner back when he ran a club over on the north side of town. That one was closer to where I live. He bought Trudy's and asked me to supervise the bartenders. Just never could pull up and move to this side of town."

"How old is your daughter?"

"She's twenty-five."

"Wow. Were you a teen mother?"

"Not really. We adopted Sarai from Korea when she was six. She stayed with me when my husband and I broke up. She's been overseas for three and a half years, but now she's back living with me. Sarai's been sick. I think she needed some moral support this morning."

Andrew yawned and swerved.

"Easy cowboy. You may be getting a little too old to party all night."

"I was never the all-night guy even in my youth."

"You did pretty good for a lightweight."

"Would you do it again?"

"You mean stay out all night?"

"No, model for me."

"Maybe."

"I'd make it worth your while."

"You don't have to do that."

"Hey, I know it's hard work. It deserves a fair wage. How does $500 a day sound."

"I'm free every night this week," she said enthusiastically. Her demeanor changed a bit. "What exactly would I have to do for that kind of money?"

"Nothing more than you did last night." Andrew enjoyed the idea of being generous with a friend. He didn't need it and Fanny did.

"I'm in. You'd better update your wardrobe."

The GPS hailed their arrival at Fanny's residence.

"Here we are. Thanks Fanny. Thanks for being a friend. I appreciate you watching out for me last night. The painting session was great. By the way, here's last night's wage." Andrew pulled five $100 bills out and handed them to Fanny.

Fanny's eyes widened slightly. She looked at Andrew and slowly pulled the money to her.

"Thanks." She smiled. "Who'd a known that the day would end the way it did?"

"I hear you. I hope your daughter gets better."

The thought broke Fanny out of her mindset. "Oh, yes. Gotta go. I'll see you soon." Fanny got out and hurried to the door. She glanced back and waved. Sarai met her at the door and looked out toward the driveway. He waved, but Sarai didn't see him.

"To the house." Andrew said to no one.

Andrew threw his keys on the kitchen counter and dialed the phone.

"Mitch, how you doin'? What is the IORRF?"

"IORRF? Did they call you?"

"Actually, they sent a card thanking me for taking part in their annual shindig. What have you gotten me into?"

"Oh, it's nothing really. They are on me constantly to provide original art for their auction and I figured you needed an outlet for some of your personal work. I hear that some substantial buyers actually attend the function. Besides, you can keep 10% of the sale price on anything you provide. Throw them a few bones. You never know, you might even feel good about helping a worthy cause. Listen, can we talk about this later on today? I am right in the middle of a sale."

"Oh, sure. Sorry for the interruption. Talk to you later."

Andrew was suddenly tired after talking to Mitch. Nothing that a shower and a few hours' sleep wouldn't fix. First, he walked out to his studio to review the night's work. The painting was good. He was satisfied, but Andrew couldn't get over how much better the expression was captured on one of the preliminary drawings he did. Fanny communicated compassion without pity or condescension, like one who had such things deep in her soul. He was honor bound to convey it in his depiction of her. It would probably take a few attempts, but Andrew assumed he'd do more than one painting of Fanny anyway. He'd look over the digital pictures and see if they helped at all. What a mess this studio was. Andrew promised to clean it up tomorrow.

# Chapter 2

The Excelsior Hotel, Atlanta

Andrew adjusted the black tie. Ever since he had one tailor-made, he actually liked wearing this suit. Andrew planned to simply send over several paintings that had been in storage. But, at the last minute, he decided to go to the auction. Maybe his presence would enhance sales. He could even throw in a few bids to jack up the prices. What the heck. If he accidentally outbid the crowd, he would be stuck with his own painting. Renee, his latest trophy girlfriend, already stated that she was busy all evening. He would have to go alone. Stiffing him on his show the other night and now this.

When he entered the meeting hall, he noticed people from all social segments. Obviously, many were folks that only traveled away from the mission field for this annual occasion. One middle-aged man wore an ill-fitting suit that was out of style in the 80's. His wife shopped at the same outlet mall. Andrew wondered if the new suit might have been a bit much. Oh well, some people were dressed up, such as several individuals Andrew recognized from the money crowd. This could get interesting. No complementary alcoholic beverages, however.

He'd make a note of everyone who bid and bought his paintings at the auction. They would receive a nice communiqué from Mitch. One or two could become collectors. Andrew summoned the knowledge he had gained from Stella as he scanned the crowd. The buyers were not hard to spot. He'd have to renew a few acquaintances tonight.

"Mr. Isaacson. Thank you for coming tonight."

Andrew turned to see a woman maybe in her late 30's walk toward him.

"It's my pleasure, Miss …"

"Bhaniel Tretechi. I am a member of the IORRF. The auction organizers allowed us to view the pieces on sale tonight, and I was very impressed by your work."

"Thank you. How did you know I am the artist?" He probably wouldn't hit on her. She was pleasant, in good physical shape, nice bone structure but she didn't pose like she wanted people to see her. It looked like she made the dress herself. He rated her in the mid 6's. And he was being kind. She will probably try to introduce me around to the prospective buyers. "I'd like to say that it's my own keen sense, but someone told me."
"Your accent. Where is it from?" Andrew glanced around the room as he talked with her.
"Africa. I was born and raised in the Congo."
"You speak English very nicely. Were you educated in the States?"
"No. The various preparatory schools I attended in my country taught a little English. I did spend two years living with a family in Minneapolis. Now, I enjoy coming to America so that I can practice speaking the language." Miss Tretechi studied Andrew for a moment.
"Mr. Isaacson, may I ask you a question?"
"Sure."
"What do your paintings mean?"
"They mean a thousand things to a thousand different people."
"What do they mean to you?"
The intensity of her attitude made him feel uncomfortable. He'd been asked similar questions innumerable times and it had never challenged him in this way. She gave no signs this was just small talk. Miss Tretechi was looking him in the eye and she wanted an answer. Andrew realized at that moment he had never revealed to anyone the true meaning behind his personal work. Some of it went deeper than "Man Sipping Coffee".
"You act like you really want to know."
"I do. And I have a valid reason."
"Most people don't actually want to hear the truth when they ask that question."
"I'm guessing even you don't know the whole truth behind your paintings Mr. Isaacson."
Andrew admired her energy. She wasn't taunting him, yet Ms. Tretechi wanted him to react.
"How are you inspired to paint?"
"I enjoy painting people that just happen to cross my path." Mostly true. The gavel rapped the podium and signaled the start of the auction.
"I'm sorry Mr. Isaacson, I am due back stage. Will you be here afterward?"
"Yes."
"Until then."
Miss Tretechi moved through the crowd smoothly. Andrew was impressed with her grace. He didn't particularly want to talk further with her, but kind of felt obligated now. He wasn't sure if he should be invigorated or concerned.

Andrew found a seat toward the back of the auditorium. He had registered as a representative of AD Isaacson so he didn't have to give away his identity when he picked up his bidding paddle. No sense in getting people all worked up for nothing. The couple to his right was all business. Both were immaculately dressed. This was the outing of the day. They spoke very little to each other, much like married couples who have been together for half a hundred years. The lady held the brochure and was still memorizing it as the first item was placed on the stage. The gentleman had his hat on his lap and was studying the people scurrying around with last minute chores as well as the potential foes he would encounter during the bidding. Andrew surmised they might need a little encouragement.

"Are you folks here for any particular works?"

"Yes and no. We came initially to look at the bronzes by Torre Jennings, but I am intrigued by the paintings by, uh," she looked at the brochure, "Andrew Isaacson."

Hello.

"Yes. That's why I came as well." Andrew brightened as he talked.

"Oh, really? Do you know the artist?"

"I am familiar with him, yes."

"How old is he? Is he about to die?"

Andrew smiled. "I hope not. He's only in his forties."

The lady was visibly disappointed.

"Don't worry about that, though. His work has doubled in price within the last three years."

Nice save, Andrew. I think I see the gleam in her eye again.

"That's good to know." She turned to see if her husband had caught that tidbit.

The auctioneer called for everyone's attention, and the bidding began on a three by five foot impressionism derivative. Nicely done, but not all that clever. They were just getting the crowd warmed up.

The event went well and went quickly. The auctioneer didn't wait around for indecisive people. If they weren't raising their paddles or calling in with a bid, then he moved on. Five of Andrew's paintings went for more than the target price which was good. The other three started out well, but faded at the end. No problems, it was for a good cause. The elderly couple almost bought one, but the price got too much for them. The wife was ready to go to the mat for it, but her husband didn't feel they had that kind of cash for an investment that might not pan out.

After the auction, three of the IORRF members spoke. Ms. Tretechi was the last to talk and her words still rang in his ears. As he rose from his seat, he admitted to himself how moving the speech had been. She illustrated such a compelling picture of the necessity for the citizens of the world to care for their needy. For the first time it was reasonable to believe that such actions made the society more … righteous. Was that the word she used? Ms. Tretechi talked of the numerous orphanages in the Democratic Republic of the Congo without governmental support. Although the arena was a prime opportunity for her to appeal to the attendees for further financial support, she made no plea. Hopefully, the auction would prove to be lucrative.

Andrew was a believer and now glad to be a part of her effort. He spotted her talking to a small group near the exit. The passion in her voice was the same whether she was speaking to a vast audience or a single listener. Andrew's attitude had changed during the speech. He was like a fan trying to get an autograph. He walked up and waited until there was a break in the conversation and the group thinned out.

"Your speech moved me."

"Thank you, Mr. Isaacson. How were you moved?"

"I came here a bit annoyed that I had to be a part of another fund raiser, but I am going away grateful and proud to be associated with the effort."

"Thank you. That's very satisfying to know." She paused. "Would you have time to talk before you leave? I honestly do want to know more about your work."

"Certainly, you are very busy tonight. There are probably crowds of people waiting to talk to you."

"Not at all. I want to hear your heart, and I may not have this opportunity again soon. We have the conference room next door set up with tables and refreshments. Please?"

"That's fine with me. I'd love to stay. But, don't hesitate to go when you have to."

"I was just going to say the same thing to you. Through those doors, please."

It could be fun. They were going to talk about his favorite subject. Him. Free food too.

They were met by a crowd of organization members and friends. As suspected, Bhaniel was surrounded. Andrew took the opportunity to fill a plate with food. He located a table on the edge of the room with a favorable view and a bit of obscurity. Bhaniel made her way through the food line, conversing all the way, and broke away toward Andrew's table.

"See that man in the gray jacket? He is the CEO of American Hydro, Inc. and he has come to the DRC four times in the last nine years. Not only is he dedicated to the orphanages, he is manufacturing water systems for villages in the country. It's revolutionizing the whole area."

"Impressive. I'm sure there is a great need for that."

"You'll have to forgive me. I should not assume you don't perceive the meaning of your own paintings."

"Forgiven." Andrew noted her remarkable skill at focusing her complete attention to someone at a moment's notice. Politicians were made or broken with the use of such a skill.

"So tell me. What do they mean?"

"Which one?"

"All of them, but most significantly the one of you and your father."

"There wasn't a father and son painting in the auction."

"No, I saw it on the web site. I usually do a bit of research on all of our contributors, and was fascinated by what I found on your site."

"It's not titled 'Dad and I'. How did you know it was a paternal painting?"

"Basic psychology. Original art is like most expressions. They bare the soul to the world."

"It's not my father. It's me. And my son."

Bhaniel readjusted her gaze on Andrew. She enjoyed the revelation.

"Of course, but that changes everything. Instead of the receiver, you are the giver."

"Of what?"

"All that you are. Your spirit."

"I don't think it worked. My son and I are not close. I've seen him very little since the divorce. I'm not even sure where he is now." Too much information.

"I'm sorry." She didn't look away.

"Not a problem. Maybe it will have a happy ending. Someday."

"I believe it will."

Andrew caught himself staring into Bhaniel's eyes, studying her face and the emotion behind it.

"Would it be too corny to say I would like to paint you?"

"I guess I have officially crossed your path." She smiled.

One hour turned into two, and finally their conversation was interrupted by vacuum cleaners and the rustling of busboys stacking chairs.

"Looks like we closed the place."

"Oh my. Forgive me for keeping you."

Bhaniel stood up.

"How long will you be in the States?"

"I'm leaving next week, but I'll be back in a few months. Why don't you go back with us?"

Andrew stared at her. She didn't seem to be embarrassed to ask such a crazy thing. "You mean to the DRC?"

"The orphanages can always use the help."

"I guess I had never really thought of doing something like that. Wouldn't I be in the way?"

"Not at all. Can you love children?"

Andrew felt awkward under the guileless woman's gaze. Smiling sheepishly, he said, "I came here this evening expecting to sell a few paintings and feel good about my small contribution. Now I've won a trip to Africa." He laughed.

"You are a generous, good man Mr. Isaacson. However, in my spirit, I believe that your presence with us and the perspective you will have when you leave, will affect the world – at least our part of it – in a new and dramatic way."

Her eyes belied knowledge and understanding of life that typically resides with aged people or individuals that have gone through and survived a great tribulation.

"You barely know me. What if I get over there and cause trouble? I'm just a city boy with no pioneer experience." The excuses were lame, but he was off balance.

"I'm sorry to be so direct, but I believe that you have not entered into all that you were created to be. You expose a bit of your soul in your paintings Mr. Isaacson. Even the sum of the paintings here tonight show me that you have a gift for understanding the heart of a matter and expressing important truths. You have crossed MY path Mr. Isaacson, and it is no accident. I realize I am proposing an unusual and dramatic idea. I truly wish we could spend more time together and develop a measure of trust, but unfortunately, I don't have the luxury of time right now. Who knows when we will meet again?"

The conversation had officially exceeded Andrew's comfort quotient. Ever the polite one, Andrew responded, "Can I give it some thought?"

"I'm leaving Wednesday. Please call me at this number – she handed him a card – by Tuesday. It is very difficult to send communications to our part of the DRC. Contacting me could take several days."

"If you later decide to join us, this is the number for my associate here in America. She will give you any information and help you might need. I must warn you, however. The political climate is not good. There is much unrest in our country. Our leader is an unpredictable and ruthless man, but" - she paused and looked down as if preparing to present a memorized anecdote – "Asafari Zuberi has the capacity to do what is right." She looked at him again. "Even so, if you are sure about joining us, time is of the essence."

By this time, they were at the entrance to the museum. The marble steps spread out before them to city streets lightly sprinkled with rain. The air was fresh and cool.

"Goodnight, Mr. Isaacson."

"Andrew."

"Goodnight, Andrew."

"Thank you."

"For what?"

"For helping me to see the value of authenticity."

"You value it because it is in you, Andrew."

Andrew didn't think anything fazed her.

"Can I give you a ride anywhere?"

"Thank you. I'm afraid I cannot leave yet. My assistant is inside finishing up auction details. I stay with her when I come to America."

"Very well. So long for now."

With that, Andrew shook her hand warmly, and walked down the steps. Andrew wasn't sure what had just happened. He marveled at her sincerity and dedication to her calling. It had certainly disarmed him. Could she have meant all that? Andrew had a hard time remembering when anyone had shown so much interest in him without an ulterior motive. She definitely intrigued him, but he didn't want to go to the edge of the world to paint her. Oh well, maybe he would see her again sometime. There was always the next auction. Andrew looked at her card again and slipped it into the front pocket of his suit.

# Chapter 3

Remington District, Atlanta

Toward the end of the week, Andrew drove to the Schuster Gallery. The owner, Mitch DeGuerre, was a friend from art school, and Andrew had been showing his personal work there for twelve years. Mitch purchased the gallery from the founder Evan Schuster, a fixture in the developing art community in 1975 Atlanta. Evan never married and his death at the age of 56 left several friends, but no heirs. Mitch was his lone employee at the time. Evan was not a gifted manager, which kept staff longevity at a minimum. Nobody seemed to want the gallery because Evan had developed other interests, and the gallery suffered. At the estate hearings, Mitch's only competitor for the gallery was another local art retailer trying to reduce the number of his rivals. He made a deal with the competitor and acquired the rights for the gallery from the estate. At the beginning, Mitch had big dreams to market his own work, but the customers didn't respond. Mitch had a good eye, but he never wanted to put in the time to develop his skills. After two lean years, his focus changed to marketing other artists and managing the business.

The gallery was a generous space in the refurbished section of downtown Atlanta, but Mitch was quick to point out that the gallery was there even before others determined it to be a fashionable area. The showroom/public space was a thoughtful collection of new and established artists, and all of it was original work. He had tried to sell prints in the early days, but the focus of the business went toward establishing clients and supplanting their collections. Although the browsing traffic was consistently brisk, walk-in sales had become a rarity.

Andrew pushed open the wooden storefront door and set off the bells hanging on the inside.

"How come you have not replaced those bells with an electronic buzzer or something? Every time I come in here, I feel like Floyd should give me a haircut."

Mitch just looked over his glasses at Andrew. "That gives the place charm and character. Bring me more paintings to sell and I'll put the system in just for you. What brings you in this early in the morning? I thought the tortured soul of an artist rarely stirred before 2 pm."

"I'm not an artist, I'm a business man," Andrew smirked. "You know that. What do you know about IORRF?" Andrew slouched into an overstuffed chair near Mitch's desk.

"Them again? Did something happen at the auction?"

"Not exactly. What do you know?"

"Very little actually. They've been headquartered in Atlanta for as long as I can remember. Just your standard charity organization. The only difference is that someone in the group likes art so they use auctions to raise money."

"I spent some time with one of the members the night of the auction. Interesting, but kind of out there."

"What was her name?"

"Funny. None of that happened. I'm thinking about doing a series of paintings focusing on issues surrounding their organization."

"That sounds great. What countries do they operate in?"

"Not sure. A few I think."

"Have you called them?"

"No. You're my first foray."

"Call them. Why don't you hook up with the – person – you talked with the other night?"

"She's headed back to the Democratic Republic of the Congo." Andrew said it very slowly and clearly, like the hearer had never known such a place existed until now. "She did ask me to go back with her."

"Sounds like something happened to me. Go with her. You need a vacation. The Princess of Darkness can live without you for a few weeks."

"Not you too. You're suggesting I go to the Congo? Incredible. I'm not going to an edge-of-the-world banana republic just to do a painting. And as far as Stella goes, you need to get off of her. She's not so bad. The business would not be where it is today if it weren't for her."

"You sure you want to get into this conversation again?"

"She's not. What is so bad about her?"

"Andrew, you made my point exactly. The business would NOT be where it is today if it weren't for her. She's making a joke out of you and your work. What happens when the highbrow art world realizes that AD Isaacson's paintings are produced on an assembly line? Besides, she's practically taken over the business. When's the last time you made a decision concerning the direction of the company?"

"A joke? I disagree. Very few people know about our business arrangement, and it will stay that way. Also, I am very careful about quality control. Last week."

"Last week, what?"

"I made a decision concerning the company last week. I sent out a memo forbidding any inappropriate internet activity on company computers."

"Impressive. Does Stella still make up your schedule, prepare the financials and determine the subject matter of the artwork?"

Short silence. "I don't want to talk about it anymore."

"Come on, Andrew. I'm your friend on the outside looking in. It's a lot clearer out here. Andrew, you have enough money for six people and their extended families. Cut Stella off - for your own peace of mind."

"My mind is fine. The company is fine. Life is fine." Andrew wasn't quite as convincing as he thought he would be.

Mitch had promised himself he wouldn't preach to Andrew. They had been friends too long and Andrew knew exactly what his attitude was about AD Isaacson. Oh well, Andrew had started it.

"Want something to drink?"

Mitch went for a water refill.

"So, are you going to the DRC?" He called from the other room.

"No. Absolutely not. I'm not that desperate. Anyway, she's not my type."

"Yeah, those women with brains and motivation are definitely to be avoided." Mitch peered around the corner to see if he got a response. "Do you have any plans now that the show is over?"

"Nah, not yet. You're right, I do need a vacation. Maybe I'll take Renee to France."

"There's always the Caribbean."

"Yeah, I love going down there, but I can never get Renee off the beach."

"Go somewhere that will create great inspiration and many canvases."

"Sounds good." Andrew got up. "I better run."

"Take care. Let me know if you decide to go on vacation. I'll come over and water the flowers."

"Thanks. It's a deal."

As Andrew walked out the door amid ringing bells, Mitch wondered if he should have told him that he already knew Bhaniel Tretechi. She had come to his gallery the day after the auction and spent considerable time going over every Andrew Isaacson original painting in stock and photos of work already sold. Ms. Tretechi made notes and took snapshots of all of them. Mitch answered most of her questions. But, some of her inquiries were surprisingly probing. When she asked about his personal habits, Mitch decided he'd have to get Andrew's permission to disclose those things. What did she see in him? Mitch had never considered the subject matter of Andrew's personal work to be quite so heart stopping. He had asked Ms. Tretechi if she gravitated toward artists, but she indicated this was her first experience.

He had to admit, it was more than a little weird. But, it didn't seem to be all that … personal though. She was actually an interesting lady. Her stories were entertaining, but tinged slightly with sadness. Tragedy and suffering can be funny in a perverted sort of way. She talked about it like it was simply a common feature of the life she chose to live. Her charisma was infectious. Only Andrew could let it skim off his stony surface without a response. Mitch was ready to go with her himself. He guessed the best he could do though was to try to get Andrew interested in Ms. Tretechi's vision.

# Chapter 4

IORRF Office/Warehouse, Atlanta

Bhaniel reviewed her list. The supplies would be prepackaged and sent to the airport by noon tomorrow. It was still mostly dry goods, heavy, dry goods, which made the cost to ship it from the United States astronomical. But, the quality for the price, plus shipping, was worth the headaches. Even the little kids could tell the difference in quality of the American food compared to the East European or North African products.

The warehouse/office was a leased prefab building in the Hammet South Industrial district two miles from the Air National Guard section of the airport. It was one of six hundred identical facilities that were built in 1974-75. With the steel girder construction, metal siding and near lack of windows, the structures would probably be standing well into the twenty-first century. So far, the receipts of the organization were sufficient to pay the rent and then some. If the money ran short, this would be one of the first luxuries to be jettisoned. Bhaniel had even tried to persuade the board of directors to let it go if for no other reason than to focus more finances on the homes overseas. The board always discouraged her lobby efforts however.

"Roni, do you have the invoice for the two pallets?"

"It's in the green folder." Veronica had been Bhaniel's US administrator for eleven years. Veronica was convinced she had a life before they had met, but details were fuzzy.

Bhaniel reviewed the invoice twice. "It's not here. Why is it not here?"

"What's not there? I checked the invoice against what we ordered and it matched."

"We must not have ordered it."

"What?"

"The seed."

"It's ordered, but it won't get there for ten to fourteen days. I told you that yesterday."

Bhaniel sighed. "You're right. I'm sorry. After all these years, you'd think this trip wouldn't be so stressful. I'd be done for sure without you Roni."

"Is this a bad time to ask for a raise?"

"No. Everything I have is yours."

"Great, two pallets of canned goods and an old suitcase."

They shared a laugh in the warehouse portion of the tiny industrial building. Hector, their do-it-all man, was in the office on the phone with the airline.

Break time.

"How did the auction go? I haven't remembered to ask you."

"It was wonderful. The audience seemed very receptive to all the speakers and most of the artwork sold." Bhaniel shifted her feet slightly. "I also had a nice conversation with one of the artists."

"Really? Which one? It wasn't that one guy who sends junkyard art every year was it?"

"No. He didn't participate this time. Gale asked him to cut back on using toilets in his art work and it offended him. He swore he'd never return. Are you familiar with Andrew Isaacson? He did the pieces that I mentioned had a prophetic bent to them."

"Oh yes. He's very good. The subject matter is a little weird, but very well done. What'd you find out about him?"

"Just basic info really, but there is something about him… he has a destiny to fulfill. I asked him to come to Africa."

"You what?" Roni's mouth was gaping. Her astonishment turned to humor. "You know, Bhaniel, if you wanted to ask him out you could have just invited him to dinner."

"Good point." She smiled. "I asked him to come, and I'm glad I did it. There are things he will experience there that he would not receive anywhere else."

"Like dying unnaturally?"

"Come on Roni. I believe I was supposed to encourage him to do it. If so, then the best place for him is the DRC."

"True. Was he good looking?" Roni's eyes twinkled.

Bhaniel shot her a look. "I don't remember."

Veronica laughed.

# Chapter 5

The AD Isaacson Galleries

Stella put the phone back. She would wait until after lunch to pester the accounting office. Besides, she knew exactly what the profit was from the show. But verification was always prudent. Stella spun around and leaned back in her executive chair, glancing out the window. They would be enjoying a new company record if the indecisive weaklings from DaschleHouse had shown some courage and purchased the last two pieces. Oh well, the game wasn't over yet. She'd add their purchase to the totals just as soon as they buckled under the pressure. Stella had to admit, DaschleHouse were never considered sure-thing buyers. They had been invited with the hope the event would sway them to get out their checkbooks. The night was just too short to prepare them properly. Pre-show efforts to build rapport with the organization were spotty at best. Next time. Things were progressing nicely, though. By the end of the year, she was confident the master plan could transition to the next phase. "Eugene, come in here." She said it like a caesar reclining on his bench. Stella's personal assistant was a 6 foot 3 inch slender man in his fifties who had a knack for typing. She had insisted on a man, and after a few overly macho misfires, Eugene met the need. She put up with his incessant phone calls and penchant for bad fashion sense presumably so that she could retain a man directly under her. Stella actually liked his willingness to stop at nothing to perform her will.

"Yes, ma'am. Would you like some more coffee?"

"Call Diego Garcia and tell him I want to see him. If you can't get him on the phone, then go to his house."

"I have him on your schedule for tomorrow at 10:30 a.m."

"I don't care. I want to see him now."

"What shall I tell him the meeting is about?"

"Make something up."

How about I tell him it's because you are a psychotic, control freak, Eugene thought to himself. Eugene's talent resided in his ability to deflect the consistently demeaning attitude of his boss. He realized this job was the only way he could hobnob with the upper crust, and the accompanying perks were enjoyable. Like the company car. Hello BMW.

"And take your Taurus."

"Great." Eugene fumed. Maybe Diego would answer the phone and save him a trip.

Eugene found Diego at his Southside apartment. As he waited for an answer to the doorbell, the noise on the other side of the door convinced Eugene a wild party or a home invasion was occurring. He really didn't want to travel to Diego's residence, but there was no response to numerous phone calls and an order was an order. After the third buzz, someone heard the doorbell. A relatively tall Latino who had looked as if he just rolled out of bed cracked the door open as far as the chain lock would allow and squinted at Eugene.

"Yeah?"

"Are you Diego Garcia?"

"Who's askin'?"

"I'm Eugene Burnett. I work for Stella Manchester. She has sent me here to escort you to the AD Isaacson offices. She would like to meet with you about some important issues." That sounded interesting didn't it?

"Oh yeah? Uh, I'm kinda busy. I thought we were going to meet tomorrow."

"She indicated that it was necessary to meet today. I have a car waiting to take you there."

Diego thought about it. "It's going to take a minute to get ready." Diego shut the door without waiting for a response.

"I'll wait out here," Eugene said to the door.

After only twelve minutes, a slightly disheveled blonde-haired girl in her early twenties came out the door followed by a Hispanic girl of similar age. Diego came out last looking much the way he did when he first answered the door. He was wearing a tank top undershirt and sloppy cotton pants. The chains and tattoos were a strong indication that this twenty-something watched way too much MTV. Must have been a little too warm for the stocking hat.

"So did you bring a limo or something?"

"Not quite." Eugene didn't have the heart to tell him.

When the crew got downstairs, the girlfriends seemed to lose interest.

"Diego we'll see you later, Hon." He got kisses and waved them on.

He turned to Eugene, "This better be worth it, man."

Eugene wondered most of the way to the company offices how Stella found this misdirected slacker. She was definitely developing a "My Fair Lady" complex. The guy could barely put together a complete sentence, but by the look of his girlfriends, he must have some game.
"Do you have an art background?"
Diego laughed. He wasn't quite sure what Eugene meant. "Don't think so. Stella told me she'd show me some art stuff. It don't look that hard smearing paint all over. All I know is she said I'd make more money than I ever dreamed."
Eugene decided to drop it.

"Diego, so good to see you." Stella greeted him with all the warmth of a Hollywood producer.
"Ssup, Stella? Got anything to eat?" He flopped into the nearest chair.
"Eugene, get Diego a sandwich." Stella surveyed her project. "Honey, are you still shopping at the thrift store?"
"What!? Just loosen up on Diego. Nothin' wrong with my wardrobe."
"But it's not good. You look like every other Hispanic in the 'hood."
"Tell you what. Why don't you find a way to do your art boy gig without disrespecting my look." Diego got up to leave.
"Sit down, Diego. Or you don't get the ten thousand dollars."
Diego turned and looked at Stella. "Your boy never said nothin' about ten G."
"Is it worth it?"
"What do I got to do?"
"Just be an artist."
"Give me a brush, art lady," Diego said laughing.
Stella just loved to motivate people.
First things first. Stella scribbled an address on her letterhead and handed it to Eugene. She smiled.
"Diego, you go with Eugene. He's going to take you to see a friend of mine named Cienna. You'll have a great time."
Eugene escorted Diego out the door.
Stella dialed the phone. "Lana? I had a lovely idea. Do you have plans on the 15th...?"

Eugene was jealous. He'd always wanted a makeover like the ones on E! Network. Now this loser was going to get one on the company's dime. Cienna was good too. She'd have him looking every bit like the flamboyant artist.

They walked up 17ᵗʰ Street to a boutique next to Excalibur Diner. The marquee simply stated Cienna's name with little additional description of the shop. She had built up sufficient clientele making advertisements unnecessary. Stella had sent her a number of customers. The art crowd was a fertile field for over-the-top fashion.

Cienna was waiting on them. She was average height and there was really nothing memorable in her appearance. The most remarkable thing about her was what she didn't have - wild clothes or oddly colored hair. She dressed somewhat conservatively in leather pants and a plain blouse. One surmised that she didn't want to get addicted to her product. She saved it for the clients.

"Here he is, Cienna."

"Hi, Eugene. Hello, Diego."

She had been sizing him up as Diego walked between the leather skirts and feather boas on his way to the back of the shop.

Eugene noticed Cienna had a look in her eye. "You walk like a model. Size 42 tall with a 32 inch waist. Dark gray worsted suit with a black silk shirt. Do you like chains?"

"Yeah. Got any hats?"

"I do, but you'd look better with the right haircut. What do you think about losing the piercings around the mouth? Well, the one below your mouth in the middle isn't bad. The extra earrings are nice. Let's try a couple other ideas. Come with me." Cienna led him to a different section of the shop, which was mostly men's items. Eugene browsed trying not to look too much at them.

After an hour and ten minutes, Diego emerged with a handful of sacks and clothes on hangers. Cienna looked satisfied.

"I think that ought to be enough for what Stella wants."

"Thanks, Cienna. Did you put it on the tab?"

"Always. Bye, Diego."

Diego just smiled and indicated his thanks for the new wardrobe as he turned to walk out.

Eugene was curious to see if this experiment worked.

Back in Stella's office, Eugene presented the new creation to the boss like a proud father.

Stella grinned at Diego approvingly.

"Wear that suit tonight; you've got a party to attend."

"Excellent. Where's it at?"

"Don't worry. Eugene will drive you."

Diego scowled at the thought of taking his ladies to a party in Eugene's lame ride.

"Relax, Diego. You'll get to ride in a company car tomorrow night."

How'd she know what he was thinking?

"But, I want you to go alone. No dates."

"Come on, boss lady. Why do you want to do that to me? You want me to hang out with *Eugene*?"

"Cute. Just trust me. It will be worth your while. If that's not enough then gut it out for the money."

"Yeah, whatever. What time is Slim coming to get me?"

"He'll be at your apartment at eight."

"Come on, Slim. Take me home. I've got to get geared up for the big shindig tomorrow night."

Eugene followed Diego out the door. Stella hit the intercom and called downstairs. "Yvonne, I need you to call your media sources."

"Sure, what do you have?"

"Tomorrow's party will be attended by Diego de Sousa, the up and coming new artist etc., etc. Give them whatever background on him you have ready. Do you still have the notes from the last staff meeting? That should cover it."

"Yes."

"Well, he is going to have an interlude that will be newsworthy."

"Sounds juicy. Is that all I'm going to get?"

"For now. Print, television, and especially People Magazine."

"Done. Standard budget?"

"Yeah. Try to get them to act on a promise of more scoops though. Thanks."

Stella looked forward to the party. Although it was a typical charity fund-raiser social affair, the environment for controversy was pristine. The only wild card was Lana. Young, attractive females were not completely reliable in the heat of the moment. Stella would just have to keep her on a short leash.

# Chapter 6

Bhaniel left Atlanta at noon, and after a short flight sat in the international waiting area at Dulles Airport in Washington D.C. another four hours. Now, there was about thirty minutes left before they started boarding the plane. She would be changing planes in Brussels in the morning followed by a short stop-over in Luanda, Angola. The second and third hops would be on Lufthansa. Roni tried her best to avoid certain airlines when scheduling Bhaniel's flights, but Lufthansa was alright. Roni wanted to ensure Bhaniel and the cargo was transferred efficiently and safely. Things had a curious way of disappearing as they made their way through Africa. She wasn't as worried about Bhaniel though. She would get there eventually.

Bhaniel waded through her organizer and was scanning the current month's appointments. She had faithfully executed everything she had wanted to do while in the United States. Roni was so efficient. Bhaniel wished the organization had the money to properly pay her for her effort. The eternal rewards would have to do for now. She did notice one item that did not get resolved. Bhaniel had put Andrew Isaacson's name on Tuesday's slot and it occurred to her that neither she nor Roni had heard from him. Oh well, maybe her feeling about him was for another time. Or another place. She made a note in her book to contact him the next time she came back to the United States. If she came back.

Certain thoughts of home had been buried deep in her emotions while on this trip, but with her attention focused on returning, the unresolved issues resurfaced with all the pain and uncertainty from before. There was no doubt that she would have to face him again. The visions and dreams she'd had before coming to Atlanta were again vivid in her mind. After years of learning to discern His voice, she knew the Lord had specific and critical intentions which had to be conveyed. Bhaniel dreaded the likely response of her warning. Death wasn't so bad, though. At least she'd go out doing the right thing. But since the risk of death was real, she was diligent while in the United States to make sure that her personal affairs were in order in case she met an untimely end. Roni was right. She didn't have much to her name, but she had numerous responsibilities within the organization and many children and workers that relied on her to do her job.

The airline representative called for Group 3 to board the plane, and Bhaniel gathered her things. As she recalled the faces of the children in her orphanage, she felt an anxiousness to be there which fought to replace the dread. Bhaniel looked around the airport one more time before going down the tunnel. Though Africa was her home, the thought of never coming back to the America brought a twinge of loneliness that she couldn't quite shake.

# Chapter 7

Madame Dianne Hoestedtler's residence, Atlanta

"Now, when we go in there, I want you to BE the artist." Stella was coaching.
"Yeah, okay." Diego didn't have a clue what she meant.
"Do you remember what we talked about? What kind of art you do?"
"Abstract. It won't be that tough. These people never seen anything I've done anyway. I could tell 'em I paint farm scenes on toilet seats and they wouldn't know any better."
"Not altogether true, but we can talk about it later." Stella smiled at him.
"Act like you own the place, babe."
"That won't be hard."
"I'll follow you in a few minutes. You go on ahead."
Diego got out of the car, a BMW 7 Series sedan, and strutted in the massive front door of what he assumed was a house. It looked more like a country club, but there was no golf course nearby. How did people make this much money? Probably not acting like an artist. Oh well, one thing always leads to another…
He didn't know what the fund raiser was for and really didn't care. Although he'd throw out a few art comments tonight, he wasn't all that interested in expending a lot of energy attempting to convince people he was an artist. His primary goal was to take advantage of the enormous opportunity he'd been given to hook up with some high class ladies. He was going to make the most of his good fortune. Fine clothes, clean ride, there's no way he was going to crash and burn tonight. He stopped in the entry colonnade and a maître de or some kind of butler met him.
"Hello, sir. Do you have an invitation?"
"Yeah, my name is Diego de Sousa."

The maître de looked at Diego as if he had been slapped in the face. "Mr. de Sousa, please forgive me. I did not recognize you." He was scurrying. "Let me show you into the ballroom." He opened the door and bowed slightly.

Diego was a little off balance himself, but he was cocky enough to receive the man's praise like he expected it.

Diego stepped past the columns to the atrium and quickly sized up the room. It occurred to him he did not know a soul in the place. He was going to have to start from scratch. Most people were standing, grouped in twos and threes chatting. He was definitely one of the younger ones in attendance. There was food everywhere. If he struck out in love, there was plenty of free eats to kill the pain.

Diego walked to the back of the house and noticed the bar was set up on the veranda. He made his way out there and ordered a drink. He wondered if free drinks were watered down. Near the pool, he eyed two young ladies standing by themselves. Nice looking. No obvious wedding rings and no men close by. Good. Maybe they like to have fun.

"Hello, ladies."

The women stopped their conversation for a moment.

"Hello to you." They looked him over briefly. "Are you the entertainment tonight?" The brunette was the more talkative one. The blonde was interested in scanning the crowd.

"Nah." He grinned as he said it. "I thought Aerosmith was going to be here tonight."

"That's a good one. You don't come to these parties much, do you?"

"You make it sound pretty boring. I figured everyone got wasted and jumped in the pool at the end of the night."

The girls looked at each other and laughed. "What's your name?"

"Diego de Sousa. Young and willing."

The brunette shot him a sideways look. "I'm Colette and this is Jewell. This party is just to get free dinner and see famous people. Then you go to the real parties."

"I'm in. You need a ride? I got Slick outside shining up the car right now."

"Ooh, rich boy. Are you one of the donors?"

"Not yet. I'm supposed to be one of the famous people."

The girls stopped and looked closely at him. "I don't recognize you. What do you do?"

"I'm an artist. Want to pose for me?"

"Hey, that sounds like fun." Colette was definitely willing to pursue a good time tonight. Jewell could be trouble.

"So you paint or what?"

"Yeah. Something like that."

Diego glanced away to the milling people and saw a few familiar faces. He thought they were TV stars. One caused him to catch his breath. It was the hot girl from *Baja Beach*, the swimsuit babe fest on Netflix. He made a point to binge watch the show because of her. This was a perfect chance to meet her and impress her with his manly presence. Breaking through all the losers hanging around her was going to be a challenge though.

Jewell recognized her also. "Colette, look over there, it's that bimbo from *Baja Beach*. Nice dress. She is an awful actress."

"She wasn't hired for her acting ability, honey." Colette turned to look. Diego was staring. Ahhh! She saw me eyeing her. Wait a minute. Did she smile at me? Whoa. Okay, D-Sousa. Don't sweat. How's your breath? Should I ask these girls if I have anything on my face? Ease up, now. We're alright. One more quick glance. Where'd she go? Diego looked around the veranda. Nowhere. Oh well, the party had just started.

"Ladies, I'm going to get some food. Do you want anything?"

"Not right now, thanks. Get some of the crab cakes, they're awesome."

Diego made his way to the buffet area. He caught a glimpse of Stella deep in conversation with some rich looking folks. She made a comment and the group politely turned to look in his direction. He didn't have the desire to acknowledge them right now. If she wanted him to act like a monkey tonight, Stella would have to chase him down.

He took a little bit of everything. Man, is this good. These people know how to get it done.

"Mr. de Sousa, hello. My name is Madeline Green. It is a pleasure to meet you." She held out her hand. Diego shook the aging hand of the small lady with large glasses.

"Nice to meet you, too."

"I am already a fan of your work."

"You are? Uh, I mean that's nice to know." Diego didn't know he had done any artwork yet. Stella had some explaining to do.

"I am curious though. How long does it take to recover from one of your painting sessions?"

Diego had no clue what she was talking about. He stared at her as he dreamed up a lie to tell her.

"Oh, not too long. Couple days at the most."

"That's good to hear. I must tell you I am very impressed you have used your … challenge … in such a productive way. How on earth do you do it?"

It's really hard to lie to someone when you have no idea what you are lying about.

"It's not all that bad. I take a lot of breaks." He looked at her to see if that was a passable response.

"Really? I would have thought your efforts were more … frenzied." Madeline tried to be gentle with her words.

"Yeah, I just get in there and slap it on. I've got a brush in both hands sometimes."

Madeline was eating it up.

"Fascinating. How long have you been painting?"

"Since as long as I can remember. Even in kindergarten. The other kids were out playing ball, and I'd be in class smearing paint on the wall or something."

"So you painted before you were diagnosed?"

"Diagnosed?"

"With epilepsy." Madeline was whispering.

"Who told you I had epilepsy?" Diego was almost laughing at the little lady.

"I'm so sorry. Stella told me in the strictest of confidence. I haven't repeated it to a soul."

Diego digested his food and the conversation for a moment. He'd better find Stella pretty quick before he talked to any more art people.

"Miss Madeline, it's been great talking to you. You take care now." Diego shook her hand and went in search of Stella.


"There you are. Ladies and gentlemen, this is Diego." Stella saw Diego walk up to her covey of interested buyers. She hooked his arm like a new bride presenting her husband to the extended family.

Diego acknowledged each new acquaintance, but didn't catch anyone's name. He fielded a few nonsense questions about art and Stella and then began drawing away.

"Stella, could I talk with you for a minute?"

Stella looked at Diego to see how committed he was. Very.

She turned to make her apologies to the expectant crowd and then followed Diego to a quiet corner.

"This better be important."

"You need to tell me what kind of lies you've been spreadin' around. I just found out I have epilepsy."

"Epilepsy?" Stella was mentally tallying the evening's conversations to recollect who she told what.

"Oh, Madeline, yes. She promised to keep it under her hat." Stella was a little irritated with her. She did not expect the pint-sized maven to spill her guts to Diego.

"Don't worry. That's the only embellishment we haven't talked about already."

"Epilepsy? What does it do to me?"

"It means you're fine. In real life, it's controllable with medication. The illusion is you paint while in a raging fit which makes your art sexy. You do most of your work in that state. It will never be an issue because you don't allow anyone into the studio when you're … that way."

Diego looked around the room for a moment while he thought this over. "Promise me there are no other surprises."

"None. Absolutely none." Stella hesitated for dramatic effect. "Except for one more thing… have you met Lana?"

"Lana?"

Stella looked over Diego's shoulder and smiled. Diego turned to find out who Stella had seen. It was HER.

"You know her?" Diego tried not to sweat.

Lana glanced up from her conversation. She was wearing a silk robe that went to the middle of her thigh, and in her hand were paint brushes. Stella gave her the sign, and she began to make her way toward Diego.

"Diego, would you like to show off some of your work to the audience?" He wasn't sure what she meant.

"Hello, Diego, my name is …"

"Lana Markova. Yes, I know who you are." Diego extended his hand to shake hers just to touch her. "It's my pleasure."

The answer was yes to anything she had to say.

"I love your art work. In fact, I'm going to be modeling some of it tonight."

Lana loosened the tie on her robe and opened it for him to see abstract art painted on her bikini-clad torso. Diego wasn't sure if the blood rushing to his face was obvious, but the rapid intake of air made him cough suddenly. Lana smiled at the reaction and closed her robe. Diego could only remember certain colors about the painting.

"Gather around everyone. Tonight, I want to show all of you some of the latest works by Diego de Sousa. But, with a little twist."

She nodded at Lana. Ms. Markova again loosened the tie on her robe and removed the wrap, dropping it to the ground. Stella had positioned Diego next to her so that the converging paparazzi could frame the moment appropriately. Lana was truly in her element as the center of attention and made an effective billboard. The camera flashes were furious when Lana turned and gave Diego a kiss on the cheek. He did his best to take it all in stride. While they were accommodating all the requests for pictures, two more models walked into the room and took their places next to Diego. Each sported a different painting, and the audience started firing questions at Diego, but he just smiled stupidly and put his arms around the models. When Stella sensed the moment was waning, she thanked everyone for their interest and handed out cards in the crowd. The models gathered their robes and made their way back to the dressing room. Diego noticed Lana attempting to leave and caught up with her.

"Hey, Lana. Thanks for modeling my artwork. Those paintings never looked so good."

Lana just mumbled a quick thank you as she walked.

"How about giving me your phone number? I've got some ideas for new art work."

"That sounds nice, but I'm going to be pretty busy the next few weeks." She smiled benignly and kept walking. Diego slowed down and let her go on ahead. He watched her go into the dressing room. She didn't look back. These people are playing a game, and I don't know any of the rules, Diego thought to himself. He decided to leave. As Diego made his way to the front door, the ladies he met earlier walked up to him.

"Hey Dee Ay Go, nice art work. You're not leaving, are you?" She taunted him a little.

"Yeah." He looked at them for a moment. Lana's slap in the face brought him out of his fantasy of her. "Want to go?"

They thought it over. Each one read the mind of the other to make sure it was ok. "Sure! You driving?"

"I got a guy who'll take us."

They stepped out the door together.

# Chapter 8

The AD Isaacson Galleries

"Billy, have you finished stretching the new canvases?"
"Yeah, they're in storage #6. There are two that are prepped. The others are raw still."
"No problem. I wanted a four by six. Are any that size?"
"Yes, I believe so."
"Thanks." Andrew walked down the hall toward the little used storage closet.

The company would probably have to consider an addition or begin looking for a larger facility soon. The three studios were only able to accommodate five to six people per studio at any one time. Stella's constant focus on increasing production made the premises seem inadequate for the task.

As he passed the main studio rooms, he noticed the linseed oil smell had died down some with the absence of work the last several days. It was going to change soon. Most of the workers would return from holiday by next Monday, and there was money to be made.

Andrew felt good about this next batch of paintings. Not passionate, but at least the subject matter was going to be challenging. Just slight changes from the last group. Much like Picasso's blue period. Little adjustments can effectively define an artist's work and create milestones for people to follow.

He stepped into the closet and saw the new canvases in the back. A brightly colored painting over to the right caught his eye. Andrew walked over and flipped through the stack of paintings. There were at least ten works and the style was similar. He couldn't remember anybody in the studio doing these recently. Andrew was sure he had not approved it or discussed it with anyone. He took a primed canvas and one of the strange new paintings with him back to the studio where Billy was putting out new cans for mixing paint.

"Billy, have you ever seen this before?" He held up the painting for him.

"Yeah, Sylvia did that one."

"When was it done?"

"It's been a couple of weeks."

"Where is she?"

"Gone till Monday."

Billy didn't know much. He was the utility guy. There wasn't any use in trying to beat additional information out of him. Andrew carried the painting toward Stella's office.

"Stella, what's this?"

Great. He's not supposed to see those. Stella deflected the question.

"You like? It's part of the new line we're creating."

"We've never talked about this. I wouldn't have approved it if we had."

Stella turned toward Andrew. "Yes, Andrew, we did talk about it. At the October meeting. We spent a considerable amount of time discussing a new line and a change of direction."

"But, we didn't specify what we were going to do. There was a lot still up in the air." Andrew brooded for a moment. Mitch's words began to burn in his throat. Maybe he was... right.

"You shouldn't have done this, Stella. You're not the president of this company. I'm the one who makes the final decisions on the direction we take." Andrew's temperature and volume were rising with each word.

"I don't know if I'm ready to support this 'new' direction. It's too radical of a change from where we've been."

Stella nodded her head. "I see your point. I'll put it on the agenda for the next meeting. We'll hammer out the details for sure."

Andrew cooled at the thought that Stella was seeing his side of the situation. But she was agreeing too quickly. She only conceded when she had another scheme brewing. Andrew decided to leave it. This was just a shot over the bow. He'd let her act on it and see if there needed to be another confrontation.

"Thanks. We can avoid a lot of expensive mistakes if you talk with me before you pursue new ideas."

"I agree completely. Thank you, Andrew. Are you sticking around this afternoon?"

"No, I'm going out of town for a few days."

"Sounds great. Call me when you get back."

Andrew took the painting with him.

Stella was slightly irritated. Andrew was not supposed to have access to the new line of paintings. If he recognized them in the media – along with Diego – Stella's plan to incorporate a new artist would be compromised. She'd have to destroy the painting he'd found. The imbecile that left the painting lying around would be looking for other work in twenty-four hours.

Andrew walked back toward the studios. Although the lighting in the hallway was limited, he glanced at the painting as he walked. He actually liked the work, but how on earth was he going to explain it. No successful artist would change direction so dramatically in the prime of his career. The worst thing he could do would be to tear off on a tangent and leave his collectors behind scratching their collective heads. Nearing the central studio, he passed a Hispanic kid he had not seen before. Some of the workers standing nearby seemed to know him. Nice dresser.

Andrew placed the painting back in the storage closet. As he turned to leave, he noticed something on the back of the canvas he had missed until now. Someone had scrawled the word "Diego" in charcoal pencil. Odd name for a painting he thought as he shut the closet door.

For the remainder of the evening, Andrew reviewed and revised his sketches. Unfortunately, some of them weren't as fluid as the others, but he didn't want to overwork them either. The overall theme was weaker in numbers four and seven. The color palette signified a lighter, happier tone, which really didn't suit the other works. Not that all of them had to be somber, but being all over the map emotionally gave the impression he was bipolar. Andrew put another female in number six. Number eight would be a challenge in itself. It was the only painting in the group highlighting animals. Andrew didn't particularly enjoy painting animals because it was more difficult to show expression. Number seven was resolved by making the subjects work, toil rather, instead of relaxing. Four would work better with brown tones anyway.

Andrew put away his papers. The groundwork was finished. Now, the painters could come in and work from his sketches to rough in the main colors. This group would be a series of thirteen works focusing largely on minority women. There was no question the subject matter was politically correct. And the works should sell easily. Since Andrew was leaving town for a few days, the sketches would be adequate to get the workers underway. He actually didn't have to be on site until well into the production process.

He prepared a satchel with the drawings and notes. He wrote Stella's name on it and walked down the hall to put it on her desk. It was nearly eleven o'clock, and Andrew was the only one in the building. The cleaning crew wouldn't be on site until midnight. He let himself into Stella's office, pattered across the Albanian area rug and laid the package front and center. The single halogen safety light in the center of the ceiling illuminated the space quite well in the middle of the night. Andrew stopped to look at Stella's array of photographs he'd ignored a thousand times. Stella didn't have much artwork on her walls. The items that brought her the most satisfaction were snapshots of her with famous and/or important people. Conquests all. He had to admire her drive. Andrew sauntered out and locked the door behind him.

All he had to do now was get his flight itinerary, fill his pockets with cash and pack his swim suit. Going to Aruba in January was nearly the most decadent thing a human could do. It was tantamount to sidestepping one of the few things individuals could not control. The weather. No longer did one have to endure unpleasant seasons, just get on a plane and enjoy. Which was exactly his intent. He was going alone to a place where people like to party. Maybe the Travel Channel will be there filming the revelry. Andrew smiled to himself. Surely there was more to life than this. He'd have to look into that sometime.

# Chapter 9

Hartsfield-Jackson Atlanta International Airport

Getting a decent seat on a plane to Aruba was difficult for the heathen unwashed. The lure of warm beaches and bikinis invigorated many an imagination in the winter months. Even in Atlanta. First class would be worth every penny, however. Such was the danger of living large. The moment one reaches a certain standard of living, the person will spend his last dollar trying to maintain said standard.

The long line at the ticket counter was not awesome, but he wasn't checking a bag. Andrew strolled past the impatient throng. All he brought for the trip was one change of clothes, a swimsuit, sandals, toiletries and what he wore to the airport. Just a carry-on and a lovely lunch in first class. Lying about all day did not require a studied wardrobe or accessories.

Andrew typically portrayed himself as something other than an artist when he traveled alone. If he got caught in a conversation with another traveler, he enjoyed the charade and the challenge of making it believable. He didn't consider himself to be a malicious liar, just a hobbyist.

The complementary beverages before the flight were always welcomed. He timed it pretty well. The body searches consumed most of the extra lead-time he allowed, so he only had seven minutes to wait until takeoff.

Andrew checked to see if his wallet was where it was supposed to be, took off his leather jacket and browsed the onboard reading material. Must be a new copy of the airline magazine. No one had filled in the crossword in the back. He reviewed the pictorial on Aruba and other South American destinations. His resort was not listed in the article, but Andrew knew it was every bit as inviting.

The Grand Village was little known by design. In addition to the exorbitant cost, the average tourist found few amusements aside from exquisite food and premier service. It had been established to cater to individuals who anticipated and relished limited human interaction during their stay. Andrew fit right in. Sort of. The resort environment was desirable to a point, but he typically ventured out in the evenings toward the middle of town for some entertainment. It was a nice mix.

If the pilot was worth his salt, the flight would only last about an hour and fifty minutes. Amazingly, the flight attendants prepared, served and cleaned up lunch with time to spare. For first class. Coach only received beverages. Andrew enjoyed a thick pork chop and stir fried vegetables, but only two glasses of wine. The South American gentleman to Andrew's left had a drink in both hands for most of the flight. Andrew was surprised airline policy allowed such a thing, but his neighbor barely said a word the whole flight. He just drank. Good thing it was only a short flight. The attendants were so efficient that Andrew was able to nap briefly before landing.

As they taxied to Gate 23, the attendants bid each guest sincere wishes for an enchanting stay. Andrew felt like family. He was the third person off the plane. The blast of hot, humid air always took him by surprise. It would require a day or so to adjust to the climate change. If he needed to, Andrew would stay another day to make up for it.

# Chapter 10

Bhaniel walked down the aisle toward her seat, in the middle section, row 28 of the Airbus 330. The flying gymnasium was about three quarters full. Most of the free seats had been claimed by squatters for leg room during slumber. The lady in the seat next to Bhaniel's was still asleep, but now she was slumped well into Bhaniel's space. She decided to simply find an open seat and hope the attendants didn't run her off. Twenty-four hours and counting. Another three hour leg after this and she'd be done. It was always the darkest, most difficult part of the trip. Lord please renew my mind and my spirit.

The teenage girl in the next seat stirred.

"Hey, where's Gato?"

"I'm sorry, I didn't know it was his seat. I was unable to get back to my own."

"That's okay. I don't really want him to sit next to me anyway. He's kinda immature." The girl smiled at her and rubbed the sleep from her eyes.

"What's your name? Are you staying in Luanda?" She seemed pleased to visit with someone new.

"My name is Bhaniel. I'm on my way to Kinshasa."

"Excellent. What's in Kinshasa? I don't know anyone from there." Bhaniel supposed she didn't know too many people outside of her immediate circle based on her tender age. She was an African girl around fifteen years old. She looked pretty healthy and westernized. The earphones going to a new phone, her jeans and graphic t-shirt were telling signs. The accent had to be a mix of boarding school and South Africa.

"I work in an orphanage there. Our organization has 272 kids in eight homes."

"Wow! That's unreal." She was awake and interested now. "That must be sooo interesting. Did you just find all of those kids?"

"Not really. A lot of parents bring their kids to us because they simply can't care for them anymore. Many moms and dads are dying of AIDS." The girl had to think on this for a moment. "Whoa. That just blows me away. Do you do it all by yourself?"

"No. There are many full time and part time workers. A lot of kids come from other countries to help during school holidays. It certainly gives you a different perspective on life. Where are you going?"

"Home to Johannesburg. It's semester break."

"Where do you attend school?"

"Austria. It's too cold up there, but it is really beautiful. Did you ever see Sound of Music? It really looks like that. My parents can't really afford for me to go, but there's some kind of trust fund paying for part of it." She is very comfortable telling her story, Bhaniel thought.

"By the way, what is your name?"

"Leezil."

Bhaniel smiled.

"Everybody laughs when they hear my name at school. At least the Americans do. Now you know why I know about the Sound of Music. My parents really loved that movie. They won't tell me if that's why they sent me to Austria to school. Only a year and a half left, though. Then I'm off to Paris to study art."

"Are you an artist?"

"Isn't everyone? I enjoy it. I used to tell people that I am an artist, then I saw the art in Rome and Paris and I realized I'm not in their league."

Bhaniel acknowledged she was wrong about Leezil. She was impressed with her matter-of-fact attitude and her awareness of the world.

"Hey, Leezil."

It was Gato.

"Hey, G."

Bhaniel looked up to see a fifteen year old kid with hair going in all directions and the beginnings of sideburns. He looked like he needed a nap. "I'm sorry. I have taken your seat." Bhaniel moved to the aisle and turned to Leezil.

"It's been nice to talk to you Leezil." Bhaniel pulled out a card from her pocket and handed it to her. "Let me know if you would be interested in coming to the orphanage some time. I'm sure you would inspire the kids."

"Thanks, I'd like that. I'll let you know."

Bhaniel smiled and went back to row 28. Her neighbor was awake at least and eating a snack.

# Chapter 11

The Grand Village Resort, Aruba

"Where's the bartender? Could I get a refill?" Andrew stopped by the grass-roofed kiosk to top off his beverage on the way to the beach. The waitress was in a hurry also, but quickly concocted a fresh drink.

Andrew strolled to the beach. This was the triumphal entry and he was going to enjoy it. The culmination of the travel plans and hard work over the past four months. The beach. Endless waves, sand, and sunshine. He had a lounge chair with umbrella already staked out. Hours of relaxation awaited him. Normally, Andrew just reclined on the veranda of his bungalow. It overlooked the beach, but he enjoyed the sand in his toes occasionally.

Not too far away, a group of ambitious vacationers were playing volleyball just beyond the reach of the surf. Only a few kids around. Any kids at all were unusual. The closest people to him on the beach were a couple who were lounging in a curtained bungalow. The sound of the waves and an occasional sea gull drowned out almost everything. Pretty soon it would drown out his snoring.

The clouds were gathering for the daily shower. Andrew estimated he had a solid two hours yet. Rarely did a day go by without a short cloudburst. Although it was a bit cooler, mornings were the clearest part of the day. Evenings were often enjoyable after the rain cooled things off, and the clouds made for breathtaking sunsets. Certain places along the coast afforded one the opportunity to see a sunset unhindered by trees or buildings. Nothing but the flat horizon of the Gulf waters to set off the awesome sight.

Andrew lathered on the sunscreen - no need to go back bright red – and placed his frame on the lounge chair. His hat went down over his face, and before long he was napping. A waiter replaced his drink when it was obvious the former was warm from the sun. The rustling awakened Andrew. It was a good thing since the sun was warm and it was his first day out in it. Andrew put his shirt back on and got his bearings. The volleyball game was over for now, and the couple had abandoned the bungalow. He sipped his fresh beverage and tried to think of everything but his real life. It wasn't working.

He was surprised that Mitch's comments about Stella still bugged him. He had heard them so many times before and wondered why they made him uncomfortable now. The one change was now the words had the specter of truth. Something so preposterous before was almost . . . possible. Had he really relinquished control of the company to Stella? Sure he gave her sweeping authority, but there was never a question of her faithfulness and devotion.

No. Absolutely not. How could he question her loyalty just days after the company had the most lucrative show in its eighteen year history? One insignificant misunderstanding about the next batch of paintings was a weak case for that kind of accusation. Besides, that's what he loved about her. She was aggressive and always working to make the company successful. She just needed to be reined in every once in a while. Andrew was pleased with himself. He had weighed the information without malice and arrived at a reasonable conclusion. That's what trips like this were for. A fresh perspective. Even a brief evaluation showed that Mitch was way off base. Times were good. Dismantling the company's successful structure was ludicrous. He decided not to worry anymore. The sun had slipped behind the clouds and the first drops were touching down near him. This was a good time to grab a shower of another kind, and maybe a second nap, before heading into town for dinner.

There was a newspaper on the doorstep when he reached his bungalow. It didn't have much in the way of real news, but the advertisements allowed the novice to choose a nice place to eat or socialize. Andrew knew the area fairly well, but he needed a taxi. Section C had a number of hopeful taxi services. The last one he used was weak. The driver barely spoke English and acted like he didn't even know the names of the streets. That scam works on new tourists occasionally, but Andrew was not falling for it. Of all the times he had been here, his lack of a relationship with a good taxi company was irritating. The outfit with the biggest ad got the first phone call. The Beachfront Cab Company receptionist was very polite. Good sign. She was pleased to reserve a taxi for him at 7 p.m. in front of his quarters.

Lovely. Now for some shuteye. He'd see if there were any promising new watering holes when he woke up.

# Chapter 12

## Kinshasa, Democratic Republic of the Congo

It was a relief to be on the ground. Her baggage was with her and intact, but the food pallets were somewhere in Kenya. That could be fixed. The lag time waiting for the bus to Bandundu would be the quiet before the final push in a long battle. It was all she could do to stay awake. Bhaniel did not attempt to calculate the hours of sleep she had amassed the last 36 hours. Her body told her it was not enough. A certain worn out bed 110 kilometers away was the object of her affections right now. The staff knew not to extract important information or decisions from her the first day back. No court on earth would find her mentally competent in that time period.

The heat had taken her by surprise as she descended the jetliner's stairs. It was the same every year, but it seemed more stifling now. Bhaniel wondered if she was beginning to show her age. At least it wasn't raining. Rain was welcomed almost always, but trying to travel on the unpaved roads in a rainstorm made the trip north to Bandundu nearly impossible. Kinshasa, the capital of the DRC, was an active city of ten million souls. Since its settlement by Henry Morton Stanley in 1881, it evolved into the seat of government and the center for urban activity. Bhaniel was only a few kilometers from her home, but felt as though she was light years away in this congested city. The lifestyle with cars, cellphones, and people everywhere represented nothing of her day-to-day life save for the areas of the city that were home to destitute individuals just trying to survive. The metropolis was a sour mash of privilege and suffering. Slums backed up to high priced real estate, western styles clashed with tribal tradition.

The bus station wasn't far except for the luggage. Now where were they? Then she saw them. Just a few today, must be some other flights arriving at the same time. The airport had formal, adult porters, but Bhaniel loved these boys. They could easily have been children taken in by the orphanage except for unknown circumstances. If only she had enough money to keep them all busy. To their credit, all of the young boys who hung around the airport to freelance were very industrious workers, always eager to please and grateful for whatever they could earn. Bhaniel fished around for her money. The boys especially loved American dollars. She had enough to give them all a little bit. Maybe more for the ones who actually carried the luggage.

"Carry your bags?" The fastest runner asked the first question in French. The other boys arrived as the length of their legs would allow.

"Why, yes that would be lovely. Now let me see. Which ones have not had a chance to carry much luggage today?" She surveyed the workforce and noticed the two youngest in the back. The smallest ones always had the disadvantage in this arena, but Bhaniel liked to even the playing field when she could.

"You two. You will carry my luggage."

The two boys, no more than eight years old, had the look of surprise, excitement and terror. The others worked Bhaniel for any other services they could perform.

"I don't have any other work, but here are some coins for you." She divided up change among the older boys and they were on their way to find another needful soul.

"Follow me, young sirs. We need to walk to the bus station." The eager laborers split up the luggage and fell in behind the weary traveler. To their good fortune, her luggage had wheels.

"Lady that sure is a pretty dress. You beautiful. You a movie star?"

Where do they pick this stuff up? Bhaniel wondered.

"I'm gon' be an airplane driver when I make enough money. My partner here, he's gon' be one too."

"I think you both would be fine 'airplane drivers'."

"Lady, don't know what you have in dese bags, but we pulling extra hard to get dem to de station." Eight years old and they are already maneuvering for a big tip, Bhaniel thought to herself. They aren't as helpless as I thought, but surely the older boys keep them from making as much money.

"Thank you for working so hard for me."

"We good yeah?"

At the bus station, she pulled out her money.

"Thank you, gentlemen. You have performed admirably." Bhaniel placed three dollars in each of their hands and demanded that both give her a hug before racing off. The boys would now have to decide whether to tell the others of their windfall. To brag would be sweet, but the older ones had a history of reacting poorly to such news. Sometimes it's worth the abuse. Bhaniel surveyed the bus listings and found one leaving for Bandundu in two hours. One more waiting area, and one more uncomfortable chair. She hoped the announcer was loud enough to wake her up.

Bhaniel stirred at the screeching of the bus's brakes. The pads had long since worn off and now coming to a full stop was a fifty/fifty bet. Most of the time Tirek would coast into the airport stop to reduce the tendency to overshoot the loading area when he applied the brakes.

Tirek had driven the northern route for eight years. His parents were especially proud of him. He was the only one of his extended family that could boast of steady work. Although the bus was clinically dead, Tirek navigated his daily journey faithfully with this mechanical beast. When he took his place behind the wheel, they were one soul. Truly, the bus would not run when someone else tried to drive her. He could only explain it as love. Plain and simple. He understood her moves and noises, and knew how to respond. Tirek had trained the regular fares to ride her with respect. Boisterous patrons were regularly asked to simmer down or get off.

Today was a good day. He was right on time, the bus halted without the usual shudder, and the horn was working. Tirek leaned on the horn to properly notify Kinshasa that Bus 29 was ready to move out as soon as possible.

The horn brought Bhaniel around to full awareness, and she checked her luggage one more time.

"Can you fit this one on top?"

The young men were eager to help, but were barely big enough to collectively hoist the overfilled canvas bag three meters to the top of the bus. Two kids appeared on the bus's roof chattering and waving their arms. Ten minutes, six men and twelve supervisors successfully nursed the last unit of luggage on the roof top rack.

"Is the fare the same?"

"Ten francs."

"That's fine. Here." The local currency was cheap, and getting cheaper by the day. Bhaniel only converted a small portion of her funds to reduce the impact of 60 percent inflation. The trip to America allowed her to get plenty of dollars or euros.

Bhaniel staggered to a formerly vinyl covered seat and prepared to endure the trip to Bandundu. There was just enough time to get home before dark. She had the film of 36 hours in her mouth and was too tired to rummage through her shoulder bag for the water bottle. The stench permeating the buses interior overrode her own body odor, and the man in the seat next to her didn't seem to mind. Bhaniel couldn't estimate his age. He looked older than her, but disease and starvation regularly sucked the life out of young people full of potential.

The bus roared to attention, and Tirek made a quick look for any stragglers and shoved the gear shift into first. The transmission was surprisingly reluctant, but Tirek spoke to her and she dutifully submitted. Even with the jarring rhythm of the bus over ruts in the road, Bhaniel drifted rapidly off to sleep.

Bandundu came into sight as the sun was going down. The city smelled of raw sewage and dirt, yet it was a comforting thing for Bhaniel. In a curious sort of way, it reminded her of home. Her people.

Bhaniel had barely stepped off the bus and turned to look for her luggage when he called.

"There you are! I think you need a ride home!"

It was Drago.

Drago, the only name Bhaniel had ever known him by, was elderly, small and slumped over, but his spirit was gigantic. Being around him rejuvenated her like almost no one else could. He hustled to gather her luggage and put it in his ancient bicycle taxi. Bhaniel climbed in the back next to her luggage.

"Drago! How did you know I was going to be on today's bus?"

"This is my business. Also, I did not want to miss the Great Bhaniel Tretechi. My favorite rider."

"Drago, it is so good to see you. I feel like I have been away forever."

"You have, but I am comforted now. This whole town just stops when you are gone."

"Please, Drago!" Bhaniel laughed. "As long as you are here, all will be well."

"Let's go now; I think there will be some familiar faces waiting for you on the other side of the river."

Drago stood on the pedals and headed west toward the Kwango River. Even though it was late in the day, at least one more ferry would be going to the west bank. If the captain was reluctant, Drago would work his magic. Bhaniel sat back on the hard wood perch and relaxed her mind and body. The evening was clear and warm. The breeze was light and the vibe of the city had slowed as dusk overtook the merchants and pedestrians. Bhaniel could see the hills on the opposite side of the river. The home wasn't visible from this distance, but she knew exactly where it was on the landscape. She thought a small light from one of the buildings showed through the trees.

"Drago, will the ferry be running tonight?"

"Yes, Odero promised me he would wait until after nightfall in case you came tonight."

"He's so kind. Thank you, Drago, for making it all possible."

"Anything for you my dear."

Drago turned onto the avenue parallel to the river bank. The ride got bumpier as he pedaled over the rocky dirt road. Odero was just twenty meters from shore when they pulled up to the end of the pier.

There were two other people waiting to ride to the west bank of the river. Only a few citizens of Bandundu lived on the west side of the river. Although there was plentiful land available to farmers, the river made regular access to the city less reliable, especially in the rainy season.

"Hello, Miss Tretechi! Welcome home! We have been looking for you."

"Hello, Odero. It is good to be home. Thank you for making one more trip across the river."

"It is my pleasure. After your long trip, you need to be home with your children."

Drago finished putting Bhaniel's luggage on the ferry and said goodbye. Bhaniel gave him half of the money she had left.

"Thank you Drago. I'll see you soon."

"Miss B, take care and God bless the children."

The ferry ride was not a long trip, but it felt like hours. Bhaniel scanned the far shore to see if there were any of her people waiting for her. The descending darkness made it all but impossible. Then she saw the flicker of a single flame. Then another. Before long the whole river bank was lit by small candle flames. The ferry slowly worked its way to the shore and Bhaniel began to hear the song. It was the children of the home and they were singing "Heaven is my Home".

The ferry docked at the pier and as Odero was tying the boat off, the kids ran to the edge to get the first hug from Bhaniel.

# Chapter 13

Aruba

Andrew got into the back seat of the '74 Mercedes. It wasn't a gilded chariot, but the taxi drivers here considered this the top of the line. New cars were typically out of the question, but there was always a good deal to be had on a gently used luxury car. Mercedes was available worldwide and it was a smart investment for the enterprising businessman in Aruba. All the drivers preferred Mercedes, and the tips were better. At least it was clean. The last cab he rode in looked like the driver lived in the back seat. The ride to the tourist part of town wasn't all that long. Andrew's bungalow was just a few miles north of the fancy shops that thrive in a resort area. Countless store fronts offered stylish clothes, art, coffee, and quirky cuisine. All the haunts wealthy Americans desire. Andrew let the eager driver know when he got close to his destination. The driver scampered out of the car and circled back to Andrew's door. He bowed slightly as he opened the door. Andrew's reputation for tipping well would begin at this new taxi service.

The sidewalks were already crowded and it was only 7:30. Usually the party crowd didn't beef up or wake up until 11 or 12 o'clock. Andrew thought an easy night the first time out would be fine. Andrew caught sight of his favorite watering hole. Something didn't seem right though. There was pop music wafting out the door and the flickering neon sign was gone. Andrew wondered if he had ambled up the wrong side street. Wang's Ancient Dining experience was still across the street. There absolutely weren't two of those in this town.

The folks standing outside on the stoop were noticeably younger than Andrew. He tried to act normal and went in to find a seat at the bar. The bartender was a sweaty twenty-something tossing bottles to and fro. The music was a decibel or two above a B-52 engine test plant so Andrew shouted an order for Old Charter with ice. Thirty minutes later, he was on number three and getting hungry. Suddenly, the bartender set an umbrella drink in front of him.

"I didn't order this," Andrew shouted.

"What?"

"This wasn't . . ." Andrew wasn't going to fight through the music and crowd noise. "Never mind. How much?"

The tender waved him off. "No charge. She sent it over." He pointed to the corner of the bar.

Andrew looked. Pretty. And more his age. There was inherent danger in this, but he was going to leave soon anyway. He'd see if she was a psycho first. Andrew tried to walk in a circuitous path to her table reducing the appearance of eagerness.

"Hi. Thanks for the drink."

"You're welcome. Would you like to sit down? You must be a former Crazy Eddy's customer also."

"Is it that obvious? I think I'm a little old for this crowd. But you – you fit right in."

"Aren't you sweet. I'm the same way. I had come here a couple of years ago and enjoyed it only to find a new setup this time."

"I know this sounds like a line, but would you care to go somewhere where the music is not so loud?" Andrew was shouting.

"Sure. I would love to walk a bit."

They stepped outside and even though the tropical air was heavy, the relative quiet was a relief. Andrew savored the potential for an enjoyable evening with…

"By the way, I'm Andrew."

"Sabrina. Sabrina Thomas."

"It's nice to meet you."

"I hope you don't think I'm too aggressive for sending you a drink."

"Not at all. If I had seen you first, I would have done the same thing." Sabrina laughed and put her arm in his as they walked. Andrew was a little surprised. This night could get extremely good or terribly bad. Everything was going so smoothly, he was optimistic.

"Have you eaten yet?"

"No. Do you know any good places?"

"I'm not making any promises, but there used to be a spot near the water that served the best Arctic Char with Fennel."

"Can we walk?"

"Oh yeah. It's just a few blocks."

Andrew wanted to ask her all the standard informational questions to "get to know her", but he decided it wasn't important. She didn't seem too curious about him either. Sabrina had been somewhere sunning for a few days already. She was tanned, but still a little red like someone who was catching up. The flowered wraparound skirt and tight tank top revealed she was trim without having to work at it too much.

As they came over the rise in the road, Andrew could see six two-mast sailboats in the harbor and one monster boat that dwarfed the others. It had to be one hundred feet long. It was anchored about half a mile out. The sun was going down and lights were on in the boats all across the water. The breakers could still be seen in the gathering dusk. Island music dominated the street sounds now. The pop music was far behind them.

An easy flowing group of middle-aged men and one woman played a Bob Marley cover in an area set up next to a club. People were dancing under the hanging lights.

"Let's dance."

Sabrina grabbed Andrew's hand and walked toward the shimmering throng.

"What about my bad leg?"

"How bad is it?"

"Bad enough that I should sit and watch you dance."

"Just stand there. I'll do the rest."

Stand there was about all Andrew could do to this music. He'd been raised on American rock, grunge and hip hop. Sabrina had game and Andrew got tired watching. Lots of others watched her also. The music slowed and that suited Andrew. Sabrina put her arms around his neck and kissed him on the cheek.

"You were impressed with my mad dancing skills, weren't you?"

"Always." Sabrina was comfortable embracing him and Andrew inhaled deeply enjoying her presence.

"Thank you. You know, Sabrina, you've never looked prettier…"

"We just met."

"Don't sweat the details. You're incredible. I need to go to Vegas. My luck is good right now."

"Let's go. Sounds like fun." She was halfway daring him. The music stopped, and the band elected to take a break. At these joints, it could be twenty minutes or two hours depending on the refreshments of choice.

"Still hungry?"

Sabrina flashed him a look. "Yeah."

Andrew wanted to please this woman. She was…. fun. The restaurant wasn't far and getting a table was relatively painless. They sat down with a decent view of the water.

"Do you like seafood?"

"You said the Arctic somethingorother was good. That's fine with me."
Sabrina looked at her cell phone and noticed someone had tried to contact
her. "Excuse me a sec. I'm going to go to the ladies room."
Andrew watched her walk. Quite a lady. He wasn't going to talk her into
anything though. She had a free spirit or a soul running from something.
Soon, she returned with a smile.
"Good news, I found a waiter on the way and he's going to bring us a
bottle of Argentinian wine. I've always heard it was really good."
"Great. Can't wait."
As the sun set, dinner came and went. Andrew and Sabrina talked and
laughed about everything they could think of. Andrew couldn't remember
a time he had enjoyed a date so much. As Andrew finished his story about
going to Spain, and ending up in the hospital with no money or passport,
Sabrina received a text. She had ignored most of them, but this one caught
her attention.
After reading it, she grabbed Andrew's hand and said "I must go."
"Ok. Can I take you somewhere?"
"Thank you. You are sweet. I actually have a car coming for me."
"Can I see you again?"
"I would love it. I hate to run, but I have to go." She got up to leave.
Andrew paid the bill and walked her to the street.
Sabrina turned and put her arms around him.
"Andrew, I certainly enjoyed myself tonight." Sabrina kissed him. Just
then, a Plymouth Prowler drove up with a swarthy, bodyguard type behind
the wheel. Without another word, Sabrina turned and got in the car, not
looking at the driver. Andrew stood back and memorized the make and
color. Bright yellow. How hard is that? The Prowler was a common rental
on the island. That and Harley Davidson motorcycles. People had an
affinity for exotic transport when they were in like surroundings, so the
demand was consistent.
Andrew walked through the restaurant and out to the veranda, which
overlooked the bay. It was dark, but the action on the docks was still
visible. The traffic on the Cornishe paralleling the bay was light, and
Andrew caught a glimpse of what he thought was the yellow Prowler.
Trees and hotels obstructed his sight for a moment, and then he saw it
clearly. It was Sabrina in the passenger seat speeding north toward the
Tower Docks. The car turned in at Dock 12 and Andrew lost sight of it.
Soon it emerged going to the end of the pier. Andrew noticed a speed boat
waiting for them. Only Sabrina got out of the car, and like she'd done it
before, she went down the ramp and got in the boat.

Andrew could just make out the boat as it skimmed toward one of the medium sized yachts Andrew had noticed earlier in the evening... Try as he might, Andrew couldn't see anything happen on the boat. He waited for a jealous lover to appear, but there was no way to tell. Andrew stared a while longer, feared he looked pathetic, so he headed for the exit.

He decided to walk a while. Taxis were easy to find, so he'd get one on the other side of town. Normally, Andrew would just slide into another watering hole and continue his quest for interesting life, but he had lost the motivation. Maybe something would turn up later.

Looking in the storefronts, it was the standard fare with more artwork than usual. One gallery chain that his organization had done business with was just up the street. Andrew went to see what they were offering. The security lights were on inside so browsers could browse as they walked by. Andrew was not all that impressed with Claire's selections. He did see one of his paintings from the South American group. That was two years ago. Sheesh. Are sales that bad? As he was turning away, he caught a glimpse of something in the back. Andrew did a double take and shivered at the déjà vu moment.

It had the same bright colors and color scheme as the group of paintings he'd seen in the closet at work. Surely it wasn't. That was a little too coincidental. What were the chances an unrelated artist created that painting? Perplexed, Andrew decided to check on it during business hours. The night was quiet, and maybe a little lonely. Although Andrew was a dedicated, single person, he was almost a pathetic romantic and Sabrina was surely full of intrigue. Andrew vowed to put her out of his mind tomorrow. She would be a great subject for a painting though. The evening brought many mental compositions of how he would paint her. And he did happen to know where she lived. Maybe.

# Chapter 14

Bandundu, Democratic Republic of the Congo

"Bhaniel! Bhaniel!" The kids and workers who had made the trek to the river's edge and gathered to wait on her arrival were excited to finally see her. Thankfully, Bhaniel was able to catch the ferry at this late hour so the welcoming committee didn't have to go home empty handed.

Theresa made her way through the throng to embrace Bhaniel.

"Bhaniel! Welcome back!"

Theresa had an endless supply of energy and was as strong as most men. No one crossed her or for that matter had ever seen her mad, but no one wanted to test her. The local men formed a highly fictional legend about her, but Theresa paid no attention.

"Hello, Theresa. It's great to see you."

"Let's get your stuff home and put you to bed. I know you're dead tired."

"I'm so glad the kids came with you. How is everyone?"

"Surprisingly well, although it seems like you've been away a year. Only two kids got sick while you were gone. But, they're better. Which reminds me, were you able to get plenty of medicine?"

"Yes, but it's not going to be here for a week or so. You and Danaa may have to ride in and pick it up at the airport."

"Not a problem." Theresa's face became stern. "Shera is acting up again. I don't know what is getting into that girl's head. Tamego is actually helping around the property with odd chores. He's getting pretty good at some of the maintenance jobs."

The kids hoisted Bhaniel's luggage and assorted bags onto a two-wheel cart tied to a donkey. Theresa tapped it on the hind-quarters and it walked off toward the orphanage. The throng pushed toward the home after hugs and greetings were shared. Bhaniel was in no hurry now. She was back with the ones she loved and cared for. It would take a day or two to get her feet under her, but the opportunity to reacquaint herself with the routine of life in the DRC was comforting in this moment.

"Is there any dinner left, I'm hungry."

"Sure. We may have to reheat it."

Theresa looked at her for a moment and decided to hold her tongue. Bhaniel knew what she was curious about.

"It's okay, Theresa. You can ask me how the fund raising went."

"Do I look that eager? I can wait until later, really. I know you're tired. Tomorrow at daybreak is fine."

Bhaniel laughed with her.

"We can hash over the details tomorrow, but I will tell you that it went great. One of our artists' collections sold very well. Probably as strong of an auction as we've had. Hopefully he will contribute works next year also. Most of the organizations we have dealt with for several years are pledging similar amounts, so I think we will be okay for the near future. Veronica is doing a great job working it all out."

Theresa was visibly relieved. She was a stout lady. Not afraid of man nor beast, but she was a worrier when it came to issues out of her control. And money was one of the primary issues. In the case of the orphanage and the organization as a whole, Theresa was an integral member, but with little talent for finance. It was a primary factor for her initial affiliation with Bhaniel and the organization. Always driven to the Lord's work in some fashion, her vigorous work ethic and vision for great things hurled her to the forefront wherever she went.

Unfortunately, in America, that meant executing administrative duties and handling contributions which were beyond her gifting. Many good things were accomplished with the money available, but unglamorous items like mortgages and utility bills were often forgotten. Once it was exposed, Theresa was relegated to a lower position and all the shame she could stand. Or in one instance, the nonprofit organization just went belly up. After the denial and acceptance course was concluded, Theresa moved on and repeated the scenario. She had three complete train wrecks under her belt when her reputation began to precede her. Theresa learned a curious lesson in the months that followed. There is nothing more degrading than being rejected by a nonprofit organization.

By the time she came across Bhaniel Tretechi, Theresa was willing to acknowledge her weakness. Her strengths as well. Bhaniel aggressively desired her involvement, but with limitations. It would be challenging. Theresa's strong will would test Bhaniel, but she knew it would make her a better leader. If it didn't kill her.

# Chapter 15

The Grand Village Resort, Aruba

Andrew woke up with the wind blowing in his face. Window shutters slapped hard against the siding on the covered porch, and the breeze hurried through the cabin and out the screen door. The clouds were rolling in early today. The bedside lamp was still on and Andrew lay on the couch with a drawing pad on his chest. He finished the previous evening drawing likenesses of Sabrina. Four quick sketches rested on the coffee table, and the drawing pad contained three more. Andrew sat up and righted himself. Two newspapers and a pitcher of coffee sat on a tray outside the front door. Andrew took just a brief, cool shower. The constant humidity made leisurely, steamy showers unpleasant. One did not know when the showering stopped and the sweating began. Andrew sat on the couch in his towel and tested the coffee. He set the newspapers down next to last night's drawings and something caught his eye. Drawing number 3 showed Sabrina standing between two men held at arm's length from each other. There was also a woman behind her that appeared to overshadow Sabrina. In the upper right hand corner was a perfect kiss applied with burgundy lipstick.
"How in the ..."
There were only a few explanations for the presence of lipstick on his drawing. Although his imagination was fully charged, the reality of someone sauntering through his quarters in the night was unsettling. Instinctively, Andrew checked his wallet to see if the visitor had burglarized him. His buddies Ben Franklin and Ulysses Grant were still there. He wished it had been Sabrina, and that he would have awakened. He wondered if he snored during the break in.

The intrigue had a romantic twist engaging Andrew's adrenaline. He was ready to hit the street and see what adventures lay in wait. After a big, American breakfast, he would start off by visiting the art gallery from last night. Andrew decided against a full, frontal assault on Sabrina's boat since he appeared to be the prey. For the time being, he would do his thing and look for more clues. She's pretty resourceful, he thought. Andrew had not mentioned where he was staying last night.

"Hello. Welcome to Rowena Gallery. Are you looking for anything in particular?"

Andrew elected to play dumb and see if the sales lady could give him any clues.

"Thank you. I was looking for something with bright colors."

"Well, we have several selections that might meet those criteria."

The middle-aged lady walked over to a number of landscapes that were vibrant, but not the paintings Andrew was aiming at. She was stately, yet casual. The resort locale made it acceptable to wear light cotton and remain properly dressed for fine art.

"These are lovely. Are they 'Matalans'?"

"Why, yes they are. You are a collector?" Her interest in Andrew elevated due to his familiarity with art. She had all but given up on interacting with knowledgeable people in this gallery. So far from civilization.

"Not exactly. Just a fan. Do you have something with more dramatic, primary colors?"

She looked around and spied the Diegos.

"We just received these in the other day."

Andrew took a studious look at one nearly identical to the one he carried into Stella's office.

"Diego? Do you know anything about the artist?"

"We don't know much yet. All that I know at this time is that he is a Hispanic man with epilepsy. He paints during minor seizures to achieve a more primitive feel to his work. We believe that he will be a true star in the art world."

Brother. Stella had said the same line so many times, it amazed Andrew that anyone still believed such a claim.

"How many of his paintings do you have?"

"Three now, but we'll have four more by the end of the month."

"Are they all similar to this one?"

"I believe so. My contact in the States indicated as much."

"Do you have a brochure?"

"Yes, we have a brief description of his work. There will be a more illustrative brochure coming soon. Here."

"Thank you, and thank you for your time, Ms…"

"Rowena. Claire Rowena. I own the gallery."

"Nice to meet you, Ms. Rowena. My name is … Jones. Frank Jones."

Jones? Nice. You still think on your feet, Andrew.

"Mr. Jones are you thinking about purchasing one of Diego's paintings today?"

"I can't today, but I may be back. Thank you, good day."

"So long, Mr. Jones. Do come back."

Obeying the call to fall back and regroup, Andrew caught a cab back to the bungalow. He didn't feel like socializing at the moment. Andrew was glad the cleaning crew had come and gone. He might have tried to pick a fight with one of them just to make himself feel better. Andrew stood on the porch of the hut and stared at the surf. So Mitch was right. Stella had taken total control of the business, made a concerted effort to hide it from him and was en route to rubbing his nose in it. Why so clandestine? The irony was Andrew wasn't convinced that he would have opposed taking on a new artist if Stella was willing to talk it over.

With each rehashing of the facts and suppositions, Andrew clarified his role as the fool. He had passively accepted little changes over the years, and this was the result. Andrew pulled out the brochure and looked through it. The paintings were offered by a company called SM Group. What happened to AD Isaacson? It looked like Stella was preparing to break out on her own or just operate a new business venture without Andrew's input. At the very least, Stella was navigating treacherous legal waters, but she was very astute. Why would she try something like this without tying up the loose ends? Andrew's mind raced, but questions brought only further questions.

As the morning sun rose high in the sky, Andrew wrestled with and ultimately embraced the only course of action that made sense. He picked up the phone.

"Harvey, this is Andrew. How are you?"

"Hi Andrew, I'm good. What's up? I thought you were on holiday. I called the office yesterday and they said you were out."

"I am, but I've got something on my mind."

"Shoot."

"I need to keep this between you and me for now."

"Got it."

"Could you give some thought to what we need to do to dissolve AD Isaacson?"

"Sure. Wow, are you ill? This isn't the pina coladas talking is it?"

"No." Andrew laughed. "It's nothing desperate. I'm mostly on a fact-finding mission right now."

"When will you be back?"

"A couple of days. Will you have time to sit down and talk, say Monday?"

Harvey looked at his planner. Monday was free except for a court appearance in the morning.

"That'll work fine. 2 o'clock okay?"

"Yeah, I'll see you then. Thanks, Harvey."

Andrew threw on his trunks and made for a shady spot on the beach. He notified the attendants and pre-ordered a steady stream of beverages. Andrew took a magazine with him to occupy his mind. Not that it would help. There wasn't much that would improve his disposition right now.

"Hi, stranger."

Andrew looked over his shoulder at the approaching voice. It was Sabrina. Maybe there was something after all.

"Hello. This is a surprise."

Sabrina was sheathed in a bikini and floppy hat and smelled of coconut oil. She'd been at the beach for a while already.

"Mind if I share a lounge chair?"

"Sure. My chair is your chair. You staying around here?"

"Kind of."

"You're looking very lovely today." Andrew motioned for the attendant.

"Thanks. One of these days, I'll show up with clothes on."

The attendant brought drinks and condiments.

"I'm glad you came back."

"Came back? What do you mean?"

"I'm sorry I missed you last night in my bungalow."

"I have no idea what you're talking about." Sabrina had a twinkle in her eye.

"Next time, wake me up."

"Oh, are you staying around here?"  She said in faux surprise.

"Yes, I'll show you around later."

"I'd love it."

"You know, I'm sort of an expert on lips, and there's no mistaking the kiss was yours."

"I don't believe it. You can't prove it."

"There's only one way to make sure."

Andrew leaned closer and touched his lips to hers. He dropped back thoughtfully.

"Right again."

Sabrina licked her lips and studied his face.

"Proof requires further experimentation."

This time, Andrew lingered a bit. For some reason, he didn't care if the lipstick on the drawing was hers or not.

Andrew stopped to look at Sabrina.

"This may be poor timing, but is there a 'Mr. Thomas'?"

"What if there is?"

"Does he have a gun?"

"No and no. Does that ruin the mystery and excitement?"

"I'm relieved, actually. I think you are a long way from ruining the mystery."

"I'm just a woman on the loose. Enjoying the ride."
Sabrina smiled and tossed her hair behind her shoulder. She kissed him
again, hard, scraping her teeth against his.
"Want to go swimming?"
Sabrina moved over to his chair.
"Later."

"Mmmmm, the water and the sand feel so good," Sabrina cooed as she
stepped into the surf.
Andrew followed her into the water somewhat reluctantly. He was
definitely a beach guy, but not so much a water guy.
"And another perfect day."
"I wish I could stay here forever."
"I'm willing. How does dinner under the palm trees sound?"
"Sounds great… but I may have to leave soon after dessert. My ship sails
tonight."
"Stay. I'll fly you anywhere you want to go."
"You're sweet. Maybe we can meet back in the States."
Don't beg, Andrew. Stay positive.
"I'll buy the boat and fire the crew if they sail tonight."
"Andrew, you're a madman. Besides, you'd be wasting your money. That
old bucket is barely held together with seaweed and rubber bands."
Andrew studied her for a moment. He was forming an idea.
Sabrina began to grin. "What?"
"Come on."
Andrew took their drinks and strode along the beach toward his bungalow.
"Where are we going?"
"For a ride."

# Chapter 16

The Orphanage, Bandundu, DRC

"Mmm. I forgot how much I enjoy this casserole you make, Mischa."

"Thank you, Miss B. I made it special for your first day back."

"Now I'll sleep well. Am I in the same room or has someone claimed rights on it?"

"They did for a while, but I shooed them out as it got closer to your return date. We've got your room all ready for you."

"Well, I think I'll retire then. I'll see you in the morning. What's our schedule look like for tomorrow?"

"Fairly light. Just school in the morning and the older kids have a program they are going to present in the afternoon. It's pretty good. I've watched them practice."

"Wonderful. Good night then."

Bhaniel was asleep before she could arrange the bed sheets.

The following day, the kids presented their program. Three girls sang in a trio while Janette, a worker, played the guitar. Another small group of girls presented an original dance with fairly similar outfits with necklaces and bracelets they had made themselves. Seven boys and girls performed a Christmas drama of the manger scene, and the whole population sang in the choir. During the choir finale, only Bhaniel and three other workers were left in the audience. The crowd was indeed limited for such a performance, but the kids were focused on Bhaniel alone. It was their present to her and she was moved.

"Bravo! Fantastic everyone!"

Everyone gathered around Bhaniel for hugs and to rejoice.

"You've all done so well. We need to celebrate. How about some cookies and punch fresh from America?"

The kids erupted in glee and peppered Bhaniel with questions of what else was in the bounty from overseas.

"Miss B, did you bring back any toys?" asked five-year-old Qwara.

Bhaniel gave her a thoughtful look. "Maybe a few."

Qwara's idea of toys was fairly conservative to American sensibilities. Bhaniel used to fret over whether toys were necessary when gathering supplies in America although she never had to purchase such things. But, Bhaniel could not resist the immediate gratification she received when the kids delighted over presents brought just for them. Discarded toys from the average family were the Mother Lode to kids who had nearly nothing to call their own. Bhaniel did try to select small toys or inflatable items to maximize the number of toys she brought back.

"Do you have any pictures from your trip?" thirteen-year-old Uchenna queried.

"Yes I do. I'll get those right now. Everyone who wants some cookies, have a seat and we will have them out soon."

During the cookie fest, Bhaniel showed her pictures around while holding two little ones on her lap. Most of the pictures were taken in a two-day stretch while Bhaniel had a few hours free in Atlanta. She knew her kids would ask her if she had snapshots from home, and she didn't want to disappoint. In years past, Bhaniel took pictures of buildings and sites, but the kids seemed to like pictures of the people she met while in the States. Who's that? was the standard question for every picture.

"This is Cynthia Pressler. She is very involved in raising money and other work for our organization. Uchenna, you remember her from a few years ago? She came over here for two weeks."

Uchenna gave her a blank look.

"Maybe not."

The stack shuffled down to a picture of Andrew.

"That is Andrew Isaacson. He is an artist who provided several paintings for the auction. There he his standing next to one of the paintings that sold for lots of money which we use to buy good things for our home." Actual dollar amounts would not register with these little ones in a country where life was measured by day and night, living and dying. There were no style points in basic survival mode. One of the benefits for the kids who grew up in the home from infancy was the developed sense of life beyond starvation avoidance. They began to dream about possibility and wonder about the world around them.

"Is that good?"

"Yes. It means that I was able to bring back more food, clothes and toys!"

"Yay!"

"He may come over here sometime in the future."

"Neat! Will he do a painting of me?"

"Can he bring more cookies?"

As they rolled through the stack of pictures for the third time, Theresa stood over them.

"That's enough for now. One hour playtime outside, then we will begin supper duties."

With rapid shouts and scurrying feet, the contingent was out the door for kickball and sundry games. Theresa sat down next to Bhaniel and leafed through the pictures.

Bhaniel sighed and stretched. "It's good just to sit and hold them again. Pianga is getting so big."

"When I came back from holiday last spring, I was surprised at how much I missed everyone. I think I need them more than they need me."

"When will you take another holiday, Theresa? It's been quite a while since your last getaway."

"I don't think about it much. I'm getting old. All I think about when I'm away is coming back, so it may not be worth leaving."

"I wish you could have come with me this trip. I talk about you all the time to the donors and administration. All of them want to meet you."

"They need to come over here and see me. I'll put them to work."

Bhaniel smiled, "We don't want to scare them off."

"Tell me what you found out on your trip."

"Most of it was just meetings with administration, updating them on what's going on. I wondered if the American economy would impact the giving, but it hasn't yet. Dieter Graybill is retiring at the end of the year. We may have a hard time replacing him as Administrative Officer. He has been with the organization longer than anyone. There was some talk of opening another orphanage in Rwanda. One of the directors has some ties in that country, but the government chaos has slowed the process. We'll have to continue to pray for that to open up."

"Will they have you go over there to start it up?"

"I don't know. I would rather stay here for sure, but even if I did go there it would only be long enough to get it up and running."

"Miss B!! They're coming! It's the soldiers!"

The young ones shouted the loudest as they ran inside. All the kids knew what to do. Hide. A contingent of twelve armed thugs poured out of the back of two Toyota pickups. Few had complete uniforms, but all wore something that signified their association with Asafari Zuberi's regime. A slight, well-dressed lieutenant stepped out of the cab. The soldiers had been to the home before. Nothing good resulted from these visits except the stories, which were retold regularly by the kids, making the soldiers more demonic with each telling. The lieutenant walked through the front door with two of his underlings close behind.

"Where is it?"

He demanded of Theresa and one of the resident girls.

Theresa shooed two kids toward the kitchen and out the back door.
Hopefully, the others were headed to the various hideouts around the
compound. She cursed herself for being caught unaware. Usually, kids
playing would see them coming in time to warn the others.

Theresa wouldn't look at him.

"I don't know."

The lieutenant walked over and stood in front of Theresa.

"I think you do. Where is it?"

"I wouldn't tell you even if I knew."

Theresa put her chin up and looked him in the eye. The lieutenant smiled a
gold encrusted smile. He swung his right hand in a wide arc across her
face. Theresa was momentarily off balance, startled by the impact and
unsure what else the lieutenant might do. He was almost as surprised as she
because his best swing couldn't bring her down.

"Oh, yes, strong one. You will." His shoulders were back and his chest out.
A drop of sweat rolled down his forehead.

"Please, don't hurt her." Bhaniel came into the room and knelt beside
Theresa.

"I will hit whomever I please. Now tell me where it is."

"It's not here." Bhaniel knew what they wanted. "The shipment is still in
transit. I'm not sure how long it will take to get here."

"Search the property." He turned to Bhaniel. "We'll find out if you are
lying. For the sake of some of your girls, I hope you are not."

Bhaniel shook inside, but said nothing.

The first time the soldiers came to the village, they searched and found the
cache of medicine and took everything with black market value. Bhaniel
had not hidden anything, not realizing the danger. After extended
communications with the organization's board, more medicine was
shipped under tight security.

In the years since, Bhaniel and the organization were compelled to stagger
the arrival of supplies, so that the militia could not determine a pattern.
Bhaniel's departure and return became their only tip more saleable goods
were arriving. Still, they failed. Bhaniel knew the prayers of believers were
instrumental in thwarting the plans of the soldiers. Their lack of success
caused the soldiers – namely the lieutenant – to become more and more
violent.

The organization had talked about making double shipments of medicine.
One for the kids, and one for the soldiers. The risk of theft was expected,
but now the lives of the workers and children were at risk.

Thirty minutes passed and the men could find nothing.

"Nothing, Lieutenant."

The lieutenant grabbed Bhaniel's arm and half dragged her into a nearby
room, shutting the door behind him.

The lieutenant wiped the sweat from his face and neck.

"Do you understand I can do to you what I please?"

Bhaniel was calm. Many years had passed since she last feared for her life. Her primary concern was for her coworkers and the children.

"You can only do to me what God allows you to do."

The lieutenant's face tightened.

"I don't see God in this room."

"I know you cannot."

The lieutenant took Bhaniel by the arms and pressed her close to him. She turned her head to avoid breathing his stench.

"God won't be able to save you this time."

Bhaniel turned to him and met his eyes. No fear, only resolve.

At that moment, a knock came at the door.

"Lieutenant! We found something," came the voice from one of the soldiers.

The lieutenant entertained the idea of delaying the eager searchers, but he didn't want anyone of those maggots to steal his booty. He threw Bhaniel down and stomped to the door.

"What is it?"

"Lieutenant, I think you should see this. Come quickly."

As they went out of the building, Theresa and the two workers rushed in to Bhaniel.

"I'm alright. He didn't do anything to me."

"He may later when he finds out what we did."

"Theresa, what did you do?"

"We let them find the stash."

"Oh my. We may not have much time. Are all the kids hidden?"

"Yes."

"Then all of you go too."

"Not without you."

"Please, you know I'll be ok. And if something does happen, you know what to do."

Theresa hated Plan B. It was only useful if Bhaniel was dead.

"Are you going to hide at least?"

"Yes."

"Promise."

"Yes, go."

They nodded, hugged and dispersed.

The soldiers gathered around what they thought was a supply of saleable drugs.

"Get out of my way." The lieutenant pushed his way through.

He looked over the inventory and was slightly perplexed. Although he wasn't a deeply intellectual man, he knew basic math. And something didn't add up. The leader had not lied to him before. This find was almost too easy, like it was supposed to be found. But, it looked like legitimate narcotics.

"Take it to the truck."

The gathered men began to hoist the boxes two at a time. If Theresa's idea worked, the lieutenant wouldn't know the goods were false until he tried to sell the lot. And the buyers he worked with were said to be even more violent than the lieutenant himself. The orphanage workers were praying the charade held up until then. After that, may God's will be done. If it was successful, they were fairly certain the lieutenant and whoever was with him at the time would not survive the sales meeting.

Bhaniel did hide, but she positioned herself in the trees near the entrance to make sure the soldiers continued out the gate and down the road toward the river. After a few minutes of waiting, the soldiers came out of building three with several boxes emblazoned with red 'x's on the side and some packages of food. Most were smiling and moving quickly. The lieutenant remained wary however, pacing back and forth. Hopefully, the 'medicine' would salve his irritation long enough to leave the orphanage.

Because the truck blocked her view, Bhaniel did not see the lieutenant separate from the rest of the soldiers who were loading on the truck and slip through the back door of the main building. Once the boxes were on the truck, the soldiers hopped on and the convoy began to pull away. Once they were by Bhaniel's hiding place, she looked back toward the orphanage. The truck had scarcely passed outside the gate when Theresa emerged from her hideout. She gave a cursory look toward the gate and walked toward the main building.

Bhaniel swung down from the tree and hurried toward the building as well. The impact of the sound of gun fire caused her to hesitate and her heart to stop. In a full sprint she bounded through the front door. In the middle of the room, smoke from the gunfire still swirling, the lieutenant was standing over Theresa, on her knees staring at Bhaniel. He had his gun drawn and was pointing it at Theresa.

"I will take her with me for now."

"Take me."

"I do not believe I will. There is a greater chance that you will do what I want if she goes with me."

"You have the medicine, just go."

"Do I? It was a little too convenient how we found your inventory of medicine. Until I am satisfied with our transaction, I will take her as collateral."

Theresa was calm; she didn't want to show emotion to the likes of him. As he pulled Theresa to her feet, the lieutenant tied her arms at the elbow with some stray cord and led her out the front door.

"Theresa," Bhaniel called to her.

I'll be okay, Theresa mouthed as she stepped into the sunlight.

Her eyes showed she was not entirely certain. Bhaniel wanted to do something, anything, but couldn't think of one course of action that didn't end badly. Please, God. Stop this! She tried to talk to the lieutenant as he got in the jeep, but his men pushed her back.

"If it is as you say, we will have what we want and bring your worker back. Otherwise, the next time we come, the cost will be much higher."

He drove off with Theresa and two men trying to hold her down.

Bhaniel knelt down in the middle of the compound, the dust stirred up by the departing jeep still on her face. She looked up to the sky and began to call on God. The appeals got louder, and the workers came out of their hideouts. She turned to them and motioned for them to kneel with her.

"Pray with me."

"Bhaniel what happened?"

"They've taken Theresa."

As it sank in to each one joining the group, everyone dropped to their knees almost involuntarily. Prayer evolved into groaning and calling on the name of Jesus. The others began to echo Bhaniel, deepening their resolve with every wave, desperate to lay hold of the Savior. As the burden began to lift off of them, the kneeling group noticed the children had encircled them. Everyone was with them – save one.

The sun was going down. Some of the workers went in to prepare food for the kids.

"What can we do, Ma'am?"

"I don't know yet Sasha. I will have to start by calling the organization. I'll go to town in the morning to call."

Bhaniel fought the tendency to panic. She knew that if the soldiers tested the cache of medicine before they met the buyers, it would complicate things and test her belief Theresa would be alright.

"Lord, please blind their eyes to what they have. Hand them over to their fate, like those who fall in their own trap."

# Chapter 17

The Eastern Shore of Aruba

"Ooh, these cliffs and the water are fantastic! I didn't know they existed."
Sabrina was truly enjoying the adventure.
The fact was, Andrew didn't know about the oasis either until a local
produce vendor told him where it was. Apparently, it was bad native policy
to reveal certain secrets to the tourists. Andrew knew he had made the club
when the often rumored island secrets had been disclosed. He was sure
there were more, but progress was slow.
The retreat was in the heart of Arikok National Park, but without specific
directions, access was impossible. The adventurous duo stood on some
rocks a few feet above the water, and enjoyed the beauty of the crystal
clear pool before them.
"Let's jump."
"Is it cold?"
"Noooo. It's great." Andrew was lying. "We can go together."
Sabrina was a sucker for adventure.
"On the count of three."
"Is it deep enough?"
"Sure, you can see twenty feet down."
"On three."
"One. Two. Three!"
Sabrina screamed out loud when her head popped up out of the water.
"It's freezing!"
Andrew was laughing. "Sorry. I was afraid you wouldn't get in."
"You're right." Sabrina swam to Andrew and put her arms around him.
"You'll have to keep me warm now."
Andrew smiled. The plan was a go.
"I don't know if I can get you back to the boat in time."

"No worries. I'm pretty sure they won't leave without me."
The remainder of the afternoon was spent swimming and sunning. It was their own personal Garden of Eden. No one came around and as far as Andrew was concerned, it could have lasted forever. As the sun began to set and the shadows around the waterfalls lengthened, Sabrina got up on an elbow and looked at Andrew.
"I've got to go."
Andrew ran his hand down her arm and looked at her face. He knew it was time to go as well.
"Can I drive you to the boat?"
"Sure. I'd like that."

The drive back to the main road and along the coast was beautiful in the fading light. Neither said much. Sabrina held Andrew's arm most of the way.
"There it is."
The boat wasn't hard to spot. It was anchored just a short distance from shore.
"Where do I let you off?"
"Here is good." Only sand separated them from the water. A small speed boat was motoring toward them.
As Andrew pulled over, he longed to go with her.
Reading his thoughts, "I wish you could come along."
"Swing around the point and pick me up by my bungalow in ten minutes."
"You're cute. I'll be back in the States next week. Call me."
"Deal. Is ten times a day too many?"
"I will expect nothing less. Thank you, Andrew Isaacson. I have had a wonderful time."
Sabrina kissed him passionately, got out of the car and walked to the boat. She looked around and waved as the boat's motor revved to life and sped away.

Andrew sat alone on the plane staring at the cloud formations laid out like stepping stones to the edge of the world.
"Would you like something to drink, sir?"
Andrew came back to the present and waved off any refreshments. He stretched and looked around for something to occupy his mind. As he rifled through his carry-on under the seat, he came across the Rowena Gallery brochure. Diego. Who in the world is Diego? Andrew didn't like the style. It was gaudy, too bright, unbalanced.

It's all irrelevant anyway. Andrew contemplated his future. Briefly. All he knew as a certainty was the world ahead wouldn't include Stella. He had lost any urge to fight when he next saw her. He'd let the attorneys do that. Andrew really couldn't blame her for doing what she does best. Manipulation for financial gain. Personal gain. Lots of gain. She'd always had an allergic reaction to being accountable to anyone else, however. If Stella only had a thin film of conscience to hem her in occasionally, it might make reconciliation a possibility. But, it was time. The line had irretrievably been crossed. Finis, Andrew decided. He adjusted his seat and made plans to wake up at the terminal.

"You're sure."
She drew a deep breath. "Yes, Jacque wrote it down word for word."
Stella reread the note. "Meet Harvey - Mon/Tues next week. Corp dissolution papers. Plans for potential lawsuit. Court restraining order."
"Did he say anything about this to you?"
"No, but Jacque saw him go into the Rowena Gallery and talk to the owner about the Diego paintings. Then he found the note when I was with Andrew on the beach."
"He doesn't know you saw this note?"
"No."
Stella eased a little.
"Well, your efforts are greatly appreciated. I believe this is the amount we agreed on."
Stella handed her a wire transfer receipt.
"Thank you dear. This is a bonus. I would have – almost – done it for free. He's a sweet guy. I hope you'll go easy on him."
"You can believe I will take great pains in handling him." Stella smiled without showing her teeth.
"Call me."
"Bye, Love."
Sabrina got up to leave.

Andrew pulled into the parking garage level D. He was late today, but wasn't expected back until next week. Pulling into his space, he noticed someone exiting the elevator and crossing the garage in the dim light. That looks like Sabrina! Andrew made a move to get out of his car and call her over when it hit him.
He never told her where he worked or where he lived for that matter.

"Hello, Stella."
"Andrew, hi." She was clearly startled. "What are you doing home? Weren't you going to go to Aruba for *two* weeks?"
"I was, but something came up."

"How was it? Rainy again?"

"No, it was fine. Pretty relaxing for the most part."

Andrew was unsure of how much to say.

"Did you take your girlfriend?"

"No, she doesn't come around much anymore."

Pause.

"Who was the lady I saw leaving just now?"

Stella's eyes and sphincters constricted.

"Could have been anybody."

"The lady in the blue dress. Blonde hair."

"I don't know who that is. Andrew we have all sorts of people coming and going around here."

"But not all of them leave here in your Lexus."

"What?!"

"I'm sure she's just borrowing it."

Stella scrambled through her purse for her keys.

"How did she get them …" Stella mumbled to herself.

"Who is she, Stella?"

Andrew would have enjoyed the chance to make Stella squirm, but it was becoming evident that he was the patsy in another of her schemes.

"She's … an old friend. Why do you ask?"

"How much did you pay her?"

"What do you mean?"  Stella knew she was in the crosshairs.

"Let's go back to 1998. Barbados. It was a Brazilian girl named Anna Marie. She was great, I have to admit. Must have cost the company a bundle. Or how about 2002? Daniela from the Czech Republic. What a knock out. I can just imagine the hit our bottom line took on her."

Stella decided to roll with it.

"Andrew, they weren't prostitutes. They are all friends. I considered it a blind date of sorts. I just paid their way to the same resort. You should thank me."

"It's ironic that none of them were motivated to date anymore once they got back to the States. You know the sad part? I am pathetic enough to believe the lie. Luckily, they were all fantastic while it lasted. The sinister side of it is the possibility you hired them to babysit me or keep an eye on me, whatever you want to call it."

"Call it what it is, a favor from a friend."

"But that is the problem. I didn't – don't want relational help."

"Well, you need it, trust me…"

"No. I don't. I would rather crash and burn trying to meet my own choice of companion than to continue with the handouts. You're a control freak, Stella. As my hindsight gets clearer, it is obvious you have controlled every detail of our company and evidently me for a long time."

Stella studied Andrew as he talked.

"It's time for us to dissolve the company. I need to go a different direction. Actually make my own decisions for a change."

Stella was dumbstruck Andrew had the audacity to believe she needed him and his continuing involvement for the company to be successful. So, she patronized him.

"Andrew, will you be honest with yourself? You need me."

Stella moved in front of her desk looking down on Andrew.

"It's not in your personality to go out on your own. The business side will eat you up. I'd give you eighteen months tops. Don't do this. You don't want to have to come groveling back to me." Stella was faux pleading.

Andrew either didn't care anymore, or he was completely and finally serene in his resolve.

"Sorry, Stella. There is nothing you can do or say now. We are going to dissolve AD Isaacson as quickly as possible."

Stella's demeanor cooled as she went back to her chair. "Fine. Let me know when you have it all ready for me to sign."

"And I'm taking the name with me. With 75% of the existing assets."

Oooh. That hurt Stella. Her head whipped around to see if he was joking.

"What makes you think you can do that? We're 50/50 on everything."

"Unless you begin to make decisions for the company unilaterally. Read the by-laws. Whatever you have been doing with this "Diego" person is the perfect example, and for me the final straw."

"You do this and I'll drag you to court and clean you out."

"I guessed you would threaten me. If it goes to court, I intend on making this last for 10 years and allow my attorney the opportunity to get rich on AD Isaacson's assets. If you are going to make this difficult, I would rather he get it than you."

Andrew simply had blank look on his face.

Stella was convinced Andrew was bluffing. He wasn't smart enough to pull this off. Harvey was another matter. He was a good attorney and he stood to make some money off of this feud. She needed time to think.

She threw her hands up. "You win."

"Win? Win? Stella, I don't want to win. This should have been a partnership. A team. That's why when some of my friends tried to tell me that you were playing me, I brushed it off and stubbornly believed you were above such petty tricks. Now there is no other option. You need to go your own way and I need to be free of the sham this company has become."

Stella was unemotional. "What's the next step? We split the sheets?"

"Basically. The auditors will come in and assess the company as its stands right now. Then the attorneys will get their claws in it. Harvey said my proposal for how to split the assets will be ready for your review in two weeks. Any official act on behalf of the company by yourself will have to be approved by the auditors and of course, me."

"Fine. I will talk to Martha and begin the process on my side."
"If you need me for something, I'll be in my office."
Andrew left with no more words spoken.
Stella sat motionless for several minutes while her mind red-lined. She was confident she could start a company from scratch with little noticeable change in her routine. But this was personal. She now wanted to humiliate Andrew and take from him all that he valued. Numerous plans and scenarios were mentally cataloged and evaluated for future use. The first order was to have Martha look over the by-laws and contracts and look for any possible opening which would enable Stella to impose the sleaziest, most despicable course of action on Andrew and his beloved AD Isaacson. The name. Yes, the name AD Isaacson needs to be destroyed in the process. She leaned back and rested her eyes. This might be fun, but she was getting a headache just the same.

# Chapter 18

The Orphanage, Bandundu

"Wake up, Bhaniel. It's nearly daybreak."

"Thank you, Mischa." Bhaniel tried to raise her arms. Her whole body was frozen in place on the floor where she fell asleep, finally, after holding vigil before the Lord deep into the night.

Mischa helped her up and gave her some water.

"Do you want me to go with you, Bhaniel?"

"I wish you could, dear, but I have to go alone."

Mischa knew although Bhaniel was kind and accommodating, she wouldn't budge when it came to protecting the other workers.

"How long will you be gone?"

"I don't know, dear. It became apparent to me last night that I will have to go to the capital before I contact the organization."

"The last time you did that, you were gone over a week." Mischa was concerned for Bhaniel, but also for the safety of all who were to remain at the orphanage.

"I am confident everyone will be safe. That is something I wrestled with all last night. You have provisions and I am going to send a man from town to stay with you while I am gone."

The other workers were coming into the main building now. Some had the same look as Bhaniel - like they had spent the night praying not sleeping.

Mischa went around telling young and old what Bhaniel's plans were.

Some wanted to ask more questions, but most just looked at Bhaniel as she prepared for her journey. Almost as quickly as she came back to them, the workers and kids were saying goodbye to Bhaniel.

"Try to get word to us how you are doing if you can," Mischa said.

"Miss B., I miss you already," cried young Dalani as she hugged her.

"Don't be sad, everyone. I'll be back very soon."

As Bhaniel made her way outside, Mischa touched her arm.

"Come back to us."

"I will. I love you."

The kids followed Bhaniel out to the gates and watched her as far as the Cyprus tree at the bend.

"Let's go back, children. There are chores and school work to be done." The sun had just bounded off the horizon and another day was well under way.

Bhaniel was wary of this trip. She had made it twice before in the last seven years, but this would be the first time she would make a request of her brother. During the night, the Lord had made it plain what she was to do. He opened Bhaniel's eyes to her brother's fate and clarified the purpose of going to him. She had no promise of success, but the message was simple. Bhaniel had approached him the other two times with prophetic words. To her knowledge, the negative consequences never took place which led her to believe he had heeded the Lord's direction.

Tirek was surprised to see Bhaniel again so soon. He greeted her as an old friend. The bus ride was physically tiring, but she always enjoyed the people she met or reacquainted herself with during the trip. Many of the people knew of her orphanage and wished they could help in some way. Unfortunately, as with most citizens of the country, few people had resources beyond the sparest of daily needs.

# Chapter 19

Stella's Office, AD Isaacson Galleries

"You've got to be kidding."

"No, it's right there in the contract. If Andrew can prove that he had no knowledge of certain activities by yourself, the company can be dissolved in the portions he told you."

Stella was preparing to slam the phone down on the desk when Maria made another comment almost offhand.

"There is one qualifying issue, however. If one of you dies, the company goes into a trust, but the surviving party acts as executor of the business trust. Also, the surviving party has the authority to run the company if the other party is incapacitated in some way."

The words ricocheted through her brain, gathering steam. A twinkle formed in her eye.

In Stella's best nonchalant voice, she said "I don't see that helping us. Andrew is in great health. We'll have to give it some more thought. I'll talk to you later."

Stella saw a crease in the armor. All she needed now was a plan.

# Chapter 20

The Presidential Palace, near Kinshasa, DRC

Zuberi shut the door to his chambers and removed his jacket. That small function was a welcomed part of the day for him. His uniform was getting too heavy to wear due to the dazzling array of medals he felt compelled to display on his person. He dropped the jacket on the back of the leopard skin couch and loosened his tie on the way to the drink that had been prepared for him on the Louis XIV bureau. The first was a gulp. He'd taste the next one. The dictator scarcely noticed the knock on the door. As he turned, his valet opened the door and stepped halfway into the room.
"Many pardons, Commander. We have a visitor at the gate. It is the orphanage owner again. She is begging to see you."
Zuberi never could understand why his men were unable to deal with this woman without getting him involved. She was a nuisance and he was tired of her. In reality, the men closest to the leader knew that she was the dictator's sister and any unauthorized action against her could unleash Zuberi's unpredictable wrath. The slight woman had appealed to the leader on more than one occasion and his men had been amazed at Zuberi's gentleness toward her. He looked at the servant for a moment.
"Send her in, Unifri. But this will not occur again. If you disturb me again regarding this woman, you will be removed."
Unifri bowed and backed out of the room.
The guards hustled the visitor to the main living quarters, careful not to make the leader wait. Zuberi didn't look at her when she entered. Bhaniel stepped just inside the door and remained there against the wall.
"What do you want Bhaniel."
"Thank you for receiving me, Asafari." Bhaniel drew a breath.

"I would like you to help me, brother. Soldiers came to our orphanage and took medicine again, but this time they kidnapped one of our workers as well. Lieutenant Raswa took her because he suspected us of hiding something from him."

Zuberi broke into a sideways grin when he heard the lieutenant's name. "I'm not sure what I can do. What are you prepared to do for me in return?"

"I have a word from the Lord for you that could save your life."

"That is worth nothing to me, woman. I can't eat it or sell it."

"It could be worth a great deal, brother. This time, I believe you are in mortal danger."

He sipped his drink, scarcely hearing her.

"I'm in danger every day. This is not disturbing information, and don't call me brother."

"This is different. Asafari, I pray to my God for you every day. Last night He told me very plainly that your life is in danger and you must heed the warning."

"Woman, you are as mad as your mother. My own advisors do not foresee this impending doom. Why should I believe you?"

The reference to her mother cut into Bhaniel and stirred her emotions for her family, long since cold. Bhaniel had few happy memories of her life as a child growing up with her mother and two twin brothers. She knew of a distant family tie to a brother that would eventually seize control of the military and political factions in their troubled country. Her immediate family was in constant danger, which culminated in a midnight invasion of their home by soldiers loyal to Zuberi. They took her brothers away and Bhaniel never saw them again. The apparent deaths of her two brothers had killed their mother eventually; and though she never spoke of it to Bhaniel, Zuberi's guilt was obvious. Even so, Bhaniel had been commissioned to warn him.

"I do care for you, Asafari. But I also know that you can have me killed. I would not have taken the risk to come here now if I were not completely convinced that the word was true and from the Lord."

"I rule this country and have thousands of men at my disposal to protect me and fight for me. But to avoid this danger, I must do as you say. Bah. I am tiring of this."

Bhaniel knew she only had a few seconds left.

"The Lord says, 'Cancel your meeting with the Defense Minister tomorrow. Return Bhaniel's worker to her, set free others that have been wrongfully imprisoned and distribute a portion of your reserves to the poor. If you do these things, your life will be spared and your regime will be strengthened.'"

He glanced at her.

"That almost sounds like a threat to me. Woman, go back to your orphans and quit worrying about me. You're delusional and your god has led you astray. If you come to the palace again, I will have you put in prison."
She knew there were no other words to say. Bhaniel could not honestly say she desired safety and long life for her "brother", but his unwillingness to act not only jeopardized him but also the likelihood that Theresa would be recovered quickly. Finality washed over her. She was certain his fate was sealed. Bhaniel bowed her head. Only now did she realize her heart was pounding. Bhaniel turned toward the door slowly, and left without looking at him again.

Asafari tried to shake the chill that came over him. She was a nut. Always had been. Her mother was the same way. God says this, god says that. His father, the great leader Tribien Zuberi made a mistake siring illegitimate children with the woman, but her worthless daughter had no right to call him her brother. Yet he was perplexed at her desire to fear for his safety. How did she know he was going to meet with the Defense Minister tomorrow? Maybe he would gulp the next one as well.

"Unifri, contact Lieutenant Raswa. Tell him to come to the palace, and bring the woman with him....

And wipe the door down again."

# Chapter 21

The Offices of AD Isaacson Galleries

Andrew picked up the phone. Speed dial seven.

"Hi, Harvey. Yeah. Stella and I just had the talk. No, I don't plan to talk to her again about the split. It's in your hands now. When are the accountants going to be here? Yes. I have general ledger data for today's date and am going downstairs to talk with Helen after I get off the phone. She's always been reliable. No, she won't transact any business without getting prior approval. Okay. We'll set up a room for them on Thursday. Yes, have them ask for me when they get here. Sure. Okay, thanks Harvey. What? Where are you going? Hey, that's great. I didn't realize you had the hunting trip planned. Canada? Are you going to camp at Big River Bend again? Awesome. Shoot straight. I'll see you next week."

Harvey was a good operator and a good friend. What had it been now? Twenty years? He couldn't believe how time raced forward, especially since the first few had dragged on like a chronic illness. But that was typical of life after divorce. One of Harvey's partners had been recommended by a friend to handle Andrew's divorce, but the court proceedings were rocky from the beginning. If it hadn't been for Harvey stepping in with some well-timed advice, Andrew would have lost everything. Andrew deserved to lose a fair portion, but there had to be a limit. His wife and son should be living very comfortably on the cash flow from the final decree. Rachelle never remarried – as far as he knew – so the continued support was well justified. Unfortunately, the final agreements allowed Andrew only occasional time with his son. As the months wore on, it was easier for Andrew to skip scheduled meeting times, and eventually he lost touch completely. To his best recollection, Andrew thought Rachelle and Leo had moved to Virginia eight or nine years ago. Harvey would know for sure. Leo would be. . . almost 23 now.

Wow. Andrew couldn't believe he was thinking about all of that right now. He had plowed ancient memories of such things deep into the landfill of his past many years ago. He was determined to start anew. This was another closing chapter of Andrew's life Harvey would guide him through. Good riddance. It was going to be a welcome change.

In the other office, Stella hung up the phone. She had decided to listen in on Andrew's conversations to give her whatever advantage could be gained. That was quick, she thought to herself. Andrew has served up his attorney to me on a silver platter. Big River Bend. Never heard of it, but I'll soon find out.

"Eugene! Get in here. I've got a project for you."

"Sure. Whaddya got?"

"I need you to book a last minute hunting trip for a friend of mine."

"How many are going?"

"Just one."

"One?"

"Yes. He's going to meet some friends there."

Stella was pleased with herself. The war of attrition had begun.

# Chapter 22

The Presidential Palace

The oversized door of the palace slammed shut behind her. Bhaniel began walking to the gate fifty meters away. As she exited the palace compound, Bhaniel paused and looked over the city from the plateau where the palace had been built. It felt as though her strength was completely gone. Her first desire was to just drop to the ground and pass out. It wasn't physical exhaustion, but the near complete destruction of hope. Bhaniel didn't know what to do next. She did not want to leave the city without finding Theresa, but Bhaniel had nowhere to turn.

"Lord, you know my heart and my need. I obeyed your word and talked to my brother. Please lead me by your Spirit and give me understanding for the next step."

As an act of her will, she began to walk on the side of the road downward toward town. Whatever was going to happen, she believed it would be better to get away from the palace.

The sun was still high in the afternoon sky. It wasn't long before the dust from the shoulder of the road began to mix with sweat on Bhaniel's forehead and hands. Cars occasionally passed her, and one cart drawn by a slender bovine operated by a boy with a whip crossed over the road in the direction of the foothills.

The city was in the distance about three kilometers. Not that making it there was going to improve Bhaniel's situation, but she was hopeful some water was available to buy. Staying overnight didn't seem reasonable nor safe. If she found a transport, Bhaniel would sleep during the trip, but another bus ride was unlikely today.

Closer to the center of town, makeshift booths and tents were constructed against the sides of the buildings along the road and in the city center. The primary intersection was also clogged with tents and any manner of shanty that allowed persons to remain there throughout the day. In the center was another statue that honored the nation's leader. He was very regal and imposing, on his horse with a sword in his hand. As Bhaniel reached the edge of the plaza, a phalanx of vehicles entered from the opposite side. It was a military convoy and the lead vehicle didn't slow down even for the transition through the city center. Since they would indeed come right by Bhaniel, she stepped away from the road so that their momentum wouldn't throw dirt or gravel her way.

Just then, her body froze as recognition set in. It was the same convoy that Lt. Raswa had commanded at the orphanage, and Lt. Raswa was in the fourth car, sitting in the back seat. Bhaniel instinctively stepped back further behind a nearby tent so she would not be recognized. She peeked around the corner looking for Theresa but didn't see her. She had no choice but to follow. If the lieutenant was going to see her brother, then he might have heeded her – the Lord's – advice. Bhaniel set out to retrace her steps. The long day just got longer, but there was a renewed energy and strength in her step. It wasn't full blown hope, but certainly a spark in the darkness.

"Ride?" It was an old man with an ancient cart and half-dead donkey.

"I must go toward the palace."

He nodded and motioned for her to get on. "I am going that way."

As they neared the palace, the cart slowed.

"Thank you. You have helped me very much. I'm so sorry I can't pay you."

The wrinkled man just waved her off and smiled. Not necessary he said. Bhaniel jumped off where his path diverged from the palace road and she walked the remaining kilometer. She had seen the convoy continue up this road and go into the palace grounds. If anything positive occurred when they came out, she would be there to take advantage.

It was nearing dusk and Bhaniel wasn't sure what she was going to do once she reached the walls of the compound. There didn't seem to be anywhere for her to wait or loiter until the convoy or Theresa emerged. The trees might be her best option. If she stayed within the stand of trees, then one frail female might escape the casual view of soldiers or other people monitoring the palace grounds.

Evening turned to night and there was no activity. Bhaniel sat at the base of the biggest tree and occasionally glanced toward the gates. She was hungry and tired. Bhaniel fought the urge to sleep in case the lieutenant emerged at an inopportune time. Minutes turned into hours. Bhaniel could no longer contend with her exhaustion and she drifted into a fitful sleep.

# Chapter 23

Northern British Columbia wilderness

Harvey needed a break. He sat down on a rock outcropping and he placed his MG Arms Ultra-Light hunting rifle with the laser aided scope next to him. It was surprising to him when he went on one of these trips how tired he could get in such a short time. His workout regimen was not as efficient as it used to be. Late 40's didn't sound so old, but Harvey's knees weren't going to withstand the endless miles of tracking much longer. None of the young guys on the trip had any empathy for the aged. All of them were still ten feet tall and bullet proof. The miles of walking didn't seem to faze them at all. Unfortunately, none of his hunting buddies, young or old, were around right now. He had faded behind, which suited Harvey. Just being out in the Great White North was enjoyment enough. The Canadian Rockies extending to the Liard River were just to the west. The sun was just cresting the eastern horizon and bouncing off of the white peaks. Harvey could see for miles around, but wasn't completely sure where he was. No matter. The GPS unit would lead him home when it was time for lunch.

He didn't notice there was indeed another soul within a few klicks of his position. The assassin had tracked the attorney from the lodge and was comfortable with his invisibility. The other members of the hunting party had obliged him by creating a dramatic separation between them and the attorney. Also, his frequent stops to rest made him an easier target. The only danger was if he happened to notice him or if a herd of elk appeared out of nowhere. It would have been tidier if he was closer to the foothills. Tucked into a crag in the hills or, even better, a small canyon would make his remains almost impossible to find. The trained marksman positioned himself to see if he had a clean shot.

The rising sun warmed Harvey's face as he watched his breath dissipate. There was no other place on earth he would rather be. He tried to memorize the moment so that he could enjoy it all over again when he was toiling in his office back in the "real" world. Harvey breathed deeply and reached into his breast pocket for one of his energy bars. As he grabbed the snack he felt the impact and pressure in his rib cage. In a moment, he could no longer breathe or move. A host of things ran through his mind, but his reasoning turned to panic because his limbs had gone limp. He slumped over and saw himself fall to the ground. The bullet had entered the right side of his torso and exited the left. The trajectory had in fact punctured the right ventricle of his heart and shredded the left lung. There was not much blood after the impact because he expired seconds after he contacted the ground.

The gunman stayed low and quietly cleared his weapon. He pulled the gilley suit off and stowed it underneath a rock group and turned his jacket inside out. Suddenly, he looked like any other hunter traversing the great outdoors. Quickly, he made his way to the deceased attorney and removed his phone and GPS unit. Both were turned off and destroyed. The shooter dragged Harvey quite a distance and stowed him underneath a rock outcropping to make airborne searches unfruitful. Unless a rescue team stumbled on to him, this would be Harvey McCallum's final resting place. As stealthily as he came in, the contract killer made his way to a different area of the hunting lands. He had been looking forward to bagging an elk while he was here and felt like luck was on his side. He would leave the publication of his handiwork to the media as the missing attorney's story would ultimately be told by multiple news outlets.

# Chapter 24

The Presidential Palace

"Open the gate!" The voice came from somewhere inside the walls echoing through the trees. In the predawn quiet, the voice was clearer due to the lack of activity around the palace.

Bhaniel started and turned her head. She pulled herself up and eased near the road being careful to stay out of sight. The first of the military vehicles filed through the gate and motored down the slope heading west. As each one passed Bhaniel, she strained to see any sign of Theresa.

As the last of the vehicles rolled out of the compound and down the road, the last truck came out of the gate and slowed to a stop. The rear gate fell open and cargo of some sort was removed and laid unceremoniously to the side of the road. The bundle could have been a person, but she wasn't sure. When the truck left and things quieted down, she would make her way over there to see for sure.

"Hurry up! Don't touch her, just leave her and get in the truck!"

The soldier obeyed immediately due to his fear of the lieutenant, and the truck meshed the gears and drove away.

Bhaniel slowly worked her way over to the mass lying beside the road. The light of dawn was still too dim to know for sure what she was about to uncover. Although it could be a villain or a soldier left behind, the chance it was Theresa made it worth the risk. Bhaniel crouched next to what was now obviously a person, a woman, with light colored hair.

"Theresa!" Bhaniel grabbed her and rolled her onto her back.

"Theresa, can you hear me? Are you injured?" Bhaniel checked for blood and broken bones. Other than some bruises on her face and a cut from the fall, she looked like she could move. Theresa was semi-conscious.

"Bhaniel, is that you?"

"Let's try to move, Theresa. It is too dangerous to stay here."

Bhaniel essentially dragged Theresa away from the road and closer to the stand of trees.

"I'll be up in a minute." Theresa kept saying in a slurred voice.

By the time Bhaniel had worked her way into the trees, Theresa was nearly comatose again. They were going to have to stay here awhile. Bhaniel had nothing with her to ease Theresa's pain. No water, food or medicine.

"Lord, please make a way for Theresa to be refreshed or healed."

Bhaniel propped Theresa up on her lap and just held her for a while.

As the sun crept above the horizon, Bhaniel could see that Theresa was stirring.

"Theresa. It's Bhaniel. Can you open your eyes?"

She squinted and peeked at Bhaniel.

"Oh, Bhaniel. I can't believe it's you. Where am I?" Her voice was almost unintelligible from thirst and pain.

"You're here with me. That's all that matters. We are going to go home. Can you move?"

"Not well. I feel like a herd of wild horses just ran over me."

Bhaniel smiled, then looked around. "Try to sit up."

Theresa willed herself to sit against a tree. The process claimed all of her strength. Short bursts of energy came intermittently.

"They must have drugged me. Everything is wobbly, but I think I can walk. Let's get out of here. Wherever here is."

The next hour was invested in slow, short steps. The further they went from the palace grounds, Bhaniel feared the soldiers' return less. She began to look for someone to transport them to the city and then the bus depot. Now that the sun was in full bloom, it would be too hot for them to walk to the city center. Theresa was shuffling and leaning on Bhaniel.

They came upon an ancient truck with a men and boys sitting in the back. It appeared they were headed toward a day of hard labor. The truck was stranded at the moment and the hood was up. The driver evidently was the mechanic as well.

"Would you allow us to ride in the truck?"

"We are going nowhere right now, but when the truck is fixed, we are going to the Bandundu region to work in the fields."

Bhaniel's eyes brightened.

"Sir, we live very near there. Will you travel to Bandundu?"

He nodded.

"We would be grateful if you would let us ride."

The driver looked at them and eyed Theresa. He had never seen a white woman before.

"I guess so. You may have to wait a long time while we fix the truck."

"Thank you. We are happy to wait."

The men in the truck helped them into the back. It was a two ton truck, possibly a military cast off. Bhaniel felt as though a chariot had been summoned for their personal use.

There were eight men and boys in the truck.

A young boy opened a jug and drank from it. He held it out for them to drink.

"Thank you," Bhaniel said to the boy and to the Lord. Bhaniel gave it to Theresa to drink and then took some herself to wet her lips. To Theresa, the water tasted like life itself.

Four hours later, the truck sputtered to life and the men who had hovered over the engine let out a collective shout of triumph. They raced into the cab of the truck before the engine could die again.

The trip had all the comfort of a bareback ride on a cape buffalo. Two boys fell out of the truck and had to be rescued because of the rickety transport's violent sway.

"Bhaniel, I'm not sure I can make it." Theresa was weakening.

"I'm sorry Theresa, it has been so hard. I am praying for you."

"Thank you. Do you know where we are?"

"Yes. We are getting close. The truck passed Bulungu about half an hour ago."

"Hallelujah. I'll keep hanging on."

Finally, the truck crested the hill just to the south of Bandundu. Once they made it to the middle of town, Bhaniel tapped on the side of the truck's cab to get the driver's attention.

"Can we get off here please?"

The driver pulled the truck to a stop and waited while Bhaniel and Theresa dropped out of the back of the truck.

"Sir, we are so very thankful for your willingness to help us. We cannot pay you, but we ask the Lord's blessing on you and for the remainder of your trip."

"Thank you, Miss. Go with God."

Bhaniel and Theresa stood by as the truck lumbered down the hill toward the Kasai River.

"I need to walk, but I don't know how far I can go."

"Let's see how close we can get to the river. If we can get on the ferry, maybe someone can come out and help us home."

Just across the road, Bhaniel thought she saw a familiar face.

"You ladies look like you need a lift." Drago. Bhaniel cried as she hugged him. They had made it.

"What is this? Miss Theresa, are you ill?"

"I've had a bad day. I just need to get home."

"Let's get you in the taxi and I'll do the rest."

The ferry was still running and Drago half carried Theresa on board.
Across the river, Bhaniel left Theresa at the water's edge and raced to the
home. Bhaniel made it to the gates of the property and the wind carried a
wisp of human voices to her ears. As she shuffled closer to the main
building, it got louder. Some cries, but mostly talking. Bhaniel stood at the
door and now realized that everyone was together inside praying for their
return. She was uncertain how to make her entrance. She knocked.
The praying stopped. She knocked again. Meriba cracked the door open
and peeked outside. She threw it open and ran out to grab Bhaniel.
"Bhaniel!" The whole house erupted. Everyone ran out and surrounded
Bhaniel, peppering her with questions and trying to help her.
"Could you find Theresa?"
"Yes, she's with me, but she is down by the river resting. Can some of the
boys take the wagon and bring her back?"
The workers and kids hurried to collect Theresa and minister to both of
them.
"What can we do for you? Are you hurt?"
"Water, food and rest. Theresa may be hurt, but I don't know for sure."
The kids brought Theresa back with two workers walking along side
attempting to nurse her on the wagon. She was in bad shape, but her face
said she was just glad to be home. The next several days would be devoted
to recovery, rest and telling the story. Bhaniel was more exhausted than she
was willing to reveal, but she was doing cartwheels in her spirit. What
could have been a devastating loss had become a legendary move of God.
None of them would ever be the same.

# Chapter 25

The reports started as a missing person bit and grew into a full blown crisis with armies of people scouring the foothills and grasslands for any sign of Harvey. Two weeks went by with no evidence found and the search teams began to dwindle. The television reports were usurped by more pressing news and little by little, life went on without Harvey McCallum.

Stella clicked off the television fully satisfied no sign of Harvey had been discovered and reported. The event appeared to be a closing chapter in the bigger plan. Stella had been thinking of how to accomplish the next phase with the most efficiency. Quite possibly she could bluff Andrew into capitulating without any further effort. All she needed was for him to believe he was next. Stella didn't really need to … kill him. Just "incapacitate" him. That might be even tougher than killing actually.

"Eugene, come in here."

"Yes."

"Go down to the court house and pick up some documents for me. Here is the office and what they should give you." She handed Eugene a business card and a list. Stella turned away to work on her computer. This was Eugene's cue to leave.

And leave he did. As quickly as he could so she didn't see the beads of sweat forming on his forehead. Eugene was spineless, but he could still do simple math. His involvement in securing the travel plans for Stella to the area where Andrew's attorney disappeared made Eugene very uncomfortable. Part of him wanted to stay ignorant for deniability purposes. The other side of his mind wanted to know how deep this went. It was becoming more obvious he was going to need to get away from Stella. Far away. But he might not be able to get far enough to avoid her reach. Soon he was going to have to find a way to evaporate. Right after he completed documenting all of Stella's criminal activities. It would either make him rich or keep him alive somewhere down the road.

# Chapter 26

The Orphanage

As much as she wanted to get up and get on with life, Bhaniel did not have the strength to get out of bed. One day turned into three, and three days turned into a week. She was able to muster the will to walk across the hall to check on Theresa once. As it turned out, Theresa had some bruised maybe even broken ribs and contusions over a majority of her torso. Bhaniel didn't have any obvious physical injuries, but her recovery was going to take time.

"Bhaniel, how are you?" Theresa was moving slowly also.

"Tired." She was leaning against the door jamb and her eyes were half closed.

"You look exhausted. Is there any medicine you can take?"

"Just my regular meds and rest. I guess racing across the countryside was more strenuous than I imagined."

Theresa chuckled and winced. She settled back against her pillows and looked at Bhaniel. Studied her really.

"Thank you. For coming after me." A tear formed in Theresa's eye. The days sitting in bed had allowed her to dwell on the enormity of what Bhaniel had done for her. "How many times am I going to owe my life to you?"

Bhaniel walked over to the edge of the bed and sat down facing Theresa. She put her hand on Theresa's.

"It never entered my mind not to do it. I know you would have done the same thing for me. Or anyone else in this place for that matter."

"I would have searched the world over for you. How did you find me? I wouldn't have had a clue where to start."

"I didn't either, but the Lord told me what to do. Step by step. If it hadn't been for Him, I would have been going in circles."

"You and God are tight."

"He's certainly merciful. There was no one else to turn to."

It was Bhaniel's turn to search for the words. "Did… did they… hurt you?"

Theresa looked away, reliving some of the events in her mind. The anger and pain showed on her face. All she could do was nod her head as the tears came down her cheeks. The shame of it made it impossible for her to look at Bhaniel although she knew that Bhaniel could relate to her pain. Bhaniel reached over and embraced her for a long hug allowing Theresa to let go of the emotions that she couldn't show to anyone else.

Yes, they would never be the same.

Gradually, both Bhaniel and Theresa were able to get out of bed as the pain subsided. The new version of normal was taking shape. The workers and some of the children surrounded Bhaniel and Theresa at the dinner table. Everyone wanted to be there when they decided to tell the story of the ordeal.

Eventually the suspense was just too much. "Tell us about it." Several children asked at once. Only they could be so direct and without guile expect a full answer. Bhaniel and Theresa exchanged a glance. Bhaniel knew Theresa wasn't ready.

"I'm sure we will talk about this more than once, but I'll start."

Bhaniel began to tell her story as Theresa listened with the others.

# Chapter 27

Andrew's Office, AD Isaacson Galleries

"What?! You still haven't heard anything? What did the people who were with him say?" Andrew shouldn't have poured his frustration out on the Search and Rescue dispatcher.

"Mr. Isaacson, the hunting party and twenty other search professionals have been looking for Mr. McCallum since he disappeared. They intend to continue searching from the air, but the ground effort is going to reduce to just a few people."

"Would it be okay if I call back periodically to see if there is any news?"

"Certainly, Mr. Isaacson."

"Thanks."

Andrew couldn't believe it. He wasn't sure what he could do either. The area where Harvey was reportedly hunting was vast and the weather was going to deteriorate fairly soon. He'd have to make a few calls up in Canada. Andrew tried to put out of his mind what Harvey's disappearance meant to his personal business. Certainly a significant delay at best.

It would be bad form to rush his business to a new attorney. Some time would need to pass until it was obvious to all he wasn't coming back. On top of everything else, Andrew was going to have to talk with Stella and let her know the turn of events. She would probably try to use it to her advantage, but there was no alternative.

Andrew dialed the phone.

"Stella? It's Andrew."

"Hello Andrew. What's up?"

"I don't know if you've heard, but Harvey, my attorney, is missing."

"I'm aware of it. I've been watching the news reports. Have you heard anything new?"

"No, not really. It's such a big area where he was hunting. With each day that passes, the expectation of finding him goes down dramatically."

"Did he have a cell phone on him or a GPS?"

"Yes, that's the mystery. Those should have been working which would have made finding him fairly easy."

"So where does it leave you?"

"Back to square one, I guess. I'm not really sure. We've been focused on finding Harvey. Obviously, it will delay everything for a time. One of his associates could get the paperwork going again. The judge will have to rule on the change. It all takes time."

"Yes … time. You know, Andrew, we have business that needs to be acted upon. The arbitrator needs the freedom to do so."

"I realize that, Stella. I don't know of an easy solution. We can try to get in front of the judge as soon as possible."

"Or… you and I could come to an agreement on some things."

"Like what?"

"Andrew, we have two shows coming up which can benefit the company a lot. One is yours and one is the new artist."

"No, absolutely not. I'd rather lose the income than get into it. I'm surprised you want to split the income of your new artist's work."

"Believe it or not, it's relatively unselfish. The show is planned and to back out now will cost a lot of money. Your money. Let's do this. Everything else in the company is basically shut down. These would be the last events and then we can wait as long as you want."

"I just don't think it is a good idea. I'm pretty sure I will regret it even if it is a money maker."

Stella knew how this conversation was going to play out. She was just trying to rub it in a little for her personal enjoyment.

"Andrew." Stella made every effort to sound conciliatory. "I certainly wish we could have just gone on without all this fighting. I could have made you so much money with very little effort on your part."

"Stella, you have made the company millions, and for that I am grateful. But money isn't the prime motivator for me now. You will do just fine without me I'm sure."

"Yes, I agree." Her voice had all of the confidence of one who had read the last page of the movie script and it said she was the winner.

"Goodbye, Stella."

# Chapter 28

The Orphanage

"When we crested the hill and saw Bandundu, we knew we were home."
Everyone let out a sigh of satisfaction with some expressions of glee and
some clapping added. It was a mesmerizing story no one wanted to forget.
"All right Miss Theresa, let's hear your story." The kids were all asking at
once.
Bhaniel looked at Theresa to see how she was going to react. It did not
appear that she was ready now or any time in the near future.
"You know what, kids? Let's take a break and maybe hear from Theresa
another time."
Mischa took over. "Everyone start doing your dinner time chores. We'll eat
in one hour."
The room stretched in unison and dispersed to do their duties.
Theresa got up and went to her room without a word or gesture. The
contrast was obvious to everyone. Prior to the incident, Theresa lit up the
room with her personality. She made everyone else talk louder and more
boisterous just to keep up with her. All of the workers dreaded to know
what really happened those two fateful days, but wished it had never
occurred. They just wanted their beloved sister back which was going to be
a long, difficult process if it ever happened at all. Bhaniel stuck her head in
Theresa's room. Theresa was lying on her bed with her face to the wall.
"Can I do anything for you?"
Theresa just shook her head.
Bhaniel stepped into the room and sat on the edge of the bed.
"Theresa, I would like to arrange for you to see a doctor. That way we can
know for sure everything will heal as best as it can."
"I don't think my bones are the problem."

"We could set up an appointment for you to talk to someone about the emotional side of it also."

"I don't want to leave home."

"I'll try to have a doctor come here. Just rest for now." Bhaniel patted her on the shoulder and left the room.

Bhaniel made the trek across the river to Bandundu to call America.

"Sir, I have a call from Bandundu, The Democratic Republic of the Congo, will you accept the charges?" The operator was typically monotone.

"Certainly." Director Salvatore Hizanga was already concerned.

"Director? This is Bhaniel Tretechi. Hello, I was calling to ask for your help."

The government offices and mail facility had the most reliable phones. Bhaniel was standing in the hallway at a bank of phones.

"What can I do for you, Bhaniel?"

"We have had a difficult incident. Theresa was kidnapped by the local militia and they beat her very badly. I think they might have sexually abused her also. Would it be possible to send a doctor to see her?"

"Oh, Bhaniel, I'm so sorry. Is she back with you?"

"Yes, we were able to get her back, but it was quite an ordeal."

"Is there anything else that she might need?"

"Right now, a medical doctor is the most important."

"Let me work on that. Is there any way I can call you back as soon as I have news?"

"No. I will need to call you back in two days."

"Let's just plan on a doctor coming there immediately. If I can't find someone quickly, I'll come myself."

The director was in fact a medical doctor, but he was half a world away.

"Thank you, Director. Please hurry."

# Chapter 29

Andrew's Residence, Atlanta

It had been nearly a month since Harvey had vanished. Andrew was to the point that life, his anyway, had to go on. He had called several sources to inquire about the search and no one was offering any new information. Since the company was not officially operating, the activities vying for Andrew's time had diminished dramatically. He was spending most of his time at home working on personal art pieces, and they were beginning to stack up. The hardest part was preparing enough canvasses. He finished putting the last tacks into the edge of the frame of a 4'x6' canvas that was either going to be a self-portrait or …

"Well hello friend."

Andrew was startled by the sound of a woman's voice. He was used to the silence of solitude. Andrew reflexively turned and crouched slightly like he was ready for combat.

"Sabrina!"

"Hi, Andrew." She smiled at him shyly. "You never called me. I was so sad I decided to come looking for you."

Andrew was torn between his strong attraction to her and the realization that she was a hired hand.

"I am flattered you're here, but I truly didn't think I would ever see you again. Especially after I found out you worked for Stella."

"Oh, that. Stella told me you two talked. Would you believe me if I told you she doesn't know I'm here?"

"You came here on your own? Why?"

"Because I enjoyed being with you, and I was hoping we could make a go of it on a little more solid footing."

"That's nice to hear, but it may be difficult to get past the idea you are reporting to Stella after each visit."

Andrew turned to put his tools down and see if he had the paint he needed to start on the new canvas.

"Is there anything I can do to make it up to you?" She glided toward him. Andrew thought for a moment. This was certainly a dangerous opportunity. But what was life without a little risk?

"Well, you can start by modeling for me tonight. I have a brand new canvas and it is crying out for a beautiful woman to grace its surface."

"I would love to." Sabrina was sincerely excited. She felt like her penance was akin to winning a prize. "What do you want me to do?"

"I think I have just the wardrobe for you. Come on, let's go into the main house and we'll get you ready."

When the possibility of having her pose took form, he almost immediately envisioned her as a double agent in the vein of the traditional spy movie. He would have to paint her twice on the same canvas. She might wish she hadn't agreed to do this.

The house was dark as usual. It seemed like an event to turn on lights in the house. Andrew just didn't spend much time there. He even slept in the studio more than in the house. Of course, his studio was nicer than the average residence. Andrew entered his PIN on the alarm keypad.

"Let's go upstairs. All of my costumes are there. The other day, I had a friend come over and pose for me in a gold body suit. She laid on a piano and poured champagne on me."

"Wow. I'm looking forward to topping that."

Andrew laughed. "It's a long story, she's a good sport. She's actually a bartender on the other side of town."

Sabrina looked around the kitchen as they moved through, aware of every nook and shadow. She turned to Andrew and smiled sweetly.

"What are you thinking of for me? Do you have my size?"

"Good question. I think I do. Most of it can be adjusted for size. Since you won't actually be going out in public, we can make it work."

Andrew led her up the stairs, around the landing and into the bedroom/all-purpose room overlooking the foyer. The walls were lined with clothing for men and women. Sabrina hesitated to enter the room at first and then looked in before resolutely stepping inside. She was overcome initially by the enormity of what she saw.

Sabrina began sampling the racks of dresses. "Andrew, this is unbelievable. These clothes are worth a fortune!"

"It is a collection years in the making. I remember hearing a story about the artist Norman Rockwell who was famous for doing Saturday Evening Post covers. One time his studio caught fire and burned to the ground, and his greatest regret was his entire costume collection was lost. It really becomes an irreplaceable asset."

Sabrina was already carrying an armload of dresses into the anteroom.

"Let's see how these look. Do we have time for me to try on all of these?"

Andrew smiled. It looked as though she was enjoying this as much as he was.

"Oh, please do. I think they will look wonderful on you. Look for some shoes in there also."

Andrew waited and concluded his decision to forgive her was a good one, but this had the potential of turning into an all-nighter like the last one. Suddenly, he heard footsteps and Sabrina's whispered voice. She was talking to someone. The tone became more strident and then there were sounds of a commotion in the anteroom. The mental picture Andrew drew was of two people struggling and one falling to the floor. Andrew moved toward the door to intervene. His adrenaline made his fingers tingle.

"Sabrina, are you okay? It sounds like someone is…"

Then he heard what sounded like two shots from a gun with a suppressor and the thud of a body on the floor. The house became silent once again. Andrew froze momentarily. Odds were a stranger was going to come through the door any minute and he needed to do something. Anything. He stepped lightly to the landing and pressed against the wall in the shadow of the door. Andrew wanted to go into the bedroom and see if he could help Sabrina, but dying wasn't going to be much help. The gunman came into the main room and moved to the side with his back to the wall. He surveyed the room trying to determine how to find Andrew. There was junk piled above and below the hanging clothes all around the room making for innumerable hiding places.

Out on the landing, Andrew realized his only advantage was surprise. The gunman searched through as much of the room as he could. Yielding no targets, he turned his focus to other parts of the house. He walked quietly out onto the landing…

Andrew ran toward the gunman from behind and lowered his shoulder. He caught the intruder in the middle of his back, and the force of the impact drove both men forward and over the railing. As they went over, the gunman flailed wildly discharging his weapon several times hoping he might hit Andrew. Their trajectory drove them into the newel on the corner of the stairway. The gunman hit first and broke Andrew's fall. He caromed off and hit the hand rail on his way to the floor. The killer remained hunched over the post, with a small rivulet of blood beginning to make its way to the floor from his chest. The point of the decorative newel cap formed the killer's spine into a hump as his arms and legs hung limply. Andrew had the breath knocked out of him and his shoulder was on fire, but it did not seem that he had broken any bones. Andrew pulled himself up the stairs until he could see the gunman's face. He noticed the hitman still had life in his eyes.

"Who sent you? TELL ME!" Andrew was still on an adrenaline rush.

The gunman turned his head slightly and stared at Andrew as the final vestiges of his life ebbed away. He tried to form a word, but there was no strength or breath left. His eyes set and his skin turned gray.

Andrew fell back on the stairs and fought off hyperventilation. Ultimately, he realized he was out in the open and vulnerable. He stumbled to a protected alcove, and tried to think. The previous commotion would have drawn any other intruders to the front of the house and they would be shooting at him right now. Since there was no movement or sound in the house, he decided he was alone. Trying not to look in the killer's eyes as he went by, Andrew suffered back up the stairs to see about Sabrina.

Sabrina was lying still in the anteroom with a halo of blood around her head. Andrew felt her throat and there was no pulse. Sabrina lay awkwardly in the black chiffon dress Andrew had purchased from Stella last year. Barefoot, she hadn't been able to put the shoes on yet. Why the gunman decided to do away with her instead of wait until she and Andrew were together was a mystery. She must have found him in the room and the hitman was forced to shoot her. However, she was alive long enough to say something to the killer, but Andrew was too frazzled at the moment to remember what was said.

Andrew sat back and felt the surrealism of the evening's events wash over him. She would never know it, but Sabrina probably saved his life. The tragedy was she sacrificed her own to make it happen. He looked at her face – now contorted from the violence – and wondered if Sabrina was even her real name. Such a monumental waste. Andrew knew he had to find his cell phone and call the police.

Wait. He didn't check the intruder for a cell phone. It might yield a wealth of intel, but he wanted to do it before the authorities arrived.

Andrew struggled back down the stairs, went through the dead man's pockets and did find a small nondescript prepaid phone. There were two numbers in the database. He chose the first one with an unfamiliar area code and hit "call". It immediately went to a recorded message that stated the number was not a working number. He chose the second number and called it. Someone answered after the second ring.

"Is it done?" It was a man's voice.

Andrew tried to disguise his voice. "Yes."

"The remainder of the money will be wired to your account."

The line went dead. How was he going to trace the wire? Or the person on the other end of the phone call? Andrew wrote down both numbers, wiped the phone off and put it back. He dialed 911 on his cell phone.

"Do you know the gunman?" asked the detective.

"No, I've never seen him before."

"I would be surprised if you did. He's obviously a gun for hire. If he is who we think he is, you must have some wealthy enemies Mr. Isaacson."

The detective was very routine in his comments, but there was satisfaction in his voice. This evidently was a fish they had been tracking for a long time.

"Are you hurt? Should I call an ambulance?"

"No, I'm fine. I'll probably be sore in the morning."

"What else can you tell me about the woman?"

"Not much more than what I said to your partner. I barely knew her. She was a friend of my business partner."

"There's no car outside. How do you think she got here?"

"Really? I didn't even ask her. She just showed up at my studio behind the house."

"Based on what you said about calling his phone, you are not out of danger. You probably bought yourself a little time, but once they realize you're not dead, they'll send someone else to tag you."

"What should I do?"

"We can protect you. Protective custody, move you to another city. It's a little early for a 'witness protection' strategy though."

"That doesn't sound very efficient. Whoever is doing this probably has resources to track me down."

"We need to keep you out of sight until we do some police work. The longer the bad guys think you're dead the better."

"I've got a friend I can stay with…"

"No friends. They might give you away accidently or someone might be monitoring them."

"Okay. I'll fly out to the west coast for a few days."

"No flights and you can't use your car. Come down to the station and we'll set you up with a car from the impound lot. I suggest you drive down to Florida for a week or two. And use cash. No credit cards. You have cash handy?"

"Yeah, I have enough for a week or two. You're making it kind of tough on me Detective."

"Better safe than dead Mr. Isaacson. Here's my cell phone number. Call me in a couple of weeks, and we'll decide what to do next."

"Thanks, detective."

"Pack a bag and we'll leave in an hour."

"What about the house?"

"It will be a crime scene for a while yet. I'll make sure it is locked down after forensics are finished."

"What was the other number?"

"You mean on the gunman's phone? It's not a phone number. My partner said it looked like a bank account number. The perpetrator probably just kept it in the phone so he could remember it. We'll check it out tonight or tomorrow."

# Chapter 30

Radisson Wholesale Groceries, west Atlanta

Mitch was enthusiastic. For the first time in months, the store had fresh peaches. The wave of fresh produce was the indication of changing seasons. Andrew walked near Mitch waiting for other shoppers to get out of earshot. He had been waiting in the parking lot for Mitch knowing this was his usual day to shop for groceries. Predictability was one of Mitch's notable strengths and weaknesses.

"Anything look good today?"

"Oh, yes it is a great day for peaches… Andrew! What are you doing here?"

Andrew looked out of breath and unsure of himself. The hoodie covered most of his face which was unshaven and tired.

"I'm leaving town for a while, but I wanted to talk to you before I left. You might hear some things, and I wanted you to know the truth."

"What things?"

"That I'm dead."

"Dead!? What's going on, Andrew?"

"Someone tried to kill me last night. Do you remember me telling you about the woman I met in Aruba? She came to see me last night and while we were in the house, someone shot her and tried to get me also. Turns out, I ended up killing the killer. The police want me to leave for a while. Since the people who did this think I'm dead, I may be able to avoid them until the police can track them down. Will you help me?"

"I'll do whatever you need me to do. Why is someone trying to kill you?"

"I have no clue. I'm no threat to anyone. I'm just an artist with limited people skills."

Mitch started to get nervous.

"Let's walk to a different part of the store, we may attract attention here."

While they walked, Mitch had time to think.

"Andrew, there's only one person who would benefit from having you gone – for good."

He turned to Mitch and saw that familiar look in his eye he'd seen so many times before.

"No."

"Then who?"

"I don't know, but not her. It's just impossible."

"Tell me what she stands to gain with you gone."

Andrew considered the legal ramifications. He'd have to call Harv…

The light bulbs going on in his mind made Andrew's forehead sweat.

"It can't be."

Andrew was getting nauseous. If he embraced Mitch's point of view, everyone began to look suspicious, even Sabrina.

"You don't think Stella could have had something to do with Harvey also, do you?"

"Andrew, you know I am convinced she is capable of just about anything."

The two men walked the aisles of the store in silence for several minutes.

"Mitch, I need to get out of here. Way out of here."

"I agree. The possibility they think you're dead will give you a head start. What resources do you have?"

"A few thousand in cash, and a small amount of clothes. The police took my car and I can't go back home. I'm driving a car from the police impound lot."

"I know where you should go."

"Where? The police want me to go to Florida."

"Too close. You need to go where no one would think to check and even if they knew, they probably wouldn't want to go there to catch up to you."

"Is there a place like that?"

"The Congo."

Andrew contorted his face. "You're crazy."

"Exactly. Everyone will think so."

Andrew brooded. "How would I get there? I'm not supposed to fly."

"We'll have to get you a ride on a boat."

"Be serious. I wouldn't live long enough to get to Africa on a boat."

"Possibly, but you're not going to live long at all if you stay here."

"How will I keep track of things here? I might need to come back for some reason. The police probably don't want me to go that far away."

"What benefit are you to them if you're dead? We'll work something out so I can contact you and keep you up to date."

Long pause.

"Okay. I'm desperate so I'll go along with it. How do I get on a boat to Africa without giving myself away?"

"Let me do some checking. I can use some of the money I owe you for sold paintings to buy you passage on a freighter. That way the only time you will be seen is when you are walking up the gangplank."

"Interesting. Here, this is my new cell number." Andrew called Mitch's phone and he logged the number. "It's a pay as you go cell phone, so it's clean. Put a fake name in your phone."

"Get out of here. I'll call you when I get everything in order. Do you have somewhere to go?"

"Yes. I won't tell you where just to be safe. Thanks, buddy, with your help I may live through this."

Andrew turned and skulked out of the store looking at no one.

Let's hope we all live through this, Mitch thought to himself.


Andrew drove back across town to the only place he was sure no one in his typical circle of friends knew about. He parked the car down the street in front of a vacant lot and walked to the house on the corner.

"Fanny, hi."

Fanny answered the door with an amazed look on her face.

"I almost didn't recognize you! Are you on the run from the police or someone's husband?"

"Neither. Do you mind if I come inside?" Andrew looked around to see if there were any neighbors close by.

"Oh, sure come on in. Make yourself at home. I don't have time for another portrait if that's why you're here."

Andrew stepped in. "I wish that was why I came. It's not safe to go back to my house right now. There was an incident last night, and tragically I was killed."

"Well, you look like you could stand a shower, but your skin's pink."

"Yeah, I'm still kicking, but I'm not out of the woods yet. The police want me to leave town until they have a chance to investigate. They think if the killers believe I'm dead, it will give the detectives an edge."

"Someone tried to bump you off last night? Are you more important than I think you are?"

"No. Which is exactly the problem. Why me? I'm a self-centered artist with only a few friends. The only thing I have is some money and I'm not even sure where all of it is."

"Money is a strong motivator. Remember what Deep Throat said during the Watergate scandal, 'Follow the money'."

"Wow, 'Watergate', how old are you?"

"History Channel. You're not much of a history buff, I guess. You might have been right on target about the self-centered thing."

"I assure you, but it's not worthy of the death penalty is it?"

"Not usually." Fanny thought for a moment. "So how much danger am I in for hiding you?"

"None I hope. If you are uncomfortable with me being here, tell me and I'll leave right now. I didn't have many options."

"Nope, I'm good. I thrive on danger." Fanny was as deadpan as ever.

"My daughter is visiting her grandparents, so it's just us. I will have to go to work in a few minutes though. You're welcome to 'hide out' here as long as you need to."

"Thanks, Fanny. Your gifts as a pastor are showing."

"We take all strays here." She had a friendly smile. "There is some dinner in the fridge – chicken enchiladas – and cable television. Other than that, I can't offer you much. Don't look at the messy kitchen, I'll get to it later. You can sleep in the guest room. It's the first room on the right down the hall."

"You're awesome. I was thinking I needed to catch up on some television tonight."

Fanny went to change clothes and Andrew moved his backpack away from the entry. As he stretched out on the couch, Fanny was heading out the door.

"Hey, if the phone rings, don't answer it. The machine will get it."

"Will do."

After Fanny left, Andrew went around the house and checked the windows' visibility from the street. He shut some blinds and locked the back door. A shower and a change of clothes helped with his uneasy feeling. Hopefully, Mitch would have some success in the next 24 hours. Andrew sat down in front of the television and flipped through the hundreds of channels available. Just scrolling through the channels was a past time in itself. At eleven o'clock, he decided to watch the local news just to prove to Fanny he was aware of the world around him. Of course, he wasn't exactly sure which ones were the local channels. The anchors on channel 7 seemed capable so he chose them. The young lady with a serious look on her face read the teleprompter.

"There was a shooting on the south side of Atlanta last night at the house of internationally known artist Andrew Isaacson. Two people are dead, a male in his mid to late 40's and a female in her mid to late 30's. The police department did not release the names of the victims. When asked if it was a murder/suicide, the department spokesman had no comment."

Andrew watched as video showed his house and property from above. Evidently there had been a helicopter hovering overhead and he didn't even know it. It showed the coroner and his staff taking the bodies out of the house and many cars with flashing lights parked in the drive.

So it appeared the police department was giving very few clues to the public. The dead killer would be Andrew for the time being. Convenient. It hurt to see the second body carted away. He liked Sabrina and the memory of this night would haunt him for some time. He had to turn the channel to something else. The news had lost its appeal. Especially when one WAS the news. Andrew read two old Vanity Fair magazines and began to drift off.

The conversation between Sabrina and the killer replayed in Andrew's mind. As his body relaxed, the words became clearer, or his subconscious automatically filled in the blanks.

…not tonight… you've done your job… I won't let you…

The opening of the front door startled Andrew awake. He had dozed off while sitting on the couch and Fanny was returning home from work at 3 a.m.

"Hey, roomie. Did you see yourself on the news? You're famous, or more famous than before."

"I did. What did you hear around the bar?"

"Not much. There aren't many details floating around, but all the channels showed your picture and video of your house. No one is saying it's you who's dead, but they make you believe that's what happened."

"Benny asked about you and gave his condolences. I had to act sad in front of him."

"The evil plan is working. I'll have to tell Benny thanks for the kind words when I see him."

"Funny. So what's next?"

"I have a friend helping me with travel plans to a secret location. If you're okay with it, I won't tell you where I'm going."

"Not a problem. You're being careful. Do you think they are smart enough to track you down?"

"I don't know. The police said it was a professional killer who came to my house last night, so they aren't afraid to spend money."

"Who was the girl at the house?"

"She was a friend who just sort of showed up at the house last night. I guess she was the victim of bad timing. Best I can tell, she went into the room where he was hiding, surprised him and he shot her. The commotion is what gave me a warning to do something or get shot myself. Evidently, the killer had been waiting in the house for a while and was going to get me when I turned in for the night."

"She just 'showed up'? The timing is kind of odd. Did you give him a good old fashioned beat down?"

"Not exactly. I hid when the first shots were fired, and as he came out of the clothes room, I rushed him from behind. We both went over the railing, and he landed on the pointy thing at the base of the handrail. The routine was a little awkward, but he stuck the landing if you know what I mean. He was kind to break my fall. After, I ran upstairs to see about Sabrina, but she was already gone."

"You are a bad man. Just one surprise after another. What's next? You gonna get a special suit and fight crime?"

"You got that right. Who wouldn't be afraid of a guy that runs for his life when the going gets tough?"

Fanny laughed. "I suppose most heroes are just as scared as the next guy. Can't blame you for blowing town until things cool down. How long do you think you'll be gone?"

"I really don't know. Hopefully not long."

Andrew's phone rang. Unless he was suddenly on a telemarketer list, it had to be Mitch.

"Hey, brother. You're all set. There's a cargo ship leaving port tomorrow, er later today, from Charleston, South Carolina, going to Pointe Noire, Republic of the Congo. Apparently it's one of the bigger ports on the west coast of Africa. From there you'll sail to Matadi which is a ways inland in the DRC."

"How am I going to find her when I get there?"

"She'll have to find you I think. If the mission organization can contact her, she will meet you in Kinshasa. The orphanage is just outside the city of Bandundu if you have to go in search of her. I'll get you a picture of her to show people in case you need to activate plan B. Do you know any French? You might be able to communicate if you do. You need to be at Pier 17 at 11:30am."

"Wow, that doesn't leave me much time."

"No, it doesn't. There is no ticket, but I wired the money to the shipping company. I'll meet you east of town to give you the rest of the money and all the documents you'll need."

"I'm speechless. You are a great friend, Mitch. I'll devote the rest of my life to repay you."

"Just stay alive, that's payment enough. See you in an hour at Eller's Truck Stop in Lithonia on Interstate 20."

"Copy that."

"Fanny, thank you. I have to get going."

Fanny had been in the kitchen preparing Andrew some food to eat on his way.

"Here, you won't want to stop for food."

"This is awesome. Thank you. It'll be a great story someday."

"True."

"Just keep it under your hat for a while longer."

"I'll wait until you get back. We can get everyone together at Trudy's for a tell all."

"It's a date."

# Chapter 31

Stella's Office

"Tell us about your relationship. Sounds like things were not going well."
Stella smiled and waved off the question. "We were like brother and sister.
You know, reading each other's thoughts and so on."
"But you were dissolving the partnership. What happened?"
"We realized that the business had gone as far as we could take it. It was
time to move on so we were starting the process…"
"Then his attorney disappears."
"Yes. Is he still missing?" Stella made every effort to show concern and
confusion.
The detectives had come to the offices to interview Stella with little to go
on. They initially were just trying to understand Andrew Isaacson better so
that his enemies would come into focus.
Clarence Oliver had been on the police force for twenty four years. He was
eligible to retire, but his debts were too high. The last time he calculated
what his retirement check would be, he'd have to get another job anyway.
Bryce Tunney was the junior partner. He recently made detective and still
dressed nicely. It was his dream job and Bryce intended to be a model
employee. Civil service was in his genes. His dad served in the Army and
Bryce was a former Army Ranger.

Clarence and Bryce were on the opposite ends of the social spectrum and Bryce wasn't sure if Clarence's heart was still in it when they became partners. Clarence soothed Bryce's concerns the more they worked together. The laid-back exterior covered up a wily approach to solving criminal mysteries. Clarence had a gift when it came to sifting through lies and misinformation from suspects and even witnesses. He was never in a hurry which set his interview subjects at ease. In almost every situation, Clarence could pull back the layers and expose the truth even before the suspect realized it. He had a Master's degree in human nature. Bryce looked forward to going to school each day to learn all that Clarence could teach him.

"When did you last talk to Andrew?"

"It was just a few days ago. We have to talk regularly to work through the details of the dissolution. I guess we won't be talking anymore. I'm not sure what is going to happen now."

"Who do you think wanted to kill Andrew?"

Stella had practiced the answer to that question and always had trouble with it. There weren't many obvious choices - except her.

"Honestly, I just don't know. I have asked myself that question over and over. Andrew was just a quiet guy who stayed to himself. Sure, he dated a lot of different girls after his divorce. Maybe that was his downfall. He was not very successful in love. Maybe there was a jealous lover."

Clarence liked for people to "help" him come up with the suspect list.

"Did Andrew have any relatives close by?"

"No. Even his ex-wife's family is from out of state. She moved back there, Oklahoma I think, soon after the break up."

"Tell me about his dating life. You say there might have been a jealous lover in the past?"

"Well, he wasn't very discreet regarding the type of women he was willing to date. It ranged from recent divorcees to glorified escorts if you know what I mean. Some of them would live with him for a while and then get bored and move on. Andrew didn't seem to care if they stayed or left. He kept them around because he was lonely, I think, but he was such an independent sort he would push them away. Ironic."

This would have been a fruitful interview if Andrew was really dead. A psychological profile was always helpful, but he had Andrew to ask. Stella had revealed a few things, however.

"Did you know any of them?"

"Yes, some were my friends and I set him up with others. I just wanted him to be happy. He did better work when he was happy."

"Having a girlfriend made him happy?"

"Well, as close to happy as he was going to get. Andrew had the 'tortured artist' thing down pretty well."

"Did you know the woman who was murdered?"

"Yes, she was an acquaintance. We had some mutual friends. I thought she and Andrew would get along so I set them up once."

"Was she married or have a boyfriend?"

"She wasn't married, and I don't know if she had any boyfriends. She was a pretty lady, I'd be surprised if she didn't."

"Did you and Andrew ever date?"

"No. Well, not really. Andrew wanted to, and we did go out a few times, but it was evident a romantic relationship was not in the cards."

"But you did find a way to work together."

"Oh, yes. Andrew was a unique talent. I saw it early on and with my skills, I knew we could be successful."

And Andrew never knew what hit him, Clarence thought to himself.

Clarence looked at Bryce and gave him the signal.

"Miss Manchester, thanks for your time. If we have more questions down the road, will it be okay to come back?"

"Certainly. Come back anytime."

The detectives rose to leave.

In the elevator, Bryce asked him what he thought.

"It's pretty obvious Miss Stella tried to control Andrew's every move."

"Do you think she knows what happened?"

"I think she knows more than she's telling. No one so set on controlling someone would allow another person close enough to do harm to their meal ticket. Unless it's the controller doing the harm. Even though he probably wouldn't have been as successful as he is, she needed him worse than he needed her. Stella needs something to sell."

"Easy answer is Isaacson got tired of the arrangement and wanted out. She wasn't going to let that happen, and the only way to keep him from being successful without her was to kill him."

"If it's true, then the hard part is going to be proving it."

# Chapter 32

Director Hizanga contacted a doctor associated with the organization who happened to be in Mali. Thankfully, she had finished her southern swing through the country and was ready for what was next. The lady in her late 20's made the final hike up the hill toward the orphanage. The Director had made this trip several times in the past and was familiar with the bus routes and ferry schedule, so he did his best to explain the intricacies of the process and hoped for divine guidance. She was relatively new to the organization although not a stranger to mission work. Her parents were missionaries in Papua, New Guinea which was where she was born and grew up. Seeing the ongoing and desperate need for medical help in locations such as theirs motivated her to return to America and complete medical school.

"Hello!" The young lady waved as she entered the compound.

Kids from all directions ran to meet her. Their curiosity and excitement was similar with each new visitor. Bhaniel and the other workers came out to greet her.

"Welcome. It is very good to see you, Dr. Ratcliff." She stretched her hand out to the doctor.

"Jessica. It's good to see you again Bhaniel."

Bhaniel had acquainted herself with Jessica Ratcliff during a previous trip to America. Jessica was brand new at the time, and Bhaniel was pleased she was part of the team. It was about to pay dividends.

"How was your trip? Not too difficult I hope."

"It was really good. Only one layover, and the flights were mostly on time."

Bhaniel showed her around briefly, and answered Jessica's questions about the place and their history. Some things the director had told her, but hearing the story from Bhaniel was a bonus.

"Do you need time to rest or settle in? We have a room set up for you."

"I'll put away my luggage, but I feel fine. If Theresa is willing, I'm anxious to meet her."

"She is certainly expecting you."

"Great. I'll say hello to her and then go organize my materials. I've brought more supplies and medicine also."

"Thank you." Bhaniel showed her the way to Theresa's room.

"Theresa, there is someone here to see you. It's Dr. Jessica."

Theresa stirred, and tried to work the sleep out of her eyes.

"Hi, Doctor. Thanks for coming. Sorry, I'm such a mess. Been sleeping a lot lately."

"It's very understandable. You need extra rest. Are you able to get up and about?"

"Not really. Mostly just staying here in the room. Bhaniel and the girls have been taking care of me."

The room was dark, but sweltering. Sheets had been put over the window to block the sunlight, but it also stopped the air from moving.

"I'm going to put my bags in the room and get some things organized. Would you like to have a talk when I come back?"

"Sure Doc. That will be fine." Theresa responded with an air of resignation. She didn't have any will to resist, and everything was inevitable. She lay back down on the bed.

Bhaniel led Dr. Jessica to her room and left her to settle in.

Before long, the doctor made her way back to Theresa's room.

"If you are up to it, I would like to do some tests, take some blood, and do a short examination. Okay?"

"Sure. What do you want me to do?"

"Not a thing. You don't even have to get out of bed."

The doctor busied herself with the test packet she brought and prepped Theresa's arm for taking blood. Ultimately, she performed a full examination which left Theresa exhausted.

"You're kinda young. Have you been with the organization long?"

"Not too long. This is my first trip overseas to visit the orphanages. I was in Mali right before coming here, and I might spend some time in Tanzania next."

"Wow. Brand new, huh? Ever seen anything like me before?"

"There are some similarities. I grew up a missionary kid in New Guinea. We had our fair share of women who needed medical attention due to local diseases and sometimes abuse. My parents aided in their treatment, and as I got older, I was able to help some too. That experience was my motivation to go to medical school. My residency at the Grady Memorial emergency room in Atlanta also exposed me to all kinds of brutality people inflict on one another."

"So young and you've seen so much. Do you lose faith in people?"

"If I hadn't seen so many people changed by the power of God, I would be very disillusioned. I'm sure you have seen a lot of children come through here who have had to endure some difficult circumstances."

"Yeah, Joliba was so beat up when she got here, we weren't sure she'd live. And she walked over seventy miles from her home. Djali had been a child soldier, but was taken captive and left for dead. If it wasn't for Bhaniel, the police would have finished him off. Wild boys don't fare too well here."

"I'm sure they are thankful to have someone like you caring for them."

"No, no. I'm no good. I can't protect them. I can't even protect myself."

"You mean the kidnapping?" Doctor Jessica wasn't one to beat around the bush.

Theresa agreed simply by nodding and looking away. She was angry. Angry at herself for not fighting harder.

"It sounds like you were very courageous. Bhaniel said you gave yourself up to protect the others. It's rare to see someone willing to sacrifice so much for the safety of others. You're a true hero."

"She said that?" Theresa had been so focused on her seeming failure, she had missed the victory. Tears formed in her eyes at the realization, and a small spark of life rekindled in her soul.

"I've only seen courage like that one other time in my life. My dad had gone to another village to give medical help and work with the community leaders. While he was gone, marauders came and tried to carry off some children and animals from our settlement. My mom fought them off and freed the kids, but they got her instead. Where they took her no one knows. All of us were sure she was dead. Dad came back and searched for her, but on the evening of the third day, she walked back into the village bloody and bruised. She never regained much memory of the ordeal, and we never saw those evil men again. If it hadn't been for her, the kids would have been lost for good."

"Your mom sounds like she was an amazing woman."

"Is. She's still kicking, living back in America now. I think you and her are cut from the same cloth."

"I know someone else like her too."

"Hello ladies. How is it going?" Bhaniel stood in the doorway.

"Hi, Bhaniel. Doctor Jessica was telling me about her family. She's quite a gal."

Bhaniel could already tell a change in Theresa's countenance. The old Theresa was peeking through.

"Yes, I agree. I'm so happy you came. The first of many times I hope."

"If you don't mind, I'd like to stay a while and spend some time with the kids. We might be able to try some new medicines on the kids who have had reactions to the old HIV drugs. It has been a while since some of them have had a physical, no?"

"We would love for you to be with us for as long as you can stay."

"Yeah, Doc. You'll be good for these kids."

"It will also give me a chance to monitor Theresa's progress. By the way, I think you can make a full recovery."

"I tell you what, I feel better already." Theresa swung her legs over and sat on the edge of the bed.

Bhaniel looked at the doctor and mouthed the words 'thank you' knowing the healing power she had brought with her had gone well beyond the physical.

# Chapter 33

## Port of Charleston, Charleston, South Carolina

It had been a long night of driving, and in the morning mist he saw the cranes above the freight canisters stacked along the waterfront. Andrew could see a massive container ship moored at Pier 17. He'd have to swing around to see if the name on the rear was correct. Trouble was, there was a security gate he had not expected. It made good sense in light of the regular terrorist events around the world, but it had not come up in the planning. Andrew pulled the car up to the guard hut and rolled his window down.

"Good morning. I have a question. Do you have the manifest for the Quintana? My name is Andrew Isaacson and I am hoping my name is on it."

"That's a container ship not a cruise ship." The guard was bored, so he took the opportunity to make Andrew's life a little more difficult.

"I see your point, but I am supposed to be a passenger on that ship today."

"You working on the ship?"

"No, just hitching a ride to the west coast of Africa."

The guard looked over his paperwork.

"Don't see anything. You sure you're in the right place?"

"Yes sir. My contact said that if there were any questions, I should contact Wilhelm Stewart. Do you know him?"

"Yeah, he's the First Officer on the Quintana."

"Could we call him?"

The guard looked him over and wrestled with whether this was going to be worth his valuable time. With a roll of the eyes, he gave in.

"I'll make a call. If he's not there, I can't spend all day trying. The ship pulls out in a few hours and I got things to do."

"Thanks."

The guard made the call and Andrew sat patiently. The gulls were calling to each other and taunting Andrew with the fact they were not bound by the high fences or the lazy guard with too much authority.

"You may be in luck," the guard said as he hung up the phone. "An Andrew Isaacson is supposed to be on my ship. Now you need to show me who you are."

Andrew was a little concerned his identification would be recorded and his presence here documented. As long as it wasn't entered into a wide area network, it would be a minute needle in a big haystack.

"Ok, you need to take this paperwork to this man." The guard showed him a name on the first page. "And have him sign you in. Don't lose this stack of papers. Drive through there, and park next to Building A."

Andrew thanked him and drove toward the ship. The size of the freighter was intimidating and enhanced by the fact Andrew was not much of a sailor or a "cruise" guy.

He parked the car and looked for an office of some sort containing people in it associated with the ship. There were a few workers on the dock by the boat so Andrew asked them if they knew the name on his paper. They mostly just looked at him and kept working although one sort of cocked his head toward the ship and looked toward the gangplank.

That may have been all Andrew was going to get and it was enough. He climbed up the ramp and once on the boat, looked for a sign. There was plenty of bustle since the boat was set to break out of port in a short time. Two workers came down the hallway and he moved out of their path.

"Do you guys know Wilhelm Stewart?"

They pointed behind them and kept walking. Another stairway to the next deck, but still no signs. There was plenty of activity on the next level. Men were going in all directions and a cluster of men was huddled over some documents on a table in a large open area. The walls had charts and agendas pinned and taped to them. Work duties were written out with black marker on sheets of frayed, dingy paper. The men around the table looked up when Andrew spoke.

"Hey, good morning. Are any of you Wilhelm Stewart?"

"Yeah, that's me." A large, middle-aged man with a mustache the size of a muskrat turned to see what inconvenience Andrew was bringing to him.

"I'm Andrew Isaacson and I was supposed to find you."

"Oh yeah, you're the rider right? Wait one minute and I'll show you the passenger quarters."

One minute turned into fifteen and Andrew tried to wait as inconspicuously as possible while the ship prepared for departure.

Wilhelm Stewart issued some orders to two young men with wet trousers and dirty t-shirts and then walked toward Andrew.

"Andrew? I'm Wilhelm." He offered a massive hand to Andrew. "Need help with your gear?"

"No, I'm good, thanks. I'm traveling light."

Wilhelm Stewart led Andrew back down the stairwells to his original location and went down two more levels. Three hallways and four turns later, they arrived at the living quarters.

"Here we are Mr. Isaacson." Wilhelm Stewart pulled the key out of the door and handed it to Andrew.

"The mess hall is open 24/7, but most of the crew eats at the shift changes at Noon and Midnight. You might be our only passenger this trip. You were going to have a roommate, but I think he backed out at the last minute. There aren't any rules except the crew has a job to do and they're not used to people getting in their way, so be aware. We'll be at sea 12 days unless we run into bad weather which isn't in the forecast. You can go anywhere on the ship, but be extra careful in the engine rooms. There's a recreation room on Deck C. If you like poker, bring your money and jump in. The biggest games start right after chow following both shifts. I've got to get back upstairs, so enjoy the trip."

"So we're headed to Pointe Noire?"

"Yeah, that's our standard Eastward hop. From there we'll head up river to Matadi then on to Cape Town, Caracas and back to Miami."

"Ok, thanks. I appreciate the help. See you in the chow line."

The room had one small window, but was bare like a county jail cell before move in. It had one fluorescent light in the ceiling and a desk light on a wooden built in desk. The bunks were built in also, and maybe just long enough for Andrew to stretch out. It was only 12 days and Andrew was expecting to be other places on the ship most of the time. With a ship this big, just seeing all of it one time would take most of the trip.

After he stowed his worldly goods, he made his way to the deck for departure. Andrew tried to retrace his steps the way Wilhelm led him, but he took one wrong turn which led to three more. At last he started to smell the ocean and see daylight. A few of the crew not busy with duties lined the port side of the boat. The only ones on the dock were the workers facilitating the cast off procedures, so cruise-like goodbyes weren't going to happen.

As the ship slowly pulled away from the dock, Andrew leaned on the railing and considered the symbolism. He was leaving everything behind with no promise of return. He had been hyper-focused on staying alive until now, but the days ahead would give him plenty of time to think about the circumstances leading up to this point. Just a man on a boat sailing to a faraway place possibly more dangerous than the one he was running from. Andrew loitered on deck as the shore faded into the distance. The remainder of the day would be filled with not much of anything. He wasn't even sure if he was going to find anyone to talk to.

# Chapter 34

Stella's Office

So he's dead, Stella was thinking.

"Should we have a funeral or something?" Eugene asked.

"The police haven't released his body yet. Something to do with the investigation."

"We can have a memorial service without him. People just want to be able to say goodbye."

"I agree. We need to reinforce the fact he's gone. The deader he is the more valuable his work will be and since he met an untimely end, people will be intrigued all the more."

"How can we best capitalize?"

"Call the print company. We need to increase our print inventory. Also, we'll have to stop the painters after the current collection is done. We can sell the idea that those pieces were done before his death, but we should wait a while before we 'find' some previously unknown works and offer them for sale."

"Do you think we can keep the painters dialed in with Andrew's style?"

"They can do 'Andrew' in their sleep. I may only use Torre and Stan anyway."

"What do you want me to do for the memorial service?"

"Have Yvonne get the gossip rags on the phone. We'll make it a nationwide event. I'll call Cherise over at E! myself."

Stella was enthusiastic. She had done a pro forma of what Andrew's death could mean financially and the expense of staging a high profile memorial service would be worth the cost. The initial monetary bump would be enhanced by the consistent income stream of internet sales and by selling and reselling his originals.

Diego wasn't going to get much attention right now. At least not until Stella could get this cash flow stream up and running.

"Let's schedule the service as soon as possible. Have Yvonne tell the magazines it will be next Thursday."

# Chapter 35

Quintana, Atlantic Ocean

Andrew sat up on his bunk. He was groggy, but the nap was helpful after a sleepless night of driving. He didn't know how long he had slept until he looked at his watch. Wow! Was it really three in the morning? Atlanta time at least. Out here in the ocean, it might be the middle of the day.

It was time to eat no matter what the clock said. Andrew pulled himself together and headed toward the chow hall. Since he was in between shift changes, there probably wouldn't be many dining with him. The chow hall had four round tables. Two tables had card games going and the center of each had a decent pile of money waiting on a winner. No one looked up when Andrew entered. The food workers were in the kitchen taking a break, but there was plenty of food in the buffet line. Andrew filled a bowl with something that looked like stew and took two squares of corn bread. Andrew sat at an empty table and watched the closest card game. The men were silent and working hard not to show any emotion as the cards were turned by the dealer. Wilhelm Stewart sat down next to Andrew with a full plate of food.

"Hi, Wilhelm. I didn't expect to see any other diners at this hour."

"Me neither. I missed lunch so I'm eating late." He exhaled loudly ready to relax and enjoy the break.

"Busy day, huh?"

"We are carrying some unusual cargo, so the headaches are about double."

"Is it radioactive?"

"No, but I better not say any more than that."

"I'll keep it under my hat. How long you been working on this boat?"

"Seven years. About twenty trips. I'm hoping to be captain on my next gig. The company we work for has eleven ships. A captain slot should open up in a couple of years."

"Were you in the Navy prior to?"

"Yeah, Chief Petty Officer. I served two terms on the Destroyer USS John Paul Jones. Spent most of our time in the Persian Gulf lobbing Tomahawk missiles into Afghanistan."

"Decided not to make a career of it?"

"I wasn't very high on the food chain, so the money was never going to be 'career' good."

"You're hitting a home run now, huh?"

"Yeah sure. I love being on the water, and there's no one at home so it's all profit. And the food's pretty good too."

"Roger that. You guys know how to live on this boat."

"In between fights it's pretty boring."

"Do you play cards much?"

"Use to. After I lost my paycheck a few times, I realized I had too many 'tells'. The other players always wanted me to play though. Being well liked is expensive."

"Is it possible to control your 'tells'?"

"Yeah, for good players, but I didn't want to spend the time or more paychecks to develop the skill. Some of us get together and play dominoes, darts or chess occasionally. For fun."

"Darts? Is that hard when the boat's rocking?"

Wilhelm chuckled. "I guess so. We don't notice the movement much."

Both men ate a while.

"So why are you headed to the Congo?"

"Actually, my final destination is a small city north of Kinshasa in the DRC. I'm going to work with an orphanage there. I met the lady who runs it back in Atlanta a few months ago and she convinced me to check it out."

"Wow. That's a long way to chase a woman, my friend. She must be pretty special."

Andrew laughed. "No, no, it's not like that. She's a friend. It seemed like a good chance for a new perspective."

"Yeah, you'll get a new perspective alright. Do you know much about the Congo?"

"No, not really. I'm guessing the government is disorganized and corrupt, the people live in poverty, and I'm crazy for wanting to go there."

"So you DO know the country. The workers on the dock in Pointe Noire are for the most part organized, but the ones in Matadi are lunatics. The bosses try to extort money from us every time we come into port. The only reason we keep going there is it's the best port for taking freight to the interior of the continent. I have to say, the locals' ability to transport goods over land is much better than I would have guessed. It's archaic and crude, but they get it done."

"Do you carry food to Africa?"

"No, too dangerous. The warlords use food as leverage to control the people because the people need it so badly. The possibility of combat is very real when those boats come into port."

"Hey, Wilhelm! Wanna play?" Some new players were just sitting down for a new game.

"Funny. No thanks. I think I'll hang on to my money this month."

Wilhelm turned to Andrew. "I better go. Got plenty of work to do."

"By the way. What time is it?"

Wilhelm looked at his watch then Andrew's. "Yours is right. We stay on East Coast Time until the halfway point. Come up to the bridge later. I'll show you around."

"Sounds good, thanks."

Andrew decided he would have to adjust to daylight and dark rather than keep time. A walk sounded good. Now was as good a time as any to do a lap around the boat.

Andrew reached the leading point of the ship's deck and leaned into the wind. He had heard an air horn go off a few minutes ago from the direction of the bridge, but mostly it was just him and the sound of rushing water against the hull. Because of the rows of cargo containers stacked six high on deck, Andrew couldn't see back to the rear of the boat. The feeling of isolation was intensified by the white noise of the water. Out this far, there were no longer any sea gulls or dolphins. How could such a large ship seem so small in this water landscape?

It was unusual to think, but as Andrew looked out over the water, he could not get the vision out of his mind of the "Quintana" on dry land. Such as if the tide was higher than ever before and the ship had sailed inland. Then the waters receded, and it was left in a place where mere men would not be able to move it. Andrew let his imagination dwell on this image. He had nothing but time to kill. The ship was on high ground and there were people streaming to it. Some had already obtained valuables from the cargo and were carrying it off. People only took what they could carry in their hands. There were no trucks or wheelbarrows, donkeys or carts. And what they had in their hands were stones. All shapes and sizes. Everyone was carrying them to a construction site where builders were assembling the stones in the order they were brought to them, but the structure being built was tearing down other buildings and houses. Only destruction remained. Andrew had felt this way before. He needed to sketch this vision out, and maybe find out what they were actually carrying on this ship. The visuals faded from his mind and all that remained was the waves of water rising and falling.

# Chapter 36

The Orphanage

The sun was working its way toward the horizon. Bhaniel leaned against the post on the corner of the porch and looked out over the valley. It had been another long day of school and general drama brought on by the mystery of the lost soccer ball. All was well when they found it in the goat's feeding bin. The only reason it hadn't been eaten already was because the goats couldn't get it in their mouths.

Bhaniel usually had a short time to herself in the late evening. The kids were playing, the workers had finished cleaning up dinner, and the only thing that remained was to put the kids to bed. Until recently, she hadn't made much time for herself, but the crisis with Theresa had affected her emotionally like nothing before. Ironically, being alone on the porch was healing to her. It must have been a part of grieving she hadn't experienced in the past. Still, it didn't make sense. Bhaniel had been through many tragic events in her life. This relatively mild episode shouldn't have cut deep enough to reach such a tender place in her heart. Her younger brothers were violently taken from the family, and her mother slowly conceded the remainder of her life to disease while Bhaniel cared for her. Bhaniel's young adult years were shaped by betrayal at the hands of a husband who was often given to adultery. Curiously, it toughened her resolve to be pure and made her heart more sensitive toward the needy.

When she was just twenty three years young, Bhaniel's ever roving husband became needy himself when the HIV he had contracted evolved into AIDS and sucked the life from his body. Bhaniel stayed by his side and cared for him much the way she did for her mother. It was after that ordeal she began to work with orphaned children. Kids left behind when one or both parents' lives were cut short through disease - mostly AIDS. The first home dedicated to care for orphans was an abandoned structure with very little protection from the elements. It didn't take long to outgrow it which caused Bhaniel to seek help outside of her community. Missionaries connected her to organizations able to facilitate new locations and allow her to network and establish homes in new communities. There would always be a need. The influx of children was constant. Until the adults changed their ways, the number of needy children would not diminish.

"Hello Bhaniel." It was Dr. Jessica. "I was on a walk and noticed you over here. Do you mind the intrusion?"

"No, not at all. I come here to the porch some evenings to relax. I've always enjoyed the view."

"I can see why. It is quite lovely."

Bhaniel motioned for her to sit in one of the chairs.

"Thank you for coming to care for us."

"It is my pleasure. I just love getting to know the kids."

"They will consider you family in no time."

"I can already tell it will be hard to leave them."

"Will you be able to stay for a while?"

"I think so. The director wants me to remain until I have had a chance to see everyone here and do some treatments if necessary."

"Will you spend any more time with Theresa?"

"If she wants to, then yes I would like that. Has she ever taken a sabbatical?"

"Theresa? Not since she has been with us."

"What do you think about Theresa going back to America with me?"

Bhaniel didn't turn or act like she heard Dr. Jessica. She had dreaded the possibility of this question.

"How will that help her?" she said to the evening sky. "We are the only family she has."

"It wouldn't be for long, almost a vacation. There are some other doctors I would like for her to see."

"Is she not healing? Theresa has improved so much in the short time you have been here."

"You're right. She is making wonderful progress. I… I have some concerns about her physically though."

Bhaniel looked at the doctor although the night had fallen on them and her features were hard to discern.

"There is a chance she may have contracted HIV."

The monkeys called out as the birds settled in for the evening. Bhaniel considered the doctor's words as the muscles in her face tensed.

"She has nothing to fear here."

"I know many of the kids have HIV, but what about the other workers? What about you?"

"I am not afraid. All of us have dealt with the disease for many years. What can you do for her beyond the medicine we have?"

"We can determine the right drugs to put her on, and if it is extensive, then it might be safer for her to stay in America to get the treatment she needs."

Bhaniel gazed at the doctor for a long while as tears trickled down her cheeks.

"Yes. If it is best."

"I'm very sorry. I know she wants to stay. Hopefully it will only be for a short time. I'll say good night then."

Bhaniel had no inclination to leave the porch and fell asleep well after midnight sitting upright in the chair.

The next day, after the morning activities were done and most of the kids were playing outside before studies, Bhaniel and the doctor asked Theresa to meet them in Bhaniel's room.

"What do you want to talk about?"

Both ladies looked lovingly at Theresa, in an uncomfortable way.

"Why are you two looking at me that way? It gives me the creeps."

Bhaniel and Dr. Jessica were not sure how to say it.

"Theresa, the doctor would like for you to travel back to America with her for some more tests."

"Why? I feel great. I'm going to be fine."

Dr. Jessica decided to be blunt.

"The initial blood tests show you may have HIV."

Theresa stared at them both.

"What? How? I think your blood test was wrong."

"It may very well be wrong. More tests will tell us for sure. Would you be willing to go back with me?"

Theresa looked at Bhaniel for guidance.

"Under the circumstances, I think the best thing for you is to get the treatment you need."

"Come on, Bhaniel. What's a little HIV gonna do? Heck, everyone here has it anyway. Even…"

"Treat it like a vacation. Enjoy the rest and relaxation. They will take care of you very well. In a couple of weeks, you come back and life goes on as before."

"Sure. I know how these things work. I get shipped back to the States and then no one will approve me to come back."

"Theresa, you have my word. No matter what, we will find a way to get you back."

She looked at the two of them sternly. "Don't think I want to do this. I'm doing it to be obedient, but under protest. When does this happen?"

"I still have some of the kids to see. Maybe two more days?" The doctor offered.

"Fine." Theresa turned and left the room.

Bhaniel started to go after her. "She's been through so much. She's going to resent the trip to America because it will hinder her from living her life the way she wants to live it."

"I understand and promise you we will keep her there only as long as is necessary. She's very much like my mother."

"Thank you, Doctor."

# Chapter 37

Atlanta First United Methodist Church

"In closing, we want to thank all of you for coming today. Andrew was a person who left an indelible mark on the world and on all of us individually. Let's carry on his memory by looking for the good in each other and realize life truly is a fleeting gift. Thank you."

The clergyman was very distinguished looking in his black-on-black outfit. Stella found him through a headhunter agency even though he was semi-retired. A jazz pianist played softly as the attendees filed out.

The media reps hustled to the front of the event center to get a good view of exiting notables. There were a number of famous folks in the audience. Stella had connections with them even though most did not know Andrew. It was good for the magazines.

"Stella, the service was lovely. Andrew would have been very pleased. We will miss him. I will miss him."

"Dianna, thank you for coming. He always spoke very affectionately of you."

"He was one of my favorites. I'm just at a loss what I'm going to do now. His paintings are like my babies. There will never be another Andrew Isaacson."

"No, there will not. Thank goodness we have his work to remind us of him."

"True. I must go, dear. We'll talk soon."

She strode out to her waiting car and sped away. Stella was going to have to case her into some other artists' work so that she continued to do business with the company. Ms. Hoestedtler had a lot to gain from Andrew's untimely death. All of her original paintings went up in value almost overnight.

Stella worked the crowd for another 30 minutes and then went back to the office. She was satisfied the event accomplished the primary goal of solidifying Andrew's death for the general public.

Detective Clarence Oliver sat at his desk and read the initial accounts of the memorial service on the internet. He was entertained with the sincerity of the reports knowing all of it was a sham.

"Tunney, do we know where Isaacson is?"

"No. As far as I know, he has vanished. We have a couple of leads that might help us find out what happened."

"When we told him to disappear, he took us seriously. I didn't want him to go so far underground though. We're gonna need him sometime and it'd be nice to know where he's at," declared Oliver.

"We'll just have to keep looking. Anything more on the shooter?"

"Not much. He covered his tracks well. A real pro. The more I don't find out about him, the more I'm impressed our artist friend avoided getting popped. Do you know if Isaacson did any business separate from Stella? Surely he didn't let her control every facet of his life. Somebody is helping him be invisible. We just need to find out who it is without blowing his cover."

"I'll run the traps and see what turns up. I did check the bank account on the hitter's phone. Mr. Isaacson earned a cool $100,000 for his reverse hit."

"He'll be pleased."

# Chapter 38

Quintana

The next time Andrew woke up, it was just after sunset. All hope of a daily routine was shot. He had resigned himself to simply sleeping when he was tired and eating when he was hungry. The latter was true now. Andrew was getting familiar with the ship so he was confident he could find the mess hall. On his way, he decided to visit his new friend Wilhelm and see if there was any information he could pick up that would tell him what cargo was on the ship.

Andrew found Wilhelm talking quietly with a crew member in the hallway. The look on Wilhelm's face belied the gravity of the conversation however.

"Tell them if they won't work with the dock teams when we get to port, they won't get paid."

"They are not lazy, they are scared," said the crewman.

"There is nothing to be afraid of. The port is secure. The workers will not have to do anything more than what the dock teams tell them to do."

Wilhelm knew as well as his crewman anything could happen when they reached the port.

"It is bad enough when food comes into port. This is much worse."

"I realize this is a different situation. If there is any trouble, I'll pay them double."

"I will hold you to that. Also, they want their regular wages up front."

"Half now, half later."

"Agreed."

Both men noticed Andrew making his way toward them. The crewman decided his business was done and walked off in the opposite direction.

"Andrew, how are you doing this evening?"

"I'm good. Sorry to break up the meeting."

"Not at all. Just some employee negotiations. Are you headed to the mess hall?"

"Of course. Eating's my favorite hobby on this ship. I'm pretty sure I will have gained 10 pounds by the end of the journey."

"Who said this wasn't a luxury cruise?" Wilhelm laughed. "What else have you been up to? No card games I hope."

"No, sir. I'm staying out of the shark tank. I've toured the ship, run some laps, read a book or two, scratched out a few drawings."

"Drawings, really? So you're an artist? What kind of stuff are you finding to draw here?"

"Odd stuff actually. I know this is going to sound ridiculous, but sometimes I get visions and then I draw or paint them."

"You had a vision on the boat?"

"Yeah." Andrew thought about what he was going to say next. He didn't know Wilhelm well enough to predict how he would react. Oh well. He'd probably just laugh it off as silliness anyway. "It's actually of the Quintana in port. There are workers unloading building blocks or stones and whatever it is they are building is destroying the country. And several entities are fighting for control of the new structure." Andrew laughed. "Who knew? Chaos in the Congo, right? Not exactly a revelation."

Wilhelm looked at Andrew for a long minute.

"How long have you been doing this kind of 'vision art'?"

"Quite a while."

"Any of your paintings come true?"

"Most of them. At least the ones that that I have been able to track."

Wilhelm looked at Andrew to see if he was bragging or sincere. Andrew was almost apologetic, like he wished it wasn't so. It seemed to Wilhelm this was more of a curse than a gift to Andrew. Something he had to do as opposed to a circus trick he did for money.

"So, what's on the boat? Cement blocks?"

Wilhelm was noticeably uncomfortable but worked to cover it up.

"No, no, not at all. Mostly boring stuff."

Even Andrew knew this wasn't entirely true. The crew wouldn't be worried if the cargo was low risk. Wilhelm thought it over for a moment. "Follow me."

Wilhelm took Andrew past the Bridge into his office. He opened a locked filing cabinet and pulled out a binder with documents of many voyages in its past. Wilhelm thumbed through the pages toward the back. It was full of invoices, evidently representing the cargo on this ship.

"Here, look at the manifest. There is nothing on this boat useful for nation building. Unless cell phone parts and clothes are what you envisioned."

Andrew scanned down the list and saw nothing out of sorts, except a small block of containers with no descriptions. He decided to ask Wilhelm straight up.

"What is the crew afraid of? Are we going to face danger in port?"
Wilhelm considered Andrew's question as he formed a lie.
"It's mostly the ongoing dangers of the Congo port. Because of the lack of peacekeepers, there is always the risk of piracy and other bad agents. Another thing is we are American. No matter what is on the boat, there are certain crazies who think the boat is full of gold. You'll be fine. We are able to protect ourselves."
It wasn't the most comforting explanation, but Andrew decided to take it at face value.
"If you say it's going to be okay, then I trust you."
All the same, Andrew memorized the numbers on the manifest representing the unnamed containers.

# Chapter 39

Fulton County Medical Examiner's Office

3:00 pm. Ugh. The medical tech still had five hours left on his shift. Today was all paperwork which slowed the clock down considerably. Most of the time, the day went quickly because he was moving bodies and documenting what allegedly happened from police reports or other sources. No new bodies had come in all day, but there was a new recruit in the cooler. Medical Tech Rick Smalley scanned his file folders but didn't find any documentation on Number 28. He pulled up the check-in file for any information and there was no record of John Doe. Smalley knew the body was not here yesterday. If nothing else, Smalley was very cognizant of his inventory. It was a little irritating the night shift tech neglected the requisite paperwork. At least he could do the work his way and know it was done right.

Smalley slid the tray out of the cooler to photograph the areas of interest for the report. He snapped pictures of his face which was a little disfigured, but the obvious cause of death was the gaping hole in his chest. It looked like he had been skewered by a battering ram. From the appearance of his skin, he had been dead less than two weeks. No toe tag. This was getting more mysterious by the minute. He called his supervisor.

"Greta, I was inventorying our bodies and I don't have any documents on Number 28. He must have come in last night."

"Oh, uh, yes. You are correct Rick. We, uh, are just holding that body here for 24 hours. Then it is going to the Ellis County morgue."

"Shouldn't there be a paper trail? I've got nothing."

"They gave us nothing. I'm not sure what to tell you. Just make believe it's not here and by tomorrow, it will be gone."

"Did 'they' tell you who it was?"

"Not a peep. And 'they' are the hospital brass. It's all hush hush. Don't talk about any of this with anyone else either."

Smalley hung up the phone, intrigued. It couldn't hurt to snoop around a little. 'They' weren't going to dump a body in his cooler and not tell him what was going on. It just wouldn't be right. He'd have to delete the photos he took. Or send them to his personal email. Smalley decided to check the news reports to see who died recently in the area. Surely it was local.

Smalley finished his shift and made it back to his apartment following a stop at the gun shop and the Quizno's next door. He finished eating and settled in for an evening of research on the couch. After an hour of surfing the obituaries from news sources all over Georgia and South Carolina, he had a list of eight men between the ages of 30 and 45 who died within the last two weeks. Just their descriptions alone indicated two were African American, and one was Asian. A picture accompanying one showed he was bald and portly. John Doe had a full head of brown hair and was in good shape. A fifth one was a burn victim based on a news report. Six and seven were possibilities he would have to check into further.

The eighth candidate was the most interesting possibility. But the news reports, and there were many, showed pictures of a man who didn't quite look like his Number 28. Andrew Isaacson had been shot twice. None of it was adding up, yet the news reports indicated he went over the upstairs bannister and landed on the newel post. Bingo. That was consistent with the injuries noted on his guy in the cooler. Even so, Isaacson just didn't look like Mr. Doe.

Smalley flipped on the television and finished his sandwich. While watching back-to-back episodes of <u>Forensic Accountants,</u> he pulled up some more information on candidates six and seven. Facebook pages showed pictures and condolences for Six and Seven. Six was short, yet very muscular. And he was in a car wreck. No way on him. Seven really looked like his man. He was similar in height and appearance, but it couldn't be him. He died of a massive heart attack, and then his family took him back to Kentucky. So it didn't appear that '7' was his guy either. His best candidate was Andrew Isaacson, an artist who died under unfortunate unnatural circumstances, maybe some mystery also. He just didn't look like him. He'd have to ask Greta tomorrow.

"So who is Number 28?"

Greta wasn't the adventurous type. She enjoyed her job in no small part because it was very routine. No drama or intrigue. Processing dead people was until now an anonymous job few living people had an interest in. Number 28 was upsetting her apple cart, and it made her nervous.

Smalley could tell it in her eyes, something was up. Beads of sweat formed on her brow. She didn't want to lie, but Greta was sworn to secrecy. "Wha-what do you mean?"

"The stiff we got doesn't look anything like the pictures of Andrew
Isaacson, the artist who died. I did a little research last night. What gives?"
"I'm not talking about this. Can't talk about this."
Interesting. She was TOLD not to talk about it. Smalley loved the prospect
of a little controversy. Especially if it meant someone was defrauding the
general public. This would be great material for his blog.
"Come on, Greta. How long have we worked together? You can tell me."
"No, I can't." Greta haphazardly moved papers around on her desk, then
got up to pour a cup of coffee.
"Greta, don't keep this bottled up. You need to talk about it. It's going to
make you sick from worry."
Smalley was pushing her buttons. This was almost more enjoyable than
finding out the truth.
"If I say anything, I could lose my job." She walked out of the office to put
some space between her and Smalley, but he followed her into the
examination room.
"If you say anything to the public. That's different. I'm on the team. If this
gets out, I could lose my job also. Doesn't that qualify me to know what
the secret is?"
Greta mulled it over. What a relief it would be to get it off her chest. He
did have a point. What if this impacted him also?
"Come here."
Greta led Smalley into a cooler.
"Swear to me that you will not breathe a word of this to anyone."
"Done."
"It's not Andrew Isaacson." The release of classified information made
Greta nauseous.
"Then who is it?"
"I don't know. All I was told was to keep this body here until further
notice. The detectives said it would be resolved fairly quickly."
"So they don't want the public to know Andrew Isaacson didn't die the
other night."
A litany of possibilities scrolled through Smalley's mind. This was a cover
up, but why? For whatever reason, the police wanted everyone, maybe just
the killers, to think that Andrew was dead. He had never heard of anything
like this before. The bigger question was/is, where is Andrew Isaacson? Is
he on the run, or hiding at police headquarters?
"Greta, this is crazy. Why would they do this? We need to find out who
this other guy is."
"No we don't. What we need to do is leave locker number 28 closed and
ignore it. We have enough work to do."

Telling her secret did not have the desired effect, and now she had the unintended consequence of having to keep Smalley from overreacting. He smelled adventure. She felt queasy. Smalley couldn't go directly to the blog with this. At least not yet. But he certainly wanted to know more.

This looked like the right place. Smalley checked the marquee "AD Isaacson". Yep, this is it. Smalley learned so much about Andrew Isaacson in the last 24 hours. He was/is quite an artist, and looks nothing like Number 28 back at the office.

Surely somebody in this place knows something. He was snooping on his day off which had to be a new record. There were days he avoided work while on the clock. Now, he was going above and beyond and not getting paid. This was worth it though. It had 'breaking news' written all over it. Smalley would definitely fill out the blog- anonymously- if he got some good info. He walked in the door and smiled at the receptionist.

"Hi, I was interested in talking with someone about Mr. Andrew Isaacson." Smalley was gleefully brave in his naiveté. His quest for a story had landed him in the center of the snake pit.

The receptionist responded with a quizzical look and quickly disguised it. She made a call. "What is your name, sir?"

"R-Reggie Littrell, from the District Attorney's office." Rick almost gave his real name.

"Mr. Burnett? Yes, I have a Reggie Littrell from the DA's office, and he wants to talk with someone about Mr. Isaacson. Mm-hmm?" Long pause. The receptionist looked at Smalley to convey a message.

"Someone will be right with you." The receptionist busied herself with other duties, shooting a look at Smalley occasionally as he sat in the waiting area.

Eugene Burnett could not fathom why a representative from the DA's office would be here. A host of possibilities ran through his mind, most of them bad. Stella was out until Tuesday, so he was going to have to deal with this himself. He was equal parts excited and racked with dread. It could be nothing. Sign a few papers or something. Or it could be something diabolical and today, since Stella was out, he was the one who was 'the go to guy' 'the man' 'the chief decider'. The receptionist pointed him out even though he was the only one waiting.

"Hello, I'm Eugene Burnett, Chief Operating Officer. What can I do for you?"

The receptionist shot him a sarcastic look.

"I am here to talk with someone about Mr. Isaacson. I think there are things you need to know."

Eugene decided they should go somewhere more private.

"Please, let's talk in my office."

Smalley pulled out a picture from his pocket and slid it across the desk for Eugene to see.

"Who is this?"

That was all Smalley needed to hear.

"It's supposed to be Andrew Isaacson. I took it yesterday. This man has been at the morgue since the day of the incident. The police department apparently wants us to believe this is Andrew Isaacson."

"I can assure you it is not Andrew Isaacson." Eugene may have been too rash in showing his cards to this clerk. "Why did you come here?"

"I needed to be sure. There's something up and I don't know what. Why would the police want people to think Andrew Isaacson was dead when he evidently is alive?"

Eugene finally put the pieces of the puzzle together. He sat up in his chair.

"Wait, what? Are you saying that Andrew could be alive?"

"I'm not sure of anything, but if this guy is supposed to BE Andrew Isaacson, then where is the real one?"

Eugene soaked in the glorious information. Whether Andrew was alive or not was not the central issue. It was the fact that HE knew some thick, juicy news and Stella did not. Eugene would have to use this to its greatest advantage. Andrew alive? It could change everything. Stella did not want to know this.

"I need you to keep this quiet for the time being."

"But this needs to be exposed. It's a cover up. I just don't know why."

"There may be a good reason. Letting this out in the open could put your safety in jeopardy."

Eugene decided to lay it on thick.

"I don't know. At least the real dead guy needs to be identified."

That was a reasonable point. Who was this guy? Eugene guessed Stella would have an idea.

"Can I keep your picture? I may be able to get you an answer. How about keeping a lid on this until I can get you more info on this guy."

"Deal. Thanks for your time, Mr. Burnett. Have a good day."

Smalley left and Eugene schemed. He was firmly in the driver's seat now. Eugene needed to control this information and those who knew it. At least until he told Stella. If he told her.

# Chapter 40

The Orphanage

"Is there anything I can do for you?" Bhaniel was more nervous than Theresa.

"No, I'm all packed. I don't really have much to take. I'm just a poor church mouse. Why didn't you tell the doctor?"

"Tell her what?" Bhaniel was pretty sure what Theresa meant.

"You know. You acted like you were afraid to tell her."

"It doesn't really matter if she knows or not."

"Maybe you should go with me."

Bhaniel showed her a tired smile. "This trip is for you alone. You deserve the best care possible. And the rest will do you good."

"Don't get too comfortable without me. I'm hopping a plane just as soon as they look the other way."

"We will watch for you every day."

Theresa walked over and hugged Bhaniel.

"Do you think I have it?"

"I will pray you don't. I love you Miss Theresa. Come back to us soon."

"I love you too, Miss B."

As if on cue, the doctor poked her head in the door.

"Are we all ready?"

Sigh. "Yeah, I guess so."

The whole community walked them down to the river's edge. They had the ferry ready and waiting. It had the eerie feeling of Elijah leaving Elisha as he stood on the banks of the Jordan River. No chariot of fire however.

Bhaniel had already begun to feel the loss of her close friend, sister really, wondering what she would do without her unique brand of strength and devotion. It was a void in her soul tempting her to breathe carefully so as not to inflame the pain. The kids felt it too. Life at the home would be less vibrant because of Theresa's absence.

Maybe tomorrow would be a little better.

# Chapter 41

## Stella's Office

Stella was in a sour mood on Wednesday. The question was if someone is consistently in a sour 'mood' then is it really a mood shift or just how they are? She was supposed to be back in the office on Tuesday, but layovers and a headache pushed everything back one more day. Stella didn't really want to come in today except Eugene couldn't be trusted to run everything indefinitely.

"So what happened while I was gone? Please tell me you didn't screw anything up."

"Welcome back, Stella." Eugene didn't mean it. "Good news. The company ran smoothly while you were gone. Pretty routine stuff actually. The Diego collection is almost done except Riley is dragging his feet. I went over the McRae contract revisions you marked out with the attorneys, and it doesn't look like there will be any problems getting it finalized."

"Go get me some aspirin." Stella was done talking already.

Eugene walked out satisfied the inquisition was short.

Stella leaned back and wondered if taking Thursday and Friday off would be possible. She closed her eyes visualizing the things absolutely needing attention. Eugene had not come back with her pain reliever. He might have to give her a neck rub when he brings it.

The system was up and running again so she checked the various activity ledgers. First the time sheets, the delivery schedule, the shipping receipts and the appointment list. Everything looked standard which indicated Eugene was telling the truth. Except that.

"Eugene, come in here."

He had the ibuprofen in his hand.

"What can I do for you?"

"What is this?" Stella was pointing at the computer screen. The appointment schedule showed 'Reggie Littrell, DA's office, met with Eugene Burnett'.

Eugene looked at the screen and looked at Stella. She could tell he was shocked by the quick intake of breath.

"I, uh, met with him and he told me about some things going on in his office." He was stalling as he tried to think.

Stella was actually very curious because she had not interacted with the DA's office previously.

"What did he say? Did he have some information about Andrew?"

"Nothing new really. Just some questions about him and the business."

"Hmm."

"Anything else?" Eugene was ready to escape.

"Get Reggie Littrell on the phone for me."

Eugene gritted his teeth and just nodded. He dialed the phone and prayed that no one answered. Rick Smalley picked up the phone on the second ring.

"This is Eugene Burnett at AD Isaacson."

"Hello Eugene." Rick was excited to hear some new information on his cadaver.

"Please hold for Stella Manchester."

"Hello, is this Reggie Littrell?"

"Yes it is."

"I wanted to follow up on your visit to our office recently. You should know we will help you in any way we can."

"Oh, okay. Yes, that will be good. Did Eugene show you the picture?" Rick was anxious to hear what Stella knew about the mystery man.

"Uh, no not yet. Would it help if I looked at it first?" Stella was buzzing Eugene while she talked. She leaned away from the phone and asked Eugene to bring her picture that Rick left with him.

Eugene was cooked and he knew it. He pulled the picture out of his pocket and laid it on Stella's desk and walked out. Stella was going to verbally abuse him, but he left too quickly. She looked at the picture. He was not familiar to her.

"I have the picture in front of me. Who is he?"

"I was hoping you would be able to tell me."

"I don't get it. What does this have to do with Andrew Isaacson?"

'Reggie' spent the next few minutes telling Stella everything he told Eugene at his last visit.

Stella was stunned. Everything she based her actions on had just been turned upside down. Stella worked on getting her mind around the idea Andrew was not in the morgue. Since the real dead guy was almost certainly her 'employee', Andrew was running free. He is alive.

"I'm sorry. I just don't know who this person is. Have the police told you anything?"

"No, it's all hush hush. The real Andrew Isaacson must be on the run somewhere."

"Thank you. We'll keep trying to find out who this individual is, and we'll call with any new information."

"That's what the other guy said."

"We want to know as bad as you do. We'll be in touch."

The conversation was over. Stella waved him off and began to plan. Stella was tempted to light Eugene on fire. He had become a liability. Or had he? She was not happy her hit man was so inept. He had cost the company a bundle, and now she was going to have to take a chance on a new one. Did Andrew really get the best of her 'professional' killer? Well, good for him. But now the momentum had shifted a bit in her favor. Andrew would not know she had found out his secret. Somebody knew where Andrew was and she needed to get to that person.

A hit man was less important than someone who was able to extract information. She was hesitant to go back to the same people to get another 'mechanic'. But her options were limited. Stella liked their discretion, and the first contract worker was capable on the Harvey McCallum job. Not so good on the Andrew hit. He just didn't expect Andrew to blindside him. Stella went outside, walked to the dog-walking park down the street, and dialed her cell phone.

"Red's Barbeque."

"Let me talk to Wendell." The line clicked, transferring to somewhere in the restaurant. A middle-aged man with too much saliva in his mouth answered.

"Wendell doesn't work here anymore."

"Three Dog Night." This was the code they gave Stella last time.

"What do you want?"

"I need to find another worker."

"This is irregular."

"I realize this, and I am willing to pay for the exception."

"Wait one." The pause was awkward.

"What skills do you need?"

"Someone who can get information from a reluctant individual."

"This is going to be the last time we do business."

"Agreed." Stella knew there would be no negotiation. She had heard stories of this organization's dedication to secrecy. They'd find her and kill her if she called again.

"Call this number and give them the code 4973. Transfer fifty thousand dollars to the account number 45284672 prior to the worker's arrival. The remaining fifty thousand will be transferred upon completion."

The line went dead and Stella was hopeful. Good thing it was Andrew's money.

# Chapter 42

## Matadi, Democratic Republic of the Congo

The meeting was clandestine, and everyone was present. There were twenty men lining the walls of the windowless room. A few had experience, but most were new. Mada and Ruwan were the recognized leaders because of their success in previous raids. Success centered on surviving. They were veterans of six raids on ships which made them almost legendary. Unfortunately, the high ratio of soldier casualties required them to train new recruits on a regular basis. Ruwan finished talking to the group.

"We will neutralize the crew first and then secure the weapons cache which is below deck. Once we are able to do this, the next group will bring the barge to the ship and move the weapons. Everyone meet back here tomorrow night at dusk."

Men dispersed a few at a time to avoid notice. Mada waited until everyone had left to face Ruwan.

"Ruwan, I'm not sure this is a good idea."

"Why do you say this? We may not have this chance again. Mada, there is nothing more to talk about." Ruwan demanded.

"We don't know for sure the Quintana is the right ship."

"It is as sure as we can be. It is worth the risk."

It wasn't the level of confidence Mada was looking for. Their information was sketchy, gathered from bribing port authorities and brutalizing the right military personnel. The Quintana was the best guess based on ships coming to harbor in the next three days. It was due in port late tomorrow night. The men were ready and the rebels needed more weapons. To add to the urgency, the military had gained the advantage in the eastern border lands where the fighting was nearly around the clock. If the cache of weapons was as great as they imagined, it could change the course of the conflict. It couldn't be declared a full scale civil war because the rebels had yet to win a significant battle. Ruwan felt as though their luck was about to change.

"Get some rest, Mada. I believe it will go well."

# Chapter 43

The Schuster Gallery, Atlanta

Mitch noticed the bell as the door opened and shut. As usual, he was ready to leave for the evening, and one more browser had stopped by. He had not scheduled anyone this afternoon because there were so many details to take care of for the summer show coming up.

He had seven artists committed, a record for the gallery. Five were new relationships and all would give him exclusive showing rights in the city. Three looked like they had the talent to be stars and ability to produce quality pieces consistently.

"Pardon me, are you the owner of the gallery?"

"Yes. I'm Mitch DeGuerre."

"Fine, could I ask you a question?"

"Certainly."

"Is the steel sculpture in this side room available for sale?"

The middle aged man didn't appear to be the typical art enthusiast. He was simply dressed in a rumpled shirt and denim trousers. His glasses were holdovers from the Seventies, and his hair was cut with electric clippers. Mitch moved around the desk to walk with the man into the side room. The sculpture was the fourth in a series of pieces made of quarter inch steel and hardwood. Some looked like they were inspired from farm implements.

"This one on display is available at three thousand, and the artist has two more arriving next week."

Mitch turned to look at the item as the gentleman moved around behind him. He did not see the hypodermic needle, but felt the pinch in his neck. Mitch turned to look at the man, but his knees buckled. The nice man caught him before he crumpled to the floor and Mitch faded into a deep sleep.

The visitor put vinyl gloves on and pulled Mitch to the corner of the room out of any sightlines. He walked to the front to lock the main door and hang the "Closed" sign.

There was much to do before he and Mr. DeGuerre went for a ride.

# Chapter 44

Andrew's Residence

Detectives Oliver and Tunney stood on the front drive and took a wide angle view of the house.

"Can you believe one guy lived here?"

"Yeah, well he had a girlfriend I guess."

"This is bigger than my apartment building," Tunney mused. "What are we looking for?"

"A lead or two we can use to track this guy down."

"Who would have guessed an artsy guy would have a little ninja in him." They unlocked the front door and walked around the bloody area at the base of the staircase.

"Check the kitchen for mail or documents and I'll look for an office." Tunney toured the house on his way to the kitchen. Dude had style. HAS style he supposed. Oliver went from room to room looking for useable intelligence. Finding nothing of obvious use, he made his way upstairs to Isaacson's bedroom. About the time that he got to the top of the stairs, Tunney called to him.

"Clarence, do you know who Mitch DeGuerre is?"

"No, who is he?"

"Somebody he does business with evidently. From the look of the paperwork thrown on the island, he sold art through this guy's gallery."

"Good. Find a phone number and an address and we'll track him down."

"Roger that. We might want to talk to someone at this organization called the IORRF also."

"Gather it all up and we'll sift through it later."

Another hour of looking and the only other leads they found were an attorney's business card, phone numbers for three girlfriends, and a postcard from Isaacson's dentist.

The Schuster Gallery was fairly close so they went there first. There were a couple of good restaurants within walking distance and supper was going to happen soon.

It didn't look like anyone was home when they pulled up in front. Knocking on the glass door didn't rustle anybody's attention.
"Let's go around back and see if there is another entrance." This meant 'let's break in but do it out of the public's view.'
To their surprise, the back door was not locked. They instinctively pulled their weapons before they went in. A quick search of the place yielded no persons, and the burglar angle seemed less logical because there didn't appear to be anything missing, and all of the art work was in place. The office was noticeably disheveled, yet in a neat way. Like someone went through everything, but was not in a hurry.
Another oddity was the whole place was up and running. A fan was oscillating, the coffee maker in the kitchen had a fresh pot, and the radio next to the desk was still on. It was as if the owner stood up and walked out the back door never to return. Or he was escorted out against his wishes.
"Bryce, call this in and find out if there has been a missing person report on Mr. DeGuerre. We'll have to go to his house next."
"Officer Tunney, there was a 911 call regarding your location this evening at 1730 hours. A neighbor reported what she thought was a burglary from the back of the business. Her name is Nadine Farris and her address is 687 Prospect Avenue, Apartment 1843."
"Thank you. We'll follow up."
"Wow. We just missed him. Didn't we get to the shop at six?"
"Yeah, tough luck."
Looks like dinner would have to wait.

The apartment building was predictably on the next block over with the back of it facing the rear door of the gallery. Clarence stood at the rear door and considered all the windows in view. If Nadine wasn't helpful, they might have to go door to door to see if anyone saw something usable.
"Nadine Farris? We are Detectives Oliver and Tunney. We'd like to ask you a few questions about your 911 call this evening."
"Please, come in. Can I get you anything to drink? I just made some coffee cake." It smelled very tasty, especially since they were both hungry.
"A little coffee cake would be nice."
"I'll get you some iced tea also."
Ms. Farris was an elderly lady with a decided limp, but a sparkle in her eye. Faded pictures hung on the wall showing a younger Nadine with her husband – evidently. The apartment was decorated nicely for a home in 1963. The couch was covered in clear vinyl.
"How long have you lived here Ms. Farris?"

"Nearly eighteen years. I moved here after my husband died. We had always lived in Atlanta and I couldn't bear to leave. I have a son in Augusta who wants me to move there, but this is home. My church and the grocery store are close by. I love this part of the city. So much energy." She set the food and drink in front of the men.

"Would you tell us what you saw this evening?"

"I don't normally get involved in other people's business, but it seemed odd. I had never noticed that man coming out of the art gallery before. I love the Schuster gallery. It has been here as long as I have. They have some of the prettiest paintings and sculpture in town. The dark haired young man, the owner, always leaves at 5:15 of an evening and he didn't this time. I typically sit near the window that time of day and do the crossword from the newspaper."

Wow. The detectives knew they might have found a gold mine or a 'Rear Window' replay. She sounded plausible though.

"Another man had parked his car near the back door and came out soon after with a large bag which he struggled with. He put it in the trunk and drove away. He left the lights on, and I bet he didn't lock the door. Since there was no sign of the owner the rest of the evening, I was concerned something was wrong. That's when I dialed 911."

"Do you remember much about the car the other man was driving?"

"It was brown and older looking. I'm not much with styles or models, but it was a four door car."

Tunney walked over to the window and looked down toward the gallery door.

"Is this where you sit every day?"

"Yes."

There was a clear view of the gallery's back door. Her version had some merit.

"Thank you, Mrs. Farris, you've been a big help. We appreciate you calling the police."

After promising to come back soon, the detectives left to review street camera footage.

# Chapter 45

Pointe Noire, Republic of the Congo and Port of Matadi, DRC

The stopover at Pointe Noire was all business. Andrew watched with fascination as the cranes removed a large portion of the containers from the deck of the ship in an orchestral movement of chaos and precision. In a matter of hours, the labor and paperwork were done. The ship departed and headed south, hugging the western shores of African on its way to the mouth of the Congo River. With recent improvements to the shipping lane of the river, their mid-sized container ship could easily navigate the next leg into Matadi. Offloading some of the weight at Pointe Noire didn't hurt either.

As they closed in on Matadi, Andrew was down in his room organizing his gear which didn't take long. He was trying to get everything squared away and then go topside to watch the docking again. Suddenly, the ship groaned like a dying whale and then shuddered, screeching to a stop. How in the world does a boat this big stop on a dime anyway?

THUD!! The ship either ran into another vessel or they found the dock. If it was the latter, then there wasn't going to be much left of the dock. The impact threw Andrew across the room. The lights flickered off and on. The ventilation system stopped and started. Then the lights went off for good. Crew members ran by the room. Someone shouted angrily in French. The room was completely dark. Andrew could only feel around. If he could find his stuff, there was a pen light in his drawing materials.

Andrew found the light which didn't reveal anything new in his room other than there was comfort in being able to see. Andrew wrestled with the door, but it wouldn't open. More crew members ran by and Andrew pounded and yelled.

"Hello! Let me out of here! I'm stuck in here!"

It felt like thirty minutes of pounding. More men ran by his door as he bloodied his knuckles, but they did not stop. Finally, one heard him and attempted to free the door to no avail, then he continued on. After more futile pounding, Andrew had to stop and take a breather.

There was commotion outside his door and he heard the voice of Wilhelm Stewart. The latch ratcheted and the door cracked open. Wilhelm stood in the doorway, a silhouette by the glow of the emergency lights in the hallway. He was out of breath from running with a gun in one hand and a crowbar in the other. He slid into the room and looked down the hall for followers.

"Andrew we have to go. The ship is under attack from locals. A lot of the crew is dead and we may have run aground."

"Think we can make it off the boat?"

"Fifty/fifty, but it's our only play. They're like ants. I don't know how they got on the ship so fast. There is a service tunnel they probably don't know about. We'll have to find it and hope for the best."

Andrew put everything he had into the backpack.

"I'm ready if you are. Got an extra gun?"

"No. If we see any dead soldiers, we'll borrow his. Come on."

Wilhelm checked the hall and waved Andrew on.

They made it down two hallways and went to one lower deck. They did find a dead pirate, but he didn't have a gun. Wilhelm located the service tunnel and closed the bulkhead behind them. It was lit only by red trouble lights, but seemed uninhabited.

"This will take us to the stern and two cargo bays. It's possible no one will be there."

The men walked, jogged, and crawled through hallways, tunnels and catwalks. At the last bulkhead, Wilhelm turned and looked at Andrew.

"This leads to the cargo area. If there are bad guys in there, we'll have to be invisible."

Wilhelm turned the lever and moved in. Andrew followed almost tiptoeing to be as quiet as possible. They crouched on the catwalk overlooking the cargo area and watched as twenty men moved in and out of the bay. The hull was open to the outside.

"Great. This looks like their primary staging area," Wilhelm whispered.

"What about the other bay you mentioned?"

"Yeah, we'll have to go there. This is suicide."

It was one level up and about fifty meters away.

"It's just beyond this bulkhead," Wilhelm said as he pulled down on the latch.

As they stepped through, an invader surprised them. He was young, sweaty, and thin to the point of starvation. He yelled at them in a local language and pointed his gun nervously. Both of the men stopped dead and half raised their hands. The invader motioned for them to go back through the bulkhead, toward the original cargo bay. The pirates had not shown much propensity to take prisoners, so neither Wilhelm nor Andrew believed this was going to end well. They would have to act.

Andrew went through the opening first and Wilhelm followed. As the young pirate stepped through, Wilhelm turned and slammed the door on his arms and right leg. It stunned him, but didn't knock him out. Wilhelm pushed him back through the opening and rammed him into some exposed pipes. The pirate's rifle went off causing bullets to ricochet in the small space. Andrew ducked and then tried to leap through the doorway to aid in overcoming the pirate. Wilhelm was pressing his body against the young boy. Andrew noticed Wilhelm's gun tucked in his belt and grabbed for it. He clicked the safety and rammed it into the boy's forehead.

"Shoot Him!" Wilhelm yelled.

Andrew looked at Wilhelm wildly. He was hoping to scare him into surrendering, but the pirate fought as much as his spindly limbs would allow.

"Do it!!"

Andrew pulled the trigger and the young boy went limp as the bullet lodged in his brain. Andrew fell back to catch his breath as he watched the boy slump to the ground.

"Come on."

Wilhelm was in no mood to wait around. He took the pirate's weapon, closed and locked the bulkhead, and went toward the other cargo bay. Andrew avoided looking at the boy and followed Wilhelm.

The second cargo bay was empty, but voices sounded close. It was similar to the other one, but smaller.

"Ok. When you go down that ladder, you will be able to stay hidden all the way to the main door. There might still be some rope to lower yourself down to the water, or land. I'm not sure what you are going to find out there."

"You sound like you aren't coming."

"I'm not. I've got to go back up and see if I can find any other crew members. There are some documents I need to salvage too."

"I thought that was the captain's job?"

"He's dead. I'm the acting captain now."

"How am I supposed to open the cargo door?"

"Look to the right of the door. There is a big green button. Push it and it opens automatically. If it doesn't work, the manual override is next to it. Just crank it open far enough to crawl through."

Andrew looked down and saw blood coming from Wilhelm's abdomen. An errant bullet from the pirate's rifle had found him.

"You're bleeding pretty badly. Let me come with you. We can hold them off better with two of us."

"No, I need you to get off the boat alive. I've already lost most of my crew. I'm not going to lose my only paying customer. Go before someone comes."

Andrew decided to follow captain's orders. Both of them knew Wilhelm didn't have long.

"Thanks, Wilhelm. I owe you. Want your gun back?"

"No, take it. It will be easier to hide once you make it to land. This AK-47 has a full clip."

Andrew went through the door and climbed down the ladders as Wilhelm locked the bulkhead behind him.

He made it to the cargo door and hit the green button. Nothing. Great. He looked for the manual crank and found it nearby. Andrew turned it long enough to create a crack just big enough to slide through. He didn't find a rope, but there was a medium sized chain that would work. Andrew looked through the opening and considered his options. By the lights on the far shore, he guessed he was still about forty feet above the surface of the water. Whatever they hit must have been on the other side of the ship. Andrew would have to swim to land and the best bet was to go around the front of the boat. He needed a raft or something.

Andrew surveyed the cargo bay and found an emergency cache. There wasn't a usable raft, but there were some surfboard like floaters each about the size of one of his legs. Andrew took his pants off, stuffed them in the legs and threw it over his shoulder. He climbed to the end of the chain and dropped the final fifteen feet. Wrapping the floaters around him, Andrew started to believe he had a decent chance to make it out of this alive.

Trying to paddle without making waves was harder than it seemed when he first thought of it. The ship looked like it was a mile long also. The best idea was to stay close to the side of the boat. Once he got to the bow, he might have to go straight into the open water of the bay. Night was falling which was to his advantage. Just a small head protruding from the waves would be hard to see. The floaters could be trouble if they popped up out of the water though.

Twenty minutes later, Andrew was at the bow and it wasn't far to shore. He slid around the point to see if there were any pirates hovering overhead. No boats were tied up nearby, but he wondered about someone on deck seeing him as he swam away from the boat. It was a necessary risk and night was full upon them. Slow and steady and he could go almost unnoticed. Thank God for the floaters. Andrew was already fatigued even with their assistance. Just a few minutes more and he'd be on dry land.

Surprisingly, it took less time to swim to shore than it did to go around the boat. As he looked back toward the ship, it appeared they were closer to shore than he first assumed. When his feet felt the firmness of the earth, Andrew rose up and poured the water out of his backpack and put his pants back on. No one on shore was close by so his arrival in the Democratic Republic of the Congo was void of fanfare or notice. From his vantage point, Andrew could only see a rusty boat tethered next to the ship, but no pirates. He was just glad to be on land and alive. Odds were the pirates' booty was going to be off loaded sometime in the night by the invaders whoever they were. It was going to have to be someone else's concern. Andrew focused on disappearing into the night.

# Chapter 46

Police Headquarters, Atlanta

It didn't take long to find a half dozen cameras in the immediate area with footage of traffic around the time Ms. Farris mentioned. The rest of the afternoon was spent scanning the data for an older, brown sedan.

"There it is. Maybe." Bryce had the video paused on a brown, mid 1980's Ford Crown Victoria. There was a middle-aged white male driving and no passengers noticeable.

"Can we get a rear view of the car and the license plate?"

"Coming up." Bryce shifted to another security camera video showing the car move into the frame and then out. The license plate was barely visible before it went past the camera shot.

"Is it possible to zoom in on the plate?"

"Some. It may be too grainy though."

"If we can get a couple of numbers, who knows? How many 1984 Crown Vic's can there be around here?"

The zoom in was generally successful.

"Something, 26, something, something, R. They're Florida plates."

"Let's see if we can get a good shot of his face too. The face recognition software might get a hit."

"I've got a couple of shots already."

"That should be enough to go on. Let's go run all of it through the database."

"Computers are awesome." Clarence loved it when they worked.

They had the vehicle, but the license plate ended up being a fake which was not a surprise. There were only fourteen cars in the whole state with the exact description. Two were owned by middle aged white guys. One had a restriction on his license for a prosthetic leg. The other looked like he could be their guy. They were still waiting on the face match.

Ding. Clarence got a text from down the hall. The name was a match for the face shot also.

"Cyrus Coolidge. He has a place south of Fayetteville on highway 85." The Google maps satellite photos showed a house and a large barn on the property.

"Let's go. I hope this is a good lead. Do you want to call the local sheriff?"

"Yeah, but tell them to just be on the lookout for the car."

# Chapter 47

Port of Matadi, DRC

Andrew spent the remainder of the night making his way into the city and away from the docks. Blending in was not an option due to his appearance, but the chances of running into more pirates or soldiers went down the further he was from the Quintana.

By dawn, Andrew was exhausted, but well within the city of Matadi. Even though it left him more exposed, he chose to stay in the city proper to increase his chances of finding transportation once the city came to life.

A ride to the orphanage was going to be tricky. At this point, just getting close would be agreeable. The only thing that Andrew knew for sure was the need to get to Bandundu. He hadn't thought this through very well, but he had a decent excuse. Andrew was running for his life. Again. He looked over the materials Mitch gave him for any clues. Most of the papers were a soggy mess thanks to the swimming event last evening. His ace in the hole was the name of the orphanage and Bhaniel Tretechi. Surely someone would be familiar with a name like hers.

A bus through Kinshasa and possibly connecting to Bandundu seemed like the smart play. In this country, all roads lead to Kinshasa. There would be plenty of buses going there. Andrew found a bus station after asking around, and after some deciphering felt confident he was picking one headed to Kinshasa.

"Kinshasa?" He asked what looked like the driver standing by the bus's door. He only received a nod in return.

Andrew pulled himself aboard and fell into the first open seat. He was still damp and would probably leave a wet spot in the seat. An older lady with her daughter slid into the seat next to him. They didn't seem concerned with his moist state. The only thing he remembered before falling asleep was the driver slamming the door shut and firing up the engine. The bus was over full and boys climbed onto the top of the vehicle for the ride to the city. He woke up as the bus's brakes squealed at the station. Andrew wanted to stay and sleep until the next stop, but duty called.

"Where are we?" He asked the driver.

"Bandundu."

"Oh, my. What happened to Kinshasa?"

"We stopped there, but you did not wake. Extra fare is forty francs."

Andrew pulled out the additional cash. He was shocked, and pleased. This was his ultimate destination, but it was only because of dumb luck. He could have easily been in Angola by the time he arose from his nap.

He walked toward a building with a fair number of people coming and going, and even more people standing around.

"Pardon me. Do you speak English?"

Andrew spoke to a relatively well-dressed man who appeared to be waiting on someone. The gentleman was a little startled and attempted to understand Andrew. He repeated his request but the man shook his head and pointed toward a one-story building with official, government-like signs near the door.

He noticed a small man who stood against a wall scarred by posters and the remnants of various news items. He was barefooted and talked on a cell phone. Andrew made his way to him and went through the same English question.

"Yes, I speak English. What can I do for you?"

"I was told that you could help me get to this orphanage." Andrew showed him the papers he had and Bhaniel's name.

"Oh yes, I know of it. You are closer than you think, my friend."

"Do you know if there is someone who can drive me from here? I am willing to pay."

"I will take you, sir. It is not far. Please, follow me." The aged man motioned for him to follow him outside.

"So you have a car?"

"No, no. We will not need a car. I can get you there in my taxi. Drago is my name." He turned and shook Andrew's hand.

"Andrew. You have a taxi, but it's not a car. What is it?"

Drago stopped in front of a three wheeled bicycle with a bench seat on the back complete with awning for shade. He beamed with pride as Andrew inspected the vehicle.

"It will be only fifty American dollars for the trip. I will show you all the sites on the way as well."

"Fifty dollars?! Too high." Andrew knew it was the first volley of negotiations. Drago expected it and would respect him less if he just accepted the first offer. Andrew liked Drago even though it was unlikely he would ride with him.

"No, no, Mr. America. This is a reasonable rate. Anything less would be too costly for me to take you there."

"Ten dollars sounds about right. And my name is Andrew. How did you know I was from America?"

"Americans are all very similar to each other. Most know only English." Drago laughed. "Since you seem like a friendly man, I'll drive you there for only sixty dollars. You must understand I am a very old man. I have twelve children and grandchildren that I care for."

He was laying it on pretty thick. Drago had already played the guilt card. "It's only one way. You should charge less for that."

"But I have to go round trip whether you ride with me or not."

"Fair point. Twenty dollars. That's pretty reasonable."

"We have a deal, sir." Drago looked into his eyes. "You drive a hard bargain Mr. America. Are you ready to go? Where are your bags?"

"This is all I have."

"You travel light. Are you staying long?" Drago made a show of assisting Andrew into the back seat.

"I have absolutely no idea."

And Andrew had absolutely no idea where they were going. Based on the sun, it was west, sort of. At least he was staying out of the ditch. Worst case, he will drive in circles and more money would be paid to another taxi driver. Best case, Drago actually knew where he was going. He didn't lack for confidence and he knew the area.

Andrew looked at his bags next to him on the seat. It was conceivable these few items were the sum total of his worldly possessions. He was homeless and traveling the world with scarcely more than the clothes on his back.

"Is the orphanage in Bandundu?"

"Just outside of the city. Across the river. We will ride the ferry to the other side. I remember when I was a boy . . .  the donkey.... I was only eight….. and covered in mud...."

Andrew had lost interest in the story. Fatigue was setting in and a flat spot to stretch out on was sounding so good. He closed his eyes for just a minute.

"Mr. America, this is the Kwango River."

Andrew started. "Huh?"

"We are not far from the orphanage."

"Will you be able to take me there?"

"I can take you across the river and walk with you from there."

Andrew looked around. The ferry was about half way across the river and coming to them. It wasn't a large vessel, almost a long canoe really, but the river appeared to be calm today. He had had enough swimming for a while. Drago was conversing vigorously with some men by the water. All of them shook their heads as he spoke, then laughed. As they talked, each one tried to be louder than the next guy. Andrew thought he heard one of them say the name Bhaniel, but it was fast and garbled. Drago walked back to the bicycle and Andrew.

"What did you say?"

"I told them who you are and why you are here. The two younger ones will walk with you the rest of the way. If you pay them, they will treat you like a king."

"That's fine. Do they take dollars?"

"Not as readily as before, but it's still better than the franc."

"You trade in francs here?"

"Congolese francs. Not great. We're never sure what it will buy from week to week."

"You're not going to go with me?"

"I will not be able to put my bicycle on the ferry. Leaving it here is not wise. It will be gone when I return."

The ferry ran aground and all those waiting paid a small fare and climbed aboard. Andrew paid for himself and his two new companions.

"Mr. America, it has been a pleasure to meet you. I look forward to seeing you again."

"Thank you, Drago. You've been a great help."

Drago waved and pedaled away.

The ferry ride was brief thankfully. Neither of the boys spoke English so Andrew sat and listened to all the different conversations occurring around him. Two women were talking to each other in rapid fire sentences. An old man had another younger man enthralled in his stories of glory on the river. His gestures made Andrew wish he could understand the language. The ferry slid up the bank and the 'captain' tied the boat off as everyone gathered their things. The boys motioned for Andrew to follow as they trotted up the bank.

"So the orphanage is up the hill?" Andrew was asking the wind mostly, because the boys had no clue what he was saying. They just kept encouraging him to follow.

"Oh well. I've come too far to stop now."

Andrew noticed a commotion down the bank. It was two kids and a lady struggling with a donkey and a cart whose wheels were entrenched in the mud by the water's edge. The donkey was not the least bit interested in pulling it out to safety. He was on a union designated break. The lady looked oddly familiar. Could it be? He had to venture closer just to be sure. The chances were decent it was she. They were theoretically close to her home. As he moved within the range of his eyesight, it became obvious. He had finally found her. Andrew waved the boys off and pointed to Bhaniel. His hand signals were only partially decipherable, but they understood enough to know he was done with them. Andrew gave each of them a dollar for their efforts.

Two young men were already doing everything they could to free the cart, but weren't making much headway. Andrew put his bags down and moved in to help. Bhaniel was distracted with other people who had gathered around offering mostly advice. He slogged into the mud and began to push the cart from behind. The three rocked it back and forth and then another grabbed the cart from the front as the momentum moved the wheels. By this time, Andrew was covered in mud and only his white skin set him apart. Even then, Bhaniel might not recognize him. The cart broke free and Andrew followed it out. He stopped to catch his breath putting his hands on his knees.

"Oh, thank you gentlemen for your help. I'm so embarrassed the donkey went wild and ended up here." Bhaniel was speaking to her companions in Lingala.

Andrew stood up and stretched his back. He was getting too old for this kind of activity. Bhaniel looked at him and at first was surprised by the color of his skin. She then began to process what foreigner would be here by the river helping her move a rusty cart. Recognition hit her, but she hesitated to accept it.

"Mr. Isaacson?" Bhaniel couldn't believe the sight. Andrew covered in mud, her donkey cart savior.

"So, I was thinking. Would it be better to take a shower or just jump in the river?"

"Mr. Isaacson, you look fine." Bhaniel was smiling. "Besides, the mud is good for your skin." After enjoying the moment way too long, she relented. "You can either jump in now, or we can carry some water up to the house and pour it on you."

"Fair enough."

Andrew walked out a ways and jumped in to his neck. Bhaniel was thoroughly entertained. The others standing close by didn't have the foggiest idea what was being said in this unknown tongue.

"We could even teach you how to fish with a net if you like the water."

"I would love it." Andrew tried to exit the water without reacquiring a new covering of mud. He walked over to Bhaniel, soaked, and thought about hugging her. Instead, he took her hand and kissed it.

"Mr. Isaacson. Welcome to Africa."

"It is truly a pleasure to be here. Or anywhere for that matter. What a story I have to tell."

"I hope you will stay long enough to tell it."

"Well, I wanted to ask you .... I sort of need a place to stay for a while."

"I think we may have an opening. Can you work?"

"The donkey and I have a similar work ethic."

"Hmmm. Good worker but a little stubborn. Fair enough, you're hired." Bhaniel laughed and then hugged him in front of everyone. "I'm so glad you are here Mr. Isaacson."

"Me too, Miss Tretechi. Me too."

# Chapter 48

South of Fayetteville, Georgia

Mitch bowed his head and leaned forward stretching the zip ties holding his hands together behind his back. The blood dripped down between his knees from his lower lip. Mitch's eyes had swollen shut a couple of hours ago.

"Are you interested in talking now?"

The mechanic was very polite. He wasn't a yeller. It had never worked for him. He preferred to sway his subjects with action and... pain. He didn't really enjoy breaking bones. It was just as effective to bruise to the bone. Apparently, Mitch still had a measure of defiance remaining.

The man in paper coveralls went to work on Mitch's feet and fingers. The important thing for him was to make as much progress as possible before the swelling reduced the feeling in Mitch's extremities. The bones in his feet were probably going to break eventually.

"Let me know when you are ready. I know it's unpleasant. I am happy to stop when you are."

"I.... just.... don't.... know....." Mitch had to breathe in between each word.

"Maybe we can narrow it down. I'm going to need something usable from you or I don't get paid. Is Andrew still in the city? Did he leave the state? How do you contact him?"

Mitch tried to form words, but they did not come out. He was drifting in and out of consciousness. One thing he was sure of. He was not going to survive this unless he could escape.

"You're.... going.... to.... kill.... me.... anyway....."

"No, that's not true. I'm going to let you rest for a few minutes, and then we'll start again."

His torturer was a very nice man. If the circumstances were different, he might be a friend. A creepy, sadistic, murderous friend. The most chilling thing about him was he acted like he had all the time in the world and was not the least bit concerned about anyone finding the two of them in this place. Mitch fought to keep his wits about him. Where was he? He had been drugged while at his shop, and woke up sitting in this chair, in this warehouse. Mitch could barely see through the swelling. An old Crown Victoria was parked in the space not far from his chair. The mechanic was sitting at a table in the corner reading the paper under a directional lamp, eating a sandwich. This was just another day at the office for him. He was completely disinterested in Mitch or his suffering. He needed answers so he could pay the rent.

Mitch had to decide whether telling lies would buy him time or hasten his death. Andrew was so far out of reach that Mitch could say just about anything. It would take the mechanic's employer time to verify his story, so there was a chance Mitch could get a break to find a way out of here. The mechanic, an average sized man with a plain appearance finished his lunch, and was walking toward Mitch.

"So, do you want to talk a while or should I continue with my efforts?"

"I want to talk." Mitch had gained some control over his speech. "I have a question. Why would you not kill me when we are done?"

"It's not in the contract. I only do what I'm paid for. Of course, you might wish you were dead sitting here in this warehouse for weeks. It works better also to keep you around so if your story doesn't pan out, I can come back and help you revise your story. Please, begin."

"I can... tell you what I know. Andrew came to me after someone tried to kill him. The police helped Andrew leave the state in a sort of witness protection program. They intend to bring him back before long I think. The only thing that I helped Andrew do was get him some cash and clothes."

"Reasonable. I have some contacts in the police department. I'll check it out and see what they know. I found some documents in your shop I wanted to ask you about. Why did you call the Atlantic Rim Shipping Company?"

Mitch felt his skin get cold.

"I called to ask them if they could ship some artifacts from Africa. They only do big box stuff so we didn't use them. It wasn't a good fit."

"Well, you did something with them. I called the dispatcher and she said you transacted business with them recently. About the time Andrew disappeared."

Mitch was done. He didn't know how to get out of this.

"I can see the look in your swollen eyes there is more to tell." The mechanic smiled at him.

He bowed his head. There was nothing more to say.

"Well, let's try something new." The mechanic went to his table and picked up a small canister of propane and opened the valve. With a pop, the torch was lit.

"I'll hold the flame away from you so it won't burn too fast."

He placed the flame under Mitch's chair until the metal began to glow red. Mitch opened his mouth to scream and nothing came out. The heat had taken his breath away. He tried to move his body away from the heat, but the chair was stationary and he was attached to it. The mechanic looked up at him and saw the threshold of pain he was working toward and pulled the torch away.

"Would you like to discuss the other things you were thinking about earlier?"

"Nhnhh...." Mitch could barely talk.

"The only other thing I found at your shop with ties to Africa is some correspondence with the IORRF and a lady named Bhaniel Tretechi. I would like to know if you sent Andrew to Africa to hide with Miss Bhaniel."

"I... don't..."

"Of course you do Mitch. If it isn't the truth, tell me so we can move on." Mitch couldn't think of a good lie.

The mechanic got up to make a call on his cell phone.

"I have some information. Yes. I will put the data together and bring it to the meeting."

The mechanic put his tools in the carrying case, placed them in the trunk, and drove out of the warehouse. Mitch was barely able to see him drive away. After many minutes of silence, Mitch began to sob.

# Chapter 49

The Orphanage

The dirt path was rutted from donkey carts and rain. Andrew took a t-shirt from his bag and made a makeshift head covering.

"I'm impressed you were down at the river trying to wrangle the donkey. Does he go across the river?"

"No, he's never been across the river. I wonder if he would stay on the boat if we tried. The only reason I was down there is because the boys were not sure what to do. Obviously, I wasn't doing all that well either."

"By the way, where are the boys and the donkey?"

"Still at the river. The donkey needs a bath. I'm sure we will see them soon."

They walked a short distance in silence. Andrew was taking everything in.

"It's so different than I imagined. Is it tough for you to leave when you go to America?"

"It is very tiring, and the kids don't like it when I'm gone. Routine is very important to everyone at the home." Bhaniel studied Andrew for a moment. "What made you decide to come Mr. Isaacson?"

"If you had told me two weeks ago I would be in Bandundu, Democratic Republic of the Congo today we would've both had a good laugh."

"You didn't intend to make this trip?"

"Not exactly. At least not this fast."

"Tell me your story."

Andrew began to tell Bhaniel his saga and tried to be as factual as possible about the assassination attempt. Even the dry facts were so salacious he was afraid Bhaniel wouldn't believe it. Andrew finished by telling of the drawings he made from his vision. They had reached the gates of the property.

"I'm speechless. And amazed that now we are part of your incredible story. Should we be concerned for YOUR safety?"

"I hope not. No one knows where I am except for Mitch. Speaking of danger, what are the chances we are going to be eaten by wild animals out here?"

"I suppose there is always a chance, but I've never known anyone to encounter wild animals in this area. It's mostly snakes we must avoid."

"Will do."

"What do you think the drawings mean?"

"Based on my near death experience on the boat, I'm guessing the weapons figure into it pretty heavily. They are trying to swing the momentum of the conflict with the theft."

"But there are guns coming into this country on a daily basis. It's truly a miracle my brother has lasted as long as he has as the dictator. What about people?"

"Don't really know about humans. The crew looked pretty standard and they were going on to their next destination within 24 hours. I didn't see anyone else on board who was out of the norm."

"Except you."

Andrew smiled. "Yes, I'm abnormal alright. Wait. Your brother is the dictator? Of the country?" He considered the news. "You should be the wealthiest lady in the whole nation."

"No, Mr. Isaacson, not me." Bhaniel told the highlights of her story.

"Maybe you are bringing a new thing to our country."

"I'm just a man on the run."

"Don't be surprised if you are part of a bigger plan Mr. Isaacson."

"If there was anyone I would believe, it is you, but I'm a nobody with nearly nothing to my name. I have no family or home, and almost everyone thinks I'm dead."

"You sound like the perfect candidate to do great things for God. By the time Moses entered service to the Lord, he was an 80 year old sheep herder who tried to talk God out of using him as Israel's liberator. He had no confidence in himself and tried to get God to find someone else."

He pondered this revelation. "I guess we'll see."

Bhaniel searched for the right words.

"Mr. Isaacson, I need to tell you something. For your... safety."

"Trust me. Nothing you can tell me is worse than what I've been through already."

"It's mostly precautionary, but I must let you know. The children. Most of them are the offspring of parents who contracted HIV and ultimately died of AIDS. Many of them inherited HIV."

"Ok, that's an unexpected twist. Am I in any real danger being around them?"

"No, except you shouldn't come in contact with their blood."

"Can do." Andrew was going to have to digest this new development.

"How do they avoid developing full blown AIDS?"

"One of the reasons I go to America regularly is to get the medicine they need to keep the disease under control."

The home was before them, but it wasn't a relaxing sight like he thought. The 'home' was actually a collection of buildings, all in very active use. Andrew had not seen so many kids running to and fro or busy with useful chores.

"Wow. This is some place."

"It's home."

# Chapter 50

South of Fayetteville

Detective Oliver knocked on the door of the house. Nothing. The barn was fifty yards behind the house and it was locked also.

"Is there a way we can get a look in there?"

"I didn't see any windows…" They both heard the sobs, and tore down the door.

"Control this is Tango 45. We have a white male approximately forty years old comatose with multiple contusions. He is handcuffed sitting down and appears to have been tortured."

The detectives attempted to do minor triage while scanning the room to see if the perpetrator was still in the building. There was very little blood, but his body was swollen and bruised from head to toe. Actually, his toes and feet were mangled, and his ankles looked like they had been dislocated. Detective Oliver thought to himself this guy was skilled and methodical. And cold blooded. He hadn't heard of this type of torture in any recent cases.

"SIR, CAN YOU HEAR ME?" The detectives were trying to rouse Mitch to no avail. They asked for an ambulance double quick.

"Nnn IInn."

"Hey, I think he's coming around." They surrounded him and patted his face while talking to him. For some reason, smacking a person's face was always considered a good way to make people wake up faster. His face was so distorted, it was like patting a bladder full of marshmallows.

"Sir, can you hear me? Can you tell us who did this?"

"I… pain…" Mitch was in so much pain breathing came only in shallow sips.

They lowered Mitch to the ground and laid him on his side. Bryce Tunney took off his jacket and put it under his head. Mitch made wailing, grunting noises with every movement.

"Crown Vic... brown..."

"Crown Victoria, brown." The detectives looked at each other.

"Was the man who assaulted you in his mid forty's, and white?"

Mitch barely nodded his head.

"Clarence, he hasn't been gone long, the chair he was sitting in is still warm."

"Call it in. Maybe there is a helo in the area we can use."

Dispatch did have a helicopter close by and the detectives also called the highway patrol giving them the description of the car. The ambulance was ten minutes out.

The mechanic was driving at a leisurely pace so as to not attract attention. Certainly, the car he was driving would not normally generate any second notices from the casual observer. He was just an average middle-aged guy driving an average middle-aged car down a sparsely used highway. He lit a cigarette and turned on the radio. It seemed fitting he should listen to music on AM radio. If only he could understand what it was they were singing.

He didn't see the officers following him immediately. They had stayed well behind since the traffic was light. The mechanic got a little nervous, however, when the Dodge Charger mimicked his turn on to State Highway 22. Their car was just too plain. A performance car trying to be nondescript made it stand out all the more. He sped up just a little and went through his escape routes in his mind. Just over this next rise should be a bail out road leading to a series of section line roads....

As he crested the hill, the road block was obvious. The highway patrolman had his car mostly on the shoulder, but they didn't have anyone stopped. This was organized just for him. He would have to ask the officers sometime in the future how they knew. The troopers stood in the road and motioned for the mechanic to pull over. Instead, he sped up and drove right at the officer. The trooper jumped behind his car as the Crown Victoria raced by. The tailing car had caught up by now and gave chase. This had all the makings of a low budget auto theft movie, and this version of the script wasn't going to end well for the bad guy.

Even the mechanic was aware the probability of success was dwindling. He'd have to make it to a more heavily populated area to disappear. But the helo overhead and the sheriff's cars directly ahead were intent on thwarting him. He dialed the phone.

"I have run into some unforeseen difficulties."

"Are you not going to be able to meet?"

"It does not appear so."

"Tell me what you know."

"You haven't paid me yet."

"I paid half already. Give me half of what you know."

"Your boy went to Africa. To an orphanage. On the cargo ship Quintana. I'll tell you the rest later."

He hung up and made a quick turn on a gravel road. The law dogs were close behind with at least one officer shooting at the fleeing car's tires. One bullet found its mark and the left front tire deflated and began to pull off the rim. The mechanic didn't slow down when the Crown Vic began to swerve. A sudden jerk to the left and the car rolled over and over again down the country road. The mechanic popped out of the driver's side window on the third roll and he hit the gravel just as the car made another rotation on top of him. The car came to rest seventy feet further with the remaining contents of the car strewn all over the immediate countryside.

"Well that didn't go exactly like I thought it would." Detective Oliver stopped the car near the mechanic's body.

"Let's get a forensic crew out here. I don't think he is going to make it." They walked over to the unknown man and determined that yes he was dead.

"Any ID?"

"Yeah, but it's probably fake. We'll have to run prints through the database. He's most likely a ghost."

"Cell phone?"

"Probably."

"I hope he wasn't texting. I'll have a look around."

The next three hours are filled with searching the scene, gathering evidence, and impounding the body and the car. Tunney found Oliver evaluating some of the tools of torture tagged and awaiting transport.

"Hey, I found the cell phone," Tunney proclaimed.

"You mean I've been looking all over this area for it and you had it all the time?"

"It was in his shirt pocket. It didn't fare too well in the wreck. But we can get it to the tech nerds."

"Let's get back then. This is pretty well scrubbed down. Did you get the stiff's prints?"

"Yeah. And some DNA."

"Plenty of that laying around."

# Chapter 51

The Orphanage

Andrew felt queasy. This was his ultimate destination. He had been in travel/escape mode for so long, he wasn't sure what to do now. The kids outside saw them and began to run. The older boys tried to get to Bhaniel first. It was a tradition, and it would be a shame to let an opportunity for some good old fashioned competition go to waste.

"Mr. Isaacson, you are going to get a proper welcome."

"I'm guessing they are happy to see you."

"No, not at all. We didn't expect you so everyone will be delighted."

The boys reached their finish line which was Bhaniel. They all hugged her at once as Andrew stood back and admired the scene. Just as soon as they mobbed Bhaniel, they were off to attack another challenge.

"There is no lack of love here is there?"

"No, we don't have much else, but there is always plenty of love. (in Lingala) Boys! Don't go far. I need you to help the other boys lead the donkey to the shed!"

The remaining kids arrived and gathered around Bhaniel. Everyone was talking at once commenting about Andrew.

(in Lingala) "Hey, everyone, I have a great surprise for you. Mr. Isaacson is from America, and he's going to stay with us for a while."

Since he didn't know what was being said, all he could do was smile and wave. He was a curiosity and he felt like the bearded lady at the carnival.

Aleefa, seventeen, was the oldest boy at the home. He extended his hand to Andrew.

"Hello, Mr. Isaacson. Welcome to Africa."

His English was not bad.

"Thank you, sir. It's good to be here."

Some of the kids smiled and others giggled. The younger ones didn't understand him even though they were learning English.

"Let's all go to the house and get ready for supper. Boys, the donkey please."

The donkey was obstinate and didn't want to go to the shed. He'd had a long day and he was tired. Andrew was ready to sit down also.

"Mr. Isaacson, let Rapha show you where you will be sleeping. You can change and store your things in there."

The remainder of the day and evening was devoted to the routine things and then a few presentations by the kids for their new guest/worker. The other adults sat around the table with Bhaniel and Andrew after supper listening to his stories of escaping America and the excitement on the cargo ship. Andrew finally had to put an end to it because of exhaustion. The bunk was calling to him in an influential way. He wasn't worried about fitting everything into the first day since he was going to be a fixture around here for a while. How long was anybody's guess.

# Chapter 52

Police Headquarters

The police department was busier than usual. It was hard to tell if there was a full moon (crazier) since it was the middle of the day, but it had been raining. Rain typically had a calming effect on people. They just wanted to get indoors and be out of the rain. But not today. Everything odd was happening today… more car wrecks (understandable), more domestic calls (unusual) and more fires (weird).

Detectives Oliver and Tunney walked down to the lab and looked for Sid Fellows. Sharp guy and easy going. Just their type.

"Hey, Sid. Find anything?"

"What's going on Clarence? Hi, Bryce. I'm just now putting the SIM card in the computer. I'd do more research on the phone itself, but you guys obliterated it."

"Sorry, our friend was doing backflips and it got a little out of hand."

They walked to a room with computers and video screens along two walls. Sid placed the SIM card into a reader and the data popped up on the monitor in front of them.

"There's not much on here." The phone was a generic 'pay-as-you-go' type. Single use and then throw it away. "Very hard to trace, but since we have the phone, we can look at the history. Looks like just this one number. 229-489-2034."

"Dial it and see what happens."

"We can do one better. We'll enter the number into the database."

The information coming up was not much more insightful.

"The number is another generic phone, which is not a surprise. But, here is the good news. We can pinpoint where the receiving phone was when this call was made." Sid pointed at the last call made right before the wreck.

"The receiving phone was within this twenty foot area on Newport Street, Atlanta."

"What was the exact time?"

"4:38pm."

"We should be able to run through the security cameras in the area to see if we can get a visual."

"Way ahead of you. Charlie on the third floor can get you every camera operating in that area up on multiple screens in seconds. I'll call him."

Charlie was in the dark. He lived his professional life documenting the world outside from his perch inside the video room. Charlie was young and had skills. He chose the police job over two offers from local television stations. He had wanted to work in the music industry on video production, but felt like being able to pay for groceries was an honorable pursuit while he built up some street cred.

"Hey Charlie. Thanks for putting us at the front of the line."

"No worries. It's a five minute job. I'll just gather all we can get and you guys can take it with you."

"Cool. Is it all video?"

"Yeah. The archive rate is typically seven days. Not a problem for you. So, here are the video shots for yesterday at 4:35 and beyond. I'll record while we look at them so your copy will be ready when you leave."

The initial issue in viewing the video was everyone walking the street had their phones to their ears.

"Let's disregard the people using smart phones. The data shows the receiving phone was a generic phone. Could the call have gone to someone riding in a car in the area?"

"Yes, but from what I understand about the signal strength of the call, it was probably outside rather than in a moving car."

"The signal strength? How did you find that out?"

"It's in the phone's call data."

Bryce Tunney looked at the 42 inch screen. "Hey, there's a nicely dressed lady talking on a flip phone. What are the odds?"

As they are watching her walk, she finishes the call and throws the phone into the trash in the public receptacle near the road.

The detectives looked at each other. "We need to get down there and dumpster dive."

"Charlie, you've been a big help. We'll come back later to get the disks."

The detectives hurried out the door walking and running toward the exit.

"What are the collection schedules for those trash cans?"

"I'm checking right now."

After a few clicks on his phone, and a call to the dispatcher... "Today is the collection day, but the truck isn't there yet."

They sped toward the intersection, but noticed the city trash vehicle was two blocks ahead as they drew near.

"Oh, boy. We need to hurry. Turn the lights on. I don't want to take any chances."

The flashing red and blue lights went on and they closed the gap. As they pulled up behind the truck, they reached the street where the trash can was just a half block to the right. The trash truck, however, went straight. They made the turn and noticed another trash truck was pulling away from the target can location.

"No! Quick, let's check and see if the trash was taken."

It was, so they gave chase to the truck and had them pull over.

"Atlanta Police. We have to take over the contents of your truck."

"What?" The thirtyish, bearded, pony tailed driver was not impressed with police authority. He treated it as more of an annoyance. Very possibly he had enjoyed a few run ins with the law. "How do we do that?"

"You'll just have to follow us to the impound lot and dump your load."

"What are you looking for? We just started collecting. You might be able to find it by just raking through it right here."

"Tell you what, if you're willing to get in there and look for a cell phone, we won't make you follow us to the police lot."

The driver and the collection workers looked at each other and nodded in agreement.

"There's a lot down the street we can pull into. Follow us."

Bryce climbed up the side of the truck to see how the collectors were doing. There wasn't much trash in the box. Maybe it would be easy. The big one in coveralls was raking and the driver was going through another pile by hand.

"Here it is!"

The driver held up a flip phone dripping from a recent bath of diet soda. Perfect.

"Is it the only phone?"

The driver gave him an annoyed look. "Are you kidding?"

The workers climbed out and handed over the evidence.

"Thanks fellas. You have done your city a service."

"Yeah, whatever. Are we done?" The driver was ready to move on and the large collector glared at the detectives because he wasn't happy about the fluids on his uniform pants so early in the route.

"We are. Have a good day."

Clarence checked the phone and the soda had done its work.

"Think we'll get a finger print?"

"I don't know. We'll have to check the video, but I think she was wearing gloves."

"Let's get back to Charlie and see where our mystery lady went."

"Did you find it?" Charlie was right where they left him.

"Yeah, but it was soaked. The SIM card is probably the only thing recoverable."

The detectives were coming by for the DVD's as they headed for Sid's office.

"I followed the mystery lady down the street for eight blocks. She had an umbrella so it was hard to see much. Eventually, she got into another cab and rode away."

"Anything remarkable or unusual about our suspect as she walked down the street?"

"Nothing obvious. You guys will have all of it on DVD so you can analyze it some more."

"Thanks Charlie, you do good work."

"Anytime. Not much help I suppose."

"Don't know. There might be something we haven't seen yet. See you later."


"Clarence, you think she looks like Stella Manchester?"

"Same height and build, but she was pretty average."

The detectives went back to Sid and showed him what they had. Everyone had gloves on as they handled the phone in case there was a fingerprint they could lift later.

He popped the SIM card in his reader, and scanned the data. Two numbers showed. 706 396-4005 and 817 204-9011.

"Another generic phone. Big surprise. We can check where the other phone was when she talked to them though..."

"Wait. What was the number again?" Bryce had an inquisitive look on his face. He pulled out his note pad and rifled through the pages. He was right. Clarence picked up on it also.

"That's the number of the phone we found on the stiff at Isaacson's house."

"Neat and tidy. Wonder if we followed Miss Manchester if we would catch her buying a year's supply of prepaid flip phones?"

"Worth a try partner. Everything is pointing to her right now."

# Chapter 53

The Orphanage

Andrew thought he was going to get plenty of rest at the home. This was not to be the case. Activities dominated the daylight hours, both fun and work. The days started with school work and ended with fun after the chores were completed. Andrew even found himself playing daily games of soccer with the older kids and teaching games from his childhood to the younger ones. He was either going to be in shape eventually or have a heart attack.

There was no volume control on the noise in the home which abruptly ended Andrew's tenacious attempts at slumber. It continued throughout the day until the setting sun brought everyone together for devotion time right before bed. The routine was both boring and fascinating for Andrew. He was a stranger to structure, but marveled at the consistency and efficiency. The kids looked forward to each phase and relished the chance to be an active part whether it was in school classes, a game outside, or devotions. Bhaniel finished each day with an insightful lesson from the Bible, yet easy to understand for any age. She would often allow one of the children to prepare a lesson to share and co-teach if they were a little too nervous to fly solo. Andrew found himself wanting to hear more. These were Bible stories he was mostly unfamiliar with except somewhere in the far reaches of his childhood memory. An aunt had taken him to church a few times when he visited her, and he even went to Summer Bible Camp once at her church. Otherwise, his experience with religious things was limited.

During his younger years, Andrew's parents did not exhibit much of an interest in religion or church as far as he could remember. When they divorced, Andrew was a teenager adrift. His sister left for college soon after, and Andrew didn't see her again until she graduated. Dad went to Florida, and Mom busied herself with finding someone to salve her loneliness. Andrew tried to fill his void with anyone but family. He successfully cultivated a friend group interested in partying and getting in trouble, which was satisfying at the time. All he cared about was avoiding the pain of his fractured home. As a result, spiritual things were not a focus. Aunt Rebecca would contact Andrew to invite him to spend time with her, but after several rejections the connection waned. Andrew lived for the moment and cared about one thing. Andrew. He stayed true to the mission statement throughout his adult life. Even during a stormy marriage. Unfortunately, he and his wife had one thing in common. They both loved Andrew.

But now, he was in a foreign land both physically and emotionally. Nothing he had relied upon was real and he was grasping for something to believe in. His life had been an illusion and a fraud. He was terrified at the notion, but also weirdly excited at the possibility he was seeing things clearly for the first time. His time in the African wilderness was cleansing his soul, removing the toxins of a life out of control.

Bhaniel Tretechi was becoming his muse and his spiritual guide. Only she was unaware of both. This was potentially dangerous since one of Andrew's biggest problems was allowing another person, a woman actually, to dictate his every move. Would this be the second verse of the same song? He thought no. Bhaniel had nothing to gain if Andrew did or did not adhere to her influence.

Andrew was sitting on the veranda studying the colors of the sunset. The sun had gone down below the horizon only a few minutes prior. It wasn't cool by any stretch, but it was pleasant enough. The river valley below had a certain natural beauty. The city of Bandundu was encroaching on the river's attempt to swallow up 'civilization', but the pristine wilderness spreading out on three sides had endured very little in the way of human progress.

Bhaniel saw Andrew go out to the veranda earlier, but putting the last kids down for the night was the priority before relaxation. The other workers had gathered in the dining area for a game of "Speed Monster" Bhaniel had brought back from the United States. She took the opportunity to search out their new guest.

"I see you have found my best hiding place."

"Out here on the porch?"

"Yes. It's a peaceful place to sit and rest."

"I hope I'm not sitting in your favorite chair."

"No not at all."

Andrew motioned for her to sit next to him on the other wooden chair. They sat in silence for a time just listening to the sounds of the evening: kids not quite ready for sleep, insects tuning for the night's symphony, and somebody had just won a round of the new game.

"You are doing good work here Miss Tretechi."

Bhaniel looked at Andrew and then studied the valley for a long moment.

"You are very kind to say so. I am just a small part of a big organization though."

"Maybe."

Andrew took his time between sentences. Nothing vied for their time as the evening turned to night.

"Except my narrow view says this wouldn't be here if it weren't for you."

"You mean the home?"

"Everything."

"I don't understand."

"The whole organization."

"The African air has made you silly, Mr. Isaacson."

"Actually, I believe I am thinking clearly for the first time."

"I'm just an employee."

"You are so much more than a hired hand. It's why they send you to America. You are the person who gives realism to this endeavor. Why else would I travel to the other side of the world? Because of you."

Andrew stopped and considered his words, and might have turned a little red. Such was the beauty of sitting in the dark. No one would know.

"I'm sorry. I don't mean to make you uncomfortable, but I have met very few people like you in my life. The others knew the power they possessed and used it like currency. You seem to run from it."

"Now it appears, Mr. Isaacson, you are the one being very direct. Your artistic eye makes you very observant and I was right in saying so. But I do not aspire to be powerful. Whatever power you are talking about is from God only to do the task at hand."

"Forgive me, but I have to disagree. It's not contained to a certain task. It affects everyone you meet no matter what the setting."

"The price of that 'power' has been very high, Mr. Isaacson. I'm not special. I did not pursue the circumstances of my life or even desire to pay the price."

It was evident Andrew had unintentionally pulled back the curtain on an area Bhaniel did not discuss openly.

"It must be a price you have paid in full, and now you have an authority purchased by your suffering. The spirit you have is so infectious. I can't take my eyes off of you when you deal with your coworkers or care for the kids."

Tears fell down Bhaniel's cheeks. "Your words are very refreshing and kind, Mr. Isaacson. Even so, it's still too painful to talk about my past."

"I'm so sorry. I have no desire to dredge up unpleasant memories. God knows I would like to forget my past as much as anyone. I'm beginning to look at my time here as a rebirth of sorts. The old Andrew Isaacson is gone for good."

"It is exciting to hear. To go back to America a new man will be a wonderful thing. New in mind, body and spirit."

"Who said I'm ever going back?"

Bhaniel laughed. "Mr. Isaacson you are a citizen of Bandundu, DRC for as long as you desire."

"It's Andrew, and thank you."

# Chapter 54

The Fifth Street Offices, Atlanta

"Double price?"

"Yeah. It's getting a little risky. You've been burning through our contacts and we don't like how it's been going."

Stella was like a junky. She was desperate and common sense was nowhere to be found. Why else would she have gone alone to their turf to negotiate? The Outfit representatives smelled blood in the water.

"Okay. Whatever the cost is, I'll pay."

"It's going to be double the price and something else. We want a stake in your company."

Stella shivered unconsciously and her eye twitched.

"Y-you want part of the company? How?"

"You got stock? Cut us a stock certificate. We're gonna want dividends too."

Stella was trapped. As savvy as she was, her arrogance and hatred of Andrew distracted her from the warning flags. If she followed through with it, Stella would be their slave until she found a way to get the upper hand. She fought the urge to throw up.

"I can't do it. Maybe another time." Stella turned to leave.

The spokesman behind the desk motioned for his associate to detain her.

"I don't think I made myself clear. We are partners now. Tell me about the business."

"Are you threatening me?"

"Not at all. You've got a good thing going and it can be mutually beneficial for all of us."

Stella weighed her options, then took a seat in front of the desk.

"Good. Now tell me all about the business."

Stella's terror was giving way to hyper awareness. She had surely feared for her life in a brief moment, but the synapses were operating at a new level and her adrenaline was under control. Now it was getting fun. Unless one of them arbitrarily pulled a gun and shot her without warning, she was going to own these losers.

"You see, we have a curious dilemma. I can't give you a stake in the company."

"Why not?" All of the men in the room readjusted themselves.

"Because Andrew Isaacson is not dead. Until he is, there is no way ownership can be changed. Your highly paid killers have not been very successful. To be honest, you should be giving me this third moron's services for free. How many times do I have to pay you people to get the job done?"

Maybe she was a little too aggressive. Stella backed down a little. The man behind the desk wasn't sure, but it seemed like Stella just disrespected him.

"I don't really care how hard it is, you are going to give me a cut of your business whether you want to or not."

"I'm going to pay you for another 'worker'. If he's successful, then we can talk about sharing the business. Until then, neither one of us can do anything about it. Do we have a deal?" Stella got up to leave.

"You will get a text message if we decide to provide another worker. If so, he'll be in touch."

Stella turned and strode out of the office. The lieutenants stepped out of the way so as not to be run over. She half expected the doors to fly open as she walked toward them. Three taxis appeared out of nowhere and vied for her business.

# Chapter 55

Grady Memorial Hospital, Atlanta

Mitch was sort of happy he was alive, but being alive was painful.
Recovery seemed an unreachable dream. He still couldn't move his
fingers. The burns on his back and buttocks made lying down almost
impossible. He'd make Andrew pay handsomely if they both survived.
Detectives Clarence Oliver and Bryce Tunney had come to see him. It had
been a week since the incident and Mitch was mostly coherent. The
morphine worked very well, but it had a tendency to knock him out.
"Mr. DeGuerre, we are detectives Oliver and Tunney. Can we ask you a
few questions?"
"You. ones. found. me?"
Mitch could barely make words. His jaw was immobilized and his lips and
tongue were swollen.
"Yes. How are you doing?"
"Alive. Thank."
"Glad to see it. We won't stay long. What can you tell us about the guy
who did this to you?"
"Came. to. gallery. Woke up… warehouse."
"What did he find out? Did he know where Andrew went?"
"Knew. already."
"What do you mean?"
"Documents. Gallery."
"Where'd he go?"
"Who?" Mitch wondered if they meant the bad guy.
"Andrew. The guy that did this to you is dead already. Hugged a moving
vehicle."
"He talk?"
"Sadly, no. Where is Andrew?"

Mitch just shook his head.

"So, you want everyone BUT the police to know where he is."

He made a relevant point.

"Hiding."

"We think the bad guy phoned what he knew to his contact before he died. There might be some unsavory people planning an unscheduled visit to your buddy wherever he is."

Not a great development. Mitch could only blame himself for not hiding the documents at his office.

Mitch nodded his head. "Okay. Can't. get. to. him."

"Why is that?"

"Africa. DRC."

Clarence and Bryce looked at each other.

"What is he doing there? What is DRC?"

"Hiding. IORRF." He was going to have to let them figure out the rest.

"Did you write all that down?" Clarence said to Bryce. "We'd better go. We have some homework to do. Thanks for your time, Mr. DeGuerre." The detectives turned to leave.

"Keep. him. safe?"

"We'll do what we can."

Mitch was not comforted as he tapped the button on the morphine drip then drifted into sleep.


"What do you think?"

"Well, we know where he is. I guess as long as he stays there, he's better off."

Detectives Oliver and Tunney had been working the internet to learn what they could about DRC and IORRF. There was limited information on IORRF, but the DRC had a colorful past and present.

"You think he's safe there?"

"Is anybody safe over there? Everything I have been reading says a civil war is almost a perpetual event. As far as his local enemies are concerned, I don't know."

"We need to talk to someone at the IORRF and let them in on what might be happening."

"Probably so. It's a safe bet the bad guys know as much as we do."

"Do you think they will send someone to Africa to end Isaacson?"

"Not sure. You'd have to have a real stinger for this guy to chase him all the way over there. There's no promise he would be there when they get to the orphanage either. Maybe they'll decide he's as good as dead while he's out of country."

"Could get crazy again if he decides to come back."

"Let's have the IORRF folks tell him to stay."

# Chapter 56

Bandundu

Andrew was glad to be of service. He had attempted odd jobs around the home to varied success. The leak in the roof might never be solved. He was planning on teaching the kids basic art skills which was in his wheelhouse. When the kids learned of it, they were enthusiastic. Now the daily question was, 'When are we going to start art classes?' Today, his task was to walk/ferry back to town and get supplies and a package from the organization if it came in. He was going it alone today, just he and a rickshaw type cart. Aleefa had lobbied for permission to accompany him, but Bhaniel had vetoed the proposal. Aleefa had too much to accomplish this day and was on pseudo probation due to some excessive scrapping during a soccer match.

He enjoyed the scenery on the walk, but kept a sharp eye out for crawling, slithering or prowling things. He didn't have a weapon so he selected a walking stick to improve his odds if he had a visitor. The walk to the river seemed a little longer than his first trek to the home. It could have been because he was engrossed in Bhaniel. Now it was just he and nature.

The borrowed head covering which made him look very local. Danaa, one of the younger workers at the home, showed him how to wrap the material so that it covered his head without falling apart. It was evident any uncovered skin for one as fair as he would be scorched unmercifully.

The city across the river spread out before him. There wasn't an organized approach to city growth. Buildings and residential areas just formed as the need arose. People weren't particular about the aesthetic effect of their construction choices either. Shelter was the primary motivator. Wealthier citizens accessed accepted building materials and practitioners, but the more humble folk used whatever they could find. Sewage was also an adventure. The infrastructure necessary to accommodate population of this magnitude was not and never would be established. But, most people didn't seem to care. They carried on with their lives and tolerated the inconveniences as though they knew no better.

Andrew unloaded the cart from the ferry and tipped the driver. When he got to town, the streets were nearly deserted. Andrew headed toward the general store to see if he could buy some more water. He walked in, but didn't see anyone.

"Hello?"

Nobody was at the counter. Andrew walked back outside. There was no activity in the street. He went over to the building supposedly holding the shipped goods. No one in sight.

"Anybody here?"

"Hey." Someone whispered to him from the back room. "Come here." Andrew spied a middle aged man.

"Where is everyone?"

"We hide. Soldiers, they come. You stay here."

Andrew obediently crouched down with the man.

"What will the soldiers do when they get here?"

"Not know. Soldiers come many days. Ride through." The man motioned with his hands how the convoys moved through town.

Andrew noticed a young boy and his mother further back in the structure. Evidently, there were others joining them in the building, but all were afraid to move or make noise. After about fifteen minutes, the first of the convoys rode through. Andrew counted twelve convoys and expected more, but suddenly the people hiding with him and others emerged. Somehow, they knew it was safe to move about.

"Gone?"

"No more today."

Maybe they had a lookout up the road somewhere. Andrew ventured out to do some reconnaissance. As he came to the main road, he overheard people talking. Most were in the local language, but a few used English.

"Where are the soldiers going?"

"Don't know. Never come to this part of the country. Something about to happen."

Andrew decided the best thing he could do was get his cargo and return to the home to relay the news. A middle aged man was in front of the shipping facility and appeared to be an official of some sort. After a few moments of struggling communications, he was able to gather his inventory, load it on the cart and point it toward home. The home came into view as the sun was getting low on the western horizon. Bhaniel met him at the gate.

"Welcome back. Are you okay?"

"I'm fine. I think I got everything I went for. Forgive me for taking so long."

"What happened?"

"Soldiers."

"In Bandundu?" Bhaniel was incredulous.

"Driving through. According to the town's people, convoys have been going through for days, maybe weeks. They have lookouts to tell them when to hide. I showed up as everyone was hiding. A few minutes later and I would have walked into town as the soldiers drove through."

"They've never been this close before."

"What about the Lieutenant you told me about?"

"He's a ranger. A criminal on the run, really. He does not operate with the regular army."

"Why do you think they are moving this far west?"

"I don't know, but it can't be good. We need to make preparations just in case they come this way. We'll have to have regular lookouts so we won't be surprised."

"Weapons?"

"We don't have weapons. Even if we did, it would never be enough. All we can do is run or hide. The boys and now you are in the most danger. Anyone they consider a threat, they will kill. The boys might be kidnapped and forced to be soldiers."

So much for running from danger.

# Chapter 57

Kinshasa

Through his field glasses, Sindlar scanned the target area as he stood inside the vacant second-story apartment. He couldn't see any of the snipers at their prescribed positions. It was favorable for security reasons, but he wished he had a better vantage point. Radio communications with the riflemen was too risky. Without encryption technology, the more sophisticated equipment used by the military drones would intercept their messages and the game would be over before it began. Bashar was seated at his storefront, and each sniper would watch for the sign from him until the moment the objective emerged from the residence. It had been agreed unless Sindlar relayed the "fall back" sign, the shooters were to follow through with the primary plan. Bashar had been the proprietor of his small shop since the late 1980's. His willingness to play a part in the coup was the final piece of the puzzle. Since they did not know when the dictator would show at the defense minister's residence, the rebels simply had to wait and be ready. The Commander, as the dictator was called, had made a fatal mistake. He had shown a pattern to his meetings with the defense minister. Although it was not constant, he became almost predictable. Today, he was expected and the Commander had arrived. Everyone was in their place.

Placing the snipers within three hundred meters of the residence had been tedious. The most desirable position would have been on the rooftops surrounding the city square which was directly in front of the residence, but had never been an option. The dictator's helicopters regularly flew over the city looking for anything out of the ordinary. The faction had been able to rent a third-story corner flat in the apartment building down the street, and they were in their sixth month of the lease. Chadran had been in position at the southwest window for three hours and twelve minutes with a direct line of sight to the designated exit. The .50 caliber sniper's rifle was situated six feet from the window so it wouldn't be noticeable from the street. The whole weapons package had been put in place a little at a time weeks ago to reduce the chance of drawing attention to the locale on this fateful day. Details.

Chadran required extra practice shooting his treasured weapon at such an awkward angle. Typically he was most accurate in a prone position, but the third floor vantage forced him to stand on a chair to obtain a proper view through the Schmidt & Bender scope. With the technical problems worked out, the twenty-seven year old freedom fighter was entirely confident he would find his target. Maybe twice if he worked the bolt smoothly. One tiny possibility nagged at him, however. The post-assassination necessity to rapidly vacate the flat would endanger his ability to recover his beloved weapon were the search for the killers thorough. If the faction had been better funded, he would have used a different weapon. One he could flee with and hide easier. But the need for accuracy was at its highest and there was no better rifle for this than the one he had before him. He would find a way.

The building next door to the residence would have been the best location for a secondary shooter, but it was uninhabitable largely due to battles long since passed which forced them to utilize a mobile site. The second gunman was now lying in the cargo area of a parked car positioned at the end of Glorious Revolution Street. The 1971 Volkswagen Type 147 Fridolin sat on the opposite side of the three-way intersection at a ninety-degree angle to the residence entrance seventy-five meters away. Even for Nakuru, lying in the cargo area of a compact vehicle from the pre-dawn hours until the afternoon had tested his patience at least twice. However, he would never admit it when the brothers joined again to relive their glory in restoring their homeland to the people. For someone who would drink poison and wrestle cobras to recover his homeland from a despot such as he, this inconvenience was insignificant. Nakuru rechecked his ammunition and sights again. The sight of the target through the scope on his rifle was not distorted by the window. This detail had been checked for accuracy at the faction's practice range. Nakuru insisted on shooting from inside the vehicle at the range so that any defect could be noted and adjusted. The safety was off.

The defense minister's residence was in the original section of the city on a nondescript street. There remained a small number of commercial/retail establishments close by and a number of residences, both apartments and homes. The limestone facade and twenty-four hour guard gave the inner city building a foreboding presence. Yet, the fact he lived in the city was an oddity. Most of the high-ranking officials in the current regime lived in lavish government housing north of the city. The People's Resistance Front was using this to their advantage.

The defense minister was an anomaly. Maybe it was his age. Well over seventy now, Oribe was rumored to be the only person who could question the Commander and live. But, the dictator valued the old man's advice. It had protected his control of the country many times. Consequently, the Commander met with the minister once a month, maybe more, to discuss state affairs. Historically, Oribe would make the trip to Commander Asafari Zuberi's palace three kilometers outside of the city to meet with the dictator. But, since Oribe's health had deteriorated to the point travel was no longer possible, the dictator made the trip to his residence. The dictator's quest for political wisdom was a stroke of luck for the Resistance. The seemingly random trips into the city left the leader vulnerable, if only for a few moments at a time. The challenge for the Resistance was to be ready in those fleeting moments to carry out their plan.

As was typical of a military regime ruling out of fear, the leader had to protect himself from the very people he controlled. Members of The People's Resistance Front had mapped the dictator's habits on his visits to the defense minister's residence for the past three months. Because of the orientation of the residence, the dictator left the building from the same exit each time. There was a brief window of opportunity for the faction to execute its plan. If done properly, he would never make it to the automobile.

If they missed the opening, the motorcade and his destination, the palace, were much too heavily guarded for a direct assault. Based on the growing prospect of a civil war, and the declining health of the defense minister, the People's Resistance Front had to act now. Sindlar and his staff realized their plan had many risks. Assassination of a head of state potentially exposed the country to attack by any number of nearby countries or rogue factions. And in this part of the world, governmental or tribal fighting could break out at any time. To his credit, Zuberi had built up the country's military. He now had three regiments on rotating combat-ready status. The tanks and heavy artillery were from the black market in Libya.

Failure to assassinate the dictator would be unthinkable. Sindlar and his team had labored over philosophical ramifications if something were to go wrong. Two coups had been attempted during Zuberi's rule, but he had responded to the last one by ruthlessly disposing of known and supposed dissidents in public executions. Although most of the victims were innocent citizens, no further challenges to Zuberi's government had occurred for eleven years. The previous attempts had been dissected and used as models for what not to do this time. The primary error was the plans had originated with trusted assistants to the dictator and too many people ultimately knew of the operations. The security leaks were inevitable and Zuberi learned of the schemes in time to avoid them. This time, if the snipers missed their mark, the assembled freedom fighters would have no choice but to make a full frontal assault. Suicide, but the price of his escape was too great.

The security detail appeared at the entrance to the residence as three vehicles rolled to a stop. The dictator would be emerging soon. The snipers tensed slightly. Two guards put their hands to their ears to better hear the incoming message in their earphones. They spoke to the others and the guards took their places around the car and outside the residence entrance. Three would escort the dictator from the door to the car so Nakuru's view from the sedan would be partially blocked. Although he wanted the kill, Nakuru hoped his shot would not be necessary. The primary shot would come from Chadran in the apartment. His high viewpoint allowed him an unobstructed shot at the target.

Bashar reclined in his chair at the entrance to his shop. Intermittent shoppers allowed him the luxury of remaining invisible as he interacted with them. He gave the appearance of total disinterest to the guards' movement. In reality, he was watching every move to make the final determination whether to go with the mission. Hundreds of lives were at stake. There was no need to act in desperation. Every variable was acceptable. He smiled at the prospect of the mission's success. He was careful to make no sudden moves which would raise questions in the minds of the snipers. They were to carry out the mission unless he got up and left, but in stressful times, well-meaning people reacted curiously. The riflemen gave one last look and confirmed they were to follow through with the plan.

The main doors to the residence opened and the dictator emerged at a leisurely pace. He stopped between the entrance and the car to put his sunglasses on due to the brightness of the sun. The years of peace within his country had made him confident. Unfortunately, his comfort at this pivotal moment also made him an easy target. Chadran thanked his god as he loosed the first round.

# Chapter 58

The Orphanage

"Hold still. I mean 'kamata'."

The sisters couldn't help themselves. They were excited to be the models for Mister Andrew and could not keep from smiling and goosing each other. Andrew was just going to have to adjust on the fly.

Andrew was enjoying the live sessions with different kids and workers. So far, he was only able to make drawings due to the lack of paint. Maybe there were local materials he could refine and use for colors.

The crowd behind Andrew was about three deep. Everyone loved to watch the artist work, which did more for stoking the interest in drawing and art pursuits than all the training Andrew could muster.

The session ended with the emergence of a soccer game. The girls were tired of 'kamata-ing' anyway. Andrew would finish the masterpiece on his own.

"You are doing well with the crude materials." Bhaniel was glad of his flexibility.

"Not at all, it's some of the best charcoal I've used. The real stuff. Where did you get the paper?"

"Wrapping paper from items shipped to us. I hope you like brown."

Andrew looked at Bhaniel. "I like brown very much."

"When are you going to let me draw you?"

"Mr. Isaacson, there are so many kids who cannot wait to model for you."

"And I will draw every one of them if it kills me, but I can still have a session with you can't I? How about after everyone has gone to sleep?"

"I do not want to create a scandal. What did you have in mind?"

"Many, many drawings and paintings. I have some sketches already, from observing you while you worked."

"Really? May I see them?"  Bhaniel was a little uncomfortable and intrigued.

"Sure. Meet me later on the porch."

"I will. Should I wear something special?"

"No. What you are wearing is perfect. The linen looks good on your skin. Do you have a necklace?"

"I may have to make one."

"Excellent. I can't wait."


Andrew truly couldn't wait. After supper, he wandered around and puttered in his room. He went out and tossed a ball around with the boys and showed the girls a magic trick. Finally, he went to the porch and waited.

Bhaniel was scurrying the kids toward their evening destinations, maybe a little faster than normal. She glanced up and saw Andrew making his way to the porch. He was early.

"I hope you haven't been waiting long."

Bhaniel had changed her clothes. She couldn't bear the thought of seeing drawings of herself in the daily rags. This was a gown from her distant past. Simple yet elegant. Her arms and ankles were exposed which may have been too daring.

Andrew was nervous already and then to see her in this new way was breathtaking. The dress highlighted her long neck and strong shoulders. She did not wear a necklace, but no matter. Everything about her simplicity was appealing to Andrew. If only he could capture the strength and vulnerability she exuded. As they began to talk, he watched her move to her favorite chair, the way she put both feet up under her and leaned her head back. As she told him about the day, he began to draw. The evening would be his friend and enemy. Soon the sun would go below the horizon and the fine lines and curves of her body would be impossible to discern. He would have to draw her voice and aura.

"I think I'm out of paper. I feel like I just got started."

"It's just as well, the sun retired once more. May I see your drawings before it gets too dark?"

Andrew moved close to Bhaniel and set a stack of drawings on her lap. Bhaniel spent a considerable time looking at every piece. The ones of her working included some of the children as well. His drawings were brutally honest, yet showing others and her in a vibrant way. It was as if he captured her the way she wished she was. Andrew could see tears on her cheeks. He took her hand and sat silently.

"Mr. Isaacson, your drawings are stunning. So wonderful, and yet you didn't seem to add any prophetic twist to any of them."

"True. I must admit it was so satisfying to just draw what I saw I didn't think of anything else. Do you hope to see a prophetic drawing of yourself?"

"Good question. I may not like what I see. Sometime soon, Mr. Isaacson."

"Fair enough."

"I don't see a drawing in this group I wanted to ask you about. It was of Aleefa. You drew him in a very strong pose. He was guarding other children and fighting an enemy."

"Yes, it's back in my room. I'm surprised you have seen it. I've not shown it to anyone."

Oops. Bhaniel was cornered.

"I'm so sorry. I went by your room the other day looking for you and my curiosity got the best of me. There were a few drawings I noticed and his was one of them."

Andrew smiled in the dark.

"You are always welcome in my room. I have no secrets. That one was an easy drawing to make. He may not realize it yet, but Aleefa is a leader. I don't know who the enemy will be, but when the time comes, he is going to rise up."

It confirmed what Bhaniel had believed for some time.

"Yes, I completely agree. Whenever the time is right, would you show him the drawing and tell him what it means? And to hear it from you will be all the better."

"Of course. It would be my pleasure."

Andrew and Bhaniel sat still for a time and let the light breezes wash over them.

"I cannot think of how to express my joy you are here with us Mr. Isaacson or thank you in a proper fashion."

Andrew kissed her hand. Bhaniel leaned toward him, anxious to be within the arc of his presence.

"I am the one who should be thanking you."

He spoke softly, their faces nearly touching. The children had gone silent, the wildlife was waiting in expectation, and the night air held its breath. Andrew kissed her lightly on the lips. Bhaniel did not pull away as he had feared she would, but lingered there wanting to savor the moment. Slowly she bowed her head and the tears fell onto her cherished gown. Tears of release, even joy.

Andrew gathered her in his arms and held on as she surrendered her emotions to the moment. She had opened her true self to this man and he had loved her for it. Fighting her desire, Bhaniel marshalled the will to slowly pull away. She turned to Andrew at the edge of the porch. "Pleasant dreams, Mr. Isaacson." Andrew did not say a word, but watched her flow into the night.

Andrew was completely carried away. She had such a hold on his heart he was committed to be wherever she was.

It made him hope – no pray – his drawing of her did not come true. Andrew fought to put the image out of his mind. Bhaniel was wise to decline. And he was thankful she had not stumbled upon it the other day in his room. Maybe he did have a secret or two. The drawing contained difficult, troubling images. He was compelled to do it, but afraid of the meaning. Andrew wondered if he had the courage to show it to her.

Not yet. Surely it was for another time. Hopefully, a time far from now.

# Chapter 59

IORRF Headquarters, Atlanta

"Mr. Hizanga, there is a chance his life could be in danger." Clarence Oliver and Bryce Tunney sat across from the IORRF director.

"I am grateful you both have come down here to let me know, but I'm afraid we are all too late for that. Just yesterday, the president of the country was shot and killed by rebel factions who have been attempting to gain control of the government. Not only your man, but our people may be in real danger as well."

"This just keeps getting better and better. What are you going to do?"

"There's nothing we can do right now except pray. I have been trying to communicate with our primary contact in country to no avail. It may be days or weeks, I don't know."

"Weeks? I'm guessing they don't have a sat phone?" Bryce was a bit snarky.

"Good idea, but no. Where they are is remote. Ms. Tretechi has to walk the nearby city, Bandundu, to talk on a phone."

Clarence looked at Bryce. "Well, we may have done all we can do for now. Mr. Hizanga, if you are able to communicate with them, please tell Andrew to stay there but keep an eye out for hired killers. As crazy as it sounds, the middle of a civil war may be his safe place. Thanks for your time."

Clarence and Bryce went to the car.

"I guess we'll have to keep working this thing from the other side. Maybe we can catch the bad guys and stop the next assassination attempt before it happens."

"Where do you think our would-be killer is getting these professional assassins? This is their third one."

"True. Let's work our underworld contacts and see if someone can give us a clue."

# Chapter 60

Stella's Residence, Decatur

"Mmmm. You taste good Diego."
Stella loved developing the talent. Diego pulled away from Stella and started to light a cigarette.
"Go outside please." Stella was enthralled by her new paramour, but smoking left a pesky odor in the furniture.
Diego glared at her and thought about lighting it anyway. He'd play it her way since his last paycheck was five figures. Stella checked her phone as Diego left the room. The other phone. There was the text message. It was a number and a time. Just thirty minutes from now.
Stella walked outside in her silk robe and found Diego leaning against the railing of the veranda. The valley below was still hazy with little breeze.
"Would you like something to eat?"
"Yeah, sure."
"Claire will fix you something to take with you. I have some business to attend, so you'll have to be on your way."
Diego was fine with her brush off. He didn't like hanging around the house too long anyway. All Stella did was boss him around. Sometime down the road, the weaknesses of this arrangement were going to outweigh the benefits. Then he would move on to the next thing and leave this witch behind. Except for Claire. He'd have to work something out with her before he dropped Stella.
"Got it. Claire in the kitchen?"
Stella was already gone. She made the call at the appointed time. The man on the other end asked questions only.
"Name?"
"Andrew Isaacson."
"Last location?"

"At an IORRF orphanage west of Bandundu, DRC, Africa."
He made a mental note of the extra travel cost.
"Any associates with him?"
"No, he's alone."
"Time constraints?"
"ASAP."
"Text me a picture."
The line disconnected.

The crime organization texted Andrew's picture to their asset who was currently in Southern France. He looked at the specs on the contract and calculated his costs. The profit was acceptable so he texted his acceptance. His first act was to call for a flight to Kinshasa.
"Sir they've closed the borders. Entry into the country will be impossible for the time being." The voice on the phone was simultaneously bored and concerned for this would be traveler. "There has been a flare up in the armed conflict over there."
She was simply a drone for the airline conveying the company policy for a country in chaos a million miles away. The newly hired assassin was caught off guard. He would have to improvise.
"What is the nearest country still providing visas?"
"That would be Gabon. It's just a day's drive to the DRC. But you can't get into the country."
"I remember you saying that." He was being kind and she had a flair for the obvious.
"I would like a ticket to Gabon, please. One way."

# Chapter 61

The Orphanage

Andrew awoke to a firefight. Nearly every boy in the household, and some girls, were locked in a life or death battle with weapons of sticks and fingers. The action was right outside his window. Andrew pulled himself out of bed and leaned over the window sill to see the carnage. So many were mortally wounded, but they bounced back rather quickly. Andrew called out to Embii.

"How is the fight going?"

"We're winning. The other side is dying a lot, and some of their soldiers are changing to our team."

"It looks like your weapons are better also."

"It's true! Watch this."

Embii stood and took aim. He sounded off a barrage of bullets toward a cluster of enemy soldiers. Just then, an RPG round screamed overhead and exploded beyond the tree line.

All of the kids and Andrew froze wondering what had just happened. Andrew gathered himself and climbed out of the window.

"Everybody get inside!!"

The kids had kneeled down where they were and were afraid to move. Andrew hollered again and then ran outside.

"Come inside! Everyone move. Now!"

Another round went overhead, and small arms fire was heard a few kilometers away. The lookouts were running back to the main building. Bhaniel had been out in the garden tending the crops. Everyone was moving toward the buildings for shelter. Andrew went toward the source of the shooting. He had to find out what was coming their way, but disliked the idea of a bullet wound.

Most of the kids were inside by this time. Bhaniel had gone to the river side of the property to see if there was an opposing force ready to shoot back. A company of rebel soldiers were making their way north after the first shots were fired. Bhaniel had the sick feeling this battle was going to track right through the home's property and there was nowhere to hide except inside. Bhaniel turned toward the buildings. Three others were just about inside and they were the last ones. Andrew had come back toward the garden and was searching for Bhaniel.

"Hurry! The government soldiers are coming!"

"The rebels are coming from the other direction!"

Andrew grabbed hold of Bhaniel and they ran toward the main building. Another RPG rifled over the main building and impacted at the base of a mahogany tree on the edge of the property. The explosion knocked both Bhaniel and Andrew down. They pulled themselves up and stumbled into the building. Andrew was trying not to swallow the mouthful of dirt he scooped up in the process.

"Are you hurt?" Andrew asked as he spit mud.

"I don't think so. Is everyone inside?"

"We'd better do a head count."

All the workers were accounted for and they had already checked on the kids in their groups.

"Is there anywhere to hide?"

"This building is the strongest. We will have to stay here." Andrew and Bhaniel went through the side rooms to check on kids and adults.

The small arms fire was extremely close. A pickup truck raced by carrying soldiers toward the river. The youngest children were crying and the adults were consoling them. The older kids tried to look out the gaps in the windows to see the action.

"Aleefa! Get down! No one stand in the windows!"

The rebels were returning fire and rounds were ricocheting off the out buildings. The main cluster of government trucks and foot soldiers were moving through the orphanage property and standing their ground near the river. The rebels had entrenched on the east edge of the river which was proving to be a formidable divide. It was uncertain whether this fragile stalemate was beneficial to the orphanage.

The door flew open and soldiers stepped into the main room. Three of them leveled their weapons and scanned the room for unfriendlies. The rush of combat made them wild eyed and they had no patience for anything hindering the forces' advance. The soldier in front spoke up with his weapon cocked and ready. The other two watched his back.

"Who are you people? Show us your hands."

Bhaniel eyed Andrew and motioned for him to be silent. She stepped out into the great room to face the soldiers.

"We are unarmed. We are an orphanage of children and adult workers."

She stepped out so that the soldiers could see her. The lead soldier coiled and hit her in the forehead with the butt of his gun. Bhaniel's head snapped back and she fell helplessly unconscious. Andrew tensed ready to jump, but the other workers willed him to stay put by shaking their heads at him and silently begging him to wait. The ladies rushed to Bhaniel. The fighter waited and then turned to his comrades.

"There is no one here." Then he turned to the workers tending to Bhaniel. "Stay inside the building. If anyone comes out of the building, you will be shot."

He barked at two others and commanded them to stay behind to ensure full compliance.

"Head out!"

The group of soldiers loaded up and sped away to join the effort at the river. Once the soldiers had gone, the older kids barricaded the door as best they could and everyone else ran to Bhaniel.

"Get some water from the barrel!"

"She's coming around."

Andrew was standing at the fringe of the group feeling helpless. Everything in him wanted to rush the soldiers and beat all of them senseless.

Bhaniel started to stir. There was no blood to speak of. The stock of the gun was not sharp enough to break the skin, but she was going to have an enormous bruise. The swelling had already started.

The water came and they kept her head cool and clean. Ice was a luxury only occasionally available from the city, but an impossibility as long as they were sequestered here in the main building.

The sounds of war continued through the afternoon and into the evening. It seemed to grow more distant as the sun went down. Maybe the government soldiers and rebels were moving up river where the prospects for crossing were better. Andrew kept an eye on the soldiers guarding them. The sweaty fighters were diligent for a time, but even they noticed the space between them and the rest of their platoon had widened. Finally, their radio crackled and barked an order, and they bugged out. Everyone inside the building held their breath for a time to try to hear anything outside indicating the soldiers were still nearby.

"I think they're gone."

Even so, no one wanted to go out. At least not until morning. Maybe it will all go away they thought, and they could get back to regular life.

The rest of the evening was spent sneaking over to the dormitory buildings to get bed rolls and making everyone as comfortable as possible. Lookouts were posted and the group navigated the night with fitful sleep and anxious thoughts. All of the adults had kids for sleeping companions on this night. Bhaniel was doing some final checks before she made her way to the cadre of kids awaiting her presence. Andrew, on his way to the boys grouped together, ran into her in the darkened great room.

"Maybe you should sleep alone so you can rest. Your forehead is going to hurt."

"I think I can do more staying with the kids, and yes tomorrow it is really going to be painful. Thank you."

"For what?"

"I know it was very difficult for you to stay hidden. If you had attacked them, they would have killed you and then searched the entire property for other 'soldiers'. Most of the young boys could have been taken or killed also."

Andrew had been thinking only of his own survival at the time. He didn't realize he had inadvertently saved several other lives as well.

"I'm in a game with rules I know nothing about."

"There are no rules."

"I thought those were government troops. They observe some rules don't they?"

"Possibly, but they are fighting to retain control of the country and have been losing the battle. They will do anything to keep control. The boys would have been taken mostly so the rebels couldn't get them. We should be thankful it wasn't the rebels who came to the orphanage. They would have killed many and done things to the women. The boys would have been taken for sure."

"How can you survive in a country with this kind of constant danger?"

"It hasn't been an immediate threat like today. The rebels and their makeshift armies have typically fought in the eastern side of the country. The eastern border lands are rich in valuable minerals. With a weak government, the profiteering has been rampant."

"I thought Zuberi ruled with an iron fist."

"He became more cruel as his power slipped away. I don't think there is any way to control the mercenaries. They have had the upper hand for some time now. Rebel armies have roamed the country looking for boys and men to be miners and soldiers to protect their stolen lands. Since they are this far west, I'm not sure what is going to happen next."

"Can you leave here if necessary?"

"There is nowhere for us to go. The only option is to flee to a refugee camp. For those who survive the trip, almost certainly, they would separate us. We might never see the children again."

"What if we could get all of you to America?"

Bhaniel's shoulders sagged. The weight of the day's events had taken their toll.

"Mr. Isaacson, I cannot think anymore tonight."

Bhaniel was beginning to sway. Andrew moved toward her and wrapped his arms around her. He had become her angel from above, the protector she had longed for. Andrew felt her body relax in his and then the shuddering sobs. Each time it got easier for her.

"Thank you." Bhaniel whispered. "You came to us at the perfect time. I feel as though I could not have done this without you."

She kissed him on the cheek and made her way to the waiting children. Andrew knew he had to get to his boys, he and the oldest five were standing guard tonight. He leaned against the counter and thought about what he said. How would we ever get all of these kids to America safely? What other options did they have? Staying here would be suicide. Well, if there was ever a time for a miracle, this was it. Andrew decided to ask the only miracle worker he knew.

"God, if you are willing to hear my prayer, Bhaniel and these kids need you now like never before. Please help us. We have nowhere else to turn."

We? He thought to himself. This odd collection of misfit children and adults had become his family. Andrew went in search of his boys. They needed him tonight.

# Chapter 62

Libreville Leon M'ba International Airport, Libreville, Gabon

The hired killer waited in line. The flight to Gabon was long, but uneventful, and the flight was half full. Not too many thrill seekers going to Western Africa this week. Getting through customs was usually easy. He was wearing a ratty wig and had a ten day growth of beard. The hat and glasses made him all the more forgettable.

"Passport. What is the reason for your stay?"

"I am working with the non-profit group Nature Conservancy. We are developing freshwater fisheries in the Ogooue River Basin near Franceville."

The customs worker just stared at him blankly then checked for the appropriate visa. He fed the personal information into the computer and waited on any law enforcement warnings. Nothing.

"Enjoy your stay. Next."

Well, the first phase was simple enough, on to the Owendo Station and the Trans-Gabon Railway. Although riding a train the entire width of the country promised to be tedious, it would be relatively convenient, and the railhead at Franceville was not far from the DRC border with a narrow band of the country of Congo in between.

One excessively long taxi ride later, and the hired killer was at the train station. The departure listings were not favorable. It appeared he was going to have to wait until the day after tomorrow to begin the journey. Still, it was the best option. He could practically fall off the grid riding this train. Anonymity always trumped speed. Besides, real members of the Nature Conservancy would ride the train. He found a small hotel close by and settled in for the wait.

# Chapter 63

Atlanta

"We have to get this show together as soon as possible." Stella was facing the window as she talked.

"What do you want to include?"

"The stuff he was working on at the time of his 'death'. It's more intriguing at first to sell his most recent pieces and work backward from there."

"You plan to do more than one?"

"It will be the first of many. Remember how the music industry trickled Tupac's rap out to the masses for several years? We'll do the same with Andrew's work. I'd like to have an art expert find some of his work in an out of the way place and declare it authentic, but we may have to wait a few years for that."

"I thought Andrew wasn't dead." Eugene was confused.

"It is 'disputed'. We need to have an auction before the word gets out. People will want to acquire his work because of his death. Then if it hits the news he might be alive, they will root for him to actually be dead, which will cause the value of their investment will go up, up, up. We just have to play our cards right to maximize the profits."

Stella was attempting to immerse herself in the Andrew retrospective to take her mind off of Africa. The probability for success was low. None the matter, she was going to make a pile of money anyway. The kicker was hiding the profits so her new 'partners' couldn't find it. Stella's reliance on the mob for any intel from across the ocean grated on her. Surely this assassin was the charm.

Eugene poured himself a drink.

"Want one?"

"No, I have a lunch date with a new buyer and don't want to smell like I've been drinking."

"Oh yes. I remember making the date for you. He's old money. Should be a positive connection."

"I'm counting on it. I need you to do something for me while I'm gone."

Eugene turned to receive his marching orders. Stella handed Eugene a medium sized manila envelope generously taped.

"What is it?"

"You need to be careful with it."

"Where is it going?"

Stella handed Eugene an address and a name. They meant nothing to him. He'd only been on that side of town twice and neither time was pleasant.

"When does it need to be there?"

"Today. Preferably now. Can you go now?"

"Yes. Are they expecting me?"

"Yes. Sort of. Also, park a few blocks away and walk. Don't ask."

This was getting weirder. Eugene wanted to know what was in the package even more now.

"Go."

It took Eugene longer than expected to get across town. Why do people even live over here? Don't they have any ambition? There's the address. Eugene planned to find it and circle back on foot. The whole block was run down and the address was a nameless stoop with a number painted on the door. There were three men standing on the sidewalk near the door. One was talking on his cell phone and the other two were tossing pebbles toward the street. As Eugene walked up, they came alert and transformed into a steel wall.

"Uh, hello. I am looking for Levente."

"Who?" The very large man queried.

"Levente Karmazin."

All three struck a pose and looked down at Eugene.

"Would you tell him that I am here for Stella Manchester?"

Two of the oak trees glanced at each other, one ventured inside with the news. After an awkward five minutes or so, the door swung open and the door men motioned him in.

Eugene had not brandished the envelope yet. He didn't want to reveal his ace to the grunts on the front line. Additional operatives led him down a hallway to an office where a portly man with bad skin was sitting behind a desk.

"What can I do for you?"

"I am here for Stella Manchester who asked me to bring you this."

Eugene pulled the envelope out of his jacket. Two of the men in the room reached for something in their jackets also.

"Why didn't anyone check this guy? He walked in here with a package in his coat and no one checked him?"

Oops. Eugene thought to himself. This scene had a mafia feel to it. He was ready to leave. An assistant grabbed the envelope and felt it for dangerous substances before handing it to the man.

"What is it, mail man?"

"I don't know. She acted like you were expecting it."

The man slit the envelope and looked inside. It was a stack of legal papers. He looked up at Eugene.

"Did she say anything else?"

Eugene shrugged. "No."

He motioned to the operatives in the room and they shepherded Eugene out of the office and back to the street. The door shut behind him. Eugene hustled back to the car, looking behind him occasionally to make sure he wasn't being followed. Why is Stella doing business with the likes of these mob rats? Just one more thing to add to the list. Eugene decided he had better find out the truth before it came back to haunt him. Now he was a known entity to some unsavory folk.

"Who is he?"

"Don't know yet."

Clarence Oliver and Bryce Tunney had been staking out the Fifth Street Gang offices for a couple of days. They weren't supposed to know where it was except for a grateful informant who turned over helpful information for a chance to walk free again in this lifetime. Of course, he was going to wear an orange jumpsuit for nine more years first. They were perched upstairs across the street in an abandoned building once used as a retail establishment with living quarters above. Now, it was old, dusty, and home to varmints and vagrants. Clarence tried not to touch anything for fear of acquiring an infection that wouldn't go away. This was no place for a germaphobe. He had requested hazard pay and was turned down.

Neither one of them were sure this was the right gang to target, except they were well known for supplying hitmen. Gangs were like retail stores. Some specialized in prostitution, others in illegal gambling activities. The Fifth Street Gang was known for drugs and murder for hire. It was the smart bet, so to speak, to start with the industry leader.

"Did you get a good picture of his face?"

This was going to benefit the police database for sure. Bryce was surprised at the number of people coming and going from this little nondescript door in a nondescript part of town. Most of them went in and came out almost immediately. They were the ones making payments for who knows what. To arrest all of them would have been pointless. They were the sheep being fleeced. These people were useful to lead the police to the real criminals. But this guy was different. He didn't look like the typical junkie or loan recipient. He looked out of place, like a country girl in the big city for the first time.

"Yeah." Clarence thought for a minute and flipped through his mental file. "Hey, I've seen him before. He works at the art business, A.D. Isaacson."

"Bingo! We must be livin' right. I didn't think we were going to see anything usable for weeks."

"Why do you think he came here?"

"We'll have to ask him. He's either doing Stella's dirty work or he's up to something himself."

"You know, I hadn't really thought about it before. Maybe it isn't Stella we should be watching. This guy could be setting her up as the patsy and he's the one masterminding all of this."

"I don't know. There's something about Ms. Manchester I don't like. She's definitely up to no good, but a hunch and a buck and a quarter will get you a cup of coffee."

"Clarence, a rat's about to get your cinnamon roll."

Clarence turned and grabbed his 'rat stick'. He'd been trying to rid the building of rats since they got there. So far, he had injured one and irritated four others. Bryce enjoyed seeing Clarence wear himself out chasing rats. He had to duck occasionally due to Clarence's shotgun approach to swinging that stick. The rats were a bit too wily for these amateur hunters from across the tracks.

"Come on. Let's take a break. We may have seen what we came for anyway."

# Chapter 64

The Orphanage

Andrew woke up before any of the boys. He was completely surrounded by them on the floor of his bedroom. The sun was not up yet, but the eastern sky was streaked with red and purple. Getting out of the room without waking or stepping on any of the boys would be similar to navigating a mine field in Cambodia blindfolded. The need to relieve himself made it a necessity, however.

The relatively cool predawn breeze carried the remnant odor of gunpowder. The fighting had moved north, but there were certain to be dead bodies strewn over the hills west of the home. This reality was possibly going to bring back soldiers to collect them and surely wild animals if not. Andrew walked to the high spot on the north edge of the grounds. He looked in all directions and saw no human movement. Except for Lala. She had just stepped out of the building and was stretching and looking for danger at the same time. She spied Andrew and wondered what he was doing. Lala was one of the older girls. She had developed into a great helper with the young children. Lala came to the home nine years ago simply appearing at the front door. Lala didn't have a name and would not talk for months. No one could guess her age because of her emaciated body. All she wanted was to eat and sleep at first, although sleep was fitful broken up by recurring nightmares. As Lala grew and became a part of the home, Bhaniel was able to communicate with her and find out a few vague details of her past. She was born "over there" and had no recollection of any family. Once Lala mentioned being a "wife" to soldiers and had no idea how she got to the home. Two girls had come with her but both died on the way.

It had been many years since then, and Lala was a young lady now. She had grown into a winsome leader all the younger girls revered. No one was unimportant to her or got left behind. The atrocities committed against her should have killed her spirit, but they had been turned into strengths.

"Andrew, what do you see?"

Lala walked up and stood next to him.

"Hi, Lala. I was checking to see if there were any soldiers nearby. Looks like they moved on."

Lala looked around and decided the same.

"They are gone for now. I think they will be back." She said it without emotion.

"Why do you think so?"

"I don't know. It just doesn't seem safe anymore."

"What do you think we should do?"

"I want to stay because this is my home, but to be here when the soldiers come back would be worse than leaving."

"Where are you going?" The voice was young and innocent.

Dalani had snuck up on them unnoticed. She was 10 and curious. She squeezed in between Andrew and Lala. If any more kids joined them on the hilltop, they were going to look like meerkats surveying the countryside.

"We are not going anywhere Dalani. We are just seeing if there are any soldiers nearby."

"Let's go see who else is up."

Andrew had seen enough. He went to check on Bhaniel. She was resting in her bed. The recovery was going to take a while.

"Good morning."

Andrew sat on her bed and leaned toward her. Bhaniel opened her bloodshot eyes and smiled.

"You are looking very well this morning."

The swelling had misshapen her forehead. She knew it was untrue but played along.

"Thank you Mr. Isaacson. I feel wonderful except for a small headache the size of an elephant."

Bhaniel was fortunate there were no broken facial bones. She just needed time to heal. Time they possibly didn't have. She closed her eyes and held Andrew's hand.

"I was thinking. We need some supplies, so I was going to take a couple of the boys to town."

Bhaniel stole a quick look at Andrew and nodded her head. She squeezed his hand.

"No soldiers?"

"No. I had a look this morning. So far so good. This is probably a good time to venture out."

Andrew didn't say it, but he was afraid this might be his only chance to go back to town before they left. If Lala was correct.

"Be careful."

"Will you be okay for a few hours?"

Bhaniel nodded.

"Hurry back." She looked at him although her vision was blurred still.

"I will."

Andrew wanted to please her any way he could. He was truly anxious to return to her and the kids. On his way out, he found Kalil and Tamego.

"Come on, guys. I need you to go with me to town. We won't stay long."

They were in for the adventure. Maybe they would see a soldier.

"Okay, guys. If we see anyone, we are going to hide. Understand?"

Both boys nodded their heads. Adventure was one thing, but they knew soldiers of any stripe were dangerous. They would view the soldiers from a safe distance. Hiding shouldn't be hard. The soldiers were the visitors. This was their turf.

The excitement of the trek simmered down to just another boring walk and ferry ride to the city. They had not seen a thing unusual, so they turned on each other. The stick battles waged all the way to the river, and finally Andrew had to ask them to stop.

The ferry boat was drifting out in the water, pulling at the rope tied to a wooden brace on the bank. The operators were nowhere to be found. Andrew looked up and down the course of the river and saw no human life. The oddity even stirred Kalil's curiosity.

"Where did everyone go?"

"I don't know, brother. Has this ever happened before?"

Both boys shook their heads. Their breadth of experience was understandably short, but they had not even heard stories of such a thing. Andrew retrieved the ferry and they did their best to captain the boat across the river.

The travelers walked toward to the center of town and went to the general store. The original quest was to gather a few supplies, but circumstances dictated a different focus. The impact on the home could be huge. He needed to know what was happening, yet he was concerned for the boys' safety also. Andrew evaluated his escape options if they were to encounter unfriendlies.

"Where is everyone?"

Tamego hollered over his shoulder as the boys were racing from one building to the next, looking inside and calling out for someone to answer. Andrew was at a loss. After collecting his thoughts, he went into detective mode. Assessing the crime scene with a critical eye, he noticed that things were very similar to the last time he came to town. Except, when he checked the places where people had hidden, no one was there. Andrew walked back to the general store and looked for evidence. The place was ransacked and everything useful had been looted. There was a newspaper wadded up and shoved into the corner. Kalil picked it up and handed the pages to Andrew. It was dated three days prior, and the front page had a picture of Zuberi. The headline was more frantic looking than normal, however.

"Tamego! Come here!"

"Yes, Andrew?"

"Read this for me."

Andrew handed him the paper and pointed at the lead article. Kalil came too and the boys began to read to themselves.

"Read it out loud. I want to hear what it says."

"I'm sorry Mr. Andrew. We can't read a lot of the words, but the large letters say 'Zuberi is Dead!'"

"What!? Really?"

"Who is he? Is he a soldier?"

"He was the president of the country."

The boys let that sink in. Each looked at the other to see if they were reacting properly. 'President' must have been a big deal since Andrew was so shocked.

"What does it mean?"

"I'm not sure, but it can't be good. The government soldiers don't have a leader now."

"What do we do?"

"We'd better head back."

"Aren't we going to get some supplies?"

"Doesn't look like there is anything left."

\*\*\*

The Trans-Gabon Railway train eased into Booue. Halfway to Franceville, he thought to himself. The trip had been painless. The hitman had sequestered himself, and moved from seat to seat as the train entered each station along the route. Now he was in the last seat on the last car, and the disguise was gone. Only a few souls shared the tail car with him, and fewer still cared about him or why he was there. He had disembarked briefly three stops ago to get food and supplies which would carry him until the final stop at Franceville.

The killer considered his quarry and what weapons he would need. He had built his reputation using whatever was nearby as the weapon of choice, when more traditional means were not available. The easy answer was to shoot him from long range, but carrying a rifle through three countries had not been practical. Stealth in getting close to the target was his primary weapon, and he was truly an artist. He was so forgettable, he had attended a wedding and sat next to the father of the bride at the reception before doing his work and drifting away. He wasn't enthusiastic about ruining the wedding, but his client had wanted to make a statement. Murder was an ugly, amoral business, yet it was marginally satisfying when he dispatched a soul who was unrighteous in his eyes. Killing the father of the bride did not injure his psyche in the least. He had done the world a favor.

This target was strictly for the payoff. He had no knowledge of any inherent evil requiring his hand of judgment, but Andrew Isaacson was not the average victim either. He had freed himself from the previous contractor, and it was a priority for him to properly estimate Mr. Isaacson's ability to fight back. When considering the lack of a crowd to hide within, a well-defined pattern of activities to plan for, or a solid understanding of the victim's home turf, these factors made for a challenging kill. It might take him a week just to find the orphanage.

The announcer began to make an extended statement in the local language and in French warning the passengers the train would leave the station momentarily. He settled in for the next leg of the journey.

\*\*\*

Andrew and the boys returned, but he was in no hurry to talk to Bhaniel. On the trek back to the home, Tamego read more of the story – at least the words he could make out and translate. The story could have been a near complete propagandist fabrication, but there were nuggets of truth occasionally. The harsh reality appeared to be the country's president and Bhaniel's brother was gone from this world. She would not take the news well in her weakened state, but he would have to tell her. And if he didn't, the boys were going to proclaim the news loudly and often. Chaos in the capital was going to increase and was probably why the home had found itself on the frontline of the civil war. The people who had wrestled control away from Bhaniel's brother were probably more dangerous than he had ever been. Leaving the DRC was becoming a more reasonable, if not more difficult, strategy.

"Andrew?" Lala found him on his perch atop the hill once again. "Miss B is asking for you. Do you plan on staying here for a while?"

"No, not necessarily. Just checking the landscape. How is she doing?"

"Not great. It's going to take some time for her to recover. It's a good thing you are here. She trusts you to do many things while she is recovering."

"I don't know the first thing about running an orphanage."

"But everyone looks to you when there is danger. And she loves you."
Andrew looked at her to see if she was joking. There was no hint of
playfulness in her voice.
"Why do you say that?"
"The look in her eyes when you are around. And she relaxes when you are
with her."
"I think you were right what you said earlier. She is just glad there is
someone here to take some of the pressure off of her. None of us really
understands the burden she carries as the leader of this place."
"It's more than that. You love her too, don't you?"
Andrew measured his words. "I do love her, but I love everyone at the
home."
They sat in silence for a time. Andrew chewed on what Lala said.
"How many times have soldiers come and terrorized you?" He asked her
quietly.
"Many, many times. When I was younger, they would come and take boys
from the home and sometimes the older girls. Recently, it was just the
drugs since they found out we get supplies from America."
"Things are going to change, Lala. Bhaniel's brother, the nation's
president, is dead. I'm afraid the country is going to fall into chaos which
doesn't bode well for us."
"What should we do?"
"I don't know."
"We will pray. God will tell us." To Lala, it was just a matter of fact.
Lala got up to leave without another word.

He knocked softly and heard her voice.
"We're back safe and sound."
"I'm glad. What did you find?"
"Nothing, actually."
Bhaniel gave him an inquisitive look.
"Really. No one was there. The river was abandoned, and the town was
empty."
Andrew sat on the edge of the bed, holding the newspaper in his hands.
"I think I have some bad news. We found this in the general store."
Bhaniel sat next to him. Andrew handed her the paper. She read the
headline and most of the front page while Andrew studied her face. Tears
had welled up in her eyes belying a sadness tinged with regret.
"I'm sorry."
"Thank you. God sent me to talk to him and tell him this was going to
happen. If only he would have listened to God."
"Was he the last of your family?"
"Yes. If you could call him that. He made every effort to kill my other
family members."

"But not you."

"I will never fully understand why he didn't kill me also."

"Who knows you are his sister?"

"Why do you ask?"

"I'm concerned the group who did this will come after you next."

"I am not afraid to die, Andrew."

"You are very brave, but the kids need you to live. And I as well."

"I do feel stronger today."

"Bhaniel, we may have to consider leaving the country."

"Because of my brother's death?"

"The country will be in chaos. Every military group coming through here will be dangerous and deadly. The rebel group that killed your brother may have an agenda more destructive than anything your brother was capable of. Food supplies and communication with the outside world will be most likely cut off. The longer we stay here, the more I will fear for the safety and well-being of you and the kids."

"How can we leave? This is the only home some of them have ever had."

"Home is wherever you are, Bhaniel. As long as we stay together, we will be alright."

Bhaniel searched Andrew's face for any lack of resolve.

"Andrew, I don't…"

She ached in her need for him, and knew they could not do what he suggested if he wasn't fully committed to lead them through. Yet, she felt the guilt of not begging him to leave and save himself.

"Where should we go? How can we travel with so many kids?"

"I know it is overwhelming, but the prospect of soldiers coming and taking kids away from us would be too much. We can't fight. So the only alternative is to flee. With the country now in a full scale civil war, there will be others seeking refuge in neighboring countries. First, we go to Kinshasa and try to get across the river to Brazzaville. If we can make it out of the country and contact your organization, they can meet us there."

Bhaniel took Andrew's hand in both of hers.

"You are so valuable to me. You have been an angel sent from God. The things you are saying are very wise, but before we do anything, we need to ask for God's wisdom."

"Agreed." Andrew kissed her hand and got up to leave.

"Would you pray with me?"

Andrew was uncomfortable with the proposal, but wanted to please Bhaniel.

"Um, yeah, sure. I don't know what to do, but I'm willing."

"We are going to visit with the Almighty and tell Him our needs."

"You make it sound simple."

"As easy as you talking to me."

Bhaniel led them to the throne of grace and they stayed for a long while.

# Chapter 65

Franceville, Gabon

The conductor walked through the final car and announced the train would arrive in Franceville in a matter of minutes. The sun had been up for two hours, and warmed the assassin's face as he wiped the sleep from his eyes. He surveyed the buildings, and shacks – they were at first just occasional then becoming more concentrated as they neared the train station. He took a long drag on his water bottle, and checked on his hiking boots stowed in his backpack. If he could not find transportation to the airport, he would walk until a ride was found.

The train eased into the station and let out a satisfied sigh as the air brakes relaxed. The professional killer gathered his things and without making eye contact, stepped onto the landing and merged into the crowds of people. At the street, he found a line of taxis with drivers waiting. So much for walking.

"Airport?" He said in French.

The driver in the lead taxi nodded and moved to open the trunk.

"How far?" He knew to ask before they began rolling.

"Thirty kilometers west."

"Let's go."

The hitman did not intend to fly commercial. Which is why he didn't fly from the capital to Franceville. Since he possessed a private pilot's license, he hoped to find a small charter craft to do some aerial recon, and then land in Bandundu.

"We are here, sir."

The killer snapped awake unaware he had drifted off riding in the backseat of the unairconditioned car. Dust wafting in from the open window had powdered his face.

"Take me to the charter aircraft."

The driver looked confused.

"Small planes." The assassin made a motion with his hands of a spinning propeller and wings.

The driver clued in and stepped on the gas. The airport wasn't unusually large, but it did service several commercial carriers. The charter aircraft was at the other end of the runways within a cluster of metal buildings and wooden structures.

"This is good."

He looked at the meter and peeled off the cash plus tip. The hitman walked into an open hangar and found two mechanics taking a smoke break.

"I need to charter a single engine plane."

The men just stared at the stranger. Evidently neither man knew French.

"Two hangars down."

A third man emerged from a filthy, broken down office next to the hangar's entrance.

"He's a bush pilot. Knows the area very well. Where are you going?"

"DRC, Bandundu."

"Yes, yes. No problem."

The killer just nodded his head and walked out. He found the pilot reassembling the landing gear of an ancient plane inside a hangar considerably larger than the last.

"Are you a pilot?"

"Oui."

"I would like to charter a plane today."

"Sorry, sorry. Today is no good. How about tomorrow?" His French was like the first tries of an elementary student learning the language.

"I am a pilot also. May I lease a plane for one or two days?"

The pilot shook his head. "No, sir. I cannot do that. The last time I leased a plane to someone, they never brought it back. Besides, the only plane I have ready to fly is her." He pointed to a World War I era biplane with faded insignia on the sides and wings.

"In fact, I trained to fly in a similar plane. I am well versed in how to fly biplanes."

The pilot smiled, but did not appear swayed by the killer's confidence. This was an unpleasant circumstance. The hitman was not an indiscriminate killer, but he was willing to do whatever it took to accomplish his mission. He wasn't inclined to wait until the pilot was ready.

"I must go today. Can you make an exception? I am willing to pay double your price."

That may have done it. The pilot looked up from his work and a grin formed at the edge of his mouth.

"You know, the man I was going to take to Brazzaville said he could wait until Thursday to go. You would be willing to pay five hundred francs?"

The hitman nodded and picked up his backpack.

"Where are we going, friend?"

"Bandundu."

"Excellent. I have flown to Bandundu many times. We'll be there before dark."

The pilot grabbed his goggles, made a horrible mess fueling the plane and climbed into the front seat. He put a tobacco-like wad in his mouth, spit over the side of the cockpit and yelled 'Contact!'.

The hitman flipped the propeller, but nothing happened.

"It may take a few tries, my friend. It has not flown for many months." Two more attempts and it turned over for several seconds. The next turn did the trick and the killer ran to the side and jumped into the back seat. The killer coiled around in his seat to reach his backpack. He pulled out his GPS and strapped it to his wrist. Close to the airport and going southeast, there were very few landmarks for him to reference because of the rural landscape; but there would be no mistaking the mighty Congo River. It would also announce their entrance into the DRC.

\*\*\*

"I have not received a comfort in my spirit about leaving."

Bhaniel had walked up behind Andrew and made her announcement without warning or fanfare. Andrew knew it was weighing on her heavily, or she would have waited until they could sit on the porch of an evening and discuss. Andrew looked up from the wagon he was working on, sat back and wiped his hands on a rag.

"It's not an easy decision to make. Certainly, there is danger in both. One thing I would like for us to do is go to Kinshasa or Matadi and contact your organization. It is important to get their input. Even if we get everyone to either of those two cities; unless the organization is working successfully to facilitate the journey to the U.S., the trip stops there."

Bhaniel nodded. "Yes, I agree." She evaluated her words and looked at Andrew. "I know you would like to leave this place, and your reasons are upright and good. To lose another child to disease, or to see them taken away by rebels would be almost too much to bear. Going to America would bring safety in so many ways for these children, but what about the children who are abandoned after we leave? Who takes care of them?"

Andrew realized Bhaniel could not live anywhere else but here. If there was one more child needing a safe harbor, it was reason enough to stay. For Bhaniel to act any other way would be a contradiction to who she was. Andrew stood up to face Bhaniel, to search her face for any uncertainty. All he saw was sincerity and resolve based in love.

"As much as I would like to see you and the children live where you are not in constant danger, I understand why you must stay. And I want to remain as well."

Bhaniel accepted Andrew's hand and looked into his eyes. Although she wanted to do it, Bhaniel was hesitant to wrap her arms around this man in front of any children or workers who were looking. It was an unfounded check born out of tradition and someone else's rules. Andrew didn't live by those rules. He embraced her with all of his strength and emotion. He would apologize later.

"What do you think about contacting the organization? Just to let them know we are alive."

"It is a good idea. You could call from the government office in Bandundu if the phone is working properly. If not then you will need to go to Kikwit or Kinshasa. Should we go together?"

"It might be easier if I went alone."

"Yes, yes I think you are right. Are you going soon?"

"The sooner the better. The soldiers are not close, so this may be the best time."

"I'm not sure. Based on your recent trip, it is unknown what you will be able to do in Bandundu. If you have to go to the capital, the best plan might be to secure a motorbike."

Not great for 200 kilometers, but it was better than walking.

"I'll get the overseas phone number."

\*\*\*

It had been about thirty minutes since they crossed the Congo River. The exhilaration of the open cockpit in a plane only a few hundred feet above the ground made the flight into the wilds of Africa seem like a once in a lifetime safari. A tourist's dream vacation. The birds, and animals were active on the river today. The steady waters sustained life in a myriad of ways. Even a few humans working in the river noticed the plane, squinting into the sun.

"There!"

The pilot pointed over the left side of the plane as he yelled to the wind. It was the outskirts of Bandundu. He gestured as he spoke. They were coming in from the northwest, and the pilot began a wide circle around the city. The killer tapped the pilot's shoulder and yelled to him.

"There is an orphanage outside of the city. We need to find it before we land."

The pilot acknowledged what he said, but had to think a minute. They didn't have enough fuel to circle the area indefinitely. He remembered a group of buildings south and west, but had not known what they were. As long as the airport was open and available, they could search until the last minute.

He brought the plane low over the cluster of buildings so they could get a good look. It could be an orphanage, but neither saw any kids running about. The hitman motioned for the pilot to keep going. He turned to his rider and shrugged. They had made an entire circuit around the city to no avail.

"What about the other side of the river?"

The pilot checked his gas level. "We only have a short time left."

He banked to the west and began to crisscross the tree covered hills. The first time they flew overhead, they had barely noticed the orphanage structures nestled against the hills on the eastern slope. The blue roof and white walls caught the killer's eye and he motioned for the pilot to swing back around. The second time confirmed it. He had found the orphanage. The two men nodded and the pilot headed for the airport. Considering the depleted fuel level, he was hoping this plane was able to glide the last few miles.

\*\*\*

"Miss B! Miss B! Look up there!"

The kids watched in awe as the small biplane rumbled overhead. It looked so close they thought the wheels might scrape the treetops. Everyone stopped to watch as it made a slow circle in the sky around them. Two men were in the plane. Both had goggles on, and one wore a leather hat. They seemed very interested in the orphanage, but neither one waved back. Finally, the plane turned toward the river valley as if going away. Most of the kids wanted to watch until the plane disappeared. The tree line kept them from seeing the final descent toward the Bandundu airport. The kids lingered for a moment and one or two asked if they could give chase, but eventually they returned to their work or play.

The pilot allowed the plane to glide a little longer than was necessary. He was anxious about the runway after seeing some potholes on the initial flyover. Only a few feet off the ground, the pilot eased back on the throttle and kissed the dirt with the front wheels. The biplane taxied to the terminal with only a vapor of gasoline left in the tank.

"Here is your payment."

The pilot looked at the offering, adding up the bills in his head.

"Thank you, sir. Shall I wait on you?"

"No." The hitman pulled his back pack and walked away without another word.

The flyover allowed him to locate the orphanage. He got his bearings and began the walk toward the west end of the city. He noted the decided lack of humanity, but wasn't too concerned. Less interaction with locals the better. Still, a ride would not be a bad thing.

# Chapter 66

Bandundu

Andrew walked down the empty street toward the Domestic Ministry building. Even though there were no citizens milling about, surely the phones still worked. He heard a radio playing what Bhaniel called Ndombolo music through open windows of a cinder block house. The government building was just a couple of blocks further on the right. Very close to the airstrip as it turns out. Made good sense for government officials who could do their business and then bug out as quickly as possible. Andrew stepped into the government offices and still no human activity.

"Hello! Anyone here?"

"Hello! Is there anyone working here today?"

No answer. Andrew made himself at home and searched for a telephone. The biggest office behind the door with the 'do not enter' sign had a phone and Andrew sat down to call, but no dial tone. Two offices later, he found a phone with a dial tone. Andrew began the arduous task of accessing international operators and dialing numbers. Twice he was cut off after eight and fourteen minute waits, forcing him to start over from the beginning. Obviously no one else was there needing the telephone, so he waded in again. Finally, it seemed to work. The crackling on the line sounded like American static to him. Andrew held the phone gingerly, not wanting to endanger the connection in any way.

"Hello, International Orphan and Refugee Relief Foundation. How may I direct your call?"

"Hi, I'm calling from the Congo. Could I speak with Director Salvatore Hizanga please?" Andrew talked a little too loudly believing it was necessary due to his remote location.

"Certainly. May I tell him who is calling?"

"Andrew Isaacson."

"I will put you through."

There was a short wait with several clicks and electronic noises filling the void. While he waited, Andrew heard what he thought was a plane flying close by.

"Mr. Isaacson?"

"Yes, it's me."

There was a great sound of relief on the American side.

"Thank God you're alive. Is everyone safe?"

"Director, hello. Yes we're fine. Things are getting kinda crazy here though. Bhaniel and I thought it would be best to call and let you know how we are doing, but also to see what you thought we should do next."

"It's so good to hear your voice. We haven't been able to do anything but pray. Most communications and access to the country have been shut down."

"The chaos is affecting even Bandundu. The whole town has disappeared. I haven't seen a soul here since Tuesday. The Domestic Ministry office is abandoned. I'm really not sure where everyone went."

"Normally, a standard upheaval will cause a similar reaction and people will come out of hiding in a day or two. The assassination of the president is a whole new level though. International reports are saying the rebels who did it haven't been able to gain control. There are factions all over the country fighting for the upper hand. To be candid, no one is safe, Andrew."

"What can we do, Director? Should we go or stay?"

"The easy answer is to tell you to leave and go to Angola. We have other organization staff and facilities there. But, I'm not sure it's possible for you to leave right now. Is there any public transportation available?"

"Probably not until everyone comes back to town."

"Well, I would say stay put then. I will work on getting some more people into Angola and put the existing staff on alert. Why don't you make plans to come back to Bandundu every three to four days to update us? Will that be possible?"

"I think so. The only thing that will hinder us is if the soldiers come back. The fact the citizens remain in hiding tells me they could come back anytime."

"Agreed. Andrew thank you for being there. I know it's a hollow thing to say, but considering all the circumstances, you are a Godsend."

"I don't know if I have much choice at this point, but I am committed to helping Bhaniel and the kids. They've become my family in many ways."

"I'm pleased to hear it. Andrew, we'll talk soon. Go with God."

"Until then."

Well, it was a start. Now the organization was on the move, and he and everyone else at the home just had to stay alive. The chaos was going to stir up some business for the orphanage too. War means refugees, and a lot of them children. Andrew stepped out into the sunlight and noticed the biplane idling at the other end of the airstrip. What a stroke of luck. He stepped lively in hopes of catching the pilot before he left. He could just make out a second man, European maybe, leaving the plane as he made his way down the street. Unfortunately, the plane had landed and taxied a considerable distance from the terminal building. It appeared the plane was going to circle around and come back his way. Andrew arrived at the building soon after the plane did as the engine coughed to a stop.

"Hello! How are you?" Andrew's Lingala was not good. The pilot looked confused.

"Can you help me refuel the plane?" The pilot spoke broken French, which Andrew understood 'help' and 'refuel'.

"Uh, you from Congo?" Andrew knew a little more French than Lingala.

"No, no. Gabon. I'm going back now. I flew a man here to the orphanage." Andrew blinked and tried to focus on what he just said.

"The man is going to the orphanage?"

"Yes. He is meeting someone there."

Curious. Bhaniel didn't mention this event, he thought to himself. It was just odd enough to cause Andrew's adrenaline to kick in. It was time to go.

"Thank you, sir. Good day."

Andrew headed back south two blocks to get to the main road. From there, it would be a straight shot to the river. As he reached the thoroughfare, he saw the man speeding away on a motor scooter. The stranger was going to increase his lead if Andrew couldn't find like transportation. Andrew began to jog. It was a slow, old man jog, but it made him feel as though he was going faster. As he went, he looked in every shop and every alley hoping to find an abandoned bicycle, anything really, to enhance his pace. The stranger was almost out of sight. He had begun the downward approach to the river.

There. It was a tricycle much like Drago's but with no canopy. Andrew noticed it half hidden behind a pile of wood and garbage. It looked serviceable when he pulled it out into the open so off we went, squeaking and groaning with every rotation. One of the wheels was out of round so it became almost a carnival ride across town.

He zig zagged his way down to the water's edge, but there was no ferry. The stranger had taken the ferry boat leaving only two raft-like vessels used by local fishermen. Andrew peered across the river, and the stranger was still unloading his gear. Andrew drew in a breath to holler out to the stranger to wait for him, but decided against it. He watched as the stranger hiked to the tree line and out of sight.

A chill went through Andrew. None of this felt right. He untied the sturdiest raft and found a paddle. These rafts were hardly more than glorified surfboards, but they would do. Andrew straddled the craft and paddled as best he could. He was only good for minute-long bursts and then equal rest times. The current was slow, but the breadth of the river caused it to pull Andrew considerably downstream. He was not even half way across and he had lost sight of the ferry pier. The river began to turn to the west, pulling him into uncharted waters – at least for him. Granted, it looked largely the same as the known waters, but he would have to backtrack along the water's edge rather than go through the back country to safely return to familiar ground.

Andrew was exhausted. The rest times grew longer and the paddling sessions shorter. As he got closer to the shore, the current was weak which improved his effort. He pulled the raft on to dry ground vowing to return it to the rightful owner. His arms were spent, but now it was time to run. He wasn't sure how far away he drifted. The only thing to do was go as fast as he could.

The killer strolled up the path as if he didn't have anywhere to be. The first kids playing in the open area saw him and ran toward him. The fact he was white made them comfortable he wasn't a soldier. As far as they knew, soldiers were the only bad people. They were required to run and hide when soldiers came near, but this guy looked okay.

By the time he made it to the main building, the train of children following him was fifteen long. The first ones were curious and the rest joined in because it looked fun. The commotion aroused the attention of the adults, ultimately drawing Bhaniel out to meet them.

"Hello! Do you speak English? French?"

"I speak English. I am Bhaniel Tretechi. What is your name?"

"My name is Marcel Doucat. I am a representative of the International Children's Protection Protocol. We are contracted by the United Nations to go into countries experiencing political or military issues and see what we can do for indigenous orphanages and schools."

"I see. It's very kind of you and your organization to do so. Will you be staying or will you need to travel on."

"This is the only one in the Bandundu Province, but there are others east and north of here. They may not be easy to reach. If you will allow me, I will stay here tonight and continue my journey tomorrow."

"Fine. We will show you around the property. Are there certain things you need to learn from us?"

"The primary intent is to simply determine if you remain in relative safety, and see if there is a way to enhance or improve your ability to protect yourselves."

"Right now, we are safe, but soldiers have come here recently. We have developed safety measures for the children over time so they will know what to do."

"That is so important. You never know when danger will come your way."

"Rapha, Kalil, would you show Mr. Doucat where he can lay his things? You must be exhausted from your trip."

"Thank you. Actually, I was in Kinshasa yesterday so the trip wasn't long."

"Wonderful. If you are hungry, we will be having dinner in an hour."

"Thank you. I look forward to it. I haven't eaten since yesterday."

Andrew was winded from running and climbing. He could not shake the feeling of dread and anxiety which pushed him faster to the home. He reached the compound and looked for danger signs. The kids were playing and adults were doing chores. There appeared to be nothing out of the ordinary. He made his way to the main building in search of Bhaniel and the stranger.

"Hi Selah, have you seen Bhaniel?"

"Yes she's showing Mr. Doucat around the property."

"Mr. Doucat?"

"He's from the United Nations. That's all I know."

Just then, Bhaniel entered the room with their guest.

".... we did have one worker taken by the rebel soldiers, but we were able to secure her release. She is in America right now. Shortly after she left, we had a surprise arrival of a gentleman who is... Andrew! Hello. I didn't know you had returned. Have you been in the river?"

Andrew stood in the middle of the great room, wet, tired, sweaty and dirty from the cross country trek.

"Yes. I'll have to tell you about it later."

"Andrew this is Marcel Doucat. He is here from the United Nations to check on us and help us improve our safety measures."

"Andrew Isaacson. Pleasure to meet you." He moved to shake the newcomer's hand.

"Likewise."

"You American?"

"French actually, but I spent several years in America."

"Oh really, where?"

"New York mostly. I've been in Africa and Europe for the last ten years though."

"Thanks for making the effort to come here."

"It's my pleasure. There is a great need. The country is in upheaval and a peaceful solution to the chaos is not near."

"What have you heard about the takeover?"

"Not too much. There are several rival factions vying for control, but none have the strength to establish themselves as a viable government. It is unfortunately very typical. The rebels love the idea of being in charge, but don't think about the responsibilities of governing."

The hitman was marveling at his ability to play this part believably. He hadn't intended to do it this way. His initial plan was to find Andrew and kill him with little fanfare. Just a cold corporate function. While he could shut it down at any time, he was enjoying the change of pace. The cat toying with the mouse before the inevitable.

The remainder of the afternoon and dinner time was spent talking about the national chaos, the home's food and water needs, the availability of medicine and whether communications would improve. The killer played the part beautifully. The only hiccup was when he had to recite the name of his organization again. It didn't come to him immediately and he wondered if the uncertainty showed on his face.

As one would expect, the kids performed for Mr. Doucat. It was an abbreviated version with only seven groups singing or emoting on some level. He appeared to thoroughly enjoy himself, laughing and clapping along with everyone else. Lala offered the big finish with her dramatic portrayal of Mary Magdalene complete with an original song at the end. That was the cue for the crowd to break up and bedtime gyrations to begin. Andrew turned to their guest. "Mr. Doucat, I'm headed out to the porch for the sunset. Join me?"

"Yes, I'd be delighted."

Mr. Doucat was enthusiastic as they walked toward the porch.

"I'm very impressed with everything going on here at the orphanage."

"Bhaniel and her staff are a rare group for sure."

"How long have you been here with them?"

"It seems like a lifetime now. I came from America to get away from the chaos of my life and fell into a different kind of turmoil. The assassination happened not long after I arrived. The irony is, I've felt more at peace here than at any other time of my life."

"Are you planning to stay here indefinitely?"

"Probably so, yes. These people have become my family. I've walked away from people I love before. I don't intend to do it again."

"Even if the rebels come back?"

"More so then. Whether it is true or not, I believe they need me. God knows I need them."

"You and Bhaniel have a… special relationship."

"Special? In what way."

"It's obvious you came here for her."

"Does your organization offer psychological profiling as part of their wellness program?"

"It could figure into what we do. The dynamics of the leaders'
relationships has a noticeable effect on the kids."

"If you are asking 'are we sleeping together?' then the answer is no. While
I've not exactly run from the pleasures of the flesh in my life, the bond we
have developed is much deeper than that." Andrew wanted to change the
subject. "The kids seem to have responded very well to a male presence.
They've not had many men stay here."

"I can tell. They love to perform for you and look to you for approval."

"Mr. Doucat, you are very insightful."

"When you travel to so many places and need to assess the situation
quickly, you develop certain skills."

"Like I said, they've become my family. I would lay down my life for
them."

"I'm very impressed to hear that, Mr. Isaacson."

The two men sat in the growing darkness chatting about Africa and life.
The sunset was nothing short of spectacular, almost as if God knew they
had a special guest this evening. The night creatures were unusually quiet
as well. So much so, Andrew noticed it.

"Well, I'm fixing to turn in for the night. Thank you for your hospitality."

"I have one more question for you before you go."

"Certainly."

"Why are you really here?"

"What do you mean? I've told you."

"It's a lie and we both know it."

By this time, both men had given up their chairs and were standing at
opposite ends of the porch. After a short stare down, 'Mr. Doucat' smiled
and gave up the charade.

"I'm impressed Mr. Isaacson. You are the one who is insightful, I believe.
How did you see through the disguise?" At this point, the killer wasn't
concerned with what Andrew knew. All of this would be done in a few
minutes anyway.

"None of it was adding up. Kinshasa yesterday? Why would you come to
Bandundu in a biplane by way of Gabon?"

"How did you know about the plane?"

"I was in town calling our organization when you landed. There were so
few people out and about, I wanted to talk with you. I saw you ride off, but
caught up with the pilot. He told me you came from Gabon and were going
to the orphanage."

The killer made a mental note to kill the pilot next time.

"And you're 'fixing to' turn in? No one from New York says that. You're
from the South, probably right in the Atlanta area. The comment during
dinner about Waffle Houses makes Atlanta even more probable. Trust me,
after Stella tried to kill me the first time, I've developed a certain wariness
regarding strangers who simply appear out of thin air."

"Mr. Isaacson, you are so much more than I expected. Why didn't you try to capture me early on?"

"I wasn't sure at first, but if you were what I feared, I didn't want to endanger the others if we forced you to act. I decided I would get you up here on the porch alone. If you were successful, you could leave into the night and the others would be spared. Do you intend to kill anyone else?"

"I don't think there will be any need Mr. Isaacson, but your concern for the others here at the orphanage is honorable. If I didn't have an employer to satisfy, I would simply leave you here to continue your good work. Unfortunately, if I go back empty handed, my career and probably my life would be in jeopardy." The hitman contemplated Andrew for a moment. "You don't seem afraid to die."

"In a lot of ways, I'm already dead to the world. My life in America is over, and I have no family. There's no reason for me to continue on unless God has more for me to do. I have to confess to you, I don't think He's done with me yet. It might be in your best interest to leave here and start a new life somewhere besides Atlanta. Fair warning."

"Your confidence is inspiring, but I don't see how this ends any other way."

"If you don't mind telling me, how were you going to prove to Stella you killed me?"

"I don't know who Stella is. I plan to do my job, take some pictures of your face and text them to the one who set up my contract. I'll take one of your fingers with me as well."

"You sure came a long way. I hope you will be paid well."

"It has been a great trip. I've never been to Africa before. And yes, I am being paid very well."

"Stella wanted this so badly. I'm sorry it will end poorly – again."

Almost imperceptibly, the sound of another insect joined the nighttime chorus. Andrew had heard it before, and it made him smile. He glanced out into the darkness and made eye contact with Aleefa as he crouched silently. In an instant, a rush of air signaled the incoming spear. Since it was a slender rod formed from a sapling, the entrance wound was small. It hit the killer between the third and fourth rib and traveled through his torso, stopping just below his right shoulder blade.

Neither Andrew nor the killer moved. They simply stood and looked at one another for a timeless moment. Finally, Mr. Doucat realized the gravity of his situation, and instead of trying to remove the spear, he grabbed for the knife hidden in his belt and charged Andrew.

Andrew reacted by picking up the chair next to him and holding the killer off like a lion tamer in the cage. The assassin flailed wildly, but lost momentum as his wound festered and the blood flowed. The end of the spear caught on the porch post and turned the injured man slightly. Andrew saw the opening and pushed the chair and the man backward. The hitman tripped and fell, snapping the spear and eliciting a frustrated wail.

Aleefa had come to the edge of the porch to view his vanquished prey. No one spoke as the killer twitched slightly. Andrew was still in a half crouch ready for any sudden movement.

Marcel Doucat stirred and turned his head toward Andrew. He began to gasp for air as he made what would be his last remarks.

"Mr. Isaacson... I... believe... I... under... estimated... you. Indeed... God... is... not... done." Mr. Doucat was a man of blood. As a warrior of sorts, he honored a worthy foe, and had found one in Andrew although Aleefa figured heavily into the immediate outcome. Andrew knelt in front of his would be killer, not gloating, but respecting the scenario. He thought he saw a slight smile on the killer's face. At this point, there was no way they could save Mr. Doucat's life.

"It wasn't me this time. Like I said before, this is my family. Farewell Mr. Doucat."

Andrew rose and hugged Aleefa.

"Thank you. How did you know he intended to kill me?"

"I was out hunting some small animals for a cook out tomorrow and I heard your voices. I listened to most of what he said. Did you hear me sneaking up on you?"

"No, I didn't hear a thing, except for the 'insect'."

"Excellent!"

"I don't think he heard you either."

"I'm sure of it."

"You made a great throw! It couldn't have been any better." They stood and evaluated the fallen killer. Aleefa pulled the broken spear from the body of the hitman. "Aleefa, I'm sorry you had to go to this length to protect me. If you want to talk about what happened here at a later time..."

"No need Mr. Andrew. He is like the rebel soldiers who come here to hurt the women. It had to be done. If I didn't, we would have lost you."

"Aleefa, I am in your debt. We'd better tell Bhaniel what happened here."

"I'm a little bit sad. I really liked this spear."

"How about I make you a new one? It's the least I could do."

Andrew and Aleefa stepped into the main building. Bhaniel and two other workers were sitting near the stove chatting.

"Andrew! There you are." She looked confused. "Where is Mr. Doucat? Aleefa, what happened to your spear?"

"Bhaniel, we have something to tell you." Andrew and Aleefa glanced at each other.

"Mr. Doucat was not a worker from the United Nations. He was actually a hired assassin sent here to kill me."

Bhaniel's mouth fell open and her eyes widened. She looked at both of them to determine if this was a poorly planned joke. Neither men were smiling.

"Andrew, please tell me you are kidding."

"It's no joke. Aleefa saved my life. He was hunting animals with his spear and used it to, uh, stop Mr. Doucat before it was too late."

"Where is he now?"

"On the porch."

"Is he dead?"

"I believe so."

All three women gasped and the other two gathered their things and went to mother the children. Bhaniel searched Andrew's face for answers.

"What should we do now?" She asked him.

"I'm confident, aside from the pilot who brought him here, we are the only people in Africa who know he is here. The body? Bury him tonight. We will have to deal with some other issues tomorrow."

"How do you know he came to kill you, Andrew?"

"He told me."

"Pardon me?"

"He told me. I let him know I figured out his cover story was a lie and he confessed willingly. In hindsight, he was overconfident. Even so, if Aleefa had not come along, the outcome could have been significantly different."

"How did you know it was a lie? He seemed very convincing to me."

"If I had not seen him land at the airport and learn from the pilot they came from Gabon today, I might have believed him also."

"Thank you, God of Heaven. We are humbled by your protection and care for Andrew. Thank you, Aleefa you have proved yourself a mighty warrior tonight."

Bhaniel hugged him and looked at Andrew.

"Have you shown him the drawing you did?" She whispered to Andrew. The drawing made so much more sense now. He truly had fleshed out the vision.

"I will. He should appreciate it even more now."

It took longer than they thought to dig a respectable grave. While providing a proper burial seemed a little too good for this hired killer, it made sense in light of the preponderance of wild animals. The body would draw unnecessary attention to the property. Andrew and Aleefa did the majority of the digging work since the adults didn't want the younger kids to see all this.

"That should do it." Andrew tapped the dirt on the grave and threw two more rocks on the site.

Aleefa, and two workers went back to the house. Andrew and Bhaniel sat and studied the grave, resting.

"Do you think he came alone?"

"I think if there was an accomplice, he would have come to his aid when the fighting began."

"True. I wonder if the killers will just keep coming. Even for your business partner, it has to be expensive sending these men to kill you."

"It's probably my money." Andrew half laughed.

They listened to the night, wondering if it was time to go inside.

"Bhaniel, my presence here is dangerous."

"It looks as though it was more dangerous for the assassin. I agree, it is unsafe for you, but it is not more dangerous than usual for the rest of us. He was here for you."

"I disagree. It is very likely he would have harmed many of you after getting to me. They know where I am obviously."

"What can you do? Wherever you go, they will find you."

"I don't know, Bhaniel, I just don't know." Andrew took Bhaniel's hands in his. She laid her head on his shoulder.

"Let's sleep on it and discuss the options in the morning."

"Tomorrow, we need to go through his stuff. I know he had a phone. He said something about doing me in and then taking pictures and texting them to his employer."

"Really? I suppose they need proof."

Bhaniel thought it over for a minute. "Maybe we need to send them some pictures," she said raising her head.

"It's too late to send pictures of the hitman."

"Not him, you."

"You mean act dead?"

"Yes, I know it won't keep them away forever, but it will help for a while."

"It seems like I'm always just buying time, never getting completely free. Even so, it would be worth it for the temporary benefit."

"We need to make you look dead."

"Shouldn't be too hard. What will we do for blood?"

"Aleefa will have to go hunting… And I think you should shave. Stella needs to see the old Andrew."

"Agreed. I don't like it, but I agree."

Andrew kissed her before she could react. It startled Bhaniel, but he didn't care. She pulled away and caught her breath. Without saying anything, Bhaniel leaned back in for another kiss more on her terms.

"Is it weird we are kissing next to the grave of someone who tried to kill me an hour ago?"

"Mr. Isaacson, I would expect nothing less from you."

The sound of something rustling in the tall grass shocked him out of his enraptured state.

"Maybe we ought to go before Aleefa has to come out here and rescue us again."

They walked back to the house snugly arm in arm, two people glad to make it through another day.

# Chapter 67

The Orphanage

"Andrew, you have to lay still."

"I thought I was."

Andrew was covered in the blood of a small antelope which was hunted for the occasion. The meat would be welcomed as a change to their normal diet, but the adults didn't want to make it a regular part of their food supply. Poachers were already reducing the animal population at an alarming rate, and Bhaniel in particular didn't want to be a part of it. Quamanga was standing next to Andrew's shoulder wearing extra pants and shoes the killer left behind. Bhaniel held the phone out so the camera shot would include the items making it seem as though the hitman was standing right there. The ladies had been a little too generous with the blood the first time through so they had to clean off his face and try it again. This time, the blood was placed in more reasonable spots. It bothered Andrew to have the animal blood all over his face.

"I think I'm ready to be done."

"Really, Andrew. It's just a little blood."

"Actually, it's a lot of blood, and this is the second layer."

"Let's get a couple more. We don't want to do this again."

"How did I die again?"

"Hold still. You were stabbed. The knife was the only weapon we found in his back pack. But from the look of you, he must have beat you badly before killing you."

In addition to blood, Andrew had dirt rubbed on his face and arms. Everyone gathered around the phone to see the captured images. Most agreed they looked very believable. Andrew got up and had a look himself.

"I like it. The shoes and pants were a good touch. Now we just have to figure out how to get these pictures sent to the killer's boss."

"Maybe we could send the entire phone to Mr. Hizanga." It was Lala. "The phone will work in the U.S., right?"

The adults turned and looked at Lala while they thought it over.

"Do phones sent in the mail get stolen?"

"Unfortunately, electronics of any kind rarely reach their intended destination."

"That's a good idea, Lala. We may need to use it as a plan B though. We can't risk losing the phone in the mail."

Maangua spoke up. She was one of Bhaniel's best and most loyal workers. The kids loved her, but she rarely talked other than to respond to a child in need or acknowledging a request from Bhaniel. But singing was a different story. Even Andrew had said she had a beautiful voice when she sang the worship songs with the kids. She had grown up in Bandundu so the area was very familiar to her.

"You can go into town and purchase a SIM card for the phone. Then it will work here and should access international lines also."

Everyone just stared at Maangua. No one had heard her speak so authoritatively before.

"Maangua, thank you. That is a great idea."

"Where do we get such a thing?"

"Assuming someone is actually in the town now, there are many merchants who offer electronic items."

"What are we waiting for? Let's go." Andrew stopped and thought it over for a second. "You know what? I'm going to do one thing before we go. Just in case it works."

"What are you doing, Andrew?"

"I'm going to simply text the photos. Maybe we won't even need the new SIM card."

Everyone looking on agreed it was worth it. Andrew pulled out the phone and drilled down to the list of phone numbers in the contacts. There were only three numbers. He fashioned a text to all three recipients of the four best photographs and sent them one by one. The phone didn't respond immediately after it attempted to send the texts.

"It didn't reject them at least. But I'm not sure if we will be able to tell whether the texts get through."

"Why don't we go ahead and get the new SIM card just in case we need it."

Ding! The phone announced something had happened.

"One of the texts didn't go through. It says it isn't a working number. Well, one down, two to go."

"Yeah, we need to get the SIM card. I'll take Aleefa and Kalil with me."

After Andrew cleaned off most of the blood and the fake slit on his throat, he changed his shirt and they headed off toward the river. The ferry was near the other side of the river and the boys began to wave their arms to get the ferry master's attention. He was already moving in their direction, so it was going to be just a short wait.

Ding! The phone went off again in Andrew's hand. It was a return text from the second number.

[Photos received. Job done. Payment will be in primary account. Allow three days travel time.]

Andrew was stunned. It worked.

"Uh, boys. We don't have to go into town. We're done. Let's go back home."

Both boys looked at Andrew, each other and across the river. They were a little disappointed the adventure was over, but it was getting close to dinnertime anyway. They shrugged their shoulders and began the walk back. Andrew placed the now valuable phone in his pocket and followed them up the hill.


Bhaniel reviewed the text, looking for any latent shred of new information she had missed the first twelve times she read it.

"Am I wrong? Am I wrong to think you are finally free?" She was beseeching Andrew.

Andrew smiled. "Free enough. Freedom has a different meaning in the DRC, but yes I think I am free for now."

"For now?"

"They are going to expect their killer to return to the U.S. and collect his fee. Obviously, he is not going back. There will come a time, when the charade will fail and someone will begin looking for him."

The realization pulled Bhaniel down with a thud.

"Surely, his employers will not think you are to blame, since they believe you are dead."

"True. The best case is the orphanage will not be one of the places searched. The phone may not be usable though. If they are able to track it, any use will betray its location."

"So, we'll turn it off and throw it away."

"I would like to keep it in case we need it some time."

"Just hide it so the kids don't accidently turn it on."

# Chapter 68

Stella felt the vibration in her left front pocket. Eugene was in the office with her going over the sales numbers from the June show and hashing out the details for the 'found' painting releases.

"Enough for now. Rerun those numbers and call Jaime to reschedule my meeting with her for Tuesday."

"I've already done it."

"Do it again. Go."

Eugene didn't protest.

Stella pulled the phone out, fumbled with it through nervous hands and flipped it open. She gazed on the number representing the received text and held her breath. Slowly, she pushed the buttons to reveal the data.

[Call now for update.]

She speed-dialed the number.

"Well?"

"It is done. Be at the east end of Grant Park tomorrow at ten with the final payment."

"How…"

The line went dead. She was going to need proof or no deal. One text wouldn't hurt anything.

[Proof or no deal.]

The suspense would keep her up all night.

"Have you seen Stella this morning?" Marla from Sales had stopped by Eugene's office.

"No, she called earlier. Stella won't be in until after lunch, and I don't know where she is."

"Can you call me when she gets in?"

"Mm hmm." Eugene only half acknowledged her as he continued his efforts on the computer.

This had better be the last time I have to do this, Stella though to herself. She was dressed as a younger woman, almost a college student by the look of her wardrobe. Ratty jeans and a baggy coat. The crocheted hat covered her hair and the sunglasses did the rest. Sneakers and generally slouchy body language made her almost invisible to everyone else.

The bus line would take her within a few blocks of the meeting point. This time, she was not going to the main location. Way too risky. The mobsters said to meet her in Grant Park. Just anonymous enough for a casual meeting.

Stella got off the bus and made no eye contact. She readjusted her back pack and aimed for the park. Once on premises, Stella found a nearby perch for surveillance of the east end. The mob rep would have to show himself first. She sat down on a bench next to an older gentleman in a rumpled jacket, white dress shirt yellowing at the collar, polyester slacks and sensible walking shoes. He was reading the newspaper in between cat naps.

The designated time came and went. No wise guy showed.

"I have pictures if you want to see them."

Stella tried to believe the old man didn't speak. She looked away.

"I have pictures if you want to see them."

Stella shot a sideways glance at him.

"Excuse me, are you speaking to me?"

"You're here for proof aren't you?"

Stella was dumbfounded and a little impressed. They had beat her at her own game. She had no choice but to play along.

"Uh, yes. I would like to see some proof."

He slid the sports section to her with an envelope containing legal documents and some loose photographs. It was Andrew. She gasped unexpectedly. The images were gruesome and clear. And proof enough for anyone. She pulled out the envelope's remaining contents. It was a Stock Assignment. Stella scanned it quickly for the main points. If she signed this document, the mafia would own a significant stake in AD Isaacson.

"I need to take this with me and read it over."

"Sign it, Miss." The old man didn't look at her. He just read his paper.

"What if I don't?"

"You won't make it out of the park alive. I didn't come alone." He offered a conciliatory tone. "It's just business, dear." He handed her a pen. "You can keep the pictures."

Stella's hands were shaking as she signed her name. She was officially married to the mob. Stella slid the pictures into her vest, handed the sports section back to the gentleman, got up slowly and walked away.

# Chapter 69

The Orphanage

The home regained some measure of normalcy. People began to return to Bandundu, mostly because the word got out the soldiers and rebels had taken the fight to Kinshasa and in the far western regions of the country. Around the orphanage, the kids resumed their studies and the more adventurous went back to fishing in the morning. Andrew threw himself into his drawings, teaching art and establishing himself as the property manager. His time at the home was an age of discovery. Andrew had a knack for fixing things and using unorthodox materials and means to do so. The aqueduct built from bamboo was a real hit.

He and Bhaniel had developed a habit of meeting at the porch most evenings, but after Aleefa dispatched the assassin, some of the blood remained so their meetings occurred in other places. This evening was different however. Andrew ventured to the porch to catch the sunset, sensing the emotions of the previous events were waning. Bhaniel found her way there as well, still avoiding the areas where the assassin bled. Neither said anything for a long while. Finally, Bhaniel spoke softly as dusk turned to night.

"Would you tell me about it?"

Andrew gave her a quizzical look. Her voice had pulled him from pondering a commotion in the trees between two warring factions of birds. He smiled and considered her eyes. Bhaniel's eyelashes softened her unblinking gaze.

"Sure. Tell you about what?"

"The drawing."

"Aleefa?"

"No."

Andrew shifted in his seat to face her.

"You mean…?"

"Yes. I'm sorry someone went through your belongings. One of the kids…"

"I'm not upset. The only reason I haven't shown it to you is because I'm scared of what it means."

"Why would you be scared? If it is to be, then it will be. Do you think it foretells an ominous fate for me?"

Emotion was building in Andrew's chest, but he couldn't bring himself to say what he thought.

"I – I'm not sure. There are some dark images. A person – presumably you – in chains with an imposing figure overshadowing you seemingly wanting to take you away. You are surrounded by birds, like they are fighting one another."

"When I first saw it, I saw the dark figure as a protector, not as a threat. Birds are often depicted as spiritual beings in the Bible. Angels and demons. You show quite a battle going on in the spirit."

"What do you think the chains mean?"

Bhaniel didn't answer for some time.

"It's okay if you don't know."

"I'm fairly certain what the chains mean. I too have been scared to be completely honest with you."

"Why? You know you can tell me anything."

"What I have to tell you will change everything between us."

"Bhaniel, you've become my life. Through you, I've seen a glimpse of what I can be. There is nowhere else on earth I want to be except for right here. With you."

"It is why the revelation is so hard to reveal to you. I don't want anything to change. The time you have been here has been so satisfying and joyful for me."

"It won't change. Bhaniel, I love you."

Bhaniel allowed those words to hang in the night air.

"The Holy Spirit has revealed to you what I couldn't tell you myself."

"If you would rather not say, then we don't need to. . ."

Bhaniel reached for Andrew's hand.

"Andrew Isaacson you have captured my heart. You are a person I never imagined would assume such a place in my life. Not because you aren't attractive, witty, and talented, but because it's just a fantasy to expect someone as wonderful as you to take an interest in a simple African orphanage worker."

Andrew got out of his chair and knelt before Bhaniel. He took her hands in his, kissed them, and looked into her eyes.

"I've chased after so many worthless things in my life. Relationships were based on selfishness and I was unable to love because I didn't trust anyone. As I've grown to know you, everything you are, is what I wish I could be myself. The spirit within you drew me in making me want to know you more. I've found a diamond in Africa, and her name is Bhaniel. There is nothing else to do but to sell everything I own to possess that diamond."

"I love you, Andrew." The emotion was almost too much for her.

"Is that what you couldn't say?"

Bhaniel just shook her head.

"No. Even so, it was so important for me to say these things before we go any further. The chains represent something affecting me for a nearly two years. Andrew, I'm sick."

"Let's get you help. Whatever the cost."

"It won't change anything at this point. The drugs we bring from America keep me going. I, I ..."

"You have HIV."

Bhaniel was stunned. She nodded her head unable to look at him.

"How did you know?"

"It wasn't hard to figure out. You are afraid of nothing, yet there was something you couldn't bring yourself to tell me."

"I suppose I am afraid of something now. I am afraid of losing you."

"Will not happen."

"How long have you known?"

"I've known for a while."

"Ever since you made the drawing?"

"Yes."

"You kept the secret well. The chains surely represent the disease. I won't be free of it while I live. If the medicine runs out, I'll die."

Andrew searched for words to say. Nothing seemed appropriate at this moment. Andrew inched closer to Bhaniel as she moved to the edge of the chair.

"It cannot and will not change anything between us. I will only be concerned with helping you stay as healthy as possible. I don't want to lose you, Miss Tretechi."

Tears streamed down her cheeks as she wrapped her arms around his neck. In some small way, she was finally free of her unseen chains. Bhaniel held him for a long, long time.

# Chapter 70

The AD Isaacson Galleries

Eugene walked to the elevator and hit the button for the parking garage. It had been a typical day with the boss. If he could turn her into a cockroach and squash her with the heel of his Johnston & Murphy's, life would take a positive turn. Another late evening. As the elevator door opened at the garage level, he noticed only a few straggling cars. And one he didn't recognize.

He fumbled his keys, trying to hit the 'unlock' button as he balanced his dinner in its environmentally conscious container made from corn. As he prepared to open his car door, he saw the reflection of two men in the window. Startled, he turned quickly, flinging his packaged dinner at them accidently.

"Mr. Burnett, could we ask you a few questions?"

Detective Tunney picked up the container as Clarence Oliver addressed Eugene.

"Mr. Burnett, this is Detective Tunney, and I'm Detective Oliver. Would you be willing to talk with us?"

"I remember you." Eugene attempted to regain his composure. "How did you get into the garage?"

"We have our ways." Actually, they went through Andrew's stuff after the 'murder' and found his access cards for the whole building.

"Not here."

"Excuse me?"

"Not here. I'll talk to you, but not here. Follow me to my house."

"Detective Tunney will ride with you. I'll follow."

It wasn't a long drive. Eugene had lived close to downtown most of his adult life. At first, it was the lure of the night life, sharing an apartment with a friend from college. Later, he purchased a condo in a building now renovated three times. Detective Tunney didn't initiate any conversation during the ride for fear Eugene would say something both officers needed to hear.

"Make yourselves at home. Do you want something to drink?"

Both men took a seat on the couch. It was certainly a couch worthy of someone in the art industry. Stylistically, it was extremely avant-garde and almost impossible to find a way to sit comfortably. It was a fair guess the art hanging on the wall was the work of stars in the art world, but most of the paintings made Bryce nervous. Eugene was in the kitchen organizing his thrown meal.

"Mr. Burnett, have you ever gone to the Dresser District?"

"Where?"

"The Dresser District. It's a rough part of town where some of the crime families have their offices."

"I've lived here almost my entire life and I can't say I am familiar with the Dresser part of town."

"You've never been to the area south of 16th Street?"

Eugene froze. He had no idea how to deal with this situation. They knew something but he wasn't sure how much. He didn't have an option. Eugene was going to have to tell the truth. At least part of it.

"Is that the Dresser District? Huh, I'll have to make a note. You know, I do remember going down there the other day. I felt lost most of the time. Once you get past Baker Street, it's like you are in a different city. Ha ha ha ha." He was laughing stupidly. "Obviously, I haven't gone down there very often, if ever. I was just given an address and told to take a package down there for Stella. I don't even know who the people were I took it to."

Clarence just looked at Eugene. "You don't know who the people were?"

"Officer, we sell art to some of the most unusual people. But you know how it is, if their money is green we'll do business."

Eugene swallowed a little too hard.

"I did talk to them for a minute or two, but it wasn't anything significant. Just small talk while I waited for them to check the package."

"The men with guns didn't concern you?"

"I didn't see any guns."

"What was in the package?"

"No idea. I was just the mail man. Don't ask, don't tell, right?"

"Have you gone back there?"

"No. I told Stella, I wouldn't do it again. She has people who carry mail for her. Let them do it."

"Why do you think she had you do it this time?"

"I ask myself that question a lot more than I'd like to admit. What do you think she's up to?"

Eugene would not be good at poker. He had guilt plastered all over his face.

"We would like you to answer your own question."

"Stella up to something? I don't think so. Nah, it's all business with her. They probably bought paintings for their offices."

The officers looked at each other.

"Thank you Mr. Burnett. We have no more questions right now."

Clarence and Bryce stood and Eugene walked them out. Once the door was shut, Eugene slid down to the floor and tried to reign in his emotions. He was in trouble. Whatever Stella was doing, he was considered an accomplice now. The police were watching the mafia offices and he walked right into the big middle of it. Stella probably knew all of this, and she was throwing him to the wolves to save herself.

"Anything good come out of that?"

"What do you think?"

"Now they know we are on to them. Doesn't strike me as a good thing."

"Think about it. He runs back to Stella and tells her we are snooping around. She gets nervous and does something stupid, or he does."

"Seems like they would get sloppy if they thought we WEREN'T watching them."

"He won't handle it well. Our visit rattled him. Now we just need to wait for him to react."

"He looked kinda nervous."

"You're being kind. He was ready to hurl."

"Think it's him instead of her?"

"Not a chance. He'd be trying to kill her, not Isaacson."

# Chapter 71

The Orphanage

Andrew woke up with a start and a sharp intake of air. He wasn't sure, but it felt like he woke up just as the swirling water of his dreams was about to overtake him. Andrew was going to have to catch his breath before he got out of bed. Njin was standing at the side of Andrew's bed, his eyes just cresting the top of the mattress. Andrew's violent emergence from slumber looked silly to him and it made him giggle. Andrew rolled over to the edge of the bed and stared into Njin's eyes.
"Boo."
Njin wanted to run but he stayed. He shook with excitement at the possibility Andrew would grab him and tickle him. Andrew started to fake a stretch and then lunged for Njin. He squealed as he tried to escape all the while glad Andrew caught him. After a good solid tickle, he was able to break free and go out of the room hollering and laughing.
Andrew changed his shorts and put on a dirty shirt so he could help with breakfast. Several fruits were in season and Andrew was starting to acquire a taste for the cornbread-like cake (or was it bread?) they ate with every meal. He served most of the kids, those who were eating at the moment, then sat down to eat himself. Lala plopped down across the table from him without saying anything.
"Good morning, sunshine!"
Nothing.
"Are we playing a game? Is this a stare game?"
Andrew started staring back. He didn't last long.
"I'm ready."
"Ready for what?"
"I'm ready for you to draw my picture."
"I drew you just the other day."

"That's not what I mean."

"Enlighten me."

She shot him a confused look. Too big a word in English.

"Tell me what you mean."

"One of your prophetic pictures."

"What if I draw something you don't like?"

"Makes no difference." Lala looked down belying the fact she had considered this possibility, but was going all in. Andrew had just confirmed her fears a negative future was a real danger.

"Isn't there always a way for a person to avoid the bad things?"

"Yes. I have done some drawings and paintings showing some awful events. Happily, they never happened because someone involved changed their ways."

"I believe it. Miss B has taught us God will not smite us if we turn to him."

"Smite?"

"I'm not sure, but it sounds bad. Do you know anything about the prophets in the Bible?"

"Not really. Should I?"

"Aren't you one yourself? Maybe you can learn something from them."

"Possibly. I've always done my own thing. I didn't know why."

"It's a gift from God. He'll tell you why."

Lala had 'the gift' also. She saw things so clearly and stated them as a matter of fact.

"I'm not sure you need me to create a prophetic drawing for you. I think you already know yourself."

"Not until I met you."

"Hmmm?"

"Older people would get angry when I made comments. Even when I said something good, they often told me to go away. Now I spend my time with the younger kids. They don't mind me saying things to them. When you came and I saw your drawings, I realized we were a lot alike. Except I don't draw."

"It's what I do."

"I know, I'm a talker."

"Agreed. Don't move, I have something for you."

Andrew went to his room and shuffled through some drawings. He returned with a charcoal drawing on one of his bigger sheets of paper. As he laid it out on the table before Lala, her eyes widened as she studied each feature. Other kids gathered around and joined the theater. Several asked questions, but Lala was lost in the moment. She was transfixed on the central figure. It was a young woman charging up a hill with a two-edged sword in her hand and a child in her arms. She was leading people to battle, but it was as if she was healing people as she went. Interestingly, there was a young girl in front of her and Lala was stepping in her footprints.

Lala looked at Andrew.

"When did you do this?"

"A couple of weeks ago."

"Can I keep it?"

"Sure. Do you see yourself?"

"Yes. I've seen myself in this way, at least parts of it, many times. You are in touch with the Holy Spirit." Lala looked it over and thought a minute. "Have you ever been wrong?"

Andrew considered the question.

"Not really wrong, but some show things yet to come."

"See, you are a prophet."

"I'm not sure there is a need for a prophet today."

"Of course there is. Otherwise, God would not have made you for this moment in history."

"Well said, Prophet."

"Where are the paintings you are talking about?"

"Back in America. At my house. At least it used to be my house."

"Who's is it now?"

"I don't know. My life in America is kind of over."

"Over? Someone is afraid you are going to come back. Why else would they come over here to kill you? Are you going back?"

"I hadn't plan to. You think I should?"

"You need to go back and claim what is rightfully yours. There are people depending on you."

Andrew was dumbfounded. Was this really a teenage girl? She was as fearless as anyone he'd ever met.

"Don't you want me to stay? I thought there were people depending on me here."

"I want you to come back after you take care of your business. And while you're there, find the paintings. I want to see them."

"What if YOU'RE wrong, Prophet?"

"Am I? What does your heart say?"

Andrew laughed out loud. Giggled really. He felt completely exposed, but was it time to go to America? His heart was telling him Lala's words had merit.

"You've given me plenty to think about."

"Hurry back." Lala got up and walked out.

Andrew knew he'd have to go back to America sometime. He was wrestling with the idea as he battled for the soccer ball against three decidedly more athletic youngsters. How could he leave everyone? How could he leave Bhaniel? What if something horrible happened and Stella finally got to him? Andrew's willingness to run from danger allowed for a life-changing adventure in this African country, but the dark side remained. He feared confronting an unchecked evil.

Lala was right. So was the higher power she was speaking for. He had to go take care of his business. Men don't run from their responsibilities, and no one but he could do what he had to do.

Andrew got the ball on the run and made a nifty move around Kalil and kicked it in the net. The kids stopped to take the scene in. No one had seen Andrew's soccer skills on display until now. He had been the designated weak player everyone wanted on the opposing team. The symbolism was strong. It was time for Andrew to toe the line.

Bhaniel looked at him to see if he was joking. "You're serious."

"Yes."

"I thought you had no desire to go back. What is motivating you to do it now?"

"Until recently, I had only thought of myself. For me, it made sense to stay away. There was no reason to go back to America. I don't have an emotional tie to my former life. But someone helped me see there are people who may be suffering as long as I allow the people who want me dead to run free. The only person who can put an end to these things is me."

"It sounds as though you had a soul searching conversation. Lala?"

"Yeah."

"She definitely has a gift. Do you want to go sooner or later?"

"The situation is not going to get better with time. I should leave at the first opportunity."

"How long will you be gone?"

"Only as long as necessary to get Stella arrested and reestablish the company."

"It sounds like a long time. I don't want to think about you being gone for so long."

"Maybe we don't have to be apart the whole time."

Bhaniel furrowed her brow into a question and waited on Andrew to explain.

"Will you go with me?"

"Oh, Andrew. I can't, not again."

"Having you there with me is my main desire, but I also want you to see a doctor. To make sure your medication is the best it can be."

"The same thing drawing you back to America is what compels me to stay here. I also have people who need me to be here for them. The kids already are without Theresa. If we both leave… I just cannot do that to the kids. These are orphans, abandonment is their greatest fear."

"You are making me want to stay."

"I know you would if the need to go back was not so great. God is leading you back to America, so you must go."

"How can we get you the help you need?"

"All they will do is analyze my blood. Take some of my blood and let's see what they say. If you can, bring some of the right drugs back with you."

Andrew liked the idea, but hated it also. He wanted her to go with him.

"Okay. That might work. Why am I not excited?"

Bhaniel put her arms around him.

"Because you will miss me."

Andrew smiled. "True, and you flirting with me is making it worse."

She kissed his cheek.

"I'll be right here, waiting on you."

Bhaniel's dark brown eyes pulled Andrew in and he began to lose his balance. He held on to her all the more.

"Miss B!"

The disco ball quit spinning and the slow dance was over. The kids were looking for Bhaniel.

"Miss B! Are we going to have class today?"

"Yes, yes. Every day. Get the kids together and we will begin shortly."

"My budding math scientists await."

Andrew grabbed one more hug and kissed her back.

"I wish my math teacher had been as beautiful as you."

Bhaniel gave him a sideways look as she sashayed out of the room.

The enormity of the task ahead of him drove Andrew to a solitary place. He needed time to think and maybe even pray. As much as he had grown to respect God and how He worked through Bhaniel, Lala and the others, Andrew rarely sought a conversation with the Almighty himself. His desire to interact with God had increased during his stay in Africa, but like a small child, Andrew feared the unknown and lacked faith to believe God would be waiting on him. His current need was outweighing his inhibitions. He made his way to the hilltop. The 360 degree view and limited access gave it just the right amount of loneliness.

"God in heaven. I'm a man who has nothing left, yet I feel richer now than ever before. You have made yourself known to me in so many ways, and you have allowed me to begin to know myself. It would be satisfying to leave my former life behind and never go back. But as you have impressed on me through Lala's words, there are people who need me to act. Would you please give me the courage to set things right and restore justice and peace? I believe I am willing to remain in America until everything is complete and even lay down my life if it is necessary, but my heart will forever be here in Africa. I've drawn so much strength from Bhaniel and the others. I am afraid of being weak when I am away from them. Help me know your presence is with me wherever I go."

Andrew spent the remainder of the day on the hilltop. When he didn't come to dinner, a search was conducted. Aleefa saw him on the hill and sounded the all clear. The kids kept an eye on him throughout the evening to make sure he stayed put and wasn't in danger. As the sun set in the west, Kieko brought a stick to him for protection. Andrew had scarcely noticed him.

He was engrossed in thoughts of returning to America. Andrew felt as though he had evolved into a completely different person from the escaping refugee who ran for his life not so long ago. He wondered if he had changed so much no one would recognize him. The changes had been mostly on the inside, but he rarely even looked at a mirror now. He looked like a shipwreck castaway for all he knew. He was thinner and his skin was tanned, almost leathery. Actually, the anonymity might work to his advantage depending on how creative he got announcing his return. Stella deserved a bit of theater anyway.

As everyone arose in the morning, Andrew was already packing. Not that he had a lot of gear to pack, but the ritual of packing was the universal sign of 'it's time to go'. The kids got the hint and made ready their informal goodbye ceremony. The trip awaiting him was a monumental black hole mystery. All he knew was he had some money, relatively clean clothing, a passport, and a will to get there. And the killer's phone. This was evidence which should be quite valuable to the detectives.

Andrew went through the whole of the citizenry at the home hugging and saying parting words. It was a receiving line of sorts, with lots of well wishes, a few tears and a tug on his heart. Bhaniel was at the end of the line.

"There is a large group of us who are going to walk you to the river."

"Okay, good. Well, I'm ready. Shall we?"

"Yes. Do you have my blood?"

"I do. Two vials."

Bhaniel surveyed his luggage. "Is the one bag all you are taking?"

"This is every earthly thing I possess." Andrew held it out for the world to consider.

"No one would know how rich you are."

"In things money can't buy, my Dear."

"Well said."

Her smile had such a satisfied air to it. Yet the sadness crept through at the thought of him gone.

The walk to the river was much too short. Even the ferry was on time as everyone gathered close. The boys couldn't stand it and had already gotten in to the water up to their necks. Andrew and Bhaniel embraced like there were no other people about.

"Hurry back to me Mr. Isaacson."

"As fast as I can."

His family stood and watched as he crossed the river. The numbers eroded until he could only make out a lone figure at the river's edge. She was going to stay there until he went out of sight. He willed himself to get into Drago's bike and the river faded from view.

"Is the bus on time today, Drago?"

"Oh yes. Always." His optimism was refreshing. "Are you going to be in town all day, Mr. Isaacson?"

"I'm leaving the country for a few weeks." Drago looked around at him.

"We will miss you, sir. You're not going through Kinshasa are you?"

"I am."

"Be very careful, sir. The city is not safe since the killing of the president. Soldiers are not to be trusted. A man like yourself should cover his head and look at no one." Drago knew he could be kidnapped because he was a 'rich' European or American.

"I will, thanks. Drago?"

"Yes, sir."

"Would you do me a favor? Would you check in on Miss Tretechi occasionally to see if she is okay?"

"You can count on me, sir. Miss B means a lot to us here in Bandundu."

"Thank you, Drago. I'll see you soon."

Andrew got out at the bus depot, paid Drago handsomely, and waved goodbye to the last of the familiar faces in his adopted home.

Andrew raised his head as high has he could just in case it increased his chances of snagging a vein of fresh air moving through the upper reaches of the bus interior. The riders were elbow to elbow. The body odor hovering in the cabin mixed with the dust and adhered to Andrew's skin.

None of the officials at this road checkpoint appeared to be anxious to allow the bus to continue on its journey. Neither did any appear to know what they were doing. Their authority was bestowed on them by the simple fact their guns had more ammunition than the previous checkpoint officials. The driver walked the aisle collecting extortion funds, and Andrew calculated how much cash he could part with and still get an airline ticket.

"Give."

The driver shook his hat at Andrew's row. There were a few coins and wadded bills in the hat. Andrew placed forty dollars U.S. in the hat. The driver looked at the neat bills and looked at Andrew.

"Thank you."

The driver was going to keep the dollars and substitute local currency. It was more valuable than the Congolese franc and he was doing Andrew a favor. If the officials/soldiers found out an American was on the bus, his life might be in danger. Twenty minutes of demonstrative arguing later, the officials motioned for the bus to resume its progress toward Kinshasa. Andrew was hopeful for no more checkpoints even though he was learning to endure the painfully slow pace of things in this country, worse now due to the uprising. As evening came upon them, Kinshasa appeared in the distance. Although military vehicles raced by the bus several times on the pitted dirt road, there were no more stops until they reached the bus terminal. The airport was reasonably close, but Andrew took local transportation to reduce his exposure on the streets.

"You can make it if you run. I'll call ahead and ask them to hold the door open."

Andrew took off. He had endured a four hour bus ride, body searches at the entrance to the airport bordering on molestation, and an extended assessment of his passport because of a suspect visa. But now, he had a ticket on an international flight leaving in ten minutes. The weight loss and daily physical activity made him fleet of foot, at least more agile than his previous self. Gate 8 was close, but he was going to need some accommodation from the airline crew to sneak on the plane in time.

"I'm Andrew Isaacson. Here's my ticket."

The airline worker at the receiving desk was still on the phone with the ticketing official. As Andrew sprinted up to the desk, she motioned to her coworker who had turned the key on the door to the tarmac to reopen the door for the last passenger. Andrew slowed his pace and made his way to the stairs leading up to the Boeing 737. He was feeling sorry for the passengers who would ride next to him. His personal hygiene had taken a hit from the perils of travel up to this point. Oh well, it was only an eight hour flight to Manaus, Brazil.

The rumble down the runway and the leap into the air confirmed he was reentering his former life. Even if events fell in his favor, the chances were good he would not find his way back to Africa soon. The opportunity to reorganize his life in the States and create an option to return one day appealed to him. But, if it was only to tidy things up and turn the light out before leaving America forever, he was peaceful with that scenario also. Two meals, four hours of sleep, an odd movie comprised mostly of computer graphics, and the jet was on final approach. After a short layover in Brazil, Andrew was headed to Georgia. By the time he was to deplane in Atlanta, his pockets would be nearly empty.

"Sir?" The flight attendant was nudging Andrew. "Sir?"
Andrew opened one eye and through the blur saw he was the last one on the plane.
"Sir, we've arrived in Atlanta. Are you getting off here?"
Andrew grunted an answer and gathered his things. For some reason, he had absolutely conked out during the final leg. He stepped into the terminal and felt completely anonymous. Not one soul, hopefully, would be expecting him to be in this place at this time. Actually, it would be nice if Mitch were here to greet him. And maybe Fanny. Yeah, Fanny. He'd definitely have to track her down while he was in country.
First things first. He'd better head over to the police department and get an update and get his bearings. What was happening from their point of view would have a decided impact on how he proceeded on nearly all fronts. Andrew had just enough money to buy some lunch for the laboring civil servants.

# Chapter 72

Police Headquarters

At a little after eleven a.m., Andrew walked into the detectives' work area with paper bags full of sandwiches. He was accompanied by a uniformed officer who was sort of in on the ruse. Andrew positioned himself close to Detective Oliver and Tunney's desks.

"I've got a lunch order for the Atlanta Police Department, Detective Division."

All ten plain clothes officers turned to look. Free food would not be turned away no matter where it came from. They just needed to find a food taster for safety's sake. Slowly they gathered around to see what was for lunch.

"Nice, sandwiches from South Side Deli."

Three of the officers dug in immediately, and the others waited to find out more about who had financed the party.

Clarence looked the delivery man over.

"So what's the occasion? Who sent it?"

"Oh." Andrew fished around for the note. "He wanted me to read this note."

> Detectives, in honor of your hard work and tireless efforts
> to catch the people trying to kill me, please have lunch on me.
> Andrew Isaacson.

"Andrew Isaacson?! He's in Africa."

"Believe it or not, he's back."

Oliver and Tunney looked at each other.

"Where is he? He was supposed to contact us when he came back."

"He's close. I'll go get him."

Andrew walked out of the room and into the hallway. The detectives looked at the uniformed officer and he just shrugged his shoulders. Andrew walked back into the office area alone.

"Where is he?"

"Hello Detectives." Andrew went to shake their hands.

"What the...? Isaacson, is that you? You gotta be kidding me."

All of the detectives were gathered around. Some were entertained, others really didn't know what was going on. Tunney and Oliver rose to get a better look.

"Isaacson, I don't even recognize you. You're a completely different person."

"In more ways than one, Detective."

"Welcome back. Decided to get back to the real world, huh?"

"My plan is to stay for just a short while, but it was time to close the book on some things."

"You may wish you had stayed in Africa. Stella is a piece of work."

"She's why I came back. There are several people who are affected by what she's done and it was time to put an end to it. Running away seemed like a good idea at the time, but it wasn't solving the problem."

"Let's talk in here." Detective Tunney led them to a private office.

"We're going to have to watch your back while you're here. Stella has made some dangerous friends and we think the plan was to track you down and kill you in Africa."

"Funny you should mention it. I had a visitor. After he came, I knew my time at the orphanage was limited."

"A visitor? You mean a hitman? Holy cow, Isaacson. You are unbelievable. How did you avoid this one?"

"When he came, we thought he was a social worker for the United Nations. Late one evening, he and I were alone talking when he confessed he had come to kill me. He was taking his time playing the game. Maybe he was a little overconfident. Before he could finish the job, one of the boys at the home who is a great hunter, saw him make his move, killed him with a javelin and saved my life."

"You're one of those anointed people. You're indestructible."

"Only as long as God desires it. Do you know how Stella found out where I was?"

"Yes. Unfortunately, the guy you met in Africa was the THIRD hired killer. The second one found out where you were, but we ended him on a country road here in Georgia. Before we could get to him, he messed up your friend Mitch pretty good."

Andrew's heart went into his throat.

"Huh? What happened?"

The detectives detailed the mechanic's efforts and how he came about the information. They went to great lengths to tell Andrew the heights of Mitch's bravery and how he never gave in to the torture.

"Where is he? I need to see him."

"He's in a hospice facility right now. He's still under police protection, but it may not be safe."

"What if I wore a disguise? I wouldn't have to do much. You guys didn't recognize me in regular clothes. I could go with you."

Andrew needed to change the subject.

"So what has Stella been up to?"

"Nothing good. You have been very lucrative as a dead artist though. It's amazing how much 'lost' work has been found and sold since you left. If she hasn't hidden the money in Switzerland, you are going to be a rich guy again when this is all over."

"Great. Chasing money is what got me in trouble in the first place."

"I don't know what your plans are, but we would advise against meeting with Stella."

"That's exactly what I'm going to do. And you're going to be there. Well, maybe via wireless mike. I plan to put her on the spot and get a confession out of her. If she doesn't kill me with her bare hands, then I can enjoy watching you take her to jail."

"Why does this sound like a really bad idea? I need to remind you we can't help you do something illegal."

"Everything will be completely above board. You will only need to be there to escort her to jail. Do you know if I can get into my house?"

"Yeah, we have the keys. It may be in tough shape though."

"Not a problem. I just need a few things. When can we go to the hospice?"

"Can you occupy yourself until four or five? We have to meet with the Captain this afternoon."

"Sure. I'll walk around town and be a tourist."

The fact Mitch was in a hospice care facility made Andrew cringe. It sounded like he was waiting to die.

"Why is he here?"

"The people at the hospital said they've done all they can. He just needs to heal now. This place is kinda nice actually."

The detectives shepherded Andrew past the front desk and led him down the hall. Andrew eased up a little. It really was nice, like Grandma's house. Very comfortable with a hint of nursing home. Casually dressed workers patrolled the hallway.

"Here." Detective Oliver pointed to the door for room twenty three.

"We'll let you go in by yourself. Try not to be too surprised. The bad guy did his work well. The doctors say he could recover nearly all his motor skills, but it will take some time."

Andrew tensed up a little. He took a deep breath and pushed the door open. It was dim in the room. The curtains were drawn and the lights off. Only a crease of sunlight pushed around the edge of the drapes. Mitch was sleeping. His arms were completely bandaged and set at odd angles away from his body. Both feet were in padded boots, and it looked as though his trunk was suspended over the bed.

Andrew couldn't move. He stood in the dark and stared at his friend. Andrew fought the urge to make any sense of how he and his friend had come to this moment in time. In the end, it was just a cascade of helplessness and guilt. He had been overseas experiencing life changing events while Mitch had taken a sledge hammer for him. He turned to leave, almost grateful he didn't have to face him yet.

"Hello? Someone in here?"

"Hi Mitch."

Mitch turned his head slightly and peered into the shadows.

"Who is it? You sound familiar."

"It's me Mitch. Andrew." He moved closer to the bed so that Mitch could see him.

"Andrew?" Mitch had trouble catching his breath. "Andrew? Is it really you?" A tear formed in his eyes.

"Yeah, Mitch."

Mitch laid his head back on the pillow and closed his eyes. The tears fell down the sides of his face as he smiled.

"You made it."

"It was meant to be I think."

"I thought they would find you and… get you."

Andrew tried to lighten it up a little.

"What? Come on. Who are you talkin to? They came after me and I went medieval."

Mitch was almost laughing.

"Like I said, I was sure you were done for."

"Ha. Truth, if it hadn't been for Aleefa and his spear, I would have been all done."

Andrew told the whole story getting more dramatic as he went.

"Wow. I'm sincerely impressed. You are Superman."

"No, no. Remember what I said. Aleefa saved me. Anyway, you're the real Superman. The detectives told me what happened."

"He got what he wanted out of me."

"You look at it that way. I see someone who was ready to die to protect me. Brother, I'll never be able to repay you for what you did. Thank you. I know it sounds kind of hollow. So does 'I'm sorry', but it's all I got right now."

"Come on. It looks bad, but I'll be good as new in no time. By the way, I hardly recognize you. Africa agrees with you… unless you have a disease."

"No disease. I'm getting a lot of that. I walked right up to the detectives and they didn't know who I was."

"Good. Don't tell anyone you're here. It's safer that way."

"Does anyone know you're here?" Andrew couldn't say her name.

"You mean Stella? No. They are giving me the Andrew treatment. I'm off the grid. No one knows I'm here unless they have been tailing the detectives."

"Awesome. Are they getting you up?"

"Not really. The feet are pretty messed up and my bum is burned. They said it will be a couple of months before I can move around. I can see okay now and I've been moving my fingers some. I'm ready to get up and out of here so I can go see her. Show her she couldn't kill me."

"You have no doubt it's her?"

Mitch tried to form a sarcastic look on his face. "Are we going to have this conversation again? You know she had Harvey killed."

"I do now, but why?"

"Because she's insane. Probably thought it would sidetrack the company shutdown. I guess it did for a while. Look at me. She's capable of anything. You need to consider carefully what you are going to do while you're here. If you are going to confront her, she will snap. So be ready."

Thinking of Harvey and looking at Mitch was almost too much to bear. "I've got to end this. I need to stir her up so she will confess somehow."

"Understood. Just bring some help."

"I intend to my friend. I intend to."

Andrew left Mitch to rest with a plan to return often.

"Hey, guys. Do we have time to go by my house?" Andrew asked the detectives on the way to the car.

"Planning on it. You're the diva today. We'll do what you want to do."

"That's the last thing before heading to the hotel."

It was a short drive to the house. Andrew looked out the window on the way like he hadn't been home in years.

"Bryce, let's go around back just so we don't draw any attention." Clarence was being careful.

Andrew didn't think the house looked too bad. A little overgrown was all. The car wheeled around the house and stopped next to the back door.

"Here, put this over your head." Clarence tossed him an overcoat. "I don't want anyone seeing your face."

Lucky for them, it was almost dark as well. Once inside the house, the detectives made a quick safety sweep with guns out. They didn't turn on any lights, so they only went as fast as their flashlights would allow.

"Is the electricity off?"

"Just since the first of the month."

"No matter. I can find my way around in the dark. I've got to go upstairs for a minute."

"It's your house, Ace."

"Not a crime scene any longer?"

"Nope. But nothing is cleaned up from the night you were attacked. Will the blood bother you?"

"Not anymore. You should see the pictures we took of me as a dead guy. Speaking of blood, I have some blood I need analyzed. Would there be anyone in the department who could help me?"

"Whose blood is it?"

"Bhaniel Tretechi. She has HIV and I need to find out what drugs to get for her."

"Might be best to visit the CDC. At least to start with."

"Okay, will do."

Andrew went upstairs to his bedroom. It looked like he slept in the bed the night before.

Is this how I used to live? he said to himself as he looked around. The safe was hidden so well, even the crime scene detectives didn't find it. Andrew had to think for a minute to remember the combination, but inside it was still full of money and sundries. A new stack of currency would come in handy for what he had in mind. Andrew rifled through his closet for some fresh clothes to take with him. All of it was going to hang on him because of the lost weight.

"Can we go out to the studio before we leave?"

"Put the coat on."

The studio looked untouched. It never fostered much interest since everything happened in the house. There was the painting he had told Lala about. Andrew located three or four paintings he wanted to take with him. He found a sharp knife, cut around the edges of the wooden stretchers, rolled up the canvases, and put them in a plastic travel tube.

"Ready to go, detectives. Thanks for helping me out."

"Where to?"

"The hotel, I'm worn out. Can I buy you guys' dinner? It's the least I could do."

"You're right. We accept."

\*\*\*

Before Andrew turned in for the night, he made one phone call.

"Director Hizanga? It's Andrew Isaacson. I'm back in America. Atlanta actually."

"Andrew? Andrew! Andrew, welcome back. It's great to hear from you." The director rustled around from his position on the couch where he'd been napping. "You're home? Did you come alone?"

"Yes, but everyone is fine at the home. I tried to get Bhaniel to come with me, but she couldn't leave the kids."

"That's our girl." He laughed. "What has brought you back to the States?"

"I have some personal issues requiring attention."

"Can we meet soon? I would like to spend some time with you. I'm sure you have many stories to tell."

"Yes, I would love to." Andrew wondered if they would believe half the stories he carried with him. "Let's meet at the end of the week."

"Where are you staying?"

"Just an old nameless hotel." Andrew didn't want to give him the name.

"Really? Andrew, please check out tomorrow and stay with us the remainder of your time here."

"Thanks, Director. I'll stay there when I come to see you."

"I would like that."

"Uh, Director? Would you mind not telling anyone I'm back?"

His request caught the director off guard. "Sure. Not a word. Andrew, is everything all right?"

"Yes, I apologize for being mysterious, I'll explain when we meet. I would tell you right now over the phone, but it will be better to talk about it in person. It will make sense, I promise."

The director was confused and concerned, but agreed to Andrew's request. "Until then. Andrew, I'm glad you're home."

Andrew spent the next couple of days getting reacquainted with Atlanta. He rode public transportation and went by Mitch's gallery as well as his own business. He wore his everyday garb from Africa which made him nearly invisible to passersby. Most bustling citizens assumed he was homeless or a close variation. This allowed him to exist with very few people making eye contact. Andrew stayed on the bus and rode by his offices twice before getting off. It was mostly the fear of being noticed, but it also gave him time to study the place. He had a great desire to go in and walk around. That would come in due time. He loitered near the parking garage most of the afternoon, albeit in the Starbucks across the street waiting on Stella to drive out and away. He wasn't sure why exactly, but just seeing her in person felt as though it would help him put it all into perspective. Battling the specter of Stella made her bigger than life in his mind, and caused him to question his ability to overcome her. Seeing her as a human again reminded Andrew she was no more than a scared, self-absorbed, volatile individual with her world getting ready to close around her.

Thanks to the detectives, Andrew had his access fobs for the building. It was tempting to shuffle in unnoticed. If he did go in, he'd have to form a plan. A full frontal assault was flawed. The security system would show it was his own access key being used to gain entry so the element of surprise would be hindered. The plan he was concocting required him to get in at least for a short time though.

\*\*\*

"So that was when I knew I needed to return to the States and confront Stella. I didn't want to come, but here I am."

Director Hizanga was stunned. He just stared at Andrew hoping – no, fearful – Andrew would tell him more incredible stories. The whole account took Andrew over an hour to tell. He tried not to dramatize too much this time.

"Andrew, I'm fascinated and concerned at the same time. You were wise to come back. The villainy this woman has performed defies comprehension. It has put the kids and workers in more danger. As if they needed more danger."

"What do you know about the rebellion? The last we heard, the soldiers had gone to the west coast."

"The best information we have is a new coalition within Zuberi's secondary command have taken control of the army. So far, it appears to be a stalemate between them and the rebels. Concerns are, the rebels are getting additional fighters from other countries - mercenaries who have been promised riches for their help. Some say Islamic factions are beginning to pour into the country. Over the last several years, any time an African country has had a leadership vacuum, the Islamists make their play. They are for no one, fighting both the government troops and the rebels."

"Is it safe for Bhaniel and the people at the home?"

"Only God knows. We are prepared to evacuate them if the conflict moves back into their area."

"Should we bring some of them here to America?"

"What did you have in mind?"

"Some of the kids could come here and attend college. The prospects for the kids when they are old enough to attend university in country are slim especially with the uprising."

"Only one, maybe two, kids have gone on to college from the DRC home. It would be a dream come true."

"If we could get them here, I know someone who has finances to pay for their education and even a place for them to stay."

"Excellent! Who is it?"

"Me."

"Andrew you are truly a Godsend, but I thought you were bankrupt."

"Not exactly. My company continues to do well, but Stella is in control. In the perfect world, I will be able to put Stella in jail, regain control of the company, and we can move forward with the plan."

"First things first. How will you put an end to Stella? Can't you just have the police arrest her?"

"Yes and no. The police have been tracking her for months, but they haven't gathered enough evidence showing her as the decision maker and financier. That's why I'm back. To expose her."

"What's your plan?"

"It's very simple, really…."

Andrew laid out his plan for the director though it sounded very complicated to him.

"So how is Theresa?"

"Doing very well. They did the blood work on her and it came up negative for HIV."

"Wonderful. Is she planning on going back?"

"Yes. It won't be long. In fact, someone was checking out flights for her today."

"Good for her. Bhaniel will be pleased."

# Chapter 73

The Orphanage

"Miss B, is the corn ready to harvest?"

Meriba looked around the corner into the kitchen. Bhaniel was helping Ndulue stack the grain sacks.

"I don't think so. We looked at some yesterday and it needed another week."

Meriba whispered something to a cohort in the hallway out of sight. There was a short commotion and then running.

"Meriba, what are you doing?"

"Nothing, Miss B. Why?"

Somebody ran out the door. "You're not picking corn yet are you?"

"What if there was a bushel of corn already picked?"

"Meriba! Don't pick the corn yet. You and whoever was running out the door, quit picking corn! Go tell them right now."

"Yes Miss B." And Meriba was out the door in a flash.

"Those kids. I've told them over and over again to wait. I hope they are this excited about harvesting when it is time. Ndulue, let's go check on them to see what they are doing."

Bhaniel and Ndulue had been friends for several years. Ndulue was a native woman with grown children. She had lived at the home since her husband died three years ago. Bhaniel and Ndulue didn't walk fast to the garden area. The heat was stifling today and nothing was going to occur quickly. The stand of corn was nearly an acre now. It was almost too much to care for, not to mention hauling water from the river to water it, but the food source was so needed. Bhaniel walked to the edge of the field and called to the girls.

"Meriba, are you out here?"

Bhaniel looked down the row and spotted a sack full of not yet mature ears of corn. She walked into the maze of corn and bent low to pick up the sack. No kids were anywhere to be found.

"Bhaniel Tretechi. It is good to see you again."

The man's voice startled Bhaniel. Ndulue stood motionless beside her. Men were moving through the stalks of corn toward the women. All of them had guns and most were wearing uniforms.

Lieutenant Raswa was back.

# Chapter 74

Atlanta

It took Andrew three weeks to get everything organized. The extra time was useful on several fronts, but it primarily allowed him to know Stella and Eugene's schedules almost to the minute. He followed them to their homes and put electronic trackers on their cars. He built a detailed dossier on the other employees which allowed him to build an access matrix and finalize his plan.

Andrew's center of operations and 'home' was a small apartment close to the business. He needed to be within walking distance, but he had to keep an eye out for familiar faces. This gave him more flexibility for the odd times he would be in the AD Isaacson building.

When he wasn't spying, Andrew painted. The primary pieces, which were completed already, would be kids from the orphanage and some of the drawings of Bhaniel. The new paintings included interesting versions of Andrew's death photos and other scenes only he could produce. The time spent preparing also extended his beard and hair for further camouflage. Thrift stores provided all the clothing he would need. There were a number of 'delivery man' uniforms for him to repurpose.

Next step was to get into the building and bug Stella's office, copy her agenda for the next several weeks, and review security tapes.

"Excuse me. Hi, I am here to do some maintenance on the security system. I'm with OpTech."

Andrew showed the AD Isaacson receptionist his ID badge. He didn't recognize the young worker and she didn't recognize him. New employees were a plus. She checked her agenda and noted the OpTech appointment. "Sign in here please."

The receptionist shoved the log book toward him. What she didn't know was Andrew had made the appointment for the company.

"What floor will you be working on?"

"Three and four."

She prepared his Visitor access as he signed his name. While she was distracted, he also signed his name on the 'sign out' side of the book with his special pen from inside his shirtsleeve. It would show up in an hour or so.

Andrew had timed his entrance based on the receptionist's quitting time. She was leaving in forty-five minutes and a temp would take her place for the rest of the evening. By then, the log book would show the OpTech technician had signed out, and Andrew would become a ghost. First thing to do was get to the security room and disable the current day recordings, erasing Andrew's presence. He would replace it with a file from several weeks prior to cover his tracks.

Andrew didn't make eye contact with anyone, but his large awkward glasses and slouching gait allowed him to move freely in the hallways. Once he performed the security file exchange, Andrew would need to hide until the proper time. The best spot to wait was the canvas/framing room. There was an electrical service closet tucked into the back wall most people didn't even know existed. He hoped the key was still in the same place.

The evening receptionist said her usual goodbyes and double checked the log book. Since all the visitors had been accounted for, she closed it, turned off the primary lights and walked out. As planned, the log book showed the OpTech worker had left hours ago.

Andrew snapped awake. He had dozed off in the darkness of the closet against his best intentions. He still had twenty minutes until the target hour so no harm done. It was going to take some time for the feeling to come back in his left leg though.

After one more check of the timing chart, Andrew cracked the door open and tip toed down the hallway. All his senses were on hyper alert. He was straining so hard to listen for any sound of human activity, his eyes hurt.

He put on his cotton gloves as he reached the executive offices. Silently, he padded across the entry and pushed Stella's door open. Her blinds were open, but Andrew stayed in the shadows against the wall.

He didn't have to look long for Stella's schedule. Andrew scanned it for shows coming soon. The best option was a joint show with three artists he didn't recognize. He took pictures of each page and put it back. The microphone was taped to the underside of Stella's desk, and a small camera was attached to the security camera in the corner of the room.

Since everything was going so well, Andrew decided to stay a minute or two longer and scan the room for evidence. He knew of two hiding spots favored by Stella. The safe was obvious, but Stella had one other secret place she didn't realize Andrew knew of. He checked the safe, the combination was always the same, but it contained only a small amount of money and two rings. The secret spot was a hollow place behind a false wall in the built-in shelves. This was where Stella hid the contracts with two movie producers for art work in a feature film Andrew only learned of after the fact.

Andrew moved the nick knacks and juggled the wood panel. It moved with relative ease and he shined his pen light into the space. Bingo. The only item in the space was a nondescript flip phone. He turned it on hoping there was a little battery life left. The battery icon was blinking, but it had enough life to allow Andrew to scroll through the contents. He checked the call history and wrote down the numbers. The picture file was final piece of the puzzle. Even though the photos were sort of grainy due to the age of the phone, it was clear to see Stella had taken pictures of the photographs of "dead" Andrew. Most of them showed her hand holding the prints as she snapped the pictures with her other hand. Andrew texted the pictures to his cell phone and placed Stella's back in the secret cubby hole. He contemplated taking it with him, but decided against it. If everything went as planned, he would need the phone to be there at the appropriate time. The final task for the evening was to relocate the art pieces meant for the upcoming show. Studio Three had the canvases he was looking for. Thirty six pieces were tagged with information coinciding with Stella's schedule. One third of the items were paintings created by Francisco Ramirez. Average at best. He would not have approved of including him in the show because he wasn't ready yet. He can wait for another show. Andrew didn't feel like stealing the paintings, but he needed them to disappear temporarily. He removed the canvases from the frames and rolled them up. The frames were taken to the framing room, and he headed to his old office.

He stood at the door for a minute soaking in the memories. Unfortunately, there were enough bad memories to kill his desire to come back to the old life. Sentiment was a waste of time. Even so, there were some cool collectibles he wished he could take with him. But it was dangerous, he couldn't change anything for fear of being discovered. Andrew moved a portion of the drop ceiling he'd always hated, and placed the art work above and out of sight. Scanning for any evidence that betrayed the hiding place, Andrew was happy with himself. Maybe it was the perfect crime. Andrew was tired and ready to leave. His luck was surely running thin too. He looked at his watch. The window of opportunity was closing in thirty-five minutes. Andrew double checked the security camera feed, and went down to the parking garage and slid out the back door near the stairway. The logo on the jacket came off, and Andrew became just another pedestrian.

# Chapter 75

The Orphanage

"What do you want?"

"Your facility is just what we need, Miss Tretechi. I suggest you gather your workers and have them begin the preparations. I and my men are going to stay here for the time being."

Bhaniel just looked at the Lieutenant.

"Miss Tretechi, we have come too far and many are injured. I am not going to quarrel with you on this. Do as I say!"

The lieutenant walked, sort of limped, by Bhaniel and was followed by many men. Several were bleeding with makeshift bandages. All of them appeared to be hungry and weak.

Bhaniel looked at Ndulue, gathered the corn the kids had picked, and turned toward the home. The kids had instinctively run to their hiding places and the workers were scattered about. Bhaniel hollered at them to come out and attend the soldiers. Others went to the kitchen to prepare a meal.

Bhaniel opened the medicine closet and pulled out the painkilling drugs and antibiotics. She would have to appeal to Andrew to bring back a new supply. The lieutenant demanded Bhaniel attend to him. His injuries were minor except for the infection growing from a cut on his arm.

"Madame, you are a servant of your country," he said as he watched her tend to his wounds.

It was hard for Bhaniel to think of anything other than the torture and abuse this man effected on Theresa and herself. She was performing a duty only because she feared what he might do to the children.

"My country? What has happened to my country? Is there anything left of this land?"

"Oh yes. The army will have the rebels on the run in no time. We are more in number and better armed."

"It appears you and your men have not fared as well."

"We were ambushed and cut off from reinforcements."

"Lieutenant. You and your men are starving and most of these wounds are festering. You have been separated from your army for some time."

"That is not your concern, Miss Tretechi. It has been a long grueling road. We are making our way to Kinshasa for a final battle and victory over the rebels."

"What then. Who will be in charge?"

"Someone who will make this country great again."

"I'm sorry, Lieutenant. The army gaining control again does not sound much better than the rebels taking over. Both steal our medicine and take our children."

"Regardless, the army is the best option. The rebels care only about Zuberi's money and assets. The country means nothing to them. We need your medicine, but we have no use for your sons and daughters unless there are boys of fighting age. We can take them to Kinshasa with us. Otherwise, they are nothing more than additional mouths to feed."

"There are only children here. Just liabilities to you." Bhaniel hoped none of the older boys came out of hiding. "Are there rebels coming this way?"

"No. We've been walking for days away from the fighting. We ran out of ammunition and could not fight any longer."

"We do not have enough food for you to stay long."

"It will only be two or three days. The battle is going to happen soon and we must get there to make preparations."

"Some of your men do not look like they can travel any further."

"Some food and rest will rejuvenate them. If then they cannot, we will leave them behind."

Bhaniel prayed everyone would make the journey. Even so, their orphanage was a known entity now. A hostel on the road to somewhere. Regularly providing provisions to platoons of soldiers could severely hinder the survival of the home.

Bhaniel secured the final wrapping. "Well Lieutenant, let's hope all of your men recover quickly." She left to make sure the older boys were hidden.

# Chapter 76

Atlanta

Andrew hung up the phone. He had known Julie Calais for several years, but had never pulled the French accent on her. She was entirely happy to believe Andrew was Edwarde, the broker/agent for an up-and-coming artist who was interested in showing his work in the city if there was an opening. Julie worked for the Hyde Group and was contracting for AD Isaacson. She was the point person for the hosted show on Stella's calendar and was responsible for all the logistics including unplanned artist cancellations. At least Andrew was hoping that detail had not changed. She was very polite and seemed genuinely interested when Andrew/Edwarde sent images of "the artist's" work. Unfortunately, the show is booked and the only other option would be a yet to be determined show after the first of the year. Yes, AD Isaacson would keep the artist in mind for the next show.

All in all, Andrew was pleased with his performance. Now he had to stir the pot at AD Isaacson. It was in their best interest to be aware of the lost paintings as soon as possible. Andrew dredged up an Argentinian accent. "Hello, this is Francisco Ramirez. Would it be possible to visit with someone on your staff about my paintings which are intended for the upcoming show?"

The receptionist put him on hold for nearly three minutes.

"Sir, I'm going to connect you now."

"Hello? This is Bill Maserath."

Bill, or Billy as Andrew always called him, had been with the company for almost the entire time it existed. Unfortunately, when the word got out the paintings were missing, he would probably lose his job. If there was a company after all of fireworks, Andrew promised to hire him back.

"Bill, this is Francisco Ramirez. I was considering the addition of a new painting and the removal of one. Could you look through my pieces and set aside number eight? I will be in by the end of the week with the new item."

"Sure, I will locate it today and set it aside."

Andrew thanked him and hung up. That should do it. Billy will look for the paintings, not find them, contact Julie and/or Stella, and the excitement would begin.

"What do you mean, the paintings are gone?" Julie was not in the mood for this. The show was only a week away.

"They are not here. Anywhere. I looked all over the building. Did you have someone come and get them?"

"No, Bill, we don't have them, and we didn't need them until Friday. Are the other artists' paintings there?"

"Yes. It is even more of a mystery only Ramirez's work is gone."

"Don't breathe a word of this to anyone. Let me do some checking and I'll get back to you."

Julie was mortified. If she failed to deliver this show successfully, her employer might not keep her on. In her line of work, you were only as good as your last job. An irate evaluation from AD Isaacson would be a death blow.

She spent the next five hours working the phones, pulling her hair out, conniving, and praying for a miracle. It was evident the only option was to replace Francisco with another artist. The recent connection with Edwarde and his mystery artist kept demanding her attention as she raced around trying to find a solution. Finally she gave in to the idea and embraced the unfortunate reality she was going to have to call Francisco.

Understandably, Francisco was bewildered and just a little angry. He had been counting on this show to kick off his selling season. The buyers who had committed to attend would not be happy. Julie tried to let him down easy. Sure, there would be another show later in the year. No, I'm not sure what dates exactly. Yes, I'll call you as soon as I know anything. Julie hung up the phone. One detail out of a thousand, done. Edwarde was next.

# Chapter 77

The Orphanage

"Do not come out unless I say so."

"But, Miss B. It's cramped in there. We got to get out some time."

"It's only until the soldiers leave. You must stay hidden. If they see you, they'll take you with them."

Bhaniel was talking to the five boys who the Lieutenant was sure to take if he knew they were here.

"We'll bring you food. I don't know if there will be times you can get out and move around." Bhaniel glared at them. "Every one of you promise me. Promise me you will stay here out of sight until it is clear."

"We promise," they said in unison.

Bhaniel hugged all of them and went back to the house. As long as the boys were careful, they should be fine, she said to herself. The soldiers were not moving around much. Their injuries were their primary concern. The lieutenant was mobile, but he was staying close to his men.

One day turned to two and the routine centered on preparing meals, tending the soldiers, and staying away from them when possible. The corn had come in handy even though it was not completely mature. The soldiers were particularly pleased with the small animals cooked for them. Most of the soldiers were on the mend, with ample medicine and rest. The probability was high they would leave soon.

As night fell, the temptation to wander became too much. Some of the boys felt confident they could sneak out for a short peek. As the oldest of the five, Aleefa had forbidden any unsanctioned forays, but he and Rapha were asleep. Tamego and Kalil were on watch and had spent most of the time talking each other into it.

"We are only going to see how many of them there are and then come back."

"Straight back?"

"Out and back. Real quick."

"Let's go before Aleefa wakes up."

"What about Miss B?"

"She'll never know it happened."

Final plans were made and every contingency a teenage boy could think of was considered. It was already after midnight. All the soldiers should be asleep.

The time for action came. Tamego cracked the wooden door open just enough for the two to slide out. A slice of the moon allowed them to see their way toward the main house. The soldiers were housed on the other side in the boys' dorm. They moved silently toward the open window of the dorm. Candle light and sounds of sleeping soldiers were washing out into the darkness. The boys crept up and positioned themselves under the window. One of them would have to rise up and look in the window for it to be a successful mission.

The boys looked at each other, waiting on the other one to become the legend. So far, no one was sensing their date with destiny so they just sat in the darkness.

"Hey! What are you doing there?"

The boys froze. It was a soldier coming toward the dorm from the woods. He must have been relieving himself and was on his way back. The boys had not accounted for such a scenario. The soldier had his rifle with him. Probably more concerned with stray animals on his walk into the woods rather than boys on a dubious mission.

"Stand up and show yourselves!" The soldier was waving his gun around. The commotion aroused the attention of some other soldiers and the lieutenant. Four or five come out to see what it was all about.

"Lieutenant, look what I found! We have some new recruits." The soldier began to laugh.

"Well, well. Evidently Miss Tretechi was not completely truthful about the number of men who live here." The lieutenant studied the two boys standing in the light of the window. "You both will do nicely. Welcome to the glorious Army of the Democratic Republic of the Congo. Your tour of duty will begin tomorrow, but we will walk over and see Miss Tretechi tonight."

He motioned for the soldiers surrounding the boys to walk them over to the main building. The boys were disappointed and terrified at the same time. The enormity of their blunder would not hit them until the next day on their way to Kinshasa. Even so, both were vaguely aware their lives were about to change forever.

"Miss Tretechi!"

The lieutenant stepped into the main building as Bhaniel came out of her bedroom. The boys followed close behind with other soldiers bracketing them. Bhaniel looked up to see the boys. Her heart sank though she covered her emotions in front of the soldiers. The boys searched her eyes for mercy and wisdom, anything to ease the fear growing in them.

"Miss Tretechi. We have a situation. These boys were spying on my soldiers. Their curiosity makes me believe they would like to become soldiers. I am inclined to allow them this opportunity."

"They are too young…"

"No, I disagree. They will make fine soldiers, and the need is great. For the sake of the nation, we accept their application. Their training will begin immediately."

The lieutenant motioned for the soldiers to take the boys back to their quarters. The boys couldn't look at Bhaniel as they turned to leave. The unfortunate turn of events had taken all the air out of the room. Bhaniel sat down at the table as the lieutenant found a chair in the middle of the room.

"Miss Tretechi, we have some unresolved issues. When I asked you whether there were young men living at the orphanage, you were adamant there were none. This makes me wonder, what else are you hiding from me?"

Bhaniel just looked at the lieutenant with a blank stare. No amount of prodding or abuse would cause her to reveal the whereabouts of the other boys.

"You will tell me where the other young men are hiding, or I will spend the remainder of the evening extracting that same information from our newest recruits. And if not you, they will tell me eventually. Don't you agree?"

The lieutenant allowed his proposal to hang in the space between them. Bhaniel's shoulders slumped as she weighed the inevitable. She began to pray for a miracle. Yet, if it was not to be, she prayed for strength. Tragically, the prospect of the boys going to Kinshasa looked like a death warrant. A soldier appeared at the door, he had Aleefa with him.

"Lieutenant, this boy came to us in the yard just now. He has something to tell." He pushed Aleefa forward.

"I will show you where the others are."

"Aleefa!"

"Do not worry, Miss B. I know they will force the others to tell if you refuse. You would not be in this position if we had obeyed your words."

Bhaniel tried not to weep. These were her children and she wanted only for them to remain with her just a little longer. The lieutenant followed them out the door as Aleefa led the way to the hiding place.

# Chapter 78

Police Headquarters

"Have you finished the breakdown of the SIM card from the phone Isaacson brought back?" Detective Oliver tossed the remainder of his sandwich in the trash.

"Dietrich said a transcript would be done today. Here are the phone numbers that were on it."

"Did they match any of the numbers we were tracking?"

"Funny you should ask." Detective Tunney handed him the list. "Look at the fourth one."

"I don't recognize it."

"None of the numbers were direct hits, but after we saw that guy who is Stella's helper go into the mob house, we gathered up some more numbers tied to gang contacts…"

Perfect. Clarence did the math. "Our hit man was in contact with the Karmazin gang. Not a big surprise, but this is quasi proof."

"Is it enough to haul them in here?"

"Maybe. Best scenario is we get in there and find the phone they were using to call Stella."

"That'd be nice, but I'm not optimistic."

"Nor I. Have you heard from Isaacson?"

"No, it's been a while."

"We ought to call him and make sure he's not doing something stupid."

"Stupid!? Of course he's doing something stupid. He's here to confront the she-devil. And he might be kinda dangerous because he's cheated death a couple times already."

"It's still a free country, and if Isaacson wants to be the bait there's definitely an upside. We need to find out the current plan so we aren't caught in a firefight. Call him and see if he'll come in."

# Chapter 79

Atlanta

"Hello? Is this Edwarde Sacramento?" Julie spoke clearly and a little too loudly.

"Si. How can I help you?" Andrew's accent was grateful for caller id on his phone.

"Edwarde, I have an opportunity for you and your artist. The show scheduled for next week had a cancellation. Would your artist be able to show at short notice?"

"I will have to do some work to change his schedule. There is another show, but I will concede your event is most desirable. What are you willing to do to accommodate us so his work will be shown in the most favorable light?"

Julie had to think. She didn't expect the artist's rep to demand perks. She thought they were hungry, but he knew she was desperate.

"I can put you in the front of the gallery and give you more space in the brochure, but I can't change the order of the auction."

"My artist is here, let me talk with him for just a moment." Andrew covered the phone and waited for a minute. He mumbled to himself in case she could hear through his hand.

"Your offer is compelling. If you would allow him to have a time to talk to the attendees during the show, he will do it."

"Done." Julie was considering a question and answer session for the artists and this assured it.

"Then we have a deal. I will send digital images for you to use. We will be at your location next week to do the paperwork, and begin setting up his pieces."

"Wonderful. I am very happy you will be part of this show. If you can get a biographical narrative for me to include in the brochure and show materials, we will start printing tomorrow."
"Certainly, I am happy to do it."
"Edwarde, may I ask you one more question?"
"By all means."
"What is the artist's name?"
"R. des Comptes."

# Chapter 80

The Orphanage

"Where are they?" The lieutenant was growing weary of the wayward search.

"I'm sorry. This is where we were hiding. I do not know where they went." Lieutenant Raswa determined there was little to gain from further searching. He directed one of the more able men to keep the hiding place under surveillance and sent everyone else back to the barracks. The boys would spend their final night in an unceremonious fashion.

The soldiers took them to the back of the dorm and tied the boys down with coarse rope that cut into their wrists and ankles. Kalil fought off tears of pain and fear.

"Sleep well young soldiers. It may be the last rest you get for a very long time."

Most all of the soldiers settled in to their beds, because they too would not get much rest in the days ahead. The chorus of snoring coupled with fear and general discomfort kept the boys wide awake through the night. They almost longed for the sun to rise so they could be free from this makeshift prison.

"Pzgarebznt."

Aleefa snapped his head toward the direction of the sound. It was a close copy of a tree frog, but to the trained ear was definitely human. Rapha was at the open window. All three boys laid rigid in their beds anxious for what happened next. Rapha motioned for them to be perfectly still. He climbed to the sill of the window and perched there to listen for the steady snoring of the soldiers. As he dropped to the floor of the dorm, Embii followed him silently through the window. Each one had a knife presumably from the kitchen. Aleefa was impressed with their resourcefulness. They freed all three of their ties and motioned for them to stay in their beds. Still no stirring from the soldiers. One at a time, they rose slowly and moved to the window. Aleefa was last to climb to the sill. He looked around satisfied no one was awake and slipped into the night. At the tree line they finally spoke.

"Rapha where are we going?"

"To the river. Everyone else is across the river and hidden in town."

"Everyone?"

"Miss B, Miss Ndulue, all the workers and all the kids."

"How did they know to flee?"

"It was Miss B's idea. She knew the soldiers would hold them hostage if we ran without them. Aleefa, after you left the hiding place, we crawled out and watched from the edge of camp. After you were taken back to the dorm, we found Miss B."

"How will we know when it is safe to go back?"

"We will have to wait many days."

The boys reached the edge of the river and pulled the ferry to shore. Aleefa hesitated to jump on.

"Hurry, Aleefa. We must go."

"I'm not going. I am going to stay and keep watch."

"Aleefa, it isn't worth the danger."

"It is a reasonable plan. The soldiers talked of marching soon. I will stay only until the morning. Whether they leave or stay, I will come to where you are. Hopefully I will have good news."

"Look for Drago. He will tell you where we are hiding."

Aleefa pushed the ferry into the river and disappeared back into the woods. Even though he had not slept on his cot in captivity, Aleefa was not drowsy as he watched the dorm from his perch in the woods. It would be light soon. The soldiers, including the lieutenant, were sleeping soundly. Evidently, the soldier watching the original hiding place was asleep also. Their miscalculation was the boys' great fortune. If they had left even one person to stand watch, the escape might never have happened.

As the sun brightened the horizon and stirred the local creatures, there was movement in the dorm. Suddenly, one soldier appeared at the door of the dorm and ran across the compound with no shirt or shoes. He was followed by another and then the lieutenant emerged and stood at the door. The soldiers came back to the dorm to report.

"No one is here. We have searched all the buildings."

"Look again! If they are not here, we will search the woods."

The lieutenant was furious. He obviously wanted to punish someone, either Miss B or one of his soldiers. But he was sleeping within feet of the boys himself and did not wake up.

The fruitless searching went on for an hour. Hungry and now growing tired, Aleefa was anxious for them to give up and leave. Finally, the lieutenant called his men together and screamed at them until he was hoarse. Ultimately, they dispersed and began, it appeared, to prepare for the long expected exit. Twenty minutes later, the company of soldiers mustered in the square. The lieutenant assumed the head of the column and led the men south and west toward Kinshasa.

Relief flowed over Aleefa as the last of the soldiers disappeared over the hill.

# Chapter 81

Atlanta

Andrew scoured the internet for local talent and found an actor to play the part of Edwarde. Garis Pratteo. He was in his mid fifty's and had just enough of a Spanish accent to mimic Andrew's voice from the phone. His appearance was spot on. He had an unruly mane of black and gray hair matted from too much sculpting gel. Garis wore a bow tie with his jacket and trousers, and a shirt that matched none of it. But the most memorable feature was a fabulously overgrown mustache with the ends slightly oiled and curled. When he smiled, he looked exactly like a cartoon carnival barker who had just finished lunch.

"It will be two days. You'll be there to oversee the show's set up, which might only take a few hours and then the night of the show."

"So you're going to pay me by the hour?"

"No, it's two hundred dollars per day, no matter how long it goes."

'Edwarde' did the math in his head and determined it was a generous hourly wage even if it went long. Besides, it might be fun. The more flamboyant the better.

"Okay. I'll do it. When and where?"

Andrew slogged through all the details and showed him a diagram of where to put each piece. Edwarde wouldn't have to do much.

"Be as quirky as you want to be, just make sure the paintings are in the right places. If you get stuck, call me. I am the artist and my name is R. des Comptes, but my nickname is Le Meiu. These are the only names you are to use. We don't know who will overhear you talking at any time."

"Got it. I am looking forward to this event." Garis was also looking forward to the payday.

"Great. Thanks very much. I'll see you Thursday."

Thankfully, Garis showed up on time. "Edwarde, so nice to see you. I am very grateful you and Mr. des Comptes are going to be a part of the show."

"Senora Calais, the pleasure is mine. Lovely to meet you."

"Edwarde, how would you like to proceed? Are you prepared to set up today?"

"Yes I am. The artist's paintings are just outside and with a little help from your staff, we can start setting up right away."

"Perfect, I'll get our people busy."

Edwarde pulled out his diagram and walked around the gallery. All of the wall space was open and available except for the area closest to the lobby. One of the other artists' paintings covered two of the three walls.

"Julie? I have a diagram of the gallery space with the artist's desired locations for his paintings. Would it be possible to move a couple of the paintings in Gallery A?"

Julie looked up from her paperwork and considered Edwarde's plea. "Really? May I see your diagram?"

Edwarde handed the map over to Julie not sure if this was a good idea or not.

"Wow! This is a very detailed map." And it was hyper accurate. Julie shot a look at Edwarde. "How did you get such an accurate diagram of the gallery spaces?"

Edwarde had to try not to look like he was dreaming up a lie.

"Well, my artist gave the diagram to me. I must admit, where he got it, I don't know."

An idea sprang up in Julie's mind.

"He must have been to the gallery before! He is more familiar with us than I thought. I wonder what shows he has been to."

Edwarde shrugged and chuckled. He absently looked around the gallery spaces.

"Do you think this artist would be willing to share the space in Gallery A?" he asked. "Since it is the closest to the entrance, allowing each artist to have a bit of the available space seems reasonable." Edwarde very stylishly propped up his chin and covered his mouth with his left hand as he spoke. Julie studied him to see if he was serious. He had a point, she just wasn't sure if the other artist would throw a fit.

"I see what you mean. Do you mind if I call the other artist and ask her what she thinks?"

"No, I do not mind at all. Please, please."

Edwarde busied himself watching the workers unload the paintings. He checked his phone to see if Andrew had texted him. Nothing yet.

"She said it would be okay." Julie appeared relieved.

"Wonderful! Le Meiu will be very pleased. Thank you."

"Let's get these paintings hung!"

# Chapter 82

Bandundu

Aleefa found Drago negotiating the purchase of some fruit from the open market.

"Drago!"

He looked up and spied Aleefa. He made only a slight jerk of his head toward the next street over. Aleefa went between the buildings and waited. Drago walked by Aleefa and didn't slow down.

"This way."

Drago let Aleefa through a maze of single and two story structures easing into a residential area with kids playing and mothers in clusters talking. Some of the kids he recognized as his own brothers and sisters from the orphanage. Drago led him into a cinder block structure with one window and a makeshift porch. Inside were Bhaniel and the workers.

"Miss B!"

"Aleefa. Oh, my."

"Good news! The soldiers have gone. They were very angry because the buildings were empty, but after searching for a long time, they left for Kinshasa."

"Lord be praised!" All the adults were moved to hug each other and praise God.

"We can go back now, no?"

"Yes, I think so."

"Miss B, I will go ahead and make sure the home is still empty before you arrive. If there is any danger, I will hang a red scarf at the ferry dock."

Bhaniel wasn't entirely comfortable sending Aleefa back into the danger zone, but he had proven his courage and maturity. He was becoming a true leader.

"Go then. We will be close behind. Thank you, Aleefa. You have been very brave for us. Be safe."

Aleefa smiled a little bit, nodded and left. Drago followed him out the door.

"Just a minute, young sir. You are going with me. There's no need to walk when you can ride…."

Bhaniel turned to the others. "Ladies, let's gather our kids and go home."

# Chapter 83

The AD Isaacson Galleries

The show was set to begin at eight. Plenty of time before the festivities at nine. The beauty of working with AD Isaacson was the large number of wealthy patrons who participated regularly and, hopefully many were going to be present tonight. Julie was nervous and excited. This could be a pivotal moment in these artists' lives as well as her own.

Actually, Julie was more nervous than excited right now. None of the artists were present yet and she hadn't seen Stella since last Friday. Edwarde had been adamant demanding Stella's attendance. Julie was unsettled about his unbending attitude, but she passed on the message to Stella anyway.

It was 8:30pm and the gallery was full of well-dressed enthusiasts. To her great pleasure, the other two artists were milling about talking with potential customers. Unfortunately, Julie did not see des Comptes. Fashionably late arrivals were not unusual, but there were several patrons anxious to meet him. Edwarde was just across the room.

"Edwarde, good evening." Julie interjected while Edwarde was visiting with a couple from Charleston.

"Hello Julie, it is going to be a good night."

"I was wondering, have you talked to Mr. des Comptes? I have not seen him this evening and we will be starting the artist presentations soon."

"When I spoke to him earlier, he said he had an unexpected delay, but he promised to be here by nine."

Julie flushed a bit. "Okay, we can have him go last, thank you."

She hurried away to care for the details of the change clacking her heels on the hard floor as she went.

Andrew stepped into the gallery just as the first artist began to speak. Nearly all eyes were on her allowing Andrew to enter almost unnoticed. The artist expressed an interesting relationship between the suffering of man and the twisted metal sculptures placed around the gallery. Each one represented a people group and the brand of challenges they faced. As she spoke, Andrew walked quietly around the space. His painting next to the podium was covered in a black cloth and was intended to be a spectacle reveal, but the others he would be able to uncover right now. There were four paintings hanging in the anterooms which were well done but basically decoys. The intended pieces were hand painted reproductions of the photos Andrew had taken of himself as the dead assassin. During the time leading up to the show, Andrew had meticulously created and placed four false paintings over four real paintings certain to be disturbing to the casual observer. Though abstract, the fakes were surprisingly similar in shape and color to the real paintings lacking only the telltale details. But the patrons attending tonight were not the audience Andrew sought. He was chasing an audience of one, though he needed Julie's help to make it happen. If Stella didn't show, the effort might be for naught.

All of the frames were custom made by Andrew. They were fashioned with a slot in the front for the false painting and a slot behind the real piece so that the fake could slide neatly out of sight. The whole operation took only seconds, and Andrew was standing dutifully at the back of the room when the second artist finished his talk. Julie had been scanning the room feverishly hoping to catch a glimpse of Andrew. Edwarde had to point him out to her because he was so unassuming in his Homberg hat, amber-colored glasses, long hair and beard. The shabby suit of clothes looked like turn-of-the-century Goodwill. Once she spied him, her demeanor eased considerably. And just in time. The second artist offered only brief remarks, wanting the artwork to speak for itself. He gave just enough background and insight to whet the viewers' appetite, but nothing more. "Thank you, Orenthal. Your work is magnificent." Julie turned to the audience and encouraged a round of applause for the artist.

"Well, we are privileged tonight to have with us an accomplished painter from France who was a fortunate last minute addition to the show. He studied under some of the great post-modern abstractionists from the Belgian school in the mid 1970's. His work has been shown in London, St. Petersburg, Milan, and of course Paris. He intends to live here in America and continue producing work for three to five years. His work has evolved from abstract expressionism to include a dash of post modernism with a hint of romanticism. Ladies and gentlemen, I give you Reglement des Comptes."

Julie extended her arms toward Andrew and again started the applause pulling him up to the podium. The crowd followed her eyes to the back of the room to see who this mystery artist was. Andrew was void of self-promotion and the audience was conflicted with his lack of entertainment value. Based on Julie's introduction, they were cautiously optimistic of his intellectual brilliance and the possibility they were in the presence of an artistic icon. As Andrew made his way to the stage, he noticed Stella was in attendance. She was hanging back in the hallway engrossed in conversation with a favored client.

Andrew used his best French accent.

"Thank you so much. It is a pleasure to be here tonight. I did not realize until recently I would have the opportunity to share my work with all of you here in America, but here I am. Only a short time ago, I was very close to death. The experience was as you would expect, life changing. But my ordeal was not the result of disease or starvation. I was living with a small community of people in Africa when a killer came to our camp. People lost their lives that day and it was a miracle I was spared. I have chosen to make these events the central theme of the larger works on display tonight."

The attendees began to look around at the framed paintings and murmuring to each other. Most were realizing the pieces they thought were des Comptes works were now entirely different paintings.

"These aren't the same paintings."

"What happened to the other pieces?"

"They're shocking."

"I love it."

"I thought they were abstract?"

Most people were confused and trying to catch up. They wanted to join the unusual energy in the room, but no one was sure if it was the appropriate thing to do.

"Ladies and gentlemen, please forgive me. I didn't intend to create such a commotion, yet these paintings needed to be revealed. They are harsh and shocking images which simply show a murdered man in its most real form. He was hunted like an animal with little chance against a professional killer. It is a departure from my regular style, and yet the works I produce from this point forward will forever be affected by the events in Africa."

Andrew turned to the painting covered with the black cloth.

"This is the center piece of the collection. The 'Death Mask'."

He pulled the cloth back to reveal the close up of his face covered in blood and grime – Andrew had inserted his 'old' face in the paintings. There were a few gasps, but mostly silence. People would politely wait until he left to give voice to their opinions, outrage or interest.

"Thank you for coming tonight and I hope to visit with you at a later time."

Andrew embraced the crowd's measured applause as he left the stage. While he was stepping down, Andrew glanced toward the place where Stella had been. She was still there and appeared as though she mistakenly looked into Medusa's eyes. Her skin was ashen and her arms hung limply at her side. There was no indication she recognized Andrew, but the paintings had done their work. Julie hustled up to the stage in an attempt to salvage as much of the evening as she could.

"Thank you Mr. des Comptes. Your work is so challenging. And thank you to the other artists as well. All of the artists will be available for questions and further discussion throughout the evening. Please enjoy yourselves and a quick reminder: the cash bar will be open for another hour. Thank you."

Not an awesome finish, but only a few people were listening anyway. Julie hopped off the stage intent on locating Stella to smooth over any ruffled feathers possibly caused by des Comptes. But Stella had vanished.

"Did you see where she went?"

Andrew was whispering into the microphone tucked under his shirt collar. Detectives Tunney and Oliver dressed very stylishly were studying a sculpture near the stage.

"She made a beeline to the office wing after you finished. There are a couple of detectives outside waiting to follow her if she runs off."

Andrew wasn't sure what to do with himself. He didn't want to leave, but was in no mood to mingle. Too late. Several people grouped around him to dissect the finer points of his death paintings.

"Mr. des Comptes, do you consider the act of murder to be a metaphor for the oppression occurring in third world countries?"

"Not necessarily. This act of aggression was committed by a European man against an American."

And on and on it went for nearly an hour. Eventually, Andrew was exhausted. He lunged for the exit to take a break.

"Gents, I need to leave for a while. Will you holler at me if anything happens?"

"Sure. We're keeping an eye on things, but don't go far."

"Roger that."

One of the few remaining guests loitered in the back galleries. He had said little to others and blended in anonymously all evening. If ever there was a human embodiment of the fly on the wall, he was it. The receiver embedded in his ear was almost invisible as well.

"Report."

"The subject is still here in her office. There has been an unusual turn of events tonight. One of the artists has had access to the photos we received from Africa."

"The photos from the op?"

"Yes."

"How do you know?"

"He made paintings identical to the photos."

"We have a leak."

"Apparently so."

"Find out what you can on the artist. We'll send a wet team in tonight for both of them."

"I'll make the preparations."

The guest sauntered into the service/kitchen area and located the collected laundry waiting at the back door. He picked through the discarded serving smocks and chose one that was near his size. The rest of the evening would be devoted to assisting the cleaning crew and securing the subject until the other "cleaning" crew arrived.

Stella sat in her chair and stared out the window. So many emotions ran through her heart and mind. Rage and fear were the dominant ones and rage was winning the runoff. This was a setup she thought to herself. What was the angle this French man with a weird accent intended to play? Was it money? She could cover that. Was it revenge? She was going to have to face him eventually. He had made his play and was daring her to respond. How did he get access to the pictures? The paintings looked so much like the images she received from the mafia; they had to be created straight from the photos themselves. Did he make friends with the assassin? Why would the hired killer not kill him too?

There were too many questions. But one thing was sure. This mystery man came to Atlanta to rub her nose in the African killing, and she did not know what to do about it. First things first. She needed to see if the paintings were an exact match. This would prove the artist was in possession of the photos. The next step was to decide what to do if they were. Stella dialed her phone.

"Eugene, I need you here right now. We need to do some research. Not what. Who. On an artist named Reglement des Comptes. I never heard of him either, but there is no time to lose. I don't care what time it is. Okay. Start there and bring me something first thing in the morning."

It was imperative she know her enemy. Thirty minutes later, Eugene called her back.

"I have found almost nothing on this guy. There is a small blog with a few comments and pictures of paintings, no Wikipedia page, a brand new Facebook page, and hardly any references on multiple search engines. Oh, and by the way, his name seemed kind of weird so I looked it up. It means 'settlement of accounts'."

Stella dropped the phone.

# Chapter 84

Bandundu

"Wait! Wait!" Bhaniel ran to the front of the group waving her arms. The younger kids stopped just to look at her because they weren't used to her being so demonstrative.

"We must wait here until Aleefa comes back."

Aleefa had not left the red scarf at the water's edge, and the group had begun the journey up the hill to the home. Still, Bhaniel was wary and chose to hold everyone in the woods until Aleefa returned.

"Here he comes!" The bulk of the kids were acting as official lookouts.

"Miss B! I didn't find anyone. It's safe."

Bhaniel had come to trust Aleefa like he was a grown man. He had earned the respect of the adults and kids alike. Whenever any of the kids needed help or a protector, he was their first choice.

Everyone marched the final distance pleased to see the cluster of buildings. Each one went to their favorite areas to see if anything was molested. The adults went to the barracks used by the soldiers to see what needed to be fixed, burnt or destroyed.

"Bhaniel, you better come see this." Ndulue had a concerned look on her face.

All the adults had converged on the main building. Ndulue led them to the hidden medicine closet. The lock to the door had been destroyed and the door hung awkwardly to the side. Inside there was only empty boxes scattered wildly with random bottles and vials thrown to the floor.

"What did they take?"

"Everything we need."

"Everything? You mean…"

"Yes."

Bhaniel stepped in the closet and looked around. She knelt down and picked up an empty box to look at the label. She joined with the others to begin the cleanup process. The enormity of what had happened was well understood. Bhaniel had known this could happen and secretly feared what it could mean. The soldiers had taken the HIV medicine. If they didn't get replacement drugs soon, several kids would be exposed to illnesses which could easily lead to death.

The lieutenant had scored a significant parting shot. Bhaniel was surprised the soldiers had found the cache and even more astonished at what they took. They had never taken the HIV medicine before. This must have been a personal statement in response to the boys' nighttime escape. The drugs were replaceable though. To have the boys, it was a favorable tradeoff. Bhaniel would have to contact the director as soon as possible. Somehow, some way they would need an angel to bring more medicine.

# Chapter 85

Stella's Office

After a couple of extra-large drinks, Stella's nerves had eased a bit. She was slumped in her chair staring out at the night sky from her darkened office. It was possible she had even dozed off for a short time. The relentless stress of her pursuit of Andrew Isaacson was taking its toll. This had become a demon she couldn't shake.

12:30am. Surely everyone had gone home. This was as good a time as any to check the validity of the photos. Stella spun her chair around and grabbed at the desk to get to her feet. The alcohol had weakened her equilibrium slightly and she paused to allow the moment to pass. She reached up to move her trinkets off the shelf and pull the false panel back. Just as she placed her hand on the phone…

"Hello, Stella."

She spun her head awkwardly and fell back against the shelves, stunned at the voice of a man standing in the shadow of the entrance to her office. His silhouette was framed by the glass doors as he stepped into the open.

"Eugene? Is that you? Why didn't you tell me you were coming back to the office? Don't you ever scare me like that again, so help me. I ought to fire you right now…"

Andrew walked closer so Stella could see him more clearly. Stella peered at the man, processing the conflicting information. She wanted it to be Eugene, but it didn't sound like him or look like him.

"Mr. des Comptes? What are you doing here? What happened to your French accent?"

Andrew was standing close to Stella's desk as he removed the hat, glasses and jacket. If he was ever going to look like his old self, this was the best he could do on short notice.

"Stella, it's me, Andrew."

The only thing that made sense at this point was she was asleep and having a nightmare – a Scrooge-like nightmare with a ghost of Christmas Past who looked alarmingly like Andrew Isaacson.

"Who are you, really? Is this some sick joke? What do you want from me? You had no right to make those paintings. Tell me how you got those photos."

"The photos were fake, Stella. It's really me. I'm alive."

By this time, Stella was nearly hyperventilating. If the stress seemed overwhelming before, this increased it by a factor of ten.

"What? How? Andrew is dead, I saw the pictures!" Stella was shaking and had started to cry as she screamed the words.

"Actually, the hitman is dead. I think he was the third one if my math is correct. You have done some terrible things Stella. Harvey. Mitch. Sabrina. Or whatever her name was. You should have stopped while you were ahead. I didn't intend to come back to America, but you couldn't leave it alone. When the hitman showed up in Africa, it was obvious you would never rest until I was dead. What's behind the wall, Stella?"

"Who knows you're alive?"

"Everyone at the IORRF and most of the Atlanta Police. In fact, two of them are here with me tonight. Why don't you show me what's in the hole in the wall."

Stella had regained some composure and was maneuvering back to her desk. Andrew countered her movement and was stepping closer to the cubby hole. He stole a quick look into the secret compartment, but it was empty. Andrew looked back at Stella and realized she had the phone in her hand. In the other hand, was a small revolver pointed at him.

"I guess I will have to do what three other professionals couldn't do. It's going to be messy, but it doesn't matter. You're right, you should have stayed in Africa. Coming back here was foolish and now I'm going to finally win."

Just as the words left Stella's mouth, the metallic sound of a suppressed semi-automatic weapon being fired dominated the moment. Andrew flinched thinking Stella had fired her gun. He looked up to see Stella's head snap to the side and the force of the bullet entering her temple propelled her into the corner of the office between two large green palm plants.

Andrew crouched and turned toward the door. One man in black had entered the office with the weapon still leveled toward Stella's position. Two other men were close behind him. Andrew had nowhere to go. His only hope was these men were police officers.

No such luck. The gunman walked over to Stella's body and put two more slugs into her chest. This was a hit squad, cleaning up a mistake. The second man turned to Andrew.

"Who are you?"

"Andrew Isaacson."

"You look like the man we are searching for, but his name is des Comptes. Do you know who he is?"

Answering affirmatively was to ensure a bullet to the head. He was probably going to get one anyway.

"No. My name is Andrew Isaacson."

"It doesn't matter actually."

He raised his weapon to kill Andrew and eliminate the witness.

"Freeze! Atlanta Police!"

The detectives were at the door crouching with guns drawn and two others behind them.

The three killers turned and fired at the officers but in their haste, their aim was not precise. Andrew realized he was directly in the line of fire and dove behind the desk to find some semblance of cover. The officers opened fire, aiming at the perpetrators' heads since all three had extensive body armor.

The firefight was over in seconds. The killers only got off four more rounds. Three were wild and one found Detective Tunney's chest protector. He was thrown backwards as the other three men emptied their weapons into the black clad men. When the room returned to relative silence, Andrew looked up, hoping his side had won the battle. Detective Oliver crouched at his side.

"Are you hit?"

"Thankfully, no. Your timing is good."

"Couldn't you at least tell us you were coming here? We had to guess when we heard you talking to her on your mike."

"I knew you would figure it out, but I didn't plan on Stella pulling a gun on me."

He looked over at the dead team of killers.

"Who are these guys? Friends of yours?"

"Never seen them before. I was hoping you'd know."

"We have a pretty good idea. The gangsters Miss Manchester was doing business with weren't happy about the art stunt you pulled. We ID'd one of their errand boys at the gala tonight. They have been tailing Stella for about a month now. One of the other teams should have him in custody by now."

Andrew stood up and walked over to Stella. Although the scene was gruesome by all accounts, Stella looked curiously peaceful as she lay amongst the greenery. Still clutched in her hand was the cell phone which would tell the detectives everything they needed to know. Stella wouldn't be going to jail after all.

"Don't touch anything. This is a crime scene."

"I won't." Andrew kept his distance.

Andrew contemplated the finality of the evening's events. While his plan was intended to bring closure, this abrupt ending sent everything hurtling over the cliff. He was going to need a day or two to digest his new reality. It might include a new enemy to contend with.

"Detective Oliver?"

"Yeah."

"How is Detective Tunney?"

"He should be fine, except the round in his chest is going to leave a pretty good bruise."

"Thank God." Andrew thought for a moment and looked at the bodies strewn about the office.

"Should I be concerned about the people who sent these men to kill Reglement des Comptes?"

"Your friends certainly are dangerous people, but they are going to be busy saving their own skin. It appears we have all the evidence we need to cause someone to have a very bad day. Maybe several someones."

"Do you think Stella's assistant, Eugene Burnett, was in on it?"

"Could be. We are going to track him down tonight. I need you to go downtown so we can get a statement from you."

"Sure. All I have is time, Detective."

Detective Oliver laughed. "Isaacson, you did it again. You survived when most people would have been filling a body bag."

"God is good, friend." Andrew smiled but then turned serious.

"Detective?"

"Yeah."

"Thank you. You and your team. Without you, I know I would be dead."

"I'd have to agree." Oliver grinned. "You know, your plan worked to a T. And we got out of here with no casualties on our side. That's a good night."

"Perfect. I'm gonna go to the station. I'll catch up to you later."

"Just promise me you won't leave the country in the next 24 hours."

"I promise, Detective."

Andrew backed out of the office and followed a uniformed police officer to his squad car. As he got in the car, he looked back toward the building and saw his name on the sign above the door. It was time. It was time for AD Isaacson and this long chapter of his life to come to an end. But it could wait until tomorrow.

Turning to the officer, Andrew posed a request. "Could we swing over to the Grindhouse on Edgewood for a burger on the way? I'm starved."

# Chapter 86

Grady Memorial Hospital

Andrew found the room finally. The hospital was a maze of hallways and wards. Mitch had been moved back to the hospital because of complications with his feet. They were not healing well due to weak blood flow. Andrew had not been able to get back to see Mitch for over a week because of the demands of the art show.

"Mitch. Mitch." Andrew laid his hand on his shoulder. Mitch roused slightly and turned his head toward Andrew.

"Nurse? Could you adjust the pillows under my legs?"

"Mitch. It's me Andrew."

"Hey, Andrew. How are you?" Mitch seemed to be on strong medication. His speech was slow and ethereal.

"I'm good. Really good. How about you? Feeling any better?"

"Not too bad. I signed up for a slow pitch softball team, but I haven't gotten a schedule yet."

"I'll bring your glove next time."

"The doctor doesn't say much, but I think I'll be able to get out of here soon."

"Hey, how about I adjust that pillow for you."

"Sure, that'd be great."

The nurses had built a tent over the foot of the bed to remove any irritation on Mitch's legs and feet brought on by the bed covers. Andrew pulled the sheet and blanket back to get to the pillow. But there was no pillow, nor anything else. Mitch's feet were gone. His legs had been amputated just below the knee. Stunned, Andrew just looked at the empty space in silence.

"Thanks, Andrew."

Andrew could only pull the covers back over the end of the bed. His hands were shaking, and the joy and relief he had felt up to this moment had ended as quickly as a suicidal jumper hitting the concrete.

"So, I'm back in the hospital. Didn't know if you would find me or not. They had to do some work on my feet, but the doctor hasn't come by yet to give me the update."

"I had some good news to tell you." Andrew could hardly get the words out.

"Awesome. Tell me."

"It's about Stella. She's …."

There was a knock on the door, and the surgeon walked in.

"Knock, knock. Hi, Mitch. Is this a good time to talk about your surgery?"

"Yes."

Andrew got the look from the doctor. "I'll just wait outside."

"No, no, Andrew. You can stay, you're the closest thing to family I have here in Atlanta."

The doctor and Andrew exchanged a painful look. She perceived he knew the awful outcome already.

"Mitch, everything went very well. After the amputations, your blood pressure and blood flow have been very good. Even though it creates some other challenges for you, it should allow for more rapid healing in other areas of your body. So, in a few days, you can go back to the hospice. Then, you should be ready for physical therapy to get you on your new feet and out of bed."

Mitch didn't act at all surprised, and was pleased with the prognosis.

"Thank you, Doctor. I am feeling better already."

"You will have some phantom pains, which are natural."

"I had one just a few minutes ago, actually. I'll get used to it."

"If you have any issues or questions, just let the nurses know and they will contact me."

"Thanks."

"Bye for now." The surgeon slipped out to finish her rounds.

Andrew waited for Mitch to talk.

"I'm sorry, Andrew. I should have told you."

"I think I'm the one who should apologize. When I saw your legs, I was afraid you didn't know, but I couldn't bring myself to tell you. Mitch, I am so sorry. Your life will forever be changed because I wouldn't listen to you a long time ago."

"Andrew, don't carry that burden. This is not your fault. Besides, I lived through it. And I look forward to showing Stella she couldn't kill me. Even so, I'm going to need some protection until I can get up and around. I've been trying to find out if the cops are guarding my room. If they are, it's undercover."

"Don't worry. You're safe."

"You should know better than anyone. Stella will stop at nothing."

"Stella is dead."

Mitch studied Andrew's face, waiting for the joke.

"A hit squad killed her last night."

"How do you know?"

"I was standing right next to her when it happened."

"Why are you not dead?"

"I probably should be. The detectives came in right after they shot her, and they killed the hitmen in the gun battle."

"And you got through it without a scratch."

"I'm a little embarrassed to be honest."

"There is no good explanation for this, Andrew. You are still here for a reason. It's up to you to live up to the calling."

"Maybe so, but one of the things I am honor bound to do is make sure you are well taken care of for the rest of your life."

"Very kind of you, but once I get up and around, I'm going to be the bionic man. Those running blades look pretty cool. Chicks dig 'em too."

"No doubt. You are going to hit a homerun with the hero thing."

"Stella is dead." Mitch rolled the words around in his mouth to see how they felt.

Andrew spent the next hour telling the whole story so Mitch could get maximum satisfaction. He deserved it.

# Chapter 87

IORRF Headquarters

Andrew pushed the door open and walked into the reception area. The offices were humble as one would expect, but very organized and business like. It had the aura of giving the utmost care to every penny donated and striving for perfect efficiency. Pictures of the various orphanages and schools across the globe were framed and hung on the walls with updated snapshots tucked into the edges of frames.

"Hello, I'm Andrew Isaacson. I am here to meet with Director Hizanga."

"Yes, of course. Welcome Mr. Isaacson, let me tell him you're here."

The young receptionist was enthusiastic to meet Andrew, about whom she had heard so many stories. The director came out of his office before Andrew could take a seat.

"Andrew! So glad to see you." He gave Andrew a big hug. "How are you?"

"Better now. I think my unfinished business is resolved, and I can start planning to go back to the Congo."

Director Hizanga walked him back to his office and offered a worn out chair.

"That's so good to hear, Andrew." The director considered his words and gave Andrew a serious look. "Do you think anyone will be chasing you overseas anymore?"

"Not any longer, no."

One more time, Andrew told the story, but abbreviated it for time's sake.

"Is living in the Congo your destiny, Andrew? I can't say I have met anyone like you. At least no one who has survived so many attempts on their lives. Maybe you have a higher calling."

"Someone else said very similar words to me recently."

"What does your heart tell you?"

"My heart is in Africa."

"I know the kids adore you. Having a male presence there has been so beneficial to everyone."

"I do love the kids. They are the greatest. But it's... Bhaniel. She's my heart. When I'm with her, everything becomes clear. Stella, my paintings, God.... life."

The director was not necessarily surprised. Bhaniel had led many souls to an unfettered connection to God.

"Bhaniel is a rare person. We have been blessed she is a part of this family, and we may not have the privilege of knowing someone quite like her ever again. Yet, if you believe in Christ, Andrew, you have what she has, the Holy Spirit. Bhaniel would like nothing better than to know you are connected to God in the same way she is before she passes from this life. Just so you know, we did the tests on her blood. It's a good thing you brought the sample. It showed Bhaniel's viral load had increased. The drugs she will need are more powerful. There may come a time no drug will be strong enough to protect her system."

"I know she's not well, and no one knows who will live or die each day in the Congo. But, there is nowhere else I have ever been that feels so much like home. The fact her health is in question makes me want to be with her even more. How much time will we have together? If it puts my life in peril, well I've made my peace with God. Right now, the orphanage on the banks of the Kwango River is my higher calling. If everything changes the day after I get there, so be it, but I know I have to go back."

"Then you have my full support, Andrew. I appreciate your heart for what we are doing over there. At least for this season of time, you need to be in the DRC. And we need someone to carry supplies to them. I haven't talked to her in a few days, but I think Theresa is ready to go back as well. As you probably know, it won't be easy to get there. The civil war has made travel into the capital almost impossible."

Andrew was forming a plan. "How many supplies? Can we carry them?"

"Yes, it's mainly medicine. There has been an unfortunate incident at the home."

"What? What happened?" Andrew braced himself.

"Lieutenant Raswa, I think you know him, came to the home again. He was traveling with many men who had been injured from battles up river. They were marching toward Kinshasa to join the fight there. While they were at the home, the lieutenant tried to take the older boys with him, but Bhaniel escaped with them to Bandundu. The soldiers eventually left the home, but before they did, they found and stole the cache of medicine."

"All of it?"

"Yes. Even the HIV drugs."

Andrew had been at the home long enough to know what the director's words meant. Time was not their ally. He had to get there as soon as he could.

"Director, I may have a way into the country that doesn't go through Kinshasa."

"Let's hear it."

Andrew laid out the plan. Ironically, the assassin was more helpful than he would ever know.

"I do want to go back, Director. How bad is it now?" Theresa asked over the phone.

"Almost complete anarchy. There have been so many government troops going over to the rebels; some in Kinshasa believe the country will fall within weeks. My recommendation is you stay here, but I will not demand it."

"It's my home, Director. If I can save one of those kids by giving my own life, I'll do it."

"We'll never be able to repay you for your dedication to the people there."

"Good news, my payment is coming from somewhere else."

The director marveled at Theresa's willingness to go to the gates of hell itself to care for her kids.

"I didn't want to talk about it until I knew you had committed to go back, but your return may be more important than we can imagine."

"Why? What's happened?"

"It's Bhaniel. Andrew brought a sample of her blood back with him for testing. I'm afraid it is worse than we thought. Her viral levels are very high. I don't know if the new medicine you and Andrew are taking back will stop it. If the virus continues to grow, she may not live much longer." The last words were almost too difficult to say. "The kids could need you more than ever."

"Does Andrew know?"

"He knows the medicine has changed. We didn't talk much more about it than that. I just didn't have the courage to tell him. Are you comfortable going back with Andrew?"

"Yeah, I think so. We have quite a bit in common actually. He comes from a whole different world, but deep down our hearts are in Africa and we're both just homeless people in need of a family. We both love Bhaniel also."

"Have you talked to him?"

"Not yet. We're leaving soon aren't we? Is Alisha getting the plane tickets?"

"She is. You won't go directly into Kinshasa or anywhere else in the DRC. The flights will go into Libreville, Gabon. From there, Andrew says he knows a small plane pilot who will fly you to Franceville and then into Bandundu."

"I'll do whatever I need to do to get there."

# Chapter 88

Andrew's Residence

Andrew couldn't decide. There were so many supplies he wanted to take with him, but he knew the odds of getting all of it to the orphanage were low, especially the leg from Franceville to the home. How were they going to get anything in a biplane? Maybe he had access to bigger aircraft. If he didn't, Andrew expected the pilot to make more than one trip. Andrew was willing to walk, but the Congo River would prove challenging.

He sat in the middle of his studio and looked around at some of his all-time favorite paintings he wanted to keep forever and the half-finished canvases of almost great ideas. It was hard for him to think this might be the last time he would be in his studio. Andrew intended to stay in Africa indefinitely, but this time he wouldn't be running for his life. He still loved the "golden lady" painting of Fanny. Since his personal life was more resolved, maybe he would go by the bar and see her before he left. Andrew walked over and pulled the painting out in the open so he could get a clearer view. Not bad for a one-night effort. As he thumbed through the other canvases stacked against the wall, one hardly past the underdrawing stage caught his eye. He had begun to lay in the base colors, but little else. The drawing was of a man and woman at each end of the space joined in the middle by several kids of various ages. The kids, small and underdeveloped, moved toward the man and then returned to the woman, mature and healthy.

"Of course," Andrew said to himself.

He was incredulous this idea had come so far in the development phase. Considering where Andrew was in his personal life at the time, artwork with a family feel to it was inspiration from a completely different place. But it all made sense to him now. The kids were the orphans and he was the man. Andrew couldn't decipher who the woman was, but it reminded him more of Theresa than Bhaniel. Regardless, what he thought was a recent idea had been forming in him many years for a people he did not yet know. There would come a time when the kids traveled back to the U.S. to attend university. He hoped it would be an opportunity for their spirits, minds and bodies to grow strong. Maybe some would return to their home country to form a nucleus of leaders who might forever change the course of the nation.

Andrew put the canvas back in the stack. He knew without a doubt it would come to pass whether he had the painting with him or not. Next time he was home, Andrew would finish it for posterity. Actually, some of the kids might get a kick out of it just the way it is. He gathered his things and looked for a sack. More editing would be necessary before he got on the plane. Two days. He was going back in two days. There was too much to do in such a short time. . . Just as he reached for the light switches, he glanced around the space once more. In the corner of his eye he saw shapes on the wall. He spun around to look at the white wall directly, and seeing nothing specific, shrugged it off as an illusion brought on by shadows. Yet, something stirred in his heart. He'd felt this before, but how could he do it now? There was no time. It was late and he needed to do so many things tomorrow. Oh well, there was no reason to fight it. Andrew had to walk through the proverbial door and see where these stirrings would take him. If producing art for so many years had taught him anything, it was to follow inspiration whenever and wherever it presented itself. One night of inspired work was worth a month of grinding, unimaginative labor.

Bhaniel had helped him focus these feelings and take charge of them. She had shown him how to lay them out and ask for God's direction.

"God in heaven, You are the one true Creator. Please allow me to be your vessel tonight to give voice to what you have to say."

Andrew envisioned the scene nearly covering the west wall. The problem was, he didn't have a canvas that big.

"Oh well. I guess I'll just paint the wall. Now where did I put those cans of paint?"

And so the night began. As the drawing progressed, Andrew had to assemble the scaffolding for the high parts and move it himself as he filled in sections. He didn't take the time to step off and look at in from distance. There would be time for editing later. With each portion drawn, the overall composition became clearer, but Andrew still didn't understand the significance of the various parts.

Dawn came and he laid down his tools. Nearly falling off the scaffolding, Andrew pushed himself upright, and rolled the structure out of the way. Part of him didn't want to look at it. What was he going to do, change it? But his curiosity was too great. Andrew shuffled to the other end of the room and hesitated before turning around. He spun around and had to adjust his eyes to filtering sunlight and the change in distance. What arose before him left Andrew completely speechless.

# Chapter 89

The Orphanage

"Lala would you bring me a bowl?" Bhaniel was working in the kitchen today. Most of the kitchen staff were out harvesting corn. It was finally time for reaping.

"Lala?" No answer.

Bhaniel laid down the knife and walked over to the next building. Lala had been just outside the kitchen window, but was not in sight now. Bhaniel didn't find her until she poked her head in the girls' dorm. Lala was lying on her cot. This would not have been significant except Lala never rested during the day.

"Lala? Are you okay?"

"Miss B, I don't feel very well. My head hurts and I ache all over."

Bhaniel had knelt beside her bed and taken her hand. Lala's hand was hot and her whole body was covered in sweat. Bhaniel's mind raced. She wanted to help Lala as quickly as possible, but there was something new to consider. With the lack of medicine, the kids with HIV would be increasingly susceptible to illness. She needed to get Lala to a different place away from everyone else and then figure out how to treat her.

"Can you walk?"

"I think so, but I'm dizzy."

Bhaniel got her up and grabbed her around her waist. Lala put her arm around Bhaniel and the two walked outside toward the storage shed on the edge of the property.

"Miss B, why are we going to the shed?"

"Lala, I am so sorry to do this, but if we don't keep you away from the others, someone could catch your virus and have no way to fight it. Without our medicine, the HIV kids will be in more danger every day. Thank God you don't have HIV, but you will need to be alone for now."

"That's okay, Miss B. I understand. Hopefully, this will have me down just a day or so."

Bhaniel opened the shed and set Lala down on a wooden box.

"I will bring your cot out here for you to lie on and then we'll put the tent up which will be better than this shed."

Lala began to list while sitting on the box.

"And I'll get you some water." Bhaniel hurried back to the dorm.

"Ndulue, please help me. I need to move Lala's cot." Ndulue had just come back from the field.

"Yes, Miss B. Where are we moving it to?"

"The shed. She's sick."

"Oh my." Was all Ndulue said. She set her basket down and readied herself for what could turn into a campus-wide quarantine.

After relocating Lala's cot in the shed, others joined in and set up the large canvas tent in the shade of the ebony tree. The tent was a holdover from years ago. The organization had brought it over for summer missionaries to sleep under while on location. Netting on the sides made it an adventurous way to sleep in the African nighttime with all the sounds and a nice breeze. Unfortunately, the missionaries' visits had become less frequent as armed conflicts increased, but the tent was occasionally useful for various things. Today it would be the hospital.

"How bad is she? Should we take her to town?"

"I think we should watch her for a day or two and see if she gets better. We just need to make sure she doesn't get dehydrated."

Ndulue looked at Bhaniel for a moment.

"Maybe I should look after Lala."

Her meaning was understood. Ndulue didn't have HIV. It was the reasonable thing to do, although she knew getting Bhaniel to concede would be a challenge.

"No, no. I'll be okay."

"Please, Bhaniel. Let me take the first day or two and then we can talk about it then."

Bhaniel knew it was the best option, but she didn't want Ndulue to feel she had to take the extra burden.

"It's really no problem. If you take care of my kitchen duties, I'll just stay with Lala."

Bhaniel nodded without looking at her. "Okay. Thank you, Ndulue."

Her sickness had beaten her today. She accepted the defeat and was thankful for a friend who could step in to fill the void.

Lala had collapsed on the cot, glad to have a little breeze to cool her raging fever. Ndulue set up a chair and bedside table in the tent. Bhaniel turned to leave.

"I'll get some water."

# Chapter 90

Atlanta

Andrew double-checked his bags. The director had dropped off the medicine soon after Andrew had returned from the police department. Director Hizanga promised to send more as soon as possible. He had already devised a storage strategy to reduce the chances of theft or some other catastrophic loss, but it was going to require some labor on Andrew's part once he got there. Theresa texted and was going to meet him at the airport. He was ready. The detectives believed they had everything they needed to file numerous charges against the criminal organization, and Andrew's relocation to Africa wasn't going to hinder their efforts. Detective Oliver was comfortable with the methods available to contact Andrew if necessary. He had spent considerable time thanking the detectives and their whole team for their effort and bravery. Officer Tunney received special recognition due to the wounds he received in the final firefight.

His phone buzzed. The taxi was waiting at the gate. Andrew moved his luggage and locked the door. The house was dark since the utilities were turned off once more. He slid in the back seat of the van in his "African" clothes, and didn't look back as the taxi went out the gate and onto the boulevard.

"Hello, Andrew."

He had arrived early to the airport so there wouldn't be any issues with the medicine, and now was waiting at the gate. Andrew looked up from his tablet to see a physically imposing woman with a child-like, almost shy smile on her face. She offered her hand as Andrew stood.

"Hello, Theresa. It's a pleasure to meet you. How are you?"

"I'm feeling very well. I am rested up, and looking forward to getting back to the orphanage."

Andrew was fascinated. He had heard about Theresa from Bhaniel and this was a completely different woman. He had expected an aggressive, mildly impatient, socially awkward lady intent on returning to her safe zone. What stood before him was a woman with a quiet spirit about her. Maybe even a broken spirit. Regardless of how it happened, the Congo had a way of changing a person. Andrew could testify as well. He was curious to see if Theresa still had the will to endure Africa once more. Andrew cleared a seat next to him.

"We have about an hour before we board. Thank goodness we are flying at night. Maybe we can avoid jet lag."

"How many times have you been to Africa, Andrew?"

"Only once before, but it was on a container ship."

This piqued Theresa's interest. She shifted and studied him.

"What? Why? The director didn't tell me you went over on a ship. You were dead set on getting to Africa, weren't you?"

"I certainly was. I had nowhere else to go and had some unsavory people trying to kill me, so going to Africa seemed like a good idea. Sailing on a container ship gave me the opportunity to stay under the radar. I got there not long after you left I think."

Theresa looked away and focused on the many passing travelers. It was obvious to Andrew she did not want to talk about certain events from her past. Since he knew the main points of her trauma, he was sensitive not to push her.

"The director told me some of your story. You had to rescue your art business? I guess you were successful since you're here."

"For the most part. Some details are yet to be tied up, but the main issues were put to rest. God is good."

Theresa gave it some thought. "Yes, He is."

Andrew and Theresa drifted to talking about the kids at the home and watching the clock. Everyone in the waiting area dreaded the long flight, but were anxious to get on the plane rather than remain in the terminal. Finally, boarding began. Their seats were not first class, but had enough leg room to facilitate sleep.

The next eight hours included dinner, a movie, intermittent conversation, and some sleep. In the quiet moments, Andrew thought about all that had happened since he first made this trip. Maybe he'd write a book. Not a bad idea, but no one would believe it. Curiously, every thought circled back to Bhaniel. He had been so wrapped up in resolving his 'problem' there had been no time to let his mind drift back to Bandundu and the woman he adored. Until he had set foot on the airplane bound for Africa, Andrew had not let himself believe he was going back. Now, like a musician carefully opening the case to his favored violin, Andrew unlocked the longing in his heart which brought a twinge of anxiousness and excitement.

"Ma'am, can you tell me where the Air Nationale ticket counter is?" Andrew tried talking to the first uniformed service person he saw once they made it through customs in Libreville. The attendant understood 'Air Nationale' and pointed in the direction of the baggage claim area.
"So this is the mysterious part of the trip the director told me about. Are we going to be swimming some of the way?" asked Theresa
Andrew laughed. "Boy, I hope not. If we can find the Air Nationale or the Air Service ticket counters we should be able to get to Franceville quickly then it's just a short hop to Bandundu. The planes from Franceville might be the most adventurous part of the trip. We are going to do what the assassin did when he came to the orphanage. He flew a charter plane into Bandundu. A biplane actually."
"A what?" Theresa couldn't believe her ears.
"I sincerely hope we can find a larger plane to charter. A biplane won't be big enough."
"Yes, I agree. Let's hope." Theresa's voice trailed off.
"We have one flight today at 12:30 to M'Vengue."
"M'Vengue?"
"There is no airport in Franceville, but it is close."
"That's fine."
Andrew pulled out cash to pay for the tickets. The timing was rather good. They had arrived in Libreville early in the morning so the wait for the flight to M'Vengue would not be long.
"Is this what your assassin did? Did he fly across Gabon to M'Vengue?"
"I don't think so. We found rail ticket stubs in his backpack. He must have taken the Trans-Gabon Railway to stay off the grid."
"Sounds like fun."
"If we miss this flight, the railroad might be our next best option. I'm ready to get there aren't you?"
"Yeah. The sooner the better."
"How long do you plan to stay this time?" Andrew took a seat in an abandoned waiting area.

"I'm going home. The U.S. was my vacation abroad. Unless something dramatic happens, I'll never leave again. You?"

"I really don't know. I've been happy to make it to dinnertime most days. Hasn't made sense to plan too far out."

"You're not running from anything this time. Are you going just because of Bhaniel?"

"Do you mean would I even dream of going back to Africa if it weren't for her? It's hard to say. I have developed relationships with a lot of the kids and other workers, but I'd be lying if I acted like she wasn't the main reason."

"Are you going to marry her?" Theresa had regained some of her fire as she assumed the role of Bhaniel's protector. She stared at him demanding a response.

Andrew felt the pressure of her gaze. He was finally going to verbalize what he had privately contemplated many times before.

"Would I? Yes, I think so. Will we? Probably not. I'm almost afraid to change anything because it has been so perfect. Like I said, my focus isn't on the past or the future. It's only on the right now. Is that crazy?"

"No, Mr. Isaacson. It sounds about right. Africa has a way of doing that to people."

Theresa thought about the director's comments and had no idea if telling Andrew was a good thing. If he had been intent on marrying her, she would have said something. Maybe.

The waiting continued with walks around the terminal, reading and people watching. Most people were quiet and to themselves with the occasional joyous family reunion. Airport employees were busy in their uniforms of various styles. Music was playing over a speaker system somewhere in an adjoining terminal. It appeared to Andrew their flight to M'Vengue would have only a few passengers. He was hopeful for a functional plane and capable crew. Both Theresa's and his carryon luggage included a fair amount of the HIV medicine just in case they were separated from the checked bags; yet there had been no concerns from the customs officials. Finally, a man came forward near their gate and proclaimed the flight to M'Vengue would board as soon as possible, but the plane was going to be a half hour late arriving.

Andrew was reading a local newspaper he had found when he noticed the plane was rolling to a stop outside of their gate.

"Looks like we're going to fly today after all." Theresa was encouraged. She had just returned from the vendor with two bottles of water.

"I think you're right. Is this your first time through Libreville?"

"Yeah. The last time I traveled, the DRC's civil war hadn't reached the capital so there was no need to go in the back way. The nice thing about our route this time is I won't have to ride a bus to Bandundu." She looked at Andrew. "Will we?"

Andrew just shrugged as he looked up from his paper.

The last of the deplaning passengers walked through the glass door. Soon after, the airline attendants shepherded the boarding passengers on the plane and prepared for the hop to M'Vengue. Andrew and Theresa took their seats near the front of the plane. From the look of the plane's interior, this domestic airline's fleet was comprised of aircraft one step away from the salvage yard. Andrew couldn't keep his seat back upright and Theresa's seat cushion was worn nearly through to the frame. Flight attendants filled small glasses with a curiously colored beverage as the pilots joked in the front cabin. Ultimately, the plane's engines whirred to life and the craft began to taxi toward the runway. Only a few people were seated, but the movement of the plane alerted the stragglers to buckle in. Once in the air, the flight was short. As soon as the pilot reached cruising altitude, it was time to begin the descent. Andrew sat by the window and studied the countryside as they neared the earth. It was mostly rural with random residences of various quality scattered over the area. The airport was well outside of the city of Franceville which was a boon to hired drivers.

A jolt and recovery of the plane's equilibrium woke everyone up. Now, the passengers were actively attuned to the distance between plane and ground. The common consideration was how low the plane would need to be for a majority of passengers to survive a crash. Andrew was confident the pilots could glide in for a landing, but stopping effectively was anybody's guess. He just hoped they didn't overshoot the runway.

The plane kissed the ground with a resounding thud raising a question of whether the tires would stay inflated. A couple of suitcases fell from the overhead bins and a child cried out behind them. Passengers familiar with Air Nationale continued to watch out the windows indifferently as the plane raced down the runway. Others held on to the seat before them or to a loved one. Finally, either with air brakes or a lack of fuel, the plane groaned to a stop and turned back toward the small terminal. Andrew noticed a cluster of hangars and outbuildings at the end of the runway as the plane made its turn.

"Now the fun begins. When we get to the terminal, we'll need to find the area where the smaller aircraft are located. From the looks of things, it might be back there at the end of the runway."

"Will there be any customs inspection?"

"I don't know. Since we are going to get a ride in a private plane, we may not need to talk to anyone."

They gathered their luggage and stepped out to the front of the terminal and hailed a driver.

"We need to go to where the small planes are located."

Andrew wasn't quite sure how to explain himself. After repeated attempts to communicate his need, Theresa stepped in for the save and the driver finally got it and waved them into the car.

"You are going to the end of the runway."

"Yes! To the small planes."

The two travelers loaded the car with all their bags and jumped in for the short ride. The young driver was happy to have riders, but wasn't expecting to get paid much. After circling the airfield, the car went onto the tarmac and the driver drove nearly on the runway itself. Both Andrew and Theresa were scanning the skies for incoming planes. Thankfully, the pattern was clear and they reached the collection of hangars unharmed. The driver hurriedly unloaded the bags, took his fare and scurried off to find Franceville-bound riders.

Andrew looked right and left, evaluating the selection of hangars. "Well, here we are. Now we need to find a plane big enough to carry our stuff and a pilot willing to fly to Bandundu. I'm guessing your French is pretty good, based on earlier."

"It's okay. At least I can speak the DRC version of French."

"I'm sure it's better than mine."

There were signs of life inside the largest hangar which seemed as good as any place to start. Theresa addressed the grimy, mechanic carrying a piston from a radial engine as he emerged from the hangar.

"Hello. We would like to hire a plane and a pilot," Theresa said.

"There are two planes, but no pilot. He may be back later today."

"Is one of the planes big enough to carry us and our luggage?"

The mechanic nodded his head and motioned for them to follow him next door. He opened a side door and showed them what amounted to an oversized Piper Cub. It was a single engine plane with the wing over the cab, and the tires appeared to be leftovers from a monster truck event. The cargo area looked like it would be big enough to carry their luggage which was the one prerequisite.

"Does it fly?"

"Oh, yes. I just finished repairing it."

"What was wrong with it?"

"Nothing. Engine overhaul. It'll fly real nice."

"We don't have anywhere to go. Can we wait on the pilot? Is there any way to contact him?"

"No, no. He's flying right now. If there are no problems, he will be back this evening."

Theresa and Andrew exchanged looks. Well this was the wild card, Andrew thought to himself. They didn't have any other option but to sit and wait. Andrew and Theresa agreed to gut it out and hope for the best. There were a few man-made shady areas around the hangars which were akin to oversized carports. Andrew scrounged around the locale and found a couple of stools and a rickety table for their new waiting area. Theresa dug through the luggage to see what food items were handy. Pretzels, beef jerky, cheese crackers, peanuts, some hard candy and what was left in their water bottles was the day's buffet.

"Well, we won't go hungry at least."

"Unless we have to walk."

"And swim."

"I'm not even going to talk about that."

"Let's hope the pilot returns sooner than later."

The minutes turned to hours and the activities vacillated between napping, walking laps, inventorying the luggage, touring the prospective plane, and talking with the mechanic. Although the mechanic was focused on his engine overhaul, he took an occasional break and told the travelers stories about Franceville and his home which was only a bike ride away. The establishment of the Trans-Gabon Railroad and its termination in Franceville changed the culture and economy of the city forever. Now, casual travelers could come to the south easily as well as entrepreneurs. Mnambe, that was his name, was proud of the positive developments in his country. The increase in commerce allowed him to purchase toys for his children and cigarettes for himself although he wanted to quit.

Mnambe turned his head to the sky, shielding his eyes from the sun.

"Here he comes."

Andrew and Theresa had not heard a thing, but finally detected the soft whir of the biplane's engine. They searched the sky and found him approaching from the south. He stayed in the air until the plane was almost on top of them and then touched down like a mayfly on a pond. The wooden fuselage flexed and groaned as he pulled the plane to a stop near the hangar. A loud backfire accentuated the engine stop as the pilot hopped to the ground.

The pilot stretched his legs and back as he walked over to the trio.

"Welcome back, Luc. Good flight?"

"No trouble. Who are our guests?"

"This is Andrew and Theresa. They are in need of a plane."

"Where are you going?"

"The Congo. Bandundu actually," said Theresa.

The pilot looked at Andrew and recognized him.

"I remember you. I talked to you at the Bandundu airport after I flew the other man into the city. He paid very well, I hope he comes back soon."

"It probably won't happen. He had a bad experience in the Congo," replied Andrew as Theresa translated.

"The DRC is very dangerous these days."

"Agreed. So, what will it take to fly that" – Andrew pointed to the back of the hangar – "to Bandundu?"

Luc considered the proposal for a moment and calculated the wealth potential of the passengers and the lateness of the day.

"Fifty thousand francs."

Andrew didn't flinch. "Would you take dollars?"

There was a noticeable improvement in Luc's demeanor, but he was going to play it to the hilt. "I will take your dollars, but fuel is so expensive and that plane is not very efficient. Do you know what the exchange rate is for your dollars?"

"Yes. Your CFA francs are decreasing in value, but today those fifty thousand francs are worth about one hundred dollars."

Luc fretted over the offer for effect and then smiled and offered his hand. "That is acceptable. We will leave tomorrow morning."

Andrew pulled his hand back. "Oh, well actually, we wanted to go tonight."

"Sir, sir. The flight is very treacherous in the dark and as you can see the sun will set soon."

"If we leave now, we should get there in plenty of time," said Theresa.

"There are so many preparations to do before we fly. I'm not sure it can be done. Besides, I will need to fly back here as well."

Andrew looked at Theresa who shrugged her shoulders. "What's one more night, right?"

He nodded he head and moved toward his luggage, but turned with a new idea.

"Today for one-fifty?" Andrew tried his French.

"Oh, no, sir. It would have to be at least two hundred dollars."

"You have a deal."

Luc smiled even broader. "I will be happy to fly you to Bandundu today. We'd better get going."

Both men believed they had brokered a favorable deal for themselves. Theresa was just happy to be headed home.

In no time, the plane was up and running at the end of the runway and the luggage was stowed. Andrew and Theresa climbed in the tail dragger and sat on the metal bench which spanned the length of the fuselage. There were no harnesses or seat belts, and only random appendages here and there to hold on to. The pilot took his seat and radioed the tower. The pattern was clear as he revved the engine, and the missionaries hurtled toward their final destination.

# Chapter 91

The Orphanage

"Is she any better?"

"No. Bhaniel, I'm afraid we will need to take her to the hospital."

Taking Lala to the hospital wasn't a great option, but at least they could put her on an IV to restore her fluid levels. The virus had gone on long enough now Bhaniel was beginning to worry. Lala was lucid only part of the time, and she wasn't drinking enough water.

"Okay. I'll get the boys to fashion the fish net into a hammock. Will you go down to the river and make sure the ferry is on our side?"

"Sure. Are you coming straight away?"

"Yes. As soon as possible." Bhaniel sat down by Lala as Ndulue set out on her mission.

"Lala?"

She stirred and looked at Bhaniel through one sleepy eye.

"Lala, we're going to take you to town. They can give you more fluids which will help you get better quickly."

Tears filled her eyes and slid down her cheeks into each ear. "I'm sorry, Miss B. I'm supposed to be helping."

"Lala, this is not your fault. Maybe if we had the medicine. . . I don't know."

"I'll pay for it. I'll work for the hospital as long as I need to."

Bhaniel smiled at Lala. She loved her for many reasons. If nothing else, this would be a time all of them could minister to her instead.

"Let's not worry about that right now. We just need to get you some extra attention. I think you'll be up and around in a couple of days. But first we need to get your transport ready." Bhaniel squeezed her hand and headed out to find the boys.

"Drink some water, Lala." Bhaniel was walking next to the transport stretcher and held a small cup to her lips. The slouching hammock had four boys at the ends of two poles. A casual observer would have thought they were on a hunting expedition and Lala was an unfortunate antelope.

Lala tried her best to drink, but most of the water slid down the side of her face. She had never been this sick before and wondered if she was dying. Miss B had said when she showed up at the orphanage, the workers counted seven different ailments Lala was battling, including Denge Fever, but she didn't have much memory of those years. Lala concluded if she had cheated death at such a tender age, then nothing could get her. This episode had instructed her differently. Even though she didn't fear death, Lala was going to respect it more in the future.

The traveling party reached the edge of the river and the ferry was ready and waiting. The ferry operator kept his distance as best he could. He hustled to move the barge back to the east side quickly for everybody's sake. It always went better when the boys were on the ferry with him. Additional pullers, in this case four, allowed him to rest his arms occasionally. Bhaniel shaded Lala's head from the sun and tried to give her more water.

# Chapter 92

West Africa

"It's amazing." Andrew was on his knees, staring out the window. He couldn't quite see sitting down and to stand was not an option, so he knelt like a kid in front of the family's first television. Below them was the Congo River. The enormity of it made it seem as if they were heading back west over the Atlantic Ocean. He had felt this same way one time before when his passenger jet had flown over the Amazon River back in the 1990's.

His comment was more to himself than to anyone else. Theresa had found a way to sleep on some filthy canvas tarps she discovered in the tail of the craft. What was it about these people he now called his family? All of them were the toughest, most adaptive and resilient souls on earth. Nothing like the pampered, helpless, demanding illuminati with whom he was previously known to interact. His definition of beauty had changed in the process. Now he was drawn to the light that projected from a person's spirit.

"There."

"Hmm?" The pilot pulled Andrew out of his daydream.

"The eastern shore of the river. Looks like troops." Andrew followed his eyes and scanned the approaching shore. The closer they flew, more soldiers and trucks came into view. Some were wading into the water while others were lounging on their vehicles. Just to be safe, the pilot angled north so the plane wouldn't go directly over the men.

The bullets tore through the fuselage near the tail and pushed the back end sideways. Luc nearly panicked as he shouted.

"They're shooting at us!" He immediately did the only evasive maneuver he knew. He turned the plane away from the small arms fire and hit the throttle. Andrew shook Theresa and pulled her behind the luggage in case it was thick enough to slow down the bullets. Luc was intent on getting his plane as far away as possible and the angle of the plane kept Andrew from seeing the troop movements. He could hear the gun rapports in the far distance. Evidently, everyone was getting into the act of taking potshots at the plane. None of the additional rounds were finding their mark…
"They hit the wing!"
"Is it affecting control of the plane?!"
Luc checked his controls. "No, not yet."
They finally reached a distance from the soldiers where shooting at them was a waste of ammo. The plane eased over land and the three travelers scanned the horizon for any other danger.
"I did not bargain for this Mr. Andrew."
"I'm sorry Luc. We'll help you fix your plane."
"It's not the plane I'm worried about."
Andrew looked more closely at the pilot. The right side of Luc's shirt was red with blood. Theresa gasped and jumped up behind him to assess the damage in his shoulder. Luc was flying the plane with his left hand as his right arm hung limply in his lap. He was beginning to struggle with focus as shock set in.
"We've got to get him out of that seat so I can tend to his wound."
"Did he get hit by a bullet?"
"I'm not sure. Can you fly the plane?"
"What!? Fly? Are you kidding?"
Luc turned to Andrew. "You'll have to do it, but I can tell you what to do. Sit in the co-pilot's seat."
Andrew reluctantly climbed into the chair and tried to get comfortable.
"Just keep an eye on your airspeed, this gauge will show you if your wings are horizontal and this one shows you your altitude." As Luc talked, he pointed at the gauges and Andrew guessed at what he was saying. Theresa tried to translate.
"Are we going the right direction?"
Luc checked the GPS, made one adjustment to the course and turned it over to Andrew.
"You'll be fine." Theresa helped him out of the chair and set him down on the floor. She took his shirt off, mopped up some of the blood and did a quick survey. There was a jagged entry wound, but no exit. The upside was they had duffel bags full of medical supplies. The hard part was she needed to stop the bleeding. Theresa tore through the supplies and found triage materials.

"I'm going to give you a shot of pain killer and then open up the wound to see what is in there." She talked as she worked. After a quick shot, Theresa cut into the gash and felt for a bullet. She found a bullet and a mangled shard of the fuselage that was lodged underneath the scapula, but may have shattered that bone for all she knew. The metals came out easier than expected, and the blood flowed aggressively afterward. Luc slipped in and out of consciousness. There was no alternative, the bleeding had to be hindered some way so Theresa got a needle and began to sew.

"You're going to have to keep the plane steady. I've got to sew Luc's shoulder."

Ugh. Andrew turned and looked at Theresa and just nodded his head. Could this trip get any weirder? All he could do was keep the plane flying. She would have to do the rest.

"God? You know the quote where people say 'God is my co-pilot'? Well, I'm willing to give you pilot status. If you don't step in, we're going to end up in Uganda or face down in the dirt."

Since Luc had adjusted the course before he passed out, Andrew assumed he could maintain flying in a straight line for the time being. He was obsessively checking his gauges every few seconds and only had to make one adjustment to their altitude when a funky pocket of wind dropped them a few feet. It felt like a roller coaster ride, but in reality was hardly noted on the gauges. One gauge he had not considered was the fuel gauge. Still a quarter tank, but Andrew wasn't sure how fast the fuel was burning. Now another gauge was on the review circuit.

Andrew looked out the side window. What if they came across more troops with extra ammo? Could he turn the plane and escape without crashing? Maybe the further they flew away from Kinshasa the better. All he could do was keep churning toward Bandundu. "So where's Bandundu?"

Theresa climbed into the seat next to him.

"You're not Luc."

"I'm the best you got."

"God's supposed to be sitting there."

"I think He's willing to stand between us."

"Is Luc okay?"

"For now. The bleeding is under control, but he's passed out from the blood loss. I just came up here to check on you."

"So far so good."

Theresa looked out the window in the front and side searching for familiar landmarks. Nothing yet.

"Have you checked the GPS? It may show Bandundu on it."

"Thanks, I didn't even think of it." Both of them looked at it and Bandundu was closer than either imagined.

"Good, we are almost there."

Then it hit Andrew. "Is Luc going to be awake enough to land the plane?"

Theresa looked at him, then at Luc on the floor and shook her head. "You'll have to do it."

"Will he wake up at least to tell me what to do?"

"Maybe." Theresa moved back to the floor and knelt by Luc. She put her arm under his head and patted him on the cheek. "Luc? Luc? Wake up. We need you to help us land the plane."

Luc's eyes opened slightly, not focusing on anything.

"I woluflan boterchantemalathi…"

"Luc! Luc! Can you hear me?" Theresa was shaking him now.

More of the same. Luc was out of it and was not going to be any help.

"Theresa! He can't help us. I'll have to land the plane myself." Andrew let that sink in.

Theresa laid Luc back down and climbed into the co-pilot seat so she could assist in some way. If they were going down ugly, she wanted to be in there swinging.

"How close are we?"

"Twenty kilometers."

"Whoa. Can you see Bandundu yet?"

"No. Why don't you radio ahead to the airport and see if there is anyone at the terminal who can help us?"

"Good idea. Where's the radio?" Theresa was all energy, but clueless in the cockpit.

"There, by your left hand. He was talking on this frequency earlier. Maybe it will work for Bandundu."

After several tries, there was only static on the line. As far as they knew, their attempts at French and English were impossible for the receivers to understand even if they were heard.

"Forget it. We'll find the town, then the airport, then we'll land as best we can."

"What do you think you know about landing a plane?"

"Slow down, start the glide path early in the direction of the runway, flaps down and wheels down."

"Wow. It was a better answer than I was expecting."

"I've sat in enough jets staring out the window, you'd think I would learn something. The wheels are permanent so we don't have to worry about those. We'll have to figure out where the lever for the flaps is."

"Cool. Let's do this."

Andrew brought the plane down to a thousand feet. The town ahead of them evidently was Bandundu. The GPS showed them right on top of it.

"Okay, this is Bandundu. Start looking for the airstrip."

"It looks so different from up here. Hey! There's the river! Oh, and another one!"

Andrew looked out his side window for recognizable landmarks. As long as the fuel held out, he was committed to circling the city until they found the airport. There. Those buildings were familiar. The airport had to be close.

"I see it!" Theresa had spied the runway.

"Are there any planes on the runway getting ready to take off?"

Andrew did a quick scan of the skies around them for other planes. So far so good. They were alone in the air for now. He circled the airport and considered which direction to attack it. The gauges indicated the wind was from the northwest. If the compass was correct, they could come in from the east-southeast and line up with the runway nicely.

"I'm going to go out that way" – he pointed to the east – "and come in for a landing. I hope to come in shallow enough we don't have to drop the plane on the ground from a hundred feet."

"Okay." Theresa was willing but unsure. Andrew kept her informed mainly to hear himself say it. Maybe if it sounded good coming out of his mouth, the plan would work.

Andrew pulled the plane around and lined it up. He began to slow the engine and lower the flaps one notch.

Everything looked great...

"Andrew, there's a plane on the runway!"

"Yikes!" Andrew pulled the nose up and hit the throttle as he turned to the north. "We'll have to circle around again."

Suddenly, a light came on beneath the fuel gauge. The needle was almost to the 'E'.

"This next run may be our last chance." Andrew circled around and lined it up again as the other plane turned away from them, raced down the runway and climbed into the sky.

"Let's hope no one decides to takeoff in the next ten minutes."

"I'm praying."

He went through the procedures again and came in low. Andrew throttled down and increased flaps steadily as they approached the end of the runway. Just as they crossed the front end of the pavement, the plane was thirty feet off the ground. Andrew killed the throttle, and nosed the plane up to flare it in the wind. He pulled up a little too much and the plane stalled ten feet above the ground. The plane dropped to the pavement with a thud, bounced into the air and back down again; and then, now earth-bound, proceeded to race to the other end of the runway.

"What do we do now?!"

"I'm not sure."

"Hit the brakes!"

"We don't have any!"

"Turn the engine off!"

Andrew centered the airplane then looked for a cutoff switch.

"Here!" Theresa had found the key and turned it. The plane slowed easily allowing Andrew to veer off the runway and park in the grass. The two sat in silence for a few moments to soak in the successful return to earth. Then Theresa leaned over to Andrew and kissed him on the mouth.

"Thank you. The chances of getting horribly mangled in a crash were high, but you pulled it off."

"I don't want to do that again." He thought about the kiss and clarified. "I mean the landing part. The kiss was good. We'd better see to Luc."

Thankfully, there was a small truck motoring toward them with concerned individuals inside. At least they could take Luc to the medical clinic quickly.

"Is everyone okay?" The emergency person asked.

"We have a man in the back that has been injured. He needs to see a doctor."

Two of the riders jumped out carrying a makeshift gurney and went to tend to Luc.

"Is he the pilot?"

"Yes."

"We thought something was wrong since no one would respond on the radio."

"Will you be able to tow the plane to the hangar?"

"Yes, it is not a problem."

Once they collected Luc, the rescue party drove off to the clinic. Later, the car came back for Andrew, Theresa and the luggage.

"We need to go to the river, but we would like to go by and check on Luc first."

"Sure, no problem."

Sali, the driver pulled up to the main entrance of the clinic – most locals called it a hospital – but it was barely more than a cinder block office building.

"I'll wait out here for you. Will you be a long time?"

"No, we'll check on him and be right out. Thanks."

The clinic didn't have a well-defined emergency room, but they found where Luc was and surrounded his bed. He appeared to still be in a coma of sorts. They agreed to track down a nurse for some information, but Luc roused.

"How is the airplane?"

"I saved a wheel and the propeller. Did you have insurance?" Andrew said through Theresa.

"Insurance? What is insurance?"

"I'm teasing. We landed safely and the plane is at the airport in a hangar. It's a little worse for wear. The troops shot it up pretty good."

"I am in your debt. Have you flown before?"

"First time at the controls. Theresa was a first rate co-pilot."

"And a doctor too."

"Don't worry about anything. I am going to take care of your medical costs and will work with the mechanic at the airport to make sure your airplane is fixed."

"Thank you. I was not sure what I was going to do about my expenses."

"Thanks for getting us to Bandundu." Andrew shook his good hand and Theresa hugged him.

"We'd better get outside so Sali doesn't worry." The weary travelers stepped lively down the hallway and nearly ran over Bhaniel. "Bhaniel!"

"Andrew! Theresa!" She hugged both at once. "What a pleasure it is to see you. You're back safe and sound."

"We have quite a story for you."

"Another one? I cannot begin to imagine what happened this time." Bhaniel looked exhausted.

"Why are you here? Is someone hurt?" Theresa asked.

"No, it's Lala. She got so sick, we had to bring her. They have her quarantined until they can determine what the virus is. I'm not sure what tests they can run here, however. She is better now with extra fluids."

"We have a huge supply of medicine out in the truck waiting to go with us to the home." He looked at Theresa for agreement. "We'll take everything to the orphanage and come back."

"Would you be okay taking it yourself, Andrew? I think I need to stay with Bhaniel."

"Sure, I'll be back as soon as I can." He hugged Bhaniel. "It's great to see you."

"I have missed you Mr. Isaacson, and am so happy you are back."

Her tired eyes were full of so many emotions, but the joyful reunion was a healing salve for them all.

# Chapter 93

Kinshasa

"I'm hit!" Oswey called out to the other soldiers in his squad. No answer. There was a fair chance none of the fighters had heard him even though all of them would have seen him go down. He was the point man for the reconnaissance squad sent ahead because of reports of a sniper in the area. Oswey saw the gunman, at least the flash from his gun barrel, but too late to avoid the shot. If he hadn't been shot, Oswey would be kicking himself right now for being lazy and not locating the shooter beforehand. He needed someone to come up to his position, but the sniper had the whole squad ducking for cover. This one was bad. The Teflon coated bullet had gone right through his protective vest and through him also. Based on the rate of blood loss, it must have hit an artery. He wondered if the others could get help in time. Without protection from the sniper, the chances were zero.

Oswey accepted it like he did everything else, without regret or any other emotion. He had assumed an enemy's bullet would find him eventually. The young soldier fought to stay conscious, but knew sleep was coming. His mind wondered from the squad's chances of neutralizing the sniper, to the blue sky and what he ate yesterday – which appeared to be his last meal. There was no family, friends or homeland to long for. The Lieutenant had plucked him from the streets of Maadi just weeks ago, an orphan living much like a rat.

Under the protection of cover fire, two of the squad made their way to Oswey's position. Lieutenant Raswa was close behind. One of them patted Oswey on the cheek and checked his pulse. No response.

"He's dead."

"Gather up his ammo and the rifle. Check him for any other useful items, and drag him over there." The Lieutenant turned his focus to the sniper.

"Should we cover him up or something?"

"No, he's just debris now. When I open fire, you go across the street, and you" pointing to the second boy, "move up to the next storefront."

The Lieutenant stood up and poked his rifle around the corner of the building. "Now!"

The two child soldiers raced to their prescribed positions. As the younger one ran for the cover of the cinderblock building across the street, the sniper took aim from his new vantage point as the lieutenant fired on the previous perch. Two quick rounds dropped the boy in the street as the other pushed forward. The lieutenant got what he wanted.

"There you are." The lieutenant loosed the rocket propelled grenade at the location and stood to admire his work. The third story room on the corner of the building exploded in amazing Technicolor and the prospects of a successful mission improved greatly. Lieutenant Raswa motioned for the remaining squad members to move forward. Their sweep of the south side of the city would continue until dawn.

# Chapter 94

Bandundu

Andrew arrived at the home and received a hero's welcome. The adult workers immediately organized the drugs and other medicines, and set up a receiving line for all of the kids with HIV. After the hellos and hugs, Andrew found his bedroom and lay on the bed. He feared he would sleep for several hours so he set an alarm. He had to get back to the clinic so maybe both Bhaniel and Theresa might return to the home if only for a little while.

"Andrew, wake up." Ndulue shook him on the shoulder.
"Wow, that was quick." He looked at his watch. The sun was setting and his alarm had been going for twenty minutes. Andrew had slept just long enough to be sore all over and his mouth to be completely dry. "I've got to get to town."
"Please try to talk Bhaniel into coming back to rest."
"I will, and Theresa also."
He stumbled through the building and found some rice and beans to take with him. Bhaniel probably had not eaten all day. Andrew thought of Luc and the airplane. He'd have to stop by the airport to get an update on his way in.

"Bhaniel, how is she?"
Bhaniel was sleeping in a metal chair with a scarf over her head. As Andrew came into the waiting area, she looked up half expecting the nurse. "She's not improved much. We haven't heard whether they will be able to send her blood for tests either."
"Can I see her?"
"Nobody can get to her right now."

"Why don't you go back to the home for the night? I can stay over. Here, I brought you some food. Where's Theresa?"

"Somewhere close. She was sitting here a minute ago."

"Can I do anything for you?"

Bhaniel sat and looked at Andrew, studying his tired face and messy hair. "The fact you are here is all I need. With a side of rice and beans." It felt good to smile.

"Is there a room where you can lie down at least? I'll go ask." Andrew went to find a worker.

Theresa met Andrew in the hallway on her way back to the waiting area. She pointed him toward where she came from and described a very vocal nurse who could enlighten him.

Bhaniel remembered as Theresa walked into the room, "I forgot to ask you or Andrew. Did the laboratory test my blood while you were in America?" Oh boy. Theresa had rehearsed her response but it wasn't going to help. "Yes."

"So do you have the results, or are they written down somewhere?"

"They are written down and I have it with me." Theresa didn't want to do it, but she was going to find out eventually. She handed Bhaniel the envelope from her backpack.

Bhaniel took her time reading the report. It was in English, so some of the medical words were a little confusing. After a long silence, she verified her conclusion with Theresa.

"My viral levels are at an all-time high. Will the medicine you brought be able to bring the levels down?"

"We'll just have to stay on it, and check the levels. We brought some testing materials back with us." Bhaniel knew Theresa was trying to stay positive in a bleak situation. Theresa had given her a shot of the new drugs as soon as they found Bhaniel earlier in the day.

"Does Andrew know?"

Theresa shook her head. "I thought maybe you would want to tell him."

"Let's wait and see what the next blood test shows. If the numbers are good, then we need say nothing."

"Okay. I won't say a word."


"Bhaniel, I found you a room." Andrew was coming down the hall with a satisfied look on his face. "Theresa, are you staying, or going back to the home?"

"Since Bhaniel is going to stay, I'll go back. I need to see the kids. You going to be okay?" she said to Bhaniel.

"I think so. Andrew will be here also. Hopefully, all of us will be home soon." She hugged Theresa as she left.

Bhaniel went to her bed while Andrew investigated the clinic. It wasn't large, but there were several patients and visitors waiting, roaming and waiting some more. Very few looked like they had anywhere else to be, so waiting wasn't a problem. Andrew peeked into some of the rooms as he walked. Most had one or two cots and an occasional folding chair. A few patients had IV's on a stand next to their cot. With the lack of doctors, the clinic was very limited in what they could offer. All of the rooms had multiple people in them either standing or sitting. One patient was so popular, the concerned contingent spilled out into the hallway blocking Andrew's path. Some ladies were wailing and men were trying to stay out of the way. A couple of older men were so bold to smoke cigarettes on the edge of the group.

Andrew turned the corner and noticed another barrier to his casual stroll. This must be where Lala is. The facility was crude, but it performed as needed. Lala was cut off from incidental contact. Andrew noticed a man who acted as though he owned the place. Could be a doctor. The nurses were doing his bidding and he looked overworked. Andrew decided to risk a question. He'd try Lingala first.

"Excuse me, Doctor, question?"

The "doctor" looked in his direction. "I am not a doctor. I am the clinic administrator."

"Forgive me. Lala, is in there." He motioned to the quarantine area. "Will you be able to do blood tests?"

The administrator evaluated his broken Lingala and considered whether he deserved a response.

"No tests yet."

"Is she getting better?"

"Not worse. We have to send the blood out for testing. It could take several weeks."

"Thank you." Andrew bowed and left. It wasn't exactly the most desirable response.

Andrew went outside and walked around the block. The lack of street lights made walking precarious, but the moon was bright at least. Two scruffy men across the street were singing an old song about fishing (as best as Andrew could tell) in between pulls on a small glass bottle. He stood and listened for a long minute. The harmony came and went, conflicting occasionally with kids yelling at one another down the street. Andrew went back into the hospital and set up a couple of chairs in Bhaniel's room for a makeshift sleeping couch. She was sleeping quietly on a cot against the wall. Even though Andrew's bed was horribly uncomfortable, he fell into a deep sleep almost immediately.

Sunlight poured into the room through the open door. Andrew woke up, but couldn't move his head. His neck was frozen stiff in the position he assumed last night. Slowly, the muscles came around and he sat up. Bhaniel was gone, but she had laid her blanket over him before she left. Andrew found her talking to a nurse. He couldn't keep up with what was being said, but Bhaniel looked encouraged as she walked away to continue her duties.

"So what did she say?"

"Lala needs to go to Kinshasa."

"Is that possible? Isn't Kinshasa where the fighting is the worst?"

"There may not be a choice. Lala is in danger of having any number of viruses, all of them deadly. No doctor is here, and medicine is limited. The nurse said we could go to Kikwit, but their ability to treat her may not be any better. Kinshasa has the facilities to test her and an area to keep her quarantined."

"You seemed to be encouraged talking to the nurse. I was hoping Lala was getting better."

"They are doing everything in their power, and I am grateful. We are fighting against time, however. The viruses work quickly. So must we."

"We don't know if the hospital is functioning. What if the fighting has shut it down?"

"Our options are limited."

"I'll take her."

"You don't know the city, Andrew. We may have to go in after dark."

"How do we get there? The bus ride would be too rough." Andrew got a twinkle in his eye. "I know a pilot who has combat experience. And he's right here in the clinic. Will you translate if I can find him?" Bhaniel nodded. "I'll be back in a minute." Andrew took off down the hall, hoping Luc was still in the building.

He ran through the hallways checking every room. Luc was nowhere to be found so Andrew ran outside intending to hustle over to the airport. Just as he rounded the corner of the building, Luc was talking to a meat merchant under the cover of his ragged tent intent on securing some nourishment before attempting a trip back to Gabon.

"Luc!"

Luc whipped around to see what the commotion was only to see Andrew racing toward him.

"What is it, Mr. Andrew?"

"I'm so glad I caught you. Hold there for one minute." He ran back inside and collected Bhaniel.

"Have you checked on your plane yet?"

"Just heading there. Is there something wrong with it?"

"No, when I came to town, I checked on it and the mechanic said it was almost done. I have another favor to ask of you."

Luc braced himself, but felt obliged due to Andrew's heroics earlier.
"I need you to take three of us to Kinshasa. The third one is a girl who is
sick and must get to the doctors there."
"Oh Mr. Andrew." Luc was shaking his head as his whole body began to
quake from fear. "The fighting is so strong there. I am afraid we would be
shot down for sure."
"Luc, I know it is a dangerous proposition, but we have no other options. I
would offer to rent the plane and fly it myself, but I have flown a plane
only one time – today – and don't know how to communicate with the
tower there."
Bhaniel spoke to Luc quickly, way too fast for Andrew to catch it all. Luc
relaxed his shoulders like someone who could resist no further. Andrew
looked to Bhaniel for the translation.
"Luc is willing to take us, but we may need to find our own way back.
He's willing to take double the price you paid him for the trip here. Also,
he will need you to be the co-pilot."
Andrew began to protest, but after looking at both of them decided it
wasn't worth it. Luc was the only game in town one arm or not.
"I'll go with Luc to check out the plane and find someone to wheel Lala to
the airport." He left Bhaniel to secure Lala's release.

The mechanic was in the hangar when they walked up so Luc and Andrew
inspected the plane for any obvious issues. The plane still had some holes
in the fuselage, but the wings were repaired and the landing gear was in
good shape. Andrew didn't remember any problems with the engine, but
they definitely needed some fuel. The mechanic had appeared by this time,
and Luc asked him if it was ready to fly.
"It is, however, the rudder is sluggish."
Andrew studied Luc to see if he thought it was a danger to fly. Luc brushed
it off like any good bush pilot. He made plans to fuel the plane as Andrew
worked his way back to the clinic.
Bhaniel had Lala lying on a cart outside.
"Andrew, we will need to keep her away from Luc. Here, put these on."
She handed him a mask and gloves.
Andrew noticed the cart was without locomotion. "Looks like I'll be the
donkey today."
"Would you please? The fewer people – or animals – around Lala the
better, I think."
"Sure. Let's go before Luc changes his mind. By the way, shouldn't we tell
someone at the home what we're doing?"
"Yes, I sent one of the clinic workers to the home with a message. I hope it
will be enough."

Everyone settled into the plane. Andrew affixed a curtain between Lala and the cockpit. Bhaniel remained with her while Andrew assumed the right front seat.

"Mr. Andrew, I will need you to do many things during this flight. You are experienced, no?"

Andrew made a motion like he was belly laughing. "I will give it my best."

Luc was limited in his movements and strength, but Andrew had a new appreciation for his command of the aircraft as it lifted smoothly into the air. The plane may have been held together with baling wire and tree sap, but for the moment it felt solid. Luc banked the plane to the southwest and adjusted the radio frequency.

"I am not getting an answer from the tower." Luc looked nervous.

Andrew wasn't sure what to say, partly because Luc might not understand him anyway. He knew Luc had tried almost everything attempting to raise the Kinshasa N'dolo tower.

"What about the other airport?" Bhaniel stuck her head through the curtain.

"I tried. No answer. Besides, it's very far away from the hospital."

They flew in silence for a few minutes as each one considered their options.

Andrew called to the back. "How is Lala doing?"

"About the same. Luc, can we land without notifying the tower?"

"We will have to try. Before we do, I'll attempt to contact any other planes in the air around the city."

Luc twisted the radio dial, calling out to anyone who would listen.

"Nothing." Luc was out of ideas except one. "Mr. Andrew, we will need to look for airplanes as we land."

Uh oh. Andrew was bracing for this, but hoping for a miracle. Until this moment, the worst scenario he could imagine had them streaking toward the airport as anti-aircraft guns peppered the air around them. Now, they could add dodging commercial aircraft to the list of very real dangers. Such is the beauty of facing death over and over again. You make your peace knowing it's in your Maker's hands and roll with it.

"Okay. How far to the airport?"

"About ten minutes. We should begin scanning for other planes."

"Roger that." Andrew was all over it. His head was on a swivel, squinting his eyes to catch any airborne form. None so far. Luc brought the plane down to just a hundred meters. He reasoned the jet liners would not get this low until they were right on the runway. Houses were beginning to appear below. The Congo River rose up to the north. In no time, they were over the city and practically flying in between the tall buildings.

"The airport is straight ahead. But the lights are not on."

Thankfully it wasn't nighttime yet. If the sun was down, blindness could be added to the danger list.

"I haven't seen any other airplanes."

They were alone in the air. Andrew couldn't detect any movement in the streets below either. If Kinshasa was the epicenter of the battle for control of western DRC, miraculously, they were landing at halftime. Relief turned to eerie discomfort though. The enemy had hidden himself from them. They tiptoed toward the airport hoping to go unnoticed.

"Mr. Andrew you will need to help me turn the plane; and when I tell you, move the flaps and lower the throttle."

Andrew was in the zone, ready to land the plane with a blindfold if called to do so. He mimicked Luc's movements at the wheel and put his hand on the throttle.

"Full flaps, half throttle!"

"Got it."

The plane dropped even lower and the two men turned out toward the river. Circling around in a wide arc, he faced the sun and centered the plane on the first runway he saw. Andrew scanned more furiously as he manned the controls, but could not find one bogie.

"Everyone be ready, this is it! When I tell you, cut the throttle!"

Luc all but scraped the rooftops on his final descent.

"Wait! The runway is full of holes!"

Andrew saw it too. There was no way any plane could land at this airport.

"Help me! Throttle up and return the flaps!" Andrew performed and Luc pulled them back up.

"Where do we go?"

Luc searched for possibilities. Andrew saw a plethora of streets, but too many cars blocked their way.

"There is the hospital." Luc pointed at a large group of buildings to the right. Andrew noticed a spacious green area between them and the hospital.

"What is that?"

"A golf course."

"What?!" A golf course seemed so out of place to Andrew.

Luc wasn't convinced. "Too short."

"Par five. No problem."

Luc had no other ideas so he was going to have to trust Andrew.

"Show me where."

Andrew helped Luc swing the craft around for a fly by. They located the longest hole on the course with no trees or sand traps and lined up the plane.

"We must touch down at the very front or we will overshoot. Throttle and flaps now!"

The plane dropped abruptly on the tee box and bounced down the fairway. It was a slight dog leg left and Luc attempted to stay in the short grass. What was left of the grass that is. Thankfully, the par five was just enough distance. The plane came to a rest on the green with the flag resting against the right wing.

"On in one. We're putting for double eagle."

Luc had no idea what Andrew was talking about.

"There is the hospital." Bhaniel had emerged from the back. "We should find a wheel chair."

Andrew unhitched and hopped out of the plane. Luc sat back and relaxed for the first time all day. His shoulder began to throb.

"Luc, you have done a great thing today. Will you stay or go?" Bhaniel asked.

"I want to go, but I know I must stay. How will you go back if I do not?"

"It is a debt we can never repay. Thank you."

Andrew reappeared with a wheel chair, an odd caddy steering his way toward the green.

"The conditions are horrible inside, but I think there is a doctor who might be able to help us."

As the sun beamed down on them, Bhaniel and Andrew helped Lala into the rusty wheel chair. Luc stayed behind to see what he could do to camouflage the airplane.

"You're not going to like it."

"The hospital?"

"That and the lack of medical personnel. I only saw one guy who even looked like a doctor."

"We will have to trust God regardless of what it looks like."

"Fair enough."

Bhaniel was trying to hold Lala's head up as they entered the main doors of the hospital because she was nearly unconscious. She could see why Andrew's faith was damaged. The entry area and the halls leading to other wings were lined with the injured, sick and dying. Some were on the floor and others in chairs and on gurneys. The smell was like an open sewer, but no one seemed to care. No nurses or doctors were tending to the sick nor were they visible walking the halls.

"Oh my."

"Wait here. I'll walk down the hall and see if the doctor is close by."

Andrew went searching for help as Bhaniel steered Lala to an open space in the lobby. She knelt down to look into Lala's face. Lala was awake, but wanting to sleep.

"I'm sorry, Lala. This has been so hard for you. We are trying to find some people to help."

Lala mouthed the words 'thank you' and closed her eyes.

Andrew came back to the lobby with a small man who was wearing a filthy lab coat and some version of scrubs. Other patients in the room perked up a bit when he walked in hoping he would give them some attention as well.

"This is the doctor I told you about."

The hospital worker looked at Andrew when he heard doctor and began shaking his head.

"No doctor."

Bhaniel took over communicating.

"You are not a doctor?"

"No, all the doctors have been killed. Many were killed when rockets destroyed the eastern wing of the hospital. The remainder were shot by the rebels. Only a few nurses remain. Medicine is all gone."

"Sir, our sister is sick and we need to have her tested for hemorrhagic fever."

The medical man kneeled in front of Lala and studied her for a moment being careful not to touch her.

"She needs no test."

"But sir, we must try. If it is such a thing, she could be in danger of dying."

"A test would be pointless."

"Please, won't you help us?"

"The test would tell you what I already know. She has the fever, and you both have been exposed to it. We need to get her away from all these people."

"How do you know?"

"Has she been vomiting and had diarrhea? She's obviously weak, very weak."

"Yes. We have tried to keep her from becoming dehydrated."

"That's good. Do you see those bruises on her arms?"

"Yes."

"That is very typical of the fever. Follow me." Before Bhaniel and Andrew could even digest the enormity of Lala's situation, he was off and running. The 'doctor' navigated through the sea of people toward a hallway full of more people. Several of them held their arms up to him pleading for help. Andrew was sympathetic toward the overwhelming need.

"Are there any other hospital workers helping these people?" Bhaniel asked.

"A few. There is not much we can do for them. Even water is difficult to obtain. What we have must be boiled."

"What do you think can be done for Lala?"

The 'doctor' did not respond. After two more turns, he stopped.

"Here. Put her on the bed."

It was a vacant room with a simple bed and one small window. At least there would be some light when the electricity failed. He left for a moment and came back with gowns clearly used many times before.

"Put these on and don't take your masks off."

"What is your name, sir?"

"Mosungi."

"Mosungi, have you had other patients like Lala?"

"Yes. Many have come here and most of them died." Mosungi was unemotional about this provocative statement. It had lost all dramatic effect because he was surrounded by death day after day.

"Are there people here who have recovered?"

"Yes. A few. When they recover, their first desire is to leave. But, I know one girl remains. She has no family to take her home."

"How did she survive?"

"Honestly, I am not sure, but she is healthy again." Mosungi prepared some recently boiled water for Lala as he talked. "Since she is here, we can do for Lala what we have done for others."

"What did you do?"

"There is information going around that the blood from a patient recovering from 'the fever' has antibodies. If we can transfuse some of the blood to a suffering patient, there is a real chance the patient will recover."

"Have you tried it on others?"

"Yes. There has been some success, but others have died. I think the patients with matching blood types have fared the best. Also, if the disease has progressed too far, it makes survival unlikely."

"Is it possible to get some of the girl's blood for Lala?"

"Yes, we have some here. We have collected as much as we can. Unfortunately, we are not able to take plasma only. The only danger would be a conflicting blood type."

"We'll just have to risk it. We are out of options." Bhaniel stated.

"I'll get the blood. Wait here." Mosungi went in search of blood. Bhaniel began to wet Lala's mouth with the water.

"This is a little bit of a miracle. Who would guess in this place…" Andrew looked around the room for effect. "that it would contain the one thing that might save Lala. God is good."

"All the time." Bhaniel intoned.

Mosungi returned with a pint of blood, and the materials to administer an IV.

"It's a good day, I was able to find an IV. I sterilized it once more just in case."

Bhaniel breathed a silent prayer of protection against infection as the medicine man did his thing.

Mosungi set up the IV and all three stood around the bed in anticipation of new developments.

"We will wait and see. You should stay with her, but I must tend to other patients."

"Mosungi, thank you. You have been God's miracle today." Bhaniel and Andrew shook his hand.

"I will be back later to check on her."

Andrew was suddenly aware of his hunger. "I am going outside to find Luc and hopefully find some food for us."

Bhaniel stayed with Lala, praying and hoping for a sign of recovery.

"Hi." The high pitched voice startled Bhaniel. She turned to see a young girl no more than 11 or 12 standing in the doorway of Lala's room.

"Hello, what is your name?"

"Kopesa. Is she going to be okay?"

"We are not sure yet. She received some blood from a very special girl just a short time ago."

"I know. It's my blood."

Bhaniel thought it might be so.

"We are very thankful you gave your blood for us. It might save Lala's life."

Kopesa was matter of fact, much like the patient sleeping in the room. She stepped closer to the bed and gave Lala a good look.

"I think it will. She doesn't look as bad as some of the others who came here."

"Do you live here?"

"I do now. My family is gone. There is nowhere else to go. I help Mosungi and will give more blood when I can. He says when we get a centrifuge – whatever that is – we can get the plasma and give it to other fever victims. I want to be a doctor when I get older."

"You are well on your way. What else do you do for Mosungi?"

"Get bandages, boil water, clean up messes. Lots of smelly messes." She made a funny face. "Lately, I have been taking dead bodies to the 'D' wing. There are a lot of them." Kopesa was not fazed by this.

"I'm so sorry. Is it hard for you?"

"Not really. There are new ones every day. The war has taken many people. The ones who remain are like me. No families or homes. Maybe we will all live here at the hospital. I'd better go. I'm glad she is getting better. See you later." Kopesa waved and moved on down the hall. A fine doctor she would make someday, Bhaniel thought to herself.

Andrew was gone for nearly three hours. He came back with a back pack stuffed full with something. Bhaniel was asleep on the floor next to Lala's cot.

"Bhaniel. Bhaniel." He shook her lightly. "Do you want to eat?"

Bhaniel rose and looked over to Lala to see if there had been any change.

"Yes, I would like to eat. Were you able to find much?"

"Yes and no. Luc was the one who had success, but the choices were limited as you might guess. We found a vendor close to the river who was selling cooked beans and fish. I don't know if the fish is safe to eat or not. I brought some in case you wanted it. Luc said it was okay." Andrew laid out the offerings for Bhaniel.

"Did you see many people?"

"No, and the vendor said he is leaving. The word is the fighting is moving back toward the north. I don't know what the people here at the hospital intend to do, but we may have only a short time before Luc has to flee. Any change with Lala?"

"No, she is still sleeping. She took all the blood. I don't know if they will be able to do any tests."

"At this point I doubt it. Once she starts to show improvement, we may need to leave."

"Where is Luc?"

"He's eating by his plane. I told him not to come inside in case he hasn't been exposed to the virus already."

"We may need to cleanse his airplane. Thank you for getting the food."

"Sure. I feel guilty for eating when so many people here in the hospital look like they are starving."

"I understand. Maybe we can find some food for them before we go."

"Sure. How are you doing, Bhaniel? Tell me about the blood test."

Bhaniel measured her words, and decided not to avoid it.

"It showed I needed stronger medicine, but Theresa brought some testing materials so we can see if the numbers improve over time."

"I'm sorry it took so long for me to come back with the medicine." Andrew moved to take Bhaniel's hand. "If I hadn't been so obsessed with resolving my problems in the U.S., I could have come back sooner."

Bhaniel smiled. Her eyes began to water more from exhaustion than emotion, but with Andrew she was inclined to let her guard down much easier.

"You mustn't look at it that way. The time was right for you to do what you did." She didn't speak for some time. "I believe it will all work out for the best."

"You are my rock. I will believe with you. I think this area is devoted to infectious diseases, so there are a couple of empty cots in the room next door. Why don't you get some rest and I'll stay with Lala for a while."

"You've been so good to me, Andrew. I feel okay right now. Why don't you go and I will come get you in a little while. I need to pray."

"Okay. I'll be next door. Don't let me sleep all night."

Andrew was absolutely beat. He wanted Bhaniel to rest, but he had no idea how long he could have stayed awake. The cot in the next room was barely better than the cold hard floor, but it made no matter.

The alarm on Andrew's watch began to ring. If Bhaniel had not come for him prior to 4 am, he was going to spell her anyway. He stumbled toward the door and looked into the next room. Bhaniel was lying down on the floor with the back pack as a pillow. Lala was sleeping soundly and even asleep sounded better than yesterday. There was no point in waking either of them right now. Andrew wandered down the hall and explored the possibility of a private exit so he could walk outside for a bit. This hallway had very little human activity in the day time and right now was completely vacant. There, just past the admitting desk, was a metal door with a small window at eye level. Andrew stepped into the night and tried to get his bearings. Where was the plane from here? He turned the corner and by the light of the moon saw the edge of the golf course about a block away.

In the quietness of the night, he heard what at first sounded like thunder. As he focused his hearing on it, the noises were clearer and fairly obvious. Small arms fire and mortars. The fighting was getting close. The best case was Lala would show signs of real improvement and they would tear out of there at first light. It hinged on Lala. Andrew argued with himself over what would be best for her. The practical side of him supported the idea she wasn't going to get any other medical treatment here so why stay? He'd have to find out what Bhaniel's intuition was telling her. Andrew also wondered about Luc. Best way to find out was to ask him. He started toward the airplane assuming Luc was asleep in the back.

It took a while for Andrew to find the plane. Somehow, Luc was able to pull the plane over to the tree line and set some discarded items around it as a disguise. Actually, at night, it was hidden pretty well. He climbed through the roofing tin leaning against the hull and opened the door.

"Luc. Luc. Are you awake?"

Andrew could hear him snoring softly in the back. He climbed in the right side and spoke louder.

"Luc!"

"Huh? Who is it?" Luc rolled around and sat up, startled. "Mr. Andrew?"

"Luc. Please forgive." Andrew tried to speak clearly in French. "Do you think we can take off at dawn?"

"Yes. Yes. I will get the plane ready." Luc was pleased to hear of the possibility of leaving. The previous day had been a constant struggle between his interest in helping young Lala and the fear of being caught in the fighting. He had heard the sounds of war also. Dawn was coming none too soon.

"Great! Thanks, Luc. Can I help you move the plane?"

"Yes. We will need to move it back to the fairway."

For the next hour, the two men, Luc with one arm, shed the plane of its coverings and pushed the plane toward the fairway. It wasn't all the way to where they landed, but it was pointed the right way. Andrew was worn out.

"Luc, how did you do this yesterday?"

"Couple of men walking by helped me. I prayed they were not soldiers."

Andrew could see the first rays of morning in the eastern sky. His next task was to convince Bhaniel they needed to leave today. Right away.

"Luc, we will be back soon. Don't start the plane until we get here though."

"Okay."

An explosion ripped through a building maybe a kilometer to the south. The impact was strong enough to throw both men off balance.

"That was close. We will be out here as fast as we can." Andrew ran across the street and back to the door he came out of.

"Bhaniel." Andrew shook her arm. She roused and sat up, staring at him but still half asleep. "We should go."

"We don't know if Lala can travel."

"They have done all they can for her here. The fighting is coming this way and they are bombing within a kilometer of us. Right now, the best plan is to leave now."

Bhaniel got up and checked on Lala.

"Lala?"

"Hnhhh? Miss B?" Lala was practically coming out of a coma. She had no idea where she was.

"Lala. How do you feel?"

"Better. Thirsty."

Bhaniel got her some water and gave it to her in small sips.

"We may need to leave here soon. Do you think you can travel?"

"Where are we?"

"Kinshasa. We flew here yesterday."

"We?"

"Andrew and I, and our pilot."

"Andrew?"

He chimed in. "I'm right here, Lala." He took her hand.

"I'm glad." She drifted in and out, and lacked the strength to say much more.

Andrew and Bhaniel glanced at each other, and moved to the hallway.

"I know it's not the perfect plan, but our window of safety is closing. Fast. If we could continue the IV for her in the plane, she should travel okay."

Bhaniel turned toward Lala, her heart going out to her.

"I want to go." They could barely hear her say it, but Lala was ready to go.

Bhaniel smiled slightly and nodded at Andrew. "We must."

Adding an exclamation point to the decision was a mortar shell exploding nearby.

"And none too soon. Let's get Lala into the chair, and I'll try to find Mosungi to tell him we are leaving."

Everything went into high gear for Andrew. He was mindful of Lala's needs, but heartily believed fleeing Kinshasa was a great idea. Lala went into the chair and Andrew sprinted down the hall. Mosungi was nowhere to be found. He made a swipe through a wing he had not been in before, but found only waiting patients. Andrew went back toward Lala's room. When he arrived, Mosungi was there talking to Bhaniel and Lala. He was on one knee injecting something into Lala's arm.

"This will build up Lala's immune system."

"Thank you Mosungi. For all you've done."

"As she gets better, you will save many lives if you can get her plasma to a medical facility. She is now a life giver. If you develop symptoms, she is your source."

The sun was bright and the sounds of war were all around them. More people were moving up and down the streets trying to get out of the way of the fighting. Andrew stepped lively as he pushed the squeaking wheel chair. Bhaniel tried to hold Lala's head up as they went. They crossed into the golf course and stayed to the edge of the fairway. Luc was not visible, but there were few places he could be.

"I don't see Luc."

"He's there, somewhere."

Andrew pulled up next to the airplane and checked the side door. Luc was inside the plane asleep. He had gone scrounging for accessories and had found some padding for Lala to lie on during the trip home. Evidently it was effective, he was in a deep slumber.

"Luc! Wake up! We need to hit it."

Luc rolled over and came to life.

"Are you ready?"

"Yes. Very."

Andrew and Bhaniel helped Lala in as Luc got out.

"Is she feeling better?"

"Yes, I think so."

Luc gave an approving look as he circled the plane and got in the pilot's seat. He began the pre-flight procedures while Bhaniel reset the curtain. Andrew was closing the side door and heading to the co-pilot's seat when he heard the rifles cock. He turned to see at least ten soldiers form a semi-circle around the front of the plane. Luc was watching them carefully from his seat and had ceased his flight preparations.

"Get out!"

The men looked at each other resigned to the fact there was no escape. Andrew whispered to Bhaniel in the back as he moved to exit the plane. "Don't make a sound. They may not realize you are back there."

"Get out now!"

Andrew and Luc gathered at the side of the plane and the squad leader moved forward. He wanted to question Luc.

"What are you doing with this plane?"

Andrew tried to respond in French. "We brought a patient to the hospital."

"Quiet! I'll tell you when to speak!"

Suddenly, Bhaniel let out a gasp as she recognized the voice of the leader of the band of soldiers.

Lieutenant Raswa.

He heard the noise from inside the plane and motioned for two men to check inside. Before they could move any further, Bhaniel opened the door and came out, hoping they wouldn't notice Lala.

The lieutenant was dumbfounded for a moment.

"Bhaniel Tretechi! I cannot believe this! Why is an orphanage mistress in my city? You are far from home, I think."

"Hello Lieutenant."

Andrew wasn't sure what was happening.

"You know each other?"

Bhaniel just looked at Andrew and nodded.

"Oh yes, Miss Tretechi and I have known each other for many years. She provides medicine and rest for my soldiers when we come to Bandundu."

Andrew couldn't believe his eyes. This was the soldier who came to the home and brutalized Bhaniel. He owed this little man a tail whipping, but presently the soldiers had the advantage.

"We will need this plane for the military. You are the pilot?"

"Yes, but I need his help to fly the plane." Luc nodded toward Andrew.

"No, he will stay here with Miss Tretechi. You will fly me over the south side of the city to locate…"

"Lieutenant! Rebels! From the north!" A group of rag tag fighters riding in the back of three pickup trucks were headed their way. Some were already shooting at them.

"Move!" Lieutenant Raswa directed his troops to the tree line, but the rebels were already on them. Andrew got Luc's attention and motioned for him and Bhaniel to get in the plane.

The chaos of the moment worked in their favor. Neither group of soldiers acknowledged the plane's engine had roared to life as the fighters emptied their guns on each other. The window next to Andrew's head shattered from an errant round and other bullets ripped through the fuselage once again.

"Bhaniel, Lala, stay down!" Bhaniel was already on top of Lala shielding her body.

Luc gunned the engine and the plane moved forward. Everyone was hunkered down hoping they could slide out between bullets. The plane bounced and jerked, gaining speed as they rolled down the fairway.

Lieutenant Raswa noticed their escape and yelled for his soldiers to turn and shoot at the plane, but no one heard him. In his rage, the lieutenant left the protection of the trees and sprinted after the plane, squeezing off the final rounds in his pistol at the tail of the aircraft. The rebels took notice and redirected their focus on the lieutenant. The opportunity was too good to pass up. Four different shooters leveled their automatic weapons at the fleeing form and pulled the trigger. It was unclear who scored the first hit, but it slowed him down and then multiple rounds found their mark. The lieutenant lurched sideways from the force of the bullets' impact and flailed to the ground still trying to shoot the plane with an empty gun.

A slight upward incline near the tee box provided the final boost to launch the plane into the air. Luc and Andrew pulled the wheel back with all they had in hope of clearing the tree line. The plane rustled the leaves in the tree tops as they gathered height and momentum.

"Is everyone okay? Is anybody hurt?" Andrew turned to take inventory. Luc nodded that he was no worse than before as Andrew left his seat to check the ladies. Bhaniel was still covering Lala as Andrew knelt beside them. Lala was awake and looking at Andrew.

"She's hurt."

Andrew saw the blood on Bhaniel's torso as he tugged at her shoulder.

"Bhaniel!" He pulled her off Lala and turned her over, resting her head in his lap. She was taking shallow breaths in an attempt to lessen the pain.

"I'll be okay. I'll be okay."

"We've got to stop the bleeding." He laid her down on her good side and checked the wound. The bullet had entered at the base of her ribcage near the spine and come out her shoulder. It was a sure bet the jagged metal did extensive damage on its way through. Andrew took off his jacket, wadded it up and pressed it against her back. He tried to put pressure on her shoulder at the same time. The inability to stem the tide made Andrew want to panic. Bhaniel looked up at Andrew and tried to ease his concern.

"Don't worry, Andrew. It will work out for the best."

"I'm not going to lose you. Just hang in there. We'll be back home soon. Theresa will patch you up good as new."

Bhaniel had the look of someone at complete peace with no regrets.

"I love you, Andrew Isaacson. Thank you for caring for me. You are my angel."

Andrew didn't want to talk this way. It had a finality about it and he wasn't ready to concede. Even so, if events were well beyond his control, he wanted – needed – to say things to her.

"Bhaniel, you've made my life worth living again. You've taught me how to love and be the man I was intended to be. I love you." Andrew kissed her and whispered, "Please don't go."

Lala rolled over, raised her arm and put it on Andrew's knee. The three of them held on to each other as hard as they could.

# Chapter 95

Bandundu

The plane slowly came to a stop at the end of the runway. There was no welcoming party and no other aircraft was on the tarmac. No one spoke a word of gratitude for making it back to Bandundu. Andrew exited the co-pilot's seat and went to find the cart they had used the other day. He walked it back to the plane as Luc was finishing some pilot duties and checking the structure for further damage.

Andrew dragged Lala's pallet to the doorway of the fuselage and picked her up with both arms. She was awake and shielded her eyes from the sun as he took her out and placed her on the cart. Andrew climbed into the plane and knelt beside Bhaniel. She was completely and finally at rest. Bhaniel died that day not long after takeoff as Lala and Andrew held her tight. It was a suitable way for Bhaniel to enter eternity, giving everything she had to save another.

Andrew gathered her own scarf around her face and laid her gently next to Lala who put her arm around Bhaniel for the ride to the clinic. Andrew wasn't sure how far he could go. The last several days had exhausted his strength, and the finality of the trip home emptied the last stores of energy, testing his will to live. Once the adrenaline wore off, he would have nothing left.

The clinic couldn't offer much help, but at least it was somewhere to go until he was able to transport both ladies back to the home. They did have some food and fluids for Lala. She improved almost immediately with the sustenance. Somehow they were going to have to find a way to get regular measures of her plasma for others in need.

Workers at the clinic who knew Bhaniel took special care with her. One young girl offered to go to the home and bring Theresa back. Andrew declined. He felt he had to make the trip himself. On his way out of town, he checked on Luc. The pilot was almost a complete stranger, but through this ordeal Andrew and he had a unique bond only they could share. Luc's death defying courage was astounding, and it would be up to Andrew to tell the story of his legendary feats. He found him topping off the fuel tank one last time.

"Luc, is the plane able to fly?"

"Yes, Mr. Andrew. I will be able to replace the window in Gabon and the bullet holes will not hinder me. I may leave some of them to remind me." He smiled a little.

"Are YOU able to fly? How can you fly alone with one arm?"

"It feels much better. Your friend Miss Theresa is a miracle doctor." Luc bowed to emphasize his thankfulness.

Andrew wasn't going to argue with him. Chances were, Luc was in terrible pain but just couldn't bring himself to stay one day longer. The only question was the fever.

"Will you stay long enough so we can make sure you didn't get exposed to the fever?"

"I feel fine."

"If you were to get sick, we couldn't help you in Gabon."

"How long will it take to know?"

"Less than a week I think."

Luc thought it over. "I will go home and stay away from others." Luc didn't much care whether he had it or not.

"How can I repay you for all you have done? You risked your life, and saved Lala's because you stayed."

"But we were not able…." Luc couldn't bring himself to say it out loud. In a way, he felt responsible for not getting all of them out safely.

"All I can say is thank you. We will trust Bhaniel to God. She did not believe in accidents, and neither do I."

Andrew put five hundred dollars in Luc's hand. Luc considered the money and thought about giving it back.

"I think this is too much."

"It will never be enough. Will you be okay staying away from other people?"

Luc nodded. "No problem. I have no family."

"You're part of our family now. Goodbye Luc."

Andrew left him with the plane praying their heroic pilot wasn't infected.

The walk to the river was his trip to the gallows. Grief and sorrow awaited him. The elation of Lala's survival would be overshadowed by the loss of everyone's heart and soul. Andrew prayed for courage to do his duty.

The ferry slid to a stop in the muddy water on the far shore, yet Andrew couldn't remember getting on the boat. The short climb to the home lay before him. Maybe he would sit for just a minute on a rock and rest. The ferry driver faded in the distance as he returned to the city side of the river. Andrew sat and listened to the water lapping against the mud and rocks. The birds circled overhead with nothing better to do. Andrew had no idea what came next, and didn't really want to think about it very hard. He willed himself to stand and walk up the hill.

The kids were doing chores and playing. The adults were nearby working through a typical day at the home. Andrew stood and viewed the scene like one at a museum enjoying a pastoral landscape for the very last time. Life would change for everyone after this day. The ones old enough to remember would recall this day as the moment their world shifted.

"It's Andrew!" Several kids ran to him, but Andrew shied away.

"You guys will need to stay away from me for a while. I don't want to make anyone sick." The kids didn't understand, but they kept their distance.

The adults saw the commotion and walked up to greet him. Theresa came out of the main building half running to welcome the travelers home. She just ignored Andrew's warnings and went in for a hug.

"Andrew! Welcome home. Are Lala and Bhaniel with you? Are they in town?"

Andrew could only look down and shake his head.

"Andrew what happened? Andrew!"

Some of the ladies began to wail. They weren't entirely sure of the details, but their grief was certain.

Andrew broke down and went to his knees.

"I'm so sorry. I'm so sorry."

Theresa kneeled beside him and put her hands on his heaving shoulders. "Both of them?"

"No. Lala is okay."

"Bhaniel? Andrew, what happened? Bhaniel?" Theresa's voice elevated with each question.

Andrew raised his head and looked at her, tears creasing his cheeks.

"She's… gone." His throat clinched, barely letting him say the words.

Theresa's arms dropped to her sides as she looked up to heaven and cried out. The ladies gathered around them emitting a chorus of sorrow, falling to their knees or turning in circles. The kids saw this at a distance and sensed the sadness of the moment. Some of the smaller ones began to cry because they saw their family in so much pain.

"Where is she, Andrew?"

"She's at the clinic. I… I would have given my life for hers."

Theresa embraced him. "I know."

They held each other until the climax of the moment subsided.

"We need to tell the kids." Theresa rose and scanned the area to see where the kids were.

All of the ladies gathered themselves and turned toward the house.

The kids collected in the main building and Theresa went to stand in front of them.

"I know you all realize something sad has happened. As painful and difficult as it is, you deserve to know." Theresa hesitated slightly and measured her words. "Miss B… has gone to be… with Jesus."

Most of the kids weren't sure how to react, or what to do next. The older ones understood the gravity of the news. Some began to cry, others had seen so much loss in their young lives their emotions weren't as tender.

A young girl in the front of the group was confused. "Is she coming back soon?"

"No baby. She's not coming back. Miss B went to heaven."

Other kids had questions and protests as they grappled with the finality of the message.

"Why did she leave?" "I don't want her to go." "Why did Jesus take her?"

Theresa motioned for Andrew to come to the front.

"Would you tell the kids a little bit of what happened?"

The adults quieted the kids so everyone could hear Andrew.

"We took Lala to the hospital in Kinshasa by airplane. And we found someone to help her. A girl about your age." He pointed at two girls in the front. "Because she was recovering from the fever, they gave some of her blood to Lala and she got better. The soldiers were getting closer to the hospital by the second day, so we decided to leave even though Lala was still very weak. When we got to the plane, government soldiers surrounded the plane and wouldn't let us leave. Suddenly, a squad of rebel soldiers attacked, and in the confusion we jumped on the plane and tried to flee." Andrew slowed his speech. "As we were speeding up and about to take off, one of the government soldiers began to shoot at the plane and several bullets hit the back end of the plane. Miss B had laid her body on Lala to protect her and… one of the bullets hit her in the back. We tried to help her, but the damage was too great. If it had not been for Miss B, Lala would have been killed." Andrew, clothes stained with Bhaniel's blood, was turning this into a eulogy. "Miss B died the way she lived, giving herself for other people."

He sat down as the grief swept through the room.

Theresa stood up.

"I think there are several people who want to go into the city to bring her back. And Lala too."

One by one, kids all over the room stood up as a show of their solidarity.

"Me too."

"I want to go also, Miss T."

Pretty soon, even the bashful ones stood with the others. This was going to be a procession. By the time it was all done, most of the city would probably be involved. Andrew could think of nothing more appropriate.

"Let's get ready. We should leave before the sun sets."

"We'd better take candles."

And with that, they were in full planning mode. This would be a funeral event for a remarkable person who deserved all the best. The ladies began organizing the kids and gathering supplies. Theresa tried to be a part, but she was still reeling from the emotion of the loss of her beloved sister.

The afternoon progressed and all was ready. In addition to the elaborate plans, everyone found something to wear to give an air of formality to their appearance.

Andrew found Theresa hanging back.

"Ready?"

Theresa just shook her head.

"Want to stay here and wait for us to get back?"

"Staying is the only thing worse than going."

They stood and watched the first of the throng move toward the river.

"I'm sorry, Theresa. I know you and Bhaniel were so close."

"She saved my life so many times."

"I know the feeling. Wish I could have returned the favor."

"You know, it's fitting."

"What's that?"

"How she died. Someone like her shouldn't just waste away."

"Waste away? I thought she was doing well."

"What did she tell you?"

"Bhaniel said her medicine had to be increased. She was hopeful her numbers were going to improve soon."

"It was much worse. She was on the verge of developing full blown AIDS. God may have done her a favor."

Andrew had to take a minute to process this. If only he'd come back sooner with the medicine. If only he had gone to Kinshasa without her. If only.

"Don't take any personal responsibility for what happened. Bhaniel only did what she believed was God's will and believed circumstances were completely under His control."

It was as if Theresa was reading his mind.

"It may take a while to forgive myself."

"For what? If it wasn't for you, Bhaniel may not have survived as long as she did. You were the love of her life. Bhaniel was grateful she lived long enough to know you. You gave her a gift only you could give."

The last of the group was going down the hill to the river. It was time to catch up with them.

"Thank you. Ready?"

"As I'll ever be."

By the time the ferry, and a few random boats it turns out, transported everyone across the river, the sun was touching the horizon. The candles and makeshift torches were lit and a column of flame snaked its way toward the center of town. People stopped to watch and listen. The kids were singing some of Bhaniel's favorite Jesus songs as they walked. Other kids and adults joined the procession not really knowing where it was headed.

Ndulue led the group and stopped at the entrance to the clinic. A worker taking a break outside had seen the marchers coming and raced inside to warn the others. Theresa squeezed past the collected throng and stepped inside to find her people. Andrew was conflicted because of his unkempt emotions but went in anyway.

"We are here to receive Ms. Tretechi and Lala."

An elderly lady nodded and motioned for Theresa and Andrew to follow. Lala and Bhaniel shared a dimly lit room. Lala was sleeping, but quickly awoke when they entered.

"Oh, Lala!" Theresa threw her arms around her and a flood of relief rejuvenated her. The memories of her own ordeal and ultimate survival stirred again. It caused her to look over at Bhaniel. Andrew took Lala's hand as Theresa moved to Bhaniel's side. She cried tears of loss and love half expecting her to wake up and accompany them home.

Andrew sat on the edge of her bed. "Lala, forgive us for taking so long to come back. We brought some people with us."

She was still weak, but obviously greatly improved. Lala raised up on an elbow.

"Can I go to them?"

"Yes, let's get you in a wheel chair."

Andrew left Theresa with Bhaniel and wheeled Lala down the hall and in view of her brothers and sisters. It was a sincere moment of joy in the midst of the grieving. Everyone called to her wishing they could embrace Lala as Andrew stood to the side and reluctantly considered the possibility the trip was completely worth it. He was ready for the reunion to go on indefinitely, but Theresa appeared at the door with two workers pushing a gurney behind her.

They brought Bhaniel out as the crowd erupted in wails of anguish and heartache. The further they pushed her cart, the congestion of people divided and allowed them to pass through. Theresa led them down the street to an open area where they parked her body under a starlit sky. The kids and workers encircled Bhaniel and one of the adults began to sing a traditional mourning song. Those who knew it joined in while others stood silently as the flickering light of the torches and candles danced to the music.

Several songs were sung and with each new offering, more townspeople gathered. It became so raucous at times, separate groups were singing different songs and others were dancing to impromptu drumming completely disconnected from the vocal music. The rhythm section ultimately dominated the evening and nearly everyone was moving around Bhaniel to the beat. Whoever was in the city and not responding to the music, did so as an act of their will. The beat of the drums had a hypnotic effect on those who drew near, gripping them with each impact, rendering them helpless to break loose.

The event went well into the night. Andrew, completely unaware of how long it had gone on, was exhausted and sat as did many of the younger kids who were also spent. Reluctantly, the adults agreed to lead the group back to the home where Bhaniel would complete her journey. As the drumming and random singing ceased, the townspeople went their own way, leaving the members of the home to rekindle their torches for the trek back across the river.

# Chapter 96

IORRF Headquarters

The secretary stuck her head in the door and interrupted the director eating a tuna fish sandwich at his desk.

"Director, you have a call on line 2 from Andrew Isaacson. He's calling from Bandundu."

Oh boy, he thought to himself. There's no telling what is going on over there.

"Thank you, Sheri."

"Andrew! How are you?"

"Director, hi. I'm doing okay, but we've had an incident. Bhaniel and I flew Lala to Kinshasa to see about treatment for hemorrhagic fever and it looks like she's going to recover completely. But, as you know, there is fighting going on in Kinshasa."

Andrew was wavering.

"Yes, I know. It is so dangerous there right now. I'm so thankful you were able to get home safely."

"Well that is why I am calling. I'm so sorry to tell you that Bhaniel was... I mean to say... Bhaniel didn't make it."

There was silence on the other end for some time.

"Andrew, what happened?" The director's tone deepened.

Andrew began the saga from his return to the country and left out no details.

"We are going to have the funeral soon. Tomorrow or the next day maybe."

"I'll see if there is any way I can make it there."

"If you cannot, we will understand. It was almost impossible for Theresa and me to sneak back in."

"We will make every effort. Andrew, I'm so sorry. Even in the sadness, I'm very thankful you were able to find help for Lala. You saved her life."

"It certainly came at a high price."

"That was the beauty of Bhaniel Tretechi. It was always a price she was willing to pay. Thank you for calling. I hope to see you soon. So long Andrew."

Director Hizanga hung up the phone and bowed his head. Suddenly, he didn't have the energy for the two afternoon meetings planned. Salvatore Hizanga could not imagine worse news than this. The DRC had lost a member of its royalty of sorts, the organization had lost its most effective representative, and the home had lost its longtime leader. But most importantly, at least to him, he had lost a friend. A sister really. They had been like family for eleven years. He had to find a way to get to the funeral.

\*\*\*

The plans for the funeral were underway and growing as more and more kids wanted to be a part. Theresa took control and became the emotional hub for the kids and adults too. Andrew felt himself hanging back unable, maybe unwilling, to engage in the bustle of the moment. For some, the grieving process caused them to be more active. They pushed out the sharp, painful emotions with busy work. Andrew, however, spent long periods of time alone, but he couldn't bring himself to go to the porch. In the early evening of the first day, Andrew was walking toward the hilltop for some solitude and angled by the main building. Someone had helped Lala into a chair just outside the door so she could get some fresh air.

"Where are you going?"

"Just for a short walk."

"Sit here with me."

Andrew didn't have a good reason not to, so he found an overturned stool around the corner of the building.

"Are you feeling better? You look good."

"I'm alive. That's something. I do have more energy today."

"I'm glad. We came close to losing you."

"Maybe you should have just let me go."

Andrew looked at Lala in surprise.

"You know Bhaniel would never allow it."

"Going to Kinshasa cost her life. It wasn't worth it."

"Yes it was. Bhaniel always valued you and the others' lives over her own. It wasn't a hard decision for her."

"What about you? The funeral coming up could have just as easily been yours."

"True. A big part of me wishes it was me instead of her."

"I am not often weak minded, but I feel responsible for Miss B's death."
"Please don't carry that burden. I have to forgive myself too."
"Was she dying?"
"Apparently so. I was told the HIV had progressed further than she let on."
"I'm glad she didn't die of AIDS."
"Agreed. She died a hero."
"It's a debt I can never repay."
"There is a very important reason you recovered. Your blood may save hundreds of lives. We need to find a way to make it available to others who have the fever."
"Can I stay here and do it?"
"You may have to consider living somewhere else. At least for a while."
"You're right. It will be worth it. How do we make it happen?"
"I don't know. Director Hizanga said he was coming to the funeral. If he can make it here, we'll ask him."
They sat in silence for a time.
"Thank you for saving my life, Mr. Andrew."
Andrew looked at her and smiled a little. Lala wasn't given to great displays of emotion, but he reached out to her and hugged her and she cried with great sobs.
"You're worth it."
Andrew forgot about going to the hilltop, at least for now.

"I think we need to start." Ndulue offered her opinion knowing the group was struggling with what to do. No one really said anything, but most nodded in agreement. As much as they wished the director could attend, there was no way to know where he might be. The kids were ready and a fair number of townspeople had also gathered at the home.
Since the impromptu memorial service two nights ago incorporated traditional funeral customs, the members of the home decided to make this event similar to their best worship service. It would be outside, near the hill overlooking the property. The grave had already been dug and the coffin was on a bench next to it. Clouds covered the sun making for a mostly mild day. Even so, it did not appear as if it would rain.
The kids started by singing songs together. Everyone who could play an instrument accompanied the choir. Afterward, several girls offered poetry honoring Bhaniel, and a number of Andrew's protégés presented their favorite drawings and paintings. Another round of music and then the eulogies. Aleefa began, followed by Ndulue. Theresa recounted Bhaniel's journey to save her life, echoing a common theme for most of the members of the home.
"If it had not been for Bhaniel, I would not be here today."

Eventually, Andrew stood up in front of the group, but to the side of where Bhaniel lay.

"I do not want to give the impression I knew Bhaniel Tretechi better than any of you, or knew her longer. I am a relative newcomer to the home. Yet, I came as a refugee like so many of you, and like you, Bhaniel welcomed me when no one else would. In this short time, you all became my family, and this wonderful lady…" Andrew had to stop for a second, "was the love of my life."

"Bhaniel taught me the meaning of selfless love and kindness. Not by persuasive words, but by the things she did every day. It has been my privilege to have known Bhaniel Tretechi, and it is my sincere desire to remain here with you to continue the work she started. Heaven is a sweeter place today because of her. I am so happy for her, she has no disease or pain. No sorrow, no tears. We will join her someday, but until then, we press on to the high calling of the Lord Jesus Christ."

Andrew laid one of his drawings of Bhaniel on the casket and turned to help Lala reach the front. She sat down in a chair he unfolded for her. Everyone had to be extra quiet and attentive, because Lala spoke softly.

"Some of you remember when I first came to the home. I had walked for days not knowing where to go and was nearly starved to death. Miss B took me in without a second thought. Every time I woke up in the night with a bad dream, either Miss B or Momma Ndulue was right there by my side. Most of you know the story now how Mr. Andrew and Miss B took me to Kinshasa because I was almost dead. It didn't matter to them what danger was waiting on us. When we were in the plane coming back to Bandundu, Miss B was hurt and almost unable to talk. Right before she closed her eyes for the last time, she was thinking of you. She said, 'Lala, take care of my babies.' This was right after she had taken a bullet meant for me."

"I'll never be able to repay her or Mr. Andrew for what they did, but because I survived the fever, I can help those who are sick. Hopefully, for a long, long time."

With Andrew holding her, Lala went to the casket, embraced it and kissed the top. Kids and adults lined up to offer their last tributes and leave a memento behind. At the end, the casket was covered in drawings, artifacts, flowers and other handmade creations. Each one the sincerest of expressions.

The young men gathered around the casket, and with crude straps hoisted the casket and positioned it above the prepared gravesite. Slowly, they lowered Bhaniel into the ground as the cries from the living gathered steam. With each shovel of dirt, the volume and breadth increased. Finally, the gravesite became a mound of sifted soil and a temporary stone marker was placed at the head. Just then, on what had been a typically humid day, a cool breeze from the northwest blew over them. Andrew looked up to the sky and saw the sun squeeze between two clouds. He breathed in the refreshing wind, knowing who it was, but not where it was going. "Goodbye, Bhaniel."

In the days ahead, the director did make it to the home. His path was nearly as circuitous as Andrew and Theresa's, but success was measured only as pass/fail. He joined in the routines emerging with the reassigned responsibilities. Ndulue and Theresa quickly developed an impressive leadership tandem and many of the kids assumed more duties, taking pride and ownership in their home. Andrew enthusiastically took on the role of surrogate father to many of the boys often conducting spontaneous training sessions exploring the true nature of becoming a man. This involved creating unusual body noises at will, setting new records for the number of rocks in one's mouth or various and sundry feats of athletic skill. During breaks from this rigorous curriculum, Aleefa would take some of the boys hunting for small game. Almost everyone had their own handmade spears and were learning to use them. The director took a turn at target practice with someone's extra spear to the delight of the assembled group. Everyone offered tips to improve his aim and speed.
"I don't believe I'll ever get the hang of this." The director was breaking a sweat.
"Nonsense. When hunger is the price of failure, you learn quickly." Andrew spoke as an experienced hunter.
"I see your point. It's pure business to these guys." He put down his spear and encouraged Andrew to walk with him.
"Everyone seems to be functioning well."
"Yes, we are adapting."
"What's next for you?"
"Besides being here?"
"Yes. You mentioned bringing some of the older kids back to America with you when we talked before. Still interested?"
"Since Bhaniel has passed, I haven't given it much thought."
"After we talked, I did some checking. If we can work out the travel aspect, Atlanta Metropolitan State College indicated they have generous scholarship programs for international students. The fact these kids are orphans and essentially destitute makes each one who shows academic talent and the will to pursue an education very attractive to many colleges."

"I will always be willing to help financially as much as I can. What about the kids with HIV? Will they have trouble getting into the U.S.?"

"The government relaxed their rules a while back. It shouldn't be a problem with just a few kids at a time."

"What about the universities here?"

"Some are quality and others, many others, are not."

"I imagine a lot of the kids would enjoy the adventure of going to America. I can escort them I suppose. In fact, I have to go back sometime anyway."

"Really? Why?"

"Something I promised Bhaniel before she died. One of the last things she said to me in the plane was how I needed to find my son and rebuild my relationship with him. Funny how such a thing was on her mind."

"She was a unique soul. Well, we wouldn't want to disappoint her would we? I hope you will come to the states soon."

"Thanks."

# Chapter 97

The Orphanage

"Mr. Andrew. Wake up. Mr. Andrew!"
Andrew was sleeping soundly for a change and the interruption was not welcome nor was it easy to grip reality. Maybe if he feigned sleep, the intruder would give up and go away.
"Mr. Andrew! It's important."
"hhnghh." He opened one eye. Aleefa was kneeling by his bed acting like he wanted Andrew to join a band of ninjas with him. "What is it?"
"I need to talk to you."
"Is someone hurt?"
"No."
"Runaway?"
"No."
"Are the soldiers back?"
"No." Aleefa was rolling his eyes now.
"Are you sure it can't wait until morning?"
Aleefa thought it over. "Maybe, but I have decided, so I will tell you now. I am ready to go to America to continue my studies." He beamed.
Andrew opened both eyes and looked at him by the light of the small candle in Aleefa's hand.
"That's great, Aleefa. We can begin preparations tomorrow." Emphasis on tomorrow.
"Thank you, Mr. Andrew. I am stoked!"
Now where did he learn that term? Aleefa turned to leave and came back.
"Mr. Andrew."
"Hmm?"
"What college will I attend?"
"There are a few choices."

"Will I live with you?"

"Not sure."

"What should I study?"

"Time management."

"Huh?"

"Aleefa, can we talk about it in the morning?"

"Sure, Mr. Andrew. Good night. Mr. Andrew?"

"Aleefa."

"Right. See you in the morning."

Aleefa wasn't going to be able to sleep.


Andrew had been searching for Lala nearly half an hour. She must have been resting on the porch, but he didn't want to go there. It could wait. He could wait. The pain was too great still, and she would come back around soon enough. So he busied himself with chores and fixing the loose spot in the roof of the dormitory. He was up on the ladder when Lala came around the corner of the main building.

"Are you looking for me?"

"Hello, Lala. How are you feeling today?"

"Better. I'm still walking with the cane, but I'm not as tired."

"Good to hear."

"Did you want to talk with me?"

"Yes I did." Andrew got off the ladder and brought down his tools. He motioned to a bench.

"The Director has been working on a project to allow some of the older kids to go to university in America if they desire to. I wanted to visit with you to see if you were interested. Of course, there would be some testing to see if you were at an adequate educational level to qualify for college, but I think you would pass easily."

Lala was visibly pleased with the prospect, but tried to hide her emotion. Her demeanor changed a bit after considering it though.

"I would love to go. It has been a dream of mine since Miss B started teaching us."

"Great! Then I will contact the director and start the process."

"Except I can't go, at least not right now."

"Why?"

"I want to go eventually, but you and Miss B gave me a chance to live. I've got to do what I can to help other people first. I can go to university after."

Andrew studied Lala's face for a time. He had grown to appreciate everything about her, and was now seeing how much she was like Bhaniel. The link between the two was almost like Elijah and Elisha.

"What do you plan to do?"

"I told you everything I had decided so far. Not sure what to do next. I've only been praying God would tell me what to do."

"The easy answer is you find a blood donation facility and you start giving your plasma."

"Where is the nearest one?"

"We'll have to find out."

"What does giving plasma do to you?"

"Nothing really. You'll be able to do it fairly often too. I thought you could come to America and give plasma while you go to college."

"Seems like it would be best to stay here, close to the need."

"Maybe you're right. Let's find the Director. He might know where to go." The two of them walked together, slowly. It might be some time before Lala was back to full strength.

"Director!" Andrew saw him in the boys' dorm.

"Yes, Andrew. Hello, Lala. How are you feeling today?"

"Good. Better every day."

"Great. What are you two up to?"

"We were talking, and I had asked Lala about going to America to school." Andrew nodded at Lala hoping she would tell her story.

"When we were in the hospital in Kinshasa, I received a blood transfusion from a young girl there who had recovered from the fever. It was the thing that saved my life. It is a dream of mine to go to university, but before I do, I need to give my blood or plasma so others can live."

"Lala, you are willing to do a wonderful thing."

"Director, we aren't sure where she should go to give plasma. Do you know?"

"I know there is a World Health Organization hub in Brazzaville. It might be the closest and best equipped place. With the civil war going on right across the river, I'm not sure what is happening there, however. Let me do some calling. We will find a place for you, Miss Lala. You are carrying life and healing within you!" He had a big smile on his face.

"Thank you, Director."

Just then, the bell began to ring signifying lunch.

Eventually, the director went back to America, and began the process of bringing two young men to college. Aleefa was anxious to take the plunge and did admirably on the entrance tests, but Rapha was an unexpected addition. He had not said much in the early stages, but Andrew coaxed an answer out of him. Rapha was a man of few words, but had always done well in Bhaniel's classes. Because he was so dedicated to fishing, no one was sure if he would want to leave. Also, his younger brother lived at the home, and Rapha was very protective of him. He, along with all the older teenagers, took a mock entrance exam in the spring. Some did well and others struggled. Rapha nearly aced the exam, and shocked the whole community. From then on, he was dubbed a brilliant academic star. Even so, Rapha was reluctant to capitalize on his emerging capabilities. When Theresa and Ndulue both promised Rapha they would take good care of his brother, Kadeem, he agreed to go. As his decision sank in, Rapha allowed himself to be excited. He began to dream of the possibilities of what a college education could mean for him and his brother. Now he couldn't wait.

The rains subsided going into June and July, which signified to Andrew and the boys the time to leave for America was closing in on them. They didn't have much to pack so their nervous energy was spent playing games and peppering Andrew with questions about his foreign land. The only real question for Andrew was would they fly to America or hitch a ride on another container ship? The boys didn't have to wait long for their answer. With the easing of tensions between what was left of the government and the rebel soldiers, travel around the country was possible and even international flights had begun again from Kinshasa. The director was able to communicate this to Andrew as well as secure flights for them out of Kinshasa. In the meantime, he spent nearly a month working with the officials at the World Health Organization to find a place for Lala to go. Ultimately, it was Brazzaville so her impending travels promised to be relatively short. WHO authorities had worried the war-reduced supplies and effectiveness of the Brazzaville office would hinder the collection and distribution of Lala's plasma. But the near cease fire in the last 60 days, gave everyone enough confidence to proceed. No one ventured a guess how long the truce would last, but history had educated them to act when the opportunity arose.
Lala did not realize what a celebrity she had become. When the WHO learned her story and her intent to work with them, they sprang into action. The organization's personnel indicated they would travel to Bandundu, collect Lala and take her to Brazzaville.

When the WHO vehicles showed up, it created a stir in town and people immediately lined up for treatment assuming the trucks were there to provide medical help. The drivers waved off most of the hopefuls as their associates traversed the river toward the home. One young mother who had been close by when the trucks rolled in, didn't leave when the drivers dispersed the crowd. She stood there with her ailing baby in her skeletal arms holding firm to the belief the WHO workers had a miracle cure for her child.

The driver tried to tell her none of his associates were doctors and medicine was limited, but she refused to concede, propelled by desperation. It was a scene he had witnessed many times before. He didn't have to be a doctor to realize the child had a pronounced infection on his skin. It had progressed to the point he was feverish and lethargic. Finally, he poked around in the back of the SUV and found some antibiotic packages left over from their most recent trip to Angola.

"Here. Take these pills – twice a day – until they are gone. It should stop the infection."

The mother was so thankful, but unsure as she looked at the package. "How will he take them?"

The driver thought a minute and pulled another package from the vehicle. He twisted open a capsule and showed her the contents.

"Sprinkle this into water or on the child's food twice a day."

She acted very pleased as she turned away, thanking him for his mercy. The driver wasn't sure if he was helping or hurting, but he had done all he could.

On the west side of the river, the small party of workers walked in a single file toward the home. A silence came over the kids. They stopped what they were doing and lined the path toward the home. The medical workers were notable visitors and Lala was, well, Lala. Not only did she have the same charisma as Bhaniel, but Lala was one of their own. She was a kid who grew up with them. Now she was going to save the world. It was a big moment none of them wanted to miss.

Lala met them as they entered the garden area. Her belongings were limited and easy to carry.

"Miss Lala. It is a pleasure to meet you." The lone female among the four travelers extended her hand. "I'm Valerie Bacchus."

The others gathered for greetings. Andrew stepped up as well as Theresa and Ndulue.

"Do you have time to stay? We have lunch almost ready."

"You are very kind, but our colleagues are waiting for us across the river. If Lala is prepared, we have everything ready to go."

"I'm ready."

Andrew, Theresa and Ndulue circled her and hugged her hard.

"Lala, we love you. I'm so proud of you."

"Lala, if you get lonely, you just come right back here."

Andrew cupped her face in his hands. "This is your moment. God knew only a certain kind of person could handle it. Go save the world."

Lala had tears streaming down her face as she held onto Andrew just a little longer. By this time, the kids had mobbed her and everyone wanted a hug. She began to methodically hug every single one so each one would have a sweet memory of her.

# Chapter 98

N'Djili International Airport, Kinshasa

"Seriously." Andrew rolled his eyes.

Aleefa and Rapha were going through the magazines and barf bags, testing the level of recline on the seats, and rechecking their bags in the overhead bin. And boarding was only half done. It would be another half hour before they even pulled away from the gate.

"When can we order dinner?"

"Are those guys outside putting our bags on this plane?"

"Will we get a prize since this is our first time to fly?"

Andrew was amazed the airport was functioning effectively. Just a few short weeks ago, the fighting was so intense, they couldn't land their prop plane. If only Lala could have been sick a little later, he thought to himself. But now, the time was right to take these guys to America. A short hop to Gabon and then on to Manaus, Brazil.

"Relax guys. This flight will be short. The next one will have all the fun stuff on it."

No dice. They were too keyed up. Passengers though they were, their only recourse was to pester the flight attendants. Andrew was weary.

Of course, it had already been a long day. Starting at dawn, they weren't sure how long the drive from Bandundu to Kinshasa was going to take. Most of the kids made it up to say their goodbyes. It was getting to be a habit at the home. One of the young ones declared, "No one else leaves unless I say so." Fair enough.

Andrew gazed out the window and thought back to the last plane he was on. Just a few blocks away, his hopeful crew fought for their lives as bullets tore through the aircraft's skin. The shouts of the soldiers replayed in his mind as the small plane raced down the fairway trying to take off. So close. They were a hair's breadth from getting out unscathed. The pain was still too fresh for Andrew to see the greater good. It was a pain of regret. Of anger. If he had done something just slightly different, she would have survived. It might take a while to completely forgive himself. After much emotional brawling, all that remained was sadness. He longed for Bhaniel and wanted her to be with him always.

The shudder of the plane as it rolled backward pulled Andrew back to the present. The aircraft spun to the south and taxied to the runway. The boys were barely breathing in anticipation. The flight attendants checked their belts one more time. Andrew was looking forward to a long nap on the trans-Atlantic hop.

The long day became even longer due to random delays at the airport. Once the travelers made it to Atlanta, there was no time to do anything but head straight for the college. Andrew introduced Aleefa and Rapha to taxi cabs, one of which escorted them to the front door of the school's administration building. Almost on cue, a lovely school representative met them at the curb.

"Welcome to Atlanta Metropolitan State College. If you will follow me, we can get both of you set up in your dorm and registered at the bursar's office."

The boys were speechless in the presence of such a vision of beauty. Shayla, the student volunteer was very smart in her skirt and blazer set in the school's colors, and her straight black hair hung lightly on her shoulders. Aleefa was smitten as she called his name and asked about his home. Rapha tried to give the impression he was not as star struck as his counterpart.

Andrew hung back as the boys became more comfortable with Shayla. They volleyed questions at her, sometimes not even sure if they wanted to know the answer. Just conversing with their beautiful attendant was satisfaction enough. Shayla never missed a beat. She gave the impression every question was valid and necessary, and rarely did she hesitate in providing reams of information.

The tour of campus took the better part of the afternoon and came to an end at their new dorm room.

"Thank you for choosing AMSC. It was great to meet you Aleefa and Rapha. Please come by the administration office if you have any questions or need help with anything. I'll be here at 9:30 tomorrow morning and we will go to the student orientation activities together." Shayla waved goodbye and slid out the door.

"She's very nice." Aleefa said as they stared at the door.

"Yes, I agree. Very nice." Rapha was all in.

"Hey guys, it's the first day. You are going to meet so many new people and make lots of friends. Let's go eat and then we'll set up your room. Classes start in two days!"

Andrew took them to a very American restaurant which seemed appropriate on their inaugural night in Atlanta. The Varsity drive-in restaurant provided all the hamburgers and milkshakes the boys could stand. In reality, they ate so much, Andrew feared their systems would rebel. Only time would tell. The three carried the boys' luggage and supplies to their dorm, and set it up. Andrew finally called it a night and made plans to see them later in the week. He fretted for their safety and well-being as he drove away. Such a doting father.

Andrew drove around the city for a while and decided to go by the gallery just in case. It was close to the end of the day so the chances were low he would run into Mitch, but it was worth a shot. He slowed as he rolled by and the lights were still on.

The door swung open and the bell was gone. Andrew didn't expect the twinge of sentiment upon learning the era of the bell was over. He thought he would be glad. Andrew heard a faint electronic beep in the back room instead. A nice looking, well dressed, young girl came into the front gallery to greet him.

"Welcome to the Schuster Gallery. Is there something I can help you find?"

"Thank you, hello. Actually, I was looking for someone. Do you know Mitch DeGuerre?"

"Oh, yes. He's just in the back office. Can I tell him your name?"

"Andrew Isaacson."

The name clearly startled the young assistant.

"Mr. Isaacson, so glad to finally meet you. I will tell Mr. DeGuerre you're here."

She turned abruptly and escaped to the back rooms.

"Andrew, welcome back."

He looked away from a bronze of an abstract version of a man and woman to see a standing Mitch, albeit with a cane for added support.

"Mitch. How are you doing? You're standing! You look great."

"I'm doing better every day." He pulled up his pant leg to show off one of his titanium legs. "I've just started walking with the cane. I still have the wheelchair in the back, but when Elise said you were here, I wanted to show off a little."

"Well, I am impressed. I'm so happy for you."

"It's all because of you. The legs, the therapy. The pain meds."

"Even if you want to hire someone to carry you around on their back, I'll gladly pay for it."

"Speaking of that, your paintings have sold really well. I've had more than enough to cover expenses, but if you are back for a while, you may have to crank out a few more pieces."

"I'm glad to hear it. I will give it my best. How is the gallery doing overall?"

"Not bad. When I was in the hospital, the gallery was closed so the bills piled up. After a while, I was able to do some business from the hospital. Even hired Elise while I was laying on my back."

"Nice."

"Elise has been a big help. She wants to learn to run a gallery and I needed someone to do just that. Foot traffic was pretty good after word got out we were tied to you. You may not realize it, but you were something of a cult hero after the event with Stella and the local mafia. Then it died out after the news broke."

"News? What news?"

"One of the television stations ran a couple of stories on your paintings and interviewed some people who insinuated the paintings weren't authentic. Saying other people did the actual painting."

"Were they from the company?"

"One was. The other was an auction house rep."

"How believable were they?"

"Believable enough. Like I said, the traffic coming in here for your AD Isaacson work has dropped off since then. The auction houses probably won't touch your stuff until they can find out if it is true or not."

"My sins are catching up to me finally."

"What are you going to do?"

"I'm not sure."

"What will preserve your reputation and the value of your work is whether people believe the signature on the art is authentic."

"Reputation? I don't care about reputation anymore. That guy is dead."

"But you need to care because it's not over. As long as the mob is invested in your former life, you are involved."

"So what do I do about it?" asked Andrew.

"Shut the mob down."

"Not easy."

"Buy the company back."

"From a bunch of loan sharks? I'd never be able to pay enough."

"Run to Africa and never come back."

"I'm not going to run the rest of my life."

"Restore the reputation of AD Isaacson."

"And give aid and comfort to organized crime?"

"You may not have any choice. The public needs to know what you told me. Lay it all out and do away with the secrets. If there is a backlash from the art world, at least you will have comfort the truth is out," Mitch offered.

"I don't feel the comfort."

"Do it and let the chips fall where they may. There is one thing I've learned - you can't control the future. All you can do is try to do the right thing and then turn loose of it."

"You're right. This has gone on too long. It's really the last thing to drag out into the light. If it goes south, then we will deal with it then. Except."

"Except what?"

"I'm dead."

"So come back to life," Mitch counseled.

"I really ought to. When the timing is right."

"Now you're talking."

"It's a whole new world, isn't it?"

"Welcome back."

"Are you living at home now?" Andrew asked.

"Not quite. It's sort of a halfway house. They bring me down here a few hours a day and then I go back. I can't do everything myself yet."

"Would it help if I came down here and put in a few hours every day?"

"Do you have time? Are you going back to Africa?"

"Some time. I'm not sure when. I brought two boys with me who just started at Atlanta Metropolitan State College. I want to stay close, maybe for the semester."

"As long as you don't bring the mob with you, come down anytime. Elise will put you to work. I'll warn you though. She doesn't put up with laziness or trouble makers."

"Noted. Actually, I'll probably hold off for at least a while just to get settled in. When I do come in however, I'll bring my A game."

Andrew walked over and gave Mitch a hug.

"I'm sorry again to have put you through this."

"Quit talking. You can't take responsibility for Stella or anyone else. I'm better for it. I survived. The ladies love the stories, and I've got some serious street cred now."

"That's what I'm talkin' about."

"See you soon."

# Chapter 99

Police Headquarters

The trip to the police station was a little awkward, but necessary. He was interested in finding out if there had been any positive movement in the case against the mob; plus Andrew needed the detectives to know he was back.

"Hi, are detectives Oliver and Tunney here?"

The officer at the desk acted like she wasn't used to the receptionist role.

"Well, I don't know. I guess I could check."

"I would appreciate it."

The officer picked up the phone. "Are Detectives Oliver and Tunney in the building? Uh huh. Uh huh. Okay, thanks." She looked at Andrew. "They're here, but you have to wait a few minutes. They are interviewing a witness. Wait over there." She pointed to a collection of wooden chairs lined up against the wall.

"Fine, thanks."

A few minutes turned into an hour. Andrew almost got up and left a half dozen times. Suddenly, Detective Tunney burst through the door, scanned the room and noticed Andrew.

"Andrew! Big surprise! How are you?"

"Good. Really good."

"How are things in Africa? You here for a while?"

"It's always crazy in Africa. I've brought a couple of the boys with me. They are starting school at Atlanta Metropolitan State College."

"Awesome! I'm sure they'll love it. That's where my sister went."

"Oh yeah? Very cool. I wanted to stop by and let you know I'm back maybe for a few months, and to find out how the case against the Karmazin family is going."

"It's good to have you back. You probably ought to stay away from your house though."

"Really? What's happening?"

"Come on. Let's go upstairs. Oliver is up there."

"Hey Oliver! Look who's back."

Detective Oliver glanced over his computer screen and spied Andrew. "Isaacson! What's going on?" The detective got up to shake his hand.

"Hello, Detective. Good to see you." Oliver looked at Tunney. "What'd you tell him?"

"Nothing yet, except to stay away from his house."

"Tell me what?" Andrew queried.

"You'd better sit down. The case has hit a few snags. It's not a big surprise, but the Karmazin family have closed ranks and the witnesses we were lining up have either disappeared or have changed their stories. It might take a little longer to pin them down on Stella's murder."

"What about the shooters? Couldn't you tie them to the family?"

"Not well. They were out of town contractors. Cash only, no names or previous activity."

"Lucky you're dead already. If they knew you were alive, your life would be in danger."

"Why?"

"The value of the company is in question. There has been some bad press regarding the authenticity of some of your work. As long as there are questions, no one is buying your older work, which makes their investment worth less. Also, we think some of their boys have been skulking around your house. So we don't want you to go home. At least not yet."

"I'm supposed to be on the run again?"

"I guess you could go home and go about your business. Not encouraged however."

"Wouldn't you look out for me?"

"As we always do, but we're human. Still have that apartment you rented last time?"

"No, but I'm pretty sure I can get it again."

"Well, get it and lay low."

"How long?"

"Unfortunately, it could be a while the way the case is going."

"Maybe it's time for a straight up confrontation."

"What do you mean?"

"What can we do to force their hand? I don't want to be afraid to come back to Atlanta."

"Come on, Andrew. The last time you did this, Tunney just about got greased."

Tunney protested, "They couldn't kill me. It was one round, and I had my vest on."

"Sure, sure. But it's dangerous, Andrew, and I don't want them to make you dead."

"Let me worry about me. I promise I won't put any of my friends at risk. If you back my play, we might be able to end this."

"I'm not going to bet against you, but at least tell us what you're going to do this time."

"I will."

# Chapter 100

Trudy's, Atlanta

The old bar stool felt pretty much the same.

"I'll have a draft beer."

Benny pulled a glass, filled it and set it in front of the stranger. He went back to wiping down the ice box.

Andrew sat in silence for close to twenty minutes as he waited for Fanny. She was in the back room, he could hear her.

"…and he's gonna pay his tab, I guarantee it." She tossed an empty bottle in the trash for emphasis. Fanny stopped and looked down the bar at the stranger. She readjusted her eyes to make sure she was seeing straight, then made the slow walk to the end of the bar.

"Hey, friend, we got a two drink minimum here."

"I intend to abide by the rules."

"Don't think I've seen you around here before."

"It has been a while."

"You live around here?"

"No, not really. Just seemed like a nice place to have a drink on my way through."

Fanny looked at his casual dress, beard and long hair.

"You come in from the islands?"

"Not exactly. I did cross the ocean to get here though."

"Welcome to America. Staying long?"

"Not sure yet. I brought a couple of young guys to Atlanta from overseas to attend school."

"My daughter just started college this week also. She's going to AMSC."

"No kidding. That's where my guys are going!"

"Small world. She wants to study medicine, but I may have to rob a bank to pay for it."

"Ever thought of moonlighting?"

"All the time, but then I finish a shift here and don't feel like doing anything. Getting too old I guess."

"I know a guy who's looking to hire. Pays good."

"Doing what?"

"Modeling."

"Either you or he is crazy."

"No, no. This is legit. He's a painter."

"You know I had a friend who did some of that. Actually modeled for him myself once."

"Really? Is he still painting?"

"No, I don't think so. He left the country a while back. Haven't heard from him, the jerk."

"Where'd he go?"

"Africa I think. Faked his own death and then ran off like a big chicken."

"Wow! He must have had some powerful enemies. Did they catch him?"

"I doubt it. He wasn't much to look at. He probably just melted into the jungle never to be seen again."

"I'm impressed." Andrew drained his bottle.

"Want another one?"

"I think I have to, don't I?"

Fanny popped the top on the same brand of beer and slid it to him.

"Go easy on the beer, I don't want to have to call you a cab later."

"No cab for me I have my car outside."

"Tough. If I think you're tipsy, you ain't driving."

"What'll I do with my car? You going to drive me home?"

The smallest hint of a smile curled the corner of Fanny's mouth as her eyes twinkled ever so slightly.

"I will if I have to. You rich boys always expect to be taken care of."

"Rich!? Do I look like I'm rich?"

Fanny eyed him up and down as she made her way around the end of the bar.

"After a shave and a haircut." Fanny got close to him and smelled of him. "And maybe a shower, you'd probably look like a rich boy. You live in a big mansion on the other side of town too, don't you?"

"One house is as good as another."

"Where'd you say you brought those boys from?"

"I didn't."

"Well?"

"Africa. The Congo."

"You had to run into my friend then."

"What was his name?"

Fanny looked far away and taxed her memory, "Allen, Arnold… what was it?"

"Arnold?! I've only been gone for a couple of months!"
Fanny let out a howl Bennie heard in the cooler. Some of the other guests
looked to see if the two of them were going to fight. She grabbed Andrew
and hugged him so hard he couldn't get his left arm free to hug her back.
"Andrew Isaacson! I can't believe my eyes!"
"In the flesh."
"No really. I barely recognize you. You look almost like the rest of us
average folk now."
"I'll consider that a compliment."
"I thought you were dead. Had a mental funeral and everything. You must
have some great stories, and I want to hear every one of them."
"It's great to see you, Fanny. Honestly, I don't know where to begin. I
have truly lived a lifetime since I snuck away on that container ship across
the Atlantic."
"Well get ready. When my shift ends, you're going to start talking."
"You get off soon?"
"About an hour."
"Fanny!" Benny needed help with some customers.
"Be right there." She turned to Andrew. "You have to leave?"
"No, I'm good. I'll watch the news."
The hour went quickly. Fanny would come down to his end of the bar
when it slowed down to rough Andrew up a bit. She had a love/hate
relationship with the beard. Long hair, absolutely not. She ended her shift
just a shade early and went to collect Andrew.
"It may be a good thing I've been gone all this time. The news is
depressing."
"Tell me about it. The president is selling us out to some of the middle
eastern countries for a better price on a barrel of oil, interest rates haven't
gone up in years, and the jobs numbers are horrible."
"Sounds like you keep up with the news pretty well."
"The TV is on at the bar all night. It's hard not to soak up some of it. They
say the same things over and over."
"True, so where do you want to go?"
"There's a little place just a mile down the road. It's open all night."
"Perfect."
"Can you drive?"
"Yeah, sure."

It was late enough, the place was nearly empty. The bar crowd was even
thin tonight. Andrew and Fanny got a booth toward the back.
"Would it bug you if I said I am so excited to see you?"
"No, that's why I came to the bar because I knew you would be. At least I
was hoping. How have you been?"

"Couldn't be better. Like I said, my baby started school so I don't really have anyone to look after now. I'm single again. Yay!" She said laughing.

"Actually, I already miss her. It's going to be kinda lonely I think."

"Probably for a while. Everyone says you get used to it. I got a little too used to it when I was single again."

"So much water under the bridge, right? Last time I saw you, you were racing off to catch a boat. I guess you caught it."

Andrew began the saga as the coffee came to the table. He was still going strong when the waiter came to the table to see if they needed anything for the fourth time.

"Do you need to go home?"

"No, I'm good. Actually, home isn't really an option right now."

"Why don't you come over to the house? We can talk until our eyes close and then you can crash at the Fanny Motel for the night."

"It wouldn't be a bother?"

"It's just me now. Come on. Do you remember how to get to my house?"

"Yeah, but I'd better follow you just in case."

Once the two made it to Fanny's house, they had caught their second wind. Andrew talked until the first light of dawn showed through the windows. In just a few hours, Fanny truly believed she knew Bhaniel and mourned her death along with Andrew. She remembered the events on the news recounting Stella's abrupt end, and showed Andrew the newspaper clippings.

"Besides the fact I'll never forgive you for not contacting me when you came back, I am just blown away by your story."

"You know I would have if I could have. I had to go ninja."

"Sure, whatever." She smiled. "If it weren't you, I wouldn't believe half of it. It's a miracle you're still alive."

"Yeah, I get that a lot."

"Don't even start. Let's call it a night. You can sleep in the bedroom on the right. The sun won't shine in there, so you can sleep okay."

"Sounds good. I'm beat. You wore me out making me talk all this time."

"I bet it's tough working up the energy to talk about yourself."

"You know it is. I'm out of practice."

# Chapter 101

Atlanta

Andrew checked on the boys and they were doing fine. The new student committee had pre-planned enough activities, they were going to have trouble making it to all their classes. But Aleefa and Rapha were enjoying every minute. To their credit, they viewed everything about their college experience as an opportunity and a blessing. Both realized where they came from and what lay ahead. The circle of friends whom Andrew met seemed very friendly which made him glad. It would be impossible for the boys to make it through four years of college without a strong friend group. Andrew offered to take the boys out to eat, but they had to decline. Their calendar was full until week after next.

He wanted to go home. Sort of. Fanny went to work early, so he was on his own. Andrew knew without a doubt the detectives would flip out if they got wind of what he intended to do. Technically, he wasn't going to his house. Andrew just wanted to bump around the neighborhood and see if there were any mob lookouts hanging around. If he found them, then sneaking in and out of the house would be easy. There was always a benefit to having the element of surprise. The longer the mob was in the dark, the more time he would have to prepare for their demise.

He canvased the adjoining neighborhood in his nondescript rented car. The sun was low on the horizon and the light was fading. Good for him, yet bad for spotting the mafia goons. Andrew tried to think of effective places to conduct a stake out but avoid neighbor concern. He circled the area several times, but found nothing. No obvious beater car with a couple of knuckleheads in the front seat eating double cheeseburgers for the umpteenth time constantly looking over toward Andrew's house with their binoculars. Andrew didn't even see the same car twice while roaming the streets. Next time maybe he'd sneak into the studio.

Andrew sank into a funk as he drove back to Fanny's. After all this time, he was finally at the end of his rope. He was tired. Tired of fighting and tired of being strong. He hadn't let himself grieve properly either. Now, the prospect of staying alive was back on him. Yet there was no logical explanation for his remarkable durability. The Lord had determined his time had not yet come. There was more for him to do.

"God in heaven, help me see the path you've laid out for me. Help me to understand my purpose for remaining here. I need to have some confirmation I am doing the things You intended for me to accomplish. What is the point of cheating death only to miss my calling?"

Andrew let himself into the darkened house, and without even taking off his jacket slumped into a chair in the living room. A numbness settled in on him and he barely moved for an hour. As his eyes adjusted to the dim light coming from the hallway, Andrew fixed his gaze on one book amidst a bookshelf overflowing with dusty volumes untouched in years. The gold lettering on the spine indicated it was the Bible. He felt a growing persuasion to read the words of David in the early chapters of Psalms. Based on what Bhaniel had taught the children, King David was a man with a monumental calling on his life. Yet he had times when he struggled to know and understand God's will.

He opened the book and read. As if time stood still, the next thing he was aware of was Fanny coming through the front door.

"You still up? It's almost four o'clock."

"Really? I lost track of time. I've been reading."

"Oh yeah? Whatcha reading?"

Andrew held up the Bible.

"Wow. You're digging deep. Anything interesting?"

"I'm blown away. I can't put it down. It's like I found a vein of gold and I have to get all of it."

"I haven't heard anyone talk like that for a long time. A lot of people will tell you it's the truth and there's life in the pages, but they lack the passion. You keep talking and I'm going to get all enthusiastic about God again. I may have forgotten how though."

"I doubt it. You probably just haven't worked those muscles in a while."

"You might have to help me get back in shape. There is something very powerful about sincerity and it makes me want some."

"Tell me how God speaks to you."

"Oh friend, it's been a long time since I traveled down that path."

"You had as much of a calling on your life to pastor as your husband did, didn't you?"

"Maybe so."

"So share your wisdom."

"Brother. We're going to watch the sun come up again, aren't we?"

"I won't keep you long, I know you're beat. Just one question. How does he speak to you?"

"Why do you ask?"

"It's good to know I think. I was reading about David and reading his prayers to God. There were plenty of times he wasn't sure how to proceed. But he waited on God."

"Sounds like a good plan. Are you afraid to wait?"

"No…. Maybe."

"Even when he was unsure and waiting on God, David continued to do the things he knew were God's will. Waiting doesn't necessarily mean sitting still."

Andrew considered his nugget of truth and smiled. "Fanny Wilcox, you still got game! Maybe it's time you got back into it."

"Come on now."

"So, answer the question. Answer it and you can go to bed."

"It's nothing real fancy. He just talks to my heart. If you're willing to hear, it's not very complicated. What exactly are you thinking about doing?"

"Bringing down organized crime."

"Single-handedly?"

"Not exactly, but I plan to be the pot stirrer."

"All of organized crime or a portion of it?"

"Just one family."

"Should be a piece of cake then. Who is it?"

"The Karmazin family. The detectives said they are called also the Fifth Street Gang."

"I've heard of them. Is this a suicide mission?"

"Could be."

"Need me to help?"

"You already are."

"There's a mob wannabe who comes into the bar occasionally."

"How do you know?"

"He talks, I listen. Always waving a lot of cash too."

"Does he have ties to the Karmazins?"

"He's freelancing right now, but wants in."

"You know a lot."

"Like I said, he talks."

"Hmm. He might be useful."

# Chapter 102

Police Headquarters

"What do you know about the Karmazin crime family?" Andrew asked the detectives.

"I worked on the organized crime task force for six years. We chased them down and dragged half a hundred family members into court. Got several convictions, but some slipped through our fingers. They've been in Atlanta for over 50 years. Conflicts with other gangs have worked the best to thin their ranks."

"Who's the head of the family?"

"Levente Karmazin. Came to America from Hungary. Has done time twice for racketeering and murder. The murder conviction got overturned after the State's start witness disappeared during the appeal."

"What are they known for?"

"They are involved in all the activities typical for crime families. Drugs, prostitution, gambling, loan sharking, kidnapping. The Karmazins made a reputation for themselves performing assassinations, as you know, which makes it all the more impressive you are still vertical. They've begun to get into cyber-crimes and identity theft in the last few years. The best we know, they are enslaving some immigrant Asians who are in debt to them and have computer skills."

Tunney conversed like he was recounting the day's activities at the local diner. The emotional dynamic had long since faded from the constant interaction with the ungainly parts of the community.

"My anonymous friend I have been staying with told me a guy comes into her bar occasionally who is trying to get into the Karmazin gang. I want to see what I can get out of him."

"You plan to tell him who you are?"

"Funny. Got any ideas on fake names?"

"How about Vincent Van Gogh."

"Sorry, still have both ears. I'll come up with something. Gentlemen, you've given me plenty to think about. Thank you."

"And thank YOU for the food. Again." Andrew brought boxes of Chinese take-out this time.

"Like we always say, talk to us before you do something dangerous."

"You got it."

# Chapter 103

Trudy's

Andrew was getting tired of sitting. The barstool was not his friend tonight, and two hours on one was inviting bed sores. Another ten minutes and he was going to call it a night. Fanny walked nonchalantly to his end of the bar.

"That's him."

Andrew looked down the bar.

"Which one?"

"The youngish guy with the jacket and tie."

"What's his name?"

"Sammy Gallardo."

"No joke?" Andrew started laughing.

"No joke."

"Should I use a Brooklyn accent when I talk to him?"

"Be careful. He might think you are a cop if you are too obvious."

"No worries. I'll be cool, thanks."

Andrew got off the stool and made a circuitous route through the sea of people and aimed for the seat next to the wise guy. Except just as he was moving to the spot, a young girl having a good time spun in and landed on the seat. She bumped him and giggled, turning to see who it was she disrupted. It was enough for the thirty-something male to see an opportunity. Andrew held his ground and waited to see what happened. Luckily, the pair to the man's right gave up their seats as the music changed to a slow song evidently intent on sharing an intimate dance. Andrew slid into the seat and waited for the flirting to subside. The girl got up, laughing and said goodbye to her new man friend. She fluttered off with her girlfriends looking to find action in a different nightclub. The man was invigorated with the connection, turning to find someone new to benefit from his attractive qualities.

"You have good taste. She was the second runner up in the Miss USA pageant two years ago."

Sammy looked again and savored his awesomeness.

"What are you drinking?" He asked Andrew.

"Just a beer."

"Fanny? Two shots and two beers."

She stole a quick look at Andrew.

"Thanks. What are we celebrating?"

"Life is good, my friend. We are celebrating life. Women are beautiful and I'm making money." He opened his arms in a symbolic effort to bear hug the entire world.

"Congrats! I'll drink to that!" They grabbed the shot glasses and tipped them up followed by a long drink from the beer mugs.

"Ahh. Mother's milk!" Andrew's new friend was hitting on all eight cylinders.

"So how are you making money?"

"I'm a middle man for an organization here in Atlanta. (not exactly true) We offer… opportunities and entertainment for all sorts of people. I can hook you up my friend. Gambling, loans, women, drugs, you name it. We have most of the business here in the city, and we just opened up a new operation in Miami. Long term, we want to control the whole east coast." The 'we' was dubious due to his nonmember status with the Karmazin gang.

He ordered another round of drinks and Andrew was supportive. The more alcohol he had in him, the more he would talk.

Fanny had to figure out a way to water down Andrew's drinks so he wouldn't lose consciousness in an hour. Sammy was a fish.

The crowd gathered around the two men as the drinks flowed and the stories got louder. After an hour or so, Sammy got antsy and was ready for something new.

"Hey, Fanny! Come with us! We're going to go to a couple of clubs!"
Sammy was shouting everything.

"Gotta work. I don't get off for a while yet." She stepped over to Andrew
and lowered her voice. "Are you going to be alright? He'll be at it all
night."

"I think so. Thanks to you, all I've been drinking is water. I'll be in touch."
Andrew joined up with Sammy and hopped into his Jaguar. A couple of
random girls were already in the back.

"Sammy, let's go to Rio!" One of the girls said.

"Maybe later. I'm going to take my new friend to The VIP Lounge."
The girls just rolled their eyes and began to talk amongst themselves.

"So what do I call you?"

"Thad. Thad Carpenter."

"Sammy Gallardo. Pleasure. You're gonna love the VIP. Some of my
buddies hang out there almost every night."

"I don't think I've ever been."

"Not surprising. If you don't have ties to the family they probably
wouldn't let you in. But tonight my friend, full access. You're with Sammy
Gallardo!"

"Have you always been part of the family?"

"No, I'm not blood. I'm more of a freelancer. Been making a name for
myself with my computer skills."

"Everything is going digital, isn't it?"

"Yes it is. Actually, I manage a team of computer experts. We stay busy."
Andrew knew better than to ask many more questions about the 'business'.
The car pulled up to the front door of the club, and a valet raced over to the
driver's side.

"Thaddeus, when we go inside, whatever you want is on the house. Drinks,
gambling, women... enjoy!"

"Thank you. You're very generous."
Sammy put his arm around Andrew.

"I got a feeling about you. You're good people. It's a gift I have reading
people."

The doorman/bouncer eyed Sammy and turned away. Evidently, he was
not quite part of the 'in' group. Sammy fished around in his pocket for a
fifty and put it in the bouncer's hand. It must have been the ticket, because
the bouncer stepped to the side and all four filed into the club. The music
was loud, the stages were full of dancers, and the tables were covered up as
well. And on a school night no less. Andrew followed Sammy to a table
with two men and three ladies.

"Thad Carpenter, meet the crew. This is Nick, Manny and Cali. Short for California. He's always wanted to live there but hasn't ever gone!" The crew got a good laugh from that one for the hundredth time. Sammy didn't acknowledge the females and they didn't act like they cared. The ladies who rode here with them were nowhere to be found. Must be a mafia thing. Andrew nodded to each one and took a seat.

Sammy was ready to catch up with his buddies. "So did you guys have any luck with the new accounts today?"

"No. Don't want to get Sol wound up. He said the big boss doesn't want anyone to mess with them yet."

"You guys need to quit letting Sol tell us what to do."

"Don't know, Sammy. We have to keep Sol happy if we want to get in the outfit. He acted like he knew what he was talking about. Not worth the risk."

"Even the big boss will be impressed if we hack the accounts. Then we're a cinch to get in."

The other men shot looks at Andrew. They feared the conversation was too honest in front of the stranger. Actually, Andrew had heard all he needed to hear. Also, he was convinced none of these rocket scientists had a clue who he was.

"I gotta go to the can. Where is it?" Andrew tried to be nonchalant. Sammy pointed to the opposite corner of the club.

Andrew took his time. He had no desire to hustle back to Sammy's table. The club was almost a dead ringer for how Andrew had envisioned parties at the emperor's palace in Rome. Lots and lots of hedonism in the house. He contrasted this with how the orphans simply struggled to survive day after day.

Andrew called Fanny. "Hey, Fanny. It's me Andrew."

"Did they talk you into joining the family yet?"

"Close. I'm holding out for a clothing allowance. I was wondering, do you get off soon? I may need a ride back to your bar before Sammy is ready to leave."

"I kinda figured. Yeah, I'll be done in 45 minutes or so."

Andrew checked the time on his phone. "Perfect. You're the best. Text me when you get close."

Back at the table, most of the guys were gone. Evidently, they were 'dancing' with some of the help. Cali was still at the table.

"Cali, how long have you been in Atlanta?"

"Too long. Been wanting to leave for years."

"California?"

Cali shook his head. "Nah, too far away. Maybe Miami."

"You want to be part of the Miami expansion?"

"I kinda hope so. It may be a while before anything gets off the ground. Need a boat load of money to do a start-up."

Sammy came back to the table.

"Thad. Follow me."

Sammy led Andrew to a back room and then into an elevator. He hit the button with no letter on it and the car started down.

"Art collection?"

"Tables. I'm feeling it tonight and you're my good luck charm."

Andrew sucked in a breath. He'd have to risk it. Best case this casino wasn't as secure as a Las Vegas casino. Vegas has face recognition software which would blow him out of the water no matter how much weight he had lost.

The elevator doors opened to an opulent room with hundreds of people intent on their selected games. A sizable group was watching a well-dressed man throw dice in a craps game. He had done very well judging by the number of chips in front of him. Sammy wound his way through people and tables to get to a roulette wheel in the back of the room. He had a stack of chips already and dumped them on the table. He put several down on Red just as the table master began to spin the wheel.

"We're just waiting for the craps table to open up."

"Red!"

"Nice. Doubled my money. See, you are a lucky charm."

A couple more throws with varying success and the craps table opened up.

"Let's go. This is the real game." Sammy waited his turn, eventually taking the dice. He set bets on three numbers and rolled the dice between his hands.

For the next thirty minutes, Sammy threw the dice. He was up a few chips, but he had not amassed a fortune. Andrew's phone buzzed. Fanny was close.

"Sammy, I gotta blow. Have to get up early in the morning. Thanks for the great night. We'll do it again maybe."

"Thad, you just got here. I'm up five hundred bucks. Who's going to be my lucky charm?"

"I will Sammy!" A super model type with more makeup on than a circus clown stepped up and put her arms around him.

"Yeah, you'll do. See ya around Thaddy!"

"Later, Sammy."

Andrew got out of her car and leaned back in, "Thanks, Fanny."

"Not a problem. Thank you for dinner."

Andrew looked at her for a minute as he scrolled through his memory. He didn't remember offering, but knew he owed her.

"I'm hungry too. Where do you like to go at this hour?"

"Waffle House."

"Perfect. I'll follow you there."

They both ordered a mess of waffles and eggs over easy. It was surprisingly busy at this hour.

"So how'd it go?"

"Really well. I have to laugh. Sammy introduced me to his crew and then they talked about hacking some bank accounts. You steered me to the right guy."

"Andrew, you're getting too close to the flame. Someone is going to recognize you."

"Fanny, I think we're fine. I sat and talked with them and no one acted weird. Although I'm not sure it would be safe to do again. I went to the casino with Sammy…"

"They have a casino?"

"Yeah, in the basement. If they have face recognition software like some casinos, I *know* I'm not going back."

"Wow. You are just thumbing your nose at danger aren't you?"

"I didn't expect Sammy to drag me to the casino."

"Did you learn enough to make it worth your while?"

"Yes, tonight was successful."

"What's next?"

"It's time to come clean with how Stella and I ran the company. I'm going to give an interview to a reporter here in town and do a tell-all. Then I'm going to help Sammy steal some of AD Isaacson's money."

# Chapter 104

Atlanta

Andrew answered the phone. "Mr. Andrew? It's Aleefa."

"Aleefa! Great to hear from you. How are things going?"

"Mostly good. Classes are interesting and we are able to understand. Rapha and I have been very busy attending to our studies."

"So some things are not going so good?"

"It's Rapha. He seems very sad all the time. I think he is homesick."

"Do you both have time to spend an evening with Veronica and me?"

"Yes, I believe that would be fine. Tomorrow night would work well for us."

"Tomorrow it is. Five o'clock?"

"Yes."

"Okay, see you then. Thanks for calling Aleefa."

After he ended the call, Andrew realized he hadn't caught up on how things were going at the orphanage or with the home office. First, he'd call Veronica.

"Veronica? This is Andrew Isaacson. I wasn't sure if you had my number in your phone or not."

"Hello! Yes, I did have it, how are you doing?"

"Really well. I'm getting used to the flow of Atlanta again."

"I bet it is a challenge. Have you settled into your house?"

"Actually no. It's kind of complicated. I would love to tell you all about it sometime. But right now, I'm staying with a friend. Veronica, I was wondering. Have you visited with Aleefa or Rapha lately?"

"It has been a week or so. Are they okay?"

"Aleefa called and was concerned about Rapha. Said he's homesick."

"I'm so sorry. Did he ask you to help him?"

"I offered to spend tomorrow evening with them, and I was hoping you could come along."

"Yes, I would love to. Are you going out to eat? If so, I may be a little late to the restaurant. But I'll be free after."

"Great. Yes, I planned to take them to dinner. I wish there was something around here to remind him of home."

"It might make it worse if it draws him back to Africa. Maybe we can connect them to other Africans who are here in America. Kids who are doing some of the same things they are. There is a church in the city which might be just the thing. Let me do some digging and I'll see you at the restaurant."

"Thank you, Veronica. I will look forward to it. Um… where should we eat?"

"There is a nice 'little bit of everything' place fairly close to their campus called Big South Eatery."

"Perfect. See you then."


It was a popular restaurant. After an hour waiting on the front porch, a table opened up. Andrew ordered some onion ring appetizers and sweet tea.

"What is the most unusual thing you've seen since you have been here?" Veronica attempted to get the boys talking.

"So many autos."

"The grocery stores. The amount of food is plentiful."

"It is very noisy at night."

Andrew laughed. "That is what I thought when I was in Bandundu. The animals and bugs were really loud."

"It doesn't sound like home here." Rapha lamented.

"What would make it seem more like home?" asked Veronica.

Aleefa jumped in, "If I could go hunting at night."

Andrew smiled and looked at Veronica. She was wide-eyed, not sure what to say.

"Aleefa, you cannot run around Atlanta hunting animals with your spear."

"I agree. I would take only my slingshot and a mallet."

"Let me do some checking. There is probably some land you can hunt on nearby. I'm not sure what is in season right now," Andrew offered.

"Miss Veronica, have you heard anything from home?"

"No I haven't Rapha. The director should be talking with Ndulue or Theresa this week though. I will ask him to check on your brother." Veronica knew his brother was the primary concern.

"Mr. Andrew, what have you been doing since you have been back? Are you painting pictures?" Aleefa asked in between onion rings.

"I've been fairly busy. There is a group of people who have taken partial ownership of my art business. They are not so good people and I have been working to end the relationship."

"Are they the ones who tried to kill you?"

"Sort of. The man who came to the home worked for these people."

"You are in great danger. Maybe I should hunt them instead of animals." Veronica choked on her tea.

"They would never see you coming," Andrew conceded. "I have a plan though. If it works, we will finally be free of the bad people."

"I've got an idea!" Rapha was bright with excitement. "Let's jump from an airplane and fly like birds to the ground."

"Wow. How did you come up with that idea, Rapha?"

"I saw a person doing it on television. He was able to do it because he used a certain type of deodorant."

"You mean with parachutes?"

"No, these men had only wings and they flew very fast."

"Ahh." Andrew's mind was working trying to figure out how to encourage the boys' fun without killing the dream.

"How about going to the Planetary Arcade? They have a wind tunnel," Veronica brightened.

"Oh yeah, you can fly without leaving the room."

Veronica was already on her phone seeing what the hours and costs were. She tapped her phone rapidly and the boys watched with expectant fervor. "There. We have reservations for eight o'clock. We'd better eat up. It will take thirty minutes to drive there."

It was all she needed to say. The boys ate so fast Andrew was concerned they would choke on a chicken leg. He'd have to get a 'to go' box.

The next hour was spent flying in place on a massive fan. Rapha took to it immediately and Aleefa got the hang of it after a bit. Andrew was pretty sure he was going to get hit up for a return trip in the very near future. Neither Andrew nor Veronica flew, but both of them were as tired as parents at Disneyworld. Andrew drove the clan back to the boys' dorm.

"Mr. Andrew and Miss Veronica, thank you for taking us to have fun tonight. I enjoyed it very much."

"And I did too." Rapha was not going to let Aleefa talk for him. "It was better than jumping out of a plane!" Of course, Rapha had not jumped out of a plane before, but it couldn't be better than their adventure tonight.

"You guys are most welcome. I'm glad we were able to spend some time together."

"Bye fellas. I hope we can see you soon." Veronica hugged them both before they went inside.

"They're good guys. It's not easy being the first ones," Veronica pondered.

"True. They are going to pave the way for many kids coming after them."

"Which should keep me busy going forward."

"Do you think Atlanta Metropolitan State College is the best destination for future students?" asked Andrew.

"I'm not sure. The school has been very accommodating, but as this thing grows, we may have to find additional schools."

"You've got a vision!" Andrew could see it in her eyes.

"This is the next step we haven't had before. Bhaniel would have been pleased."

"I think so too. I'd better get you back to your car."

"Thanks for including me tonight."

"It wouldn't have been much of an evening without you."

Veronica considered her words. "Andrew, do you think you will go back to the orphanage?"

"I intend to, yes."

"Will your... business issues... keep you from going?"

Andrew knew where this conversation was headed. "Veronica, I know it's dangerous to try to gain control of my company again. And yes, because of the people I'm dealing with, it could result in a negative outcome. I realize the kids in Africa, and now the ones who come to America are dependent on me to care for them, financially and in other ways."

"I didn't mean to..."

"No, you don't need to apologize. I wanted to have this conversation with you since you will be overseeing the college program. I have set up a trust, a trust directed by me right now, but will automatically transfer to the organization under the control of the director if I die. I set it up the last time I was home. These are simply savings collected over many years. It is not connected to the business in any way and no one knows about it except you and the director. The 'bad men' can't touch it. The money in the trust will be enough to cover anybody who wants to go to college."

Veronica was visibly comforted by Andrew's words.

"No one will be able to repay you for your generosity."

"You know, it's funny. There are certain people's generosity I will never be able to repay as well."

# Chapter 105

The cell phone sitting on the van console buzzed. "Jim, when you're done, I need you to go to 1421 Highland Circle to do a cable install."
Jim rolled his eyes. He thought the day was all but complete. This could take a while. Oh well, the extra hours' pay would come in handy for the engagement ring he had his eye on. More importantly, the one his girlfriend had her eye on.
"Copy. They don't have any cable?"
"The homeowner has cable, but it is only operating in the house. They want to add the studio behind the house."
"You have a schematic?"
"I'm texting you a diagram right now. The homeowner won't be there, but he said use your best judgment on running the cable. Oh Jim? He said the studio was roughed in for cable a few years ago, so you just need to find the box on the west wall."
Better. The cable is already to the building, and the job will probably take half as long since the homeowner is going to be gone.
"Okay, I'll head over there in twenty to thirty minutes."
"That'll do, thanks."
Jim was mildly familiar with the neighborhood. Big houses, walls and gates. Gates. He needed a code.
"Hey, Cheri, what's the code to get in the gate at 1421 Highland?"
"Oops, my bad." She flipped through the notes on the computer screen. "It is 0934, and there is a code to get in the door to the studio also. 483754."
"Thanks."

Jim finished what he was doing and motored over to the blessed part of town. Most of the lawn care personnel had finished for the day so the streets were nearly bare. No one in this neighborhood parked their cars in the street. Actually, it was probably a covenant. They likely enforced covenants in this neck of the woods. He rolled into the drive and entered the code. The gate rolled away and Jim was in like Flint. He parked by the front door of the house and flipped through his texts. There were three well-defined pictures of the house, property and floor plan of the studio. He was going to have to run a line from the house to the studio first. Jim loaded up his arms with supplies and followed the gravel path around the east side of the house.

The studio was bigger than he thought. The pool needs work. Doesn't look like anyone lives here. There's the cable box. Jim went to his tool box and knelt down to pull out the drill.

"Excuse me, sir. Would you please stand up?"

Jim startled and twisted around reflexively. With the drill in his hand, he looked like a threat. The two Karmazin family members reached for their pistols and pointed them at Jim. He dropped the drill and jumped up with his hands raised.

"Whoa! Whoa! I'm just the cable guy! I don't want any trouble." Jim pointed at the tool box. "Take what you want."

"What's your name?"

"Jim Taylor. I work for Empire Cable."

"What is your relation to Andrew Isaacson?"

"Who?"

"Andrew Isaacson."

"I don't know him. I don't even know whose house this is. I was just told to come here and do a cable install."

The wise guys looked at each other and lowered their guns. One of them talked into a microphone in his hand.

"False alarm. Just the cable guy."

They had more questions for the installer. "What are you doing here?"

"Like I said, I work for the cable company. Dispatch called and said you wanted two cable outlets. Are you the homeowner?"

"Not exactly. It was probably a mistake. Why don't you get your stuff and get out of here."

"Yes sir. Can do. I'm gathering my tools and I'm going." Jim was gathering as he talked. Maybe he was going to live to fight another day.

"I suggest you forget what you saw here today." The tougher one said to Jim.

"Totally forgotten. Not a word."

He hustled around the side of the house and threw his stuff in the back of the van. Jim was so nervous he ripped the gears into neutral and floored it. After revving the engine, he pushed it into drive and spun the tires on the gravel drive. Jim barely allowed the gate to get out of the way before he raced onto Highland Circle and away from this parcel of fantasy island.

Through his binoculars, Andrew surveilled his house from the hill out back. Less than five minutes he thought to himself. These guys are watching the house pretty close. Actually, one or both of the goons came from the house, so they must be cycling watch dogs in the house day after day. If Andrew wanted to get in the studio, he could sneak in on the north side unnoticed. He turned to put his gear in the backpack and hike down the hill. Andrew had what he came for, although he felt bad for the cable guy.

# Chapter 106

Trudy's

"There you are. I was starting to worry. You don't call, you don't write…"
Fanny worked Andrew over a little as he took a seat at the bar.
"I know. It's weird. You'd think since I'm staying with you, we would see
more of each other. You work nights, right?"
"It's just temporary. Till I get back on my feet. Speaking of, when are you
going to put some money down and paint the lady again?"
"Just say the word and we'll start throwing paint."
"Deal. So what are you up to tonight? It's been pretty slow, your guy may
not stop by."
"No big deal. At least I got to see you."
"I'm not giving you a free drink, so stop it."
"Even one like the other night? I believe it was water on the rocks."
"You can have all those you want."
"I would love one. Water, straight."
"Coming right up."
Fanny went down to the other end of the bar to fill a glass with water. A
man in a hooded sweatshirt came into the club, kept his head down and
avoided eye contact as he strode directly to a booth well out of the way of
random foot traffic. Fanny went over to get his order and then brought
Andrew his water.
"Who's that?" Andrew pried.
"Looks like your buddy Sammy Gallardo."
"What?! I didn't even recognize him."
"Something's going on. He must be hiding from someone."
"Think he would freak if I went over to his table?"
"It's up to you. I have no idea what he'll do."

Andrew got Sammy's order and walked it over to the table. Sammy didn't look up.

"Mind if I sit down?" Andrew set his drink on the table.

"Yes, I mind. Leave."

"I'll only be a minute."

"I ain't got a minute."

"Where's your crew?"

"What crew? My computer crew?"

"Your buddies I met the other night."

"Gone. I'm a leper now. They're all out to get me now."

"Out to get you? Why? You're the man. Last time we hit the town, you were tearing it up."

"Not so much. Sit down you're drawing attention to me."

Andrew slid into the booth.

"I ran into some trouble with my hacker guys, and the family boys shut it down."

"I thought you were a freelancer."

"Yes, and no. I did my own thing, but it was sort of a tryout. When they get involved, they control everything. I'm on my way out of here. I'm going to the west coast tomorrow."

"Weren't your workers making money?"

"Yeah, but I kinda got sidetracked. Then some of the new hacker guys tried breaking into Sol's personal accounts."

Andrew gave him a quizzical look. "How'd you get sidetracked?"

"You remember that guy I told you about? Maybe I didn't tell you. I was working on hacking into some accounts of a dead guy the Karmazins had business dealings with. If I could'a done it, I figured it would get me an 'in' right?"

"So you didn't succeed?"

"No, but I felt like I was getting really close."

"What's his name?"

"Andrew Isaacson. He was a pretty well-known artist. At least around here." Sammy pulled his phone and flipped through his photos for what seemed like a long time.

"Here. I've only got one picture."

The photo was an old one. Andrew almost laughed out loud. He'd forgotten how he once looked. He could understand why someone like Sammy would never recognize him now.

"You'd think his accounts would be easy to tag."

"I agree."

Andrew gazed at himself for another minute. "What if you had some inside help with his bank accounts?"

"What?!" Sammy stopped to process what 'Thad' was saying. "How?"

"Not too hard, really. I can give you some good info."

"No, no. I'm done. If the outfit finds out I'm still working this deal, they'd shoot me in the head."

"Even if I could guarantee your success?"

Sammy had to think it over. The temptation was too great.

"Where'd you get your info?"

"I used to work there."

"You're lying to me!"

"Honest."

"Doing what?"

"Little bit of everything. Even helped on some paintings, but my work in the accounting office is probably what will help you the most."

"Why do you want to help me take their money?"

"I liked Isaacson. He seemed like a good guy. It was his business partner who offed him. This might be a way to get a little payback for him."

"Dude. This is awesome news!" Sammy was back to his old self.

"Will you be able to get your cyber crew back together?"

"No, I'll have to use some new guys. Trust me, there are thousands of them out there. So give me some intel. What do you got?"

"Account numbers mainly."

"Really? That's plenty. How many accounts?"

"Three primary operating accounts, and one savings account used for bigger purchases."

"Nice. We'll try to set up some dummy accounts and duplicate entries so they won't realize we're taking their money for a while. Any guesses on what passwords he used?"

Andrew handed Sammy the account numbers.

"Google his girlfriends' names. I know he used one as a password. Hey, I gotta run, maybe I'll see you around sometime."

"You got it, Thad. I owe you one."

Andrew just smiled, slid out of the booth and left the bar.

He texted Fanny as he pulled out of the parking lot.

[See you at the house, thanks.]

Fanny took off an hour early in case she could catch Andrew before he went to bed.

The lights were still on in the front room. Andrew was watching the original version of "The Poseidon Adventure" as she walked in.

"Remind you of your boat trip to Africa?"

"Humorous. Gene Hackman and Ernest Borgnine. Good stuff."

"Quality television. So how was your talk with Sammy?"

"I inspired him. He was in a tough spot. The organization is in process of removing him."

"Removing him?"

"Like permanently. He was obsessing over Andrew Isaacson and wasn't minding his business. The head of the family had enough and put his name on the naughty list. I offered to help him hack into AD Isaacson's bank accounts and he brightened almost immediately."

"Andrew, what will it do to your business?"

"Not much. I've set him up for success, but I'm going to have the bank monitor it and shut it down after the first break in. The accounts are small ones, so the money at risk will be limited."

"Will it be enough to save his skin?"

"I really don't know. He may not be able to steal enough money to satisfy the family, but if it does then I have an 'in' to the big boss."

"Andrew Isaacson, you are a shrewd character."

"I'm just trying to live the life I sing about. Want to pose for the artist after you get something to eat?"

"Yeah, sure. Where?"

"I have an easel set up in the living room."

"What's it going to be tonight?"

"Get the most opulent, gown-type dress you have."

"Does the color matter? 'Cause I have an unattractive brown bridesmaid dress I wore a year or so ago. I wasn't really a bridesmaid, but... never mind it doesn't matter."

"The color isn't important, just so it has a lot of creases and folds."

"Gotcha. Can do."

And the session was a go.


"Who's that?" Fanny stood back from the painting and cocked her head.

"Doesn't it look like him?"

"It looks like Sammy Gallardo."

"Good. It's supposed to."

"But I don't like him, and you made it look like we're dating, or getting married or something."

"You two have facilitated my interaction with the Karmazin gang."

"You should have painted in a little baby with your face on it."

Andrew laughed. "That would be great!"

"No, don't. It's too embarrassing already."

"You mean you don't want to hang this one up at the bar?"

"Not even in the restroom."

"We'll just have to keep it here I guess."

"On second thought, the restroom doesn't sound so bad."

"Maybe after all of this is over, I can change the guy to someone else. Someone more to your liking."

"I love it. I'll gather up some pictures of Hugh Jackman for you to work from."

"Hey, a new business line! Painting portraits of people with their fantasy boyfriend or girlfriend."

"Tacky, yet there would be no shortage of clients."

"It would get pretty tiresome painting swimsuit babes for all the men."

"I'm going to bed. Goodnight." Fanny trudged off to the bedroom.

# Chapter 107

Trudy's

"Hey, Sammy's in here asking about you." Fanny called Andrew on the phone.

"Ask him what he knows. I'm busy, I can't come to the bar right now."

"Listen 'Thad', don't put me in the middle of this. I've done too much already. You need to do your own dirty work."

"You're right. My apologies. Don't tell him anything. But just to let you know, I don't think I can come in tonight. It'll have to be another time."

"Got it. See ya."

Andrew closed the phone and considered the situation. He wanted to hear the latest on the hack into AD Isaacson, but it could wait. Probably better to maintain some distance from the illegal activity. Twisted logic would say it wasn't illegal since he was facilitating a theft of his own money. Well, maybe it wouldn't hurt to amble over to the bar and see what Sammy had to say. If he wasn't there, it didn't matter much. Andrew hopped in the car and turned it over. He'd have to look into getting a different car soon. The more anonymous the better. Any patterns noted by others could be his downfall. It was a moonless, still night. Andrew rolled his windows down as he cruised slowly through the neighborhood. The only human life he noticed were two elderly men sitting in the shadows of rickety porch, betrayed by the ember of a half-smoked cigarette. The thoughts came back to him in the quietness of the drive. Let it go. Don't risk your life for something of questionable worth. Go back to Africa. Bring more kids to America. Get on with your life. A good life.

It all sounded so reasonable except the part where a crime family was intent on exploiting his business and his name. Why did he think this plan would solve anything? The chances of ending this well had to be less than five percent, but five was better than nothing. Andrew had to break their will. Killing would breed more killing. Having the top guys arrested was going to add fuel to the fire of revenge. Something had to break in his favor. But it may not reach critical mass unless Andrew was willing to be the sacrificial lamb.

He drove into the parking lot and noticed Sammy's car. Guess he's not hiding anymore, Andrew thought to himself. Pretty sparse crowd tonight. Just a few regulars.

"Hey A… Thad." Fanny caught herself in the nick of time. "Decide to crash the party?"

"Changed my mind. Thought I'd see if Sammy was still around."

"He's in the restroom. Sit. Get you something?"

"Water. Yeah, just water."

Sammy came out and spotted Andrew.

"Thad! What's going on?"

"Hey Sammy. Fanny said you were looking for me."

"Only to tell you I owe you big time. We got in." Sammy gave him a look like he should get the clue.

"Congrats. Didn't take long."

"Not too tough with the info you had. The bank probably won't shut down the accounts for a while yet. We were able to set up the dummy accounts to cover it up. If only there was more money in the accounts."

"Really? I thought there was going to be several thousand dollars in there."

"One is a sweep account, but the other three have been pretty low balances since the assassination."

"I'll have to look at my stuff and see if there are any other account numbers."

"Yeah, if you do and we get into some real money, I'll give you a cut."

"Thanks, but I'd probably better stay out of it."

"Oh you're already in it, brother. You know, you saved my life."

Andrew gave him a quizzical look. "How so?"

"After I gathered up some tech guys and got to work, the money started to flow. I actually pulled some of it out in cash and dropped it on Sol's desk."

"How'd you get in there? I thought you were on the outs."

"Okay, I didn't drop it on his desk myself. I hired a kid to do it. But when Sol heard the story, he sent for me and said I earned another chance."

Sammy was bouncing on his bar stool he was so jazzed up.

"Great to hear. Zero to hero!"

Sammy smiled a wry, king-of-the-world kind of smile at Andrew.

"You're the best, Thad. Come on, I'm gonna take you out for the best steak in the city."

"I'm not dressed for it."

"Not a problem. They'll give you a jacket when we get there."

Sammy treated 'Thad' to an outstanding steak dinner then took him to several clubs. Andrew played along for the better part of the night. He enjoyed the ride knowing Sammy was truly indebted to him and could trust him. Sort of.

# Chapter 108

Schuster Gallery, Atlanta

"Hey, buddy!" Mitch looked up from his paperwork accompanying a stack of paintings recently delivered to the gallery. Andrew had his hands full with a large painting, gingerly working his way into the shop trying not to bump into anything.

"Hi, Mitch. How's it going?"

"You look good. No cane?"

"Nope, not so far. I might need it later. I get a little tired late in the day." Mitch was walking around in such a way, the casual observer wouldn't know he had stilts.

"Awesome."

"What do you have there?" Andrew had one of his 'Fanny' paintings in his arms.

"This is part of a series I started before I went to Africa for the first time. Her name is Fanny. She's a gal I know who tends bar not too far from here."

"I like it. She's a natural. How many are you planning to paint?"

"No idea. I'll probably go with her as long as I can. Right now, $500 per is good money to her. Once she figures up the hourly rate, I may be looking for a new model."

"I think I have a buyer in mind."

"Work your magic. I only have one stipulation. If I meet an untimely end, my cut will go to her."

"Are you planning to cheat death again?"

"You never know. As far as most people think, I'm already long dead. Even the mafia guys are still in the dark. I've actually been hanging out with a Karmazin gang hopeful who is stealing Andrew Isaacson's money."

"Even after you told him your name he didn't realize who you were?"

"No, to him I'm Thad."

"Thad!? I Love it! How'd you come up with Thad?" Mitch was laughing.

"Out of the clear blue. What? I don't look like a 'Thad'?"

"You got some stones, I'll give you that. So you're going to bring some more paintings?"

"Yeah. Probably have to bring them one at a time."

"New paintings from a dead guy. Who would've guessed?"

"They should go like hotcakes."

"Speaking of being popular, I had a browser drop by the gallery the other day asking about you. She seemed pretty harmless, but the kind of questions she was asking were almost as probing as the ones Bhaniel used to ask."

"Really? What'd you tell her?"

"Mostly standard stuff. If she is working for the bad guys, the cat's out of the bag. They know you sold stuff out of this gallery."

"It was inevitable, I guess. She must have been sent by the Karmazin family."

"Should I be concerned?"

"I'm sure they are just building a file on me and my work. Keep playing dumb, you'll be fine."

"Who's playing?"

"Do you think we ought to hold the 'Fanny' paintings for a while? You know, until this whole thing is resolved," Andrew suggested.

"Yeah, sure. Except the people I was going to market them to are long-time clients. I'm pretty sure there aren't any mafia ties."

"Just thinking about every possibility, brother."

"I get it. If they are watching the shop, you probably are in danger. Someone might put two and two together if they see the hippy guy bringing paintings in on a regular basis."

Andrew cringed. "Maybe I shouldn't have brought this in." He nodded at the Fanny piece.

"I'll keep it under wraps. And don't sign your paintings until we get this drama concluded."

"Okay."

"So what is the plan this time?"

"Not much of a plan. I'm working on getting access to the Karmazin gang, but to be honest, I don't know what will happen after that."

"Might be easier to go to a Falcons game and light yourself on fire."

"Messy. And the outcome is fairly negative. Who knows? This might go exactly as planned."

"Will you know it if it does?"

"Probably not. It's another pass/fail. Alive – good. Dead – bad."

"Will the police be joining you?"

"Not until the party has ended."

"Trust me, getting the cops there before things get out of hand is a good thing." Mitch glanced down at his feet.

"Fair point."

"When?"

"Soon. I'm getting tired of the preparations. There's one more thing to do."

"Is it too motherly to tell you to be careful?"

"No, I always appreciate the concern. And if it's worth anything, I fully intend to be as careful as possible."

"Infiltrating a crime organization and coming back to life to take back a company they stole from you?"

"You're making it sound dangerous."

# Chapter 109

WGHI – Atlanta Channel 7

Jack sat down in his cruddy chair in his stupid cubicle and stared at his idiotic computer screen. He wanted to quit so bad he was willing to bus tables just to give these drones running the local television station what they deserve. Life without him. The producer had just told the aging reporter the station was not going to renew his contract. No explanation, no message of thanks, nothing. But it was obvious. The people getting all the meaty stories were young, attractive copy-readers with no journalistic ability whatsoever.

He settled into self-loathing and resentment, pummeling himself for staying too long and not seeing the signs. What was he going to do? He had not developed viable career alternatives. This was his dream job, scratching out the story and delivering it to a grateful audience each evening. Nolan the scumbag producer offered to let him host the weekend morning show once a month which was his way of saying – "quit so I won't have to fire you".

First things first, Jack would need to find a box to compact all of his doodads and knickknacks. Then he would ignore people and eat snacks while he composed his resignation letter on the company computer. After that, a long lunch with some friends....

His phone rang. The number was unfamiliar. Probably another crack pot wanting to sell him something.

"Hello, is this Jack Johnson?"

"Yes it is." Sorry, no enthusiasm today.

"I have a story to tell and I'm looking for a reporter I can trust."

"You see a UFO? Is the President in your basement?"

"No, this is real. It's about a man who was murdered several months ago"

"Who?"

"Andrew Isaacson."

"What do you know about it?"

"Meet with me and I'll tell you."

"Come on, pal. Don't mess with me. This ain't the day for it. Why don't you try the Department of Human Services, they have programs for crazy." Jack moved to hang up the phone.

"What do you have to lose? Tell you what. Lunch is on me. I'll meet you at the diner on the corner of Mason and Eastwick in an hour. If you want the interview of your life, be there. Otherwise, I'll find someone else."

"Yeah, okay. One hour."

Jack, don't fall for this. When have these things ever panned out? It's just a bad joke.

He thought about it and decided there was nothing to lose. He had already committed to a long lunch, and it sure beat sitting in this cube all day.

"Hey, Jack whereya headed?" Charlene was an office aide and nosy.

"Just out for a while." He didn't want to say anything else.

The diner was only three blocks away, so he walked. At least this knucklehead did his homework. Jack had no idea who to look for, so he ordered a coffee and slid into a booth. He looked at the other patrons, but none of them appeared to be his mystery man.

"Jack Johnson?" A scruffy, thin, sort of middle aged man suddenly appeared at his table and it startled Jack.

"Yes."

"Mind if I sit down?"

"Sure, I guess." Jack was intrigued, but still thought this was a sham.

"I realize you probably think I'm a nut, and I don't blame you. You'll thank me when this is over."

The server came to the table and the two men ordered lunch. Jack ordered an extra side since his mystery man was paying.

What do you know about Andrew Isaacson?"

"He was a well-known artist who died ugly. It was too bad, I kinda liked him. I interviewed him for a story years ago, he told me…"

"If I ever get the chance, I'm going to sell more paintings than anybody ever has."

Jack squinted. "You could have watched the interview and memorized what was said."

"How close did you follow Andrew's murder?"

"Pretty close. I have a contact in the police force."

"Were you the lead journalist?"

"No. I was locked out. The story was flawed though."

"You know some details that didn't come out in the media then."

"A few. Some of them were rumors."

"The media never got a look at the body did they?"

"No."

"The police were unusually tight-lipped weren't they?"

"Yes, but I was able to see the police report."

"But no pictures."

"Yeah. How'd you know?"

"Because it wasn't Andrew who died. It was the assassin. He shot the girl upstairs and then the hitman and Isaacson struggled and went over the railing. The hitman landed poorly and died. The police let everyone assume it was Isaacson who was dead so he could get out of town safely. The police weren't sure who ordered the hit at the time. It ended up being Isaacson's partner."

"She got shot. What happened?"

"Stella got in too deep with the Karmazin crime family and they had her killed."

"None of this has been in the news. How do you know?"

"I was standing there when it happened. Almost took a bullet myself."

"Who ARE you?"

"Promise me you won't get up and walk out."

Jack nodded warily.

"I'm Andrew Isaacson."

Jack's eyes widened and he sat back in the booth.

"This is so wrong, and full on insane. What's your angle posing as a dead guy?"

"That's just it. He's not dead. He never died."

"If you're you, where have you been? And why are you back?"

"I've been overseas, and now I'm back to square things."

Jack studied Andrew as he chewed his food.

"Is this why we're here? So you can clear up some details from your supposed death?"

"No. I need you to believe I am Andrew Isaacson so I can tell you my story. There have been some reports in the news lately insinuating my paintings are not authentic, and it's time to clear the air. Are you interested in the interview?"

Jack thought of the possibilities. If this is legit, I could break this story and then go to work anywhere I want.

"I'm interested."

"Great."

"But I want to tell the whole story. Not just the stuff about the paintings."

"Agreed."

"Can I see your driver's license?"

Andrew anticipated this and slid it across the table.

"I'll do you one better. When we meet for the interview, I'll pull out some art work."

Jack actually felt a little twinge of excitement.

The next meeting was at the Schuster Gallery. The small conference room allowed Andrew to lay out several press clippings from years gone by, and there were a number of art pieces in the gallery for Jack to view. The newspaper man pored over the material remembering some of the coverage when it ran.

"Well, if you're not you, you are an extremely good imposter."

"Okay. With that settled, we can go into the real reason we're here."

"I'm going to record this if you're comfortable with it."

"Yeah, fine."

"I've done some research since we talked last and the art world is upset to put it mildly. Do you want to refute the allegations?"

"It's not my intention to shout them down. I simply want to set the record straight as best I can. From there, the situation is out of my control."

"Tell me your story."

"Stella Manchester and I began a partnership in college spanning over 20 years. I was the typical artist producing work and showing it in galleries. I, we, developed a clientele who were very active in purchasing original and reproduction pieces. So much so, I could barely keep up. I know, it's the poor little rich boy syndrome. We made a lot of money in those days, and Stella wanted to make even more. Stella devised a plan pulling in some staff artists who would block in colors and lay in the preliminary subjects in the work after I worked out the concept. Later, I would come in and put finishing touches on paintings. The strategy allowed AD Isaacson to almost double the art output. Stella was in the process of replicating the process with a younger artist when everything went crazy last year."

"Do you think you would have done this on your own if Stella had not pushed you?"

"Was it a bad idea? I think yes, but none of this would have happened if I had stood my ground and had a little backbone. Ultimately, the responsibility is mine."

"Are all the paintings out there with your name on them worthless?"

"I will never be able to answer that, but what I do know is every single one of them were conceived by me and the style is all mine. If any of my assistants had performed work I didn't approve of, I either redid it or started over."

"Would it surprise you to know artists have done this since the beginning of history?"

"It's not a surprise. I realize Renaissance artists had student/assistants who did large parts of the masters' work, and there are modern artists who had paid assistants flesh out their artistic visions. The difference for me is people were under the impression I did all of my artwork from start to finish and I did nothing to dispel the belief."

"Why now? Why are you interested in speaking publicly about this?"

"The last several months has been a time of great transformation for me. In the process, I was confronted with the lack of truthfulness in my life. For me, this is just another step to remove any doubts about my desire for complete authenticity regardless of the consequences. I will no longer produce large quantities of art for the sake of higher profits. My hope going forward is not to salvage the ability to sell art at a high level, but rather to appeal to those people who have invested in my art in the past to believe in the pieces they own. Each one was my vision and executed to my satisfaction."

"Where do you go from here?"

"I will continue to do work and show it here at the Schuster Gallery as well as continue my work with the IORRF."

"Several of your pieces are here and I was able to see them. They look so different from the work produced through AD Isaacson."

"It is a completely different focus. There is a timely quality to the work with many involving contemporary people and issues. Some have said they have a prophetic bent because most were produced before the events depicted in the paintings occurred."

"Wow. Very intriguing. Do you have any pieces currently showing events yet to happen?"

"Yes and no. I have a completed mural showing many provocative scenes, but it would be unwise to discuss it right now."

"When you are ready, will you let me know?"

"You'll be the first."

"Thank you. I'm nearly speechless."

"Which brings me to my last point. I need you to promise me you won't run the story until I'm ready."

"Why?"

"There are people who will try to kill me if they find out I am alive."

Jack searched his face for sarcasm. After everything he had heard so far, it wasn't a stretch to believe it was possible.

"How long do I have to wait?"

"Hopefully not long. Will you keep a lid on it? As in telling no one?"

"Yeah, I can do it, but why set up this interview?"

"Because I may not live to tell it later. And it was necessary."

"I won't wait forever."

"Fair enough. Thanks."

"When am I going to hear the full story of your fake death and the real death of your partner?"

"Soon."

"What if you're dead?"

"I'll make sure the people who know the story tell you every detail."

Andrew threw down a fifty and slipped out the door.

# Chapter 110

Fanny's Residence

Andrew's phone buzzed and woke him up. It was a newish phone with almost no contacts in it. The incoming call was not one of them. Andrew waited for the message.

"Andrew Isaacson, I know who you are." It was a young lady's voice, but unfamiliar. "We need to meet. I will wait here with your friend, Rapha, until I hear from you."

He stared at his phone as his mouth went dry. He had been found, but even worse, this – female – had found the boys. Well, Rapha at least. But, how did she find them? It was a fair guess she was the lady asking around about him, and this was a new game. Whatever he had to do to secure their safety was Andrew's only job. The master plan, for what it was worth, would have to wait.

Andrew's mind was racing. Should he call immediately or wait? While he was wrestling with his options, he heard Fanny up and about in the kitchen. He leaned against the island counter with his head down. Fanny glanced at him and then took a longer look. She saw the strain in his face. "What's up?"

"They know I'm alive."

"Who?"

"The mafia."

"How?"

He just shook his head.

"Andrew, you were dancing right under their noses. You knew that was risky, right?"

"Actually it's not me… they have Rapha."

Fanny set the milk on the counter and stared at Andrew. Rage, fear, sympathy, and disgust all took their turns center stage in her emotions. She reigned them in before she spoke, but screamed 'you're an Idiot!' with her eyes.

"Did they call you?"

"Yeah. Well, they left a message." He handed the phone to Fanny so she could replay it.

"What are you going to do?"

"Call them, and try to get Rapha back."

"Andrew, this is bigger than you now. You gotta call the cops."

The stress of the conflict boiled within him. Rapha's safety was the goal, but Andrew still wanted to do it all himself. Involving the police would force him to surrender control of the situation.

Then it hit him, he didn't have control. He never had it. As this objective reality settled in on him, he felt the full weight of what he had done. Andrew slumped into a chair.

"You're right." His voice was barely audible.

"Where is Aleefa?" Fanny was working the problem now, all business and considering every variable.

"I don't know."

"Do you know if the kidnappers have him also?"

"Not sure. All she mentioned was Rapha."

"She either doesn't know Aleefa exists, doesn't care or couldn't catch him. How can we get in touch with him?"

"They have a cell phone."

"Did the kidnapper call you with it?"

"No, it was an unknown number."

"That's good news. Maybe she doesn't have their phone."

Andrew was starting to come out of his funk. Fanny's fighting attitude was rubbing off. This wasn't over. Far from it. Then he had an idea.

"The cell phone. We can track it with an app I downloaded recently - assuming it's on."

Andrew ran into the other room and grabbed his phone. After a few keystrokes, a map appeared and he waited. Fanny moved in close to see. Finally, a dot appeared on the screen, pulsating the phone's location.

"He – the phone – is moving. Away from campus."

"We need to follow it."

"You're right. We…." Andrew stopped to look at Fanny. "Fanny, this is getting kinda wild. It's not right for me to expect you to be involved."

"What!? I am not staying home! We're going to find Aleefa and call the cops. And you need a wing wo-man, so let's go. And if we run into the kidnapper girl, I'm going to give her a beating myself." Fanny got her things and walked out the door.

Andrew smiled a nervous smile. "Lord, help!"

"He should be just ahead," Andrew said.

"You mean on the road?"

"I don't know. I don't think this thing gets close enough to tell."

"We'll just have to drive around until we see something."

"Go slow, I don't think they're in a car. The dot isn't moving fast enough."

"Maybe we ought to get out and walk."

"What if the kidnapper has the phone?"

"Then I'm going to pound her with it," declared Fanny.

"Go around the block. Wait stop! There, in the bushes. I saw a phone screen."

"Is it Aleefa?"

"I can't tell. I'm going to walk over there."

"What if it's the kidnapper?"

"Then I'll give myself up for Rapha."

"That's not a plan!"

"What else can I do? I didn't bring a gun, and I don't know kung fu."

"We'll rush her together. If Rapha gets loose, I'll take him and call the cops."

Andrew thought it over.

"Agreed. I think."

"Go, go!"

Andrew edged out of the car as he took another look at the locator. It still hadn't moved, so Andrew went to where he saw the phone screen light up. When he got to the bushes, he slowed and called to Aleefa.

"Aleefa!" Andrew whispered as loud as he could. Nothing. "Rapha!"

The bushes rustled and Aleefa showed himself. He waved at Andrew to join him in the bushes.

"Aleefa, are you safe? Do you know where Rapha is?"

"Yes, I've been tracking them since the woman called you."

"Of course. I'm such an idiot! I had her number. I could have been tracking her phone."

"No worries. You were tracking me and I am tracking her."

"Where are they?"

"Just over the hill."

"Are they in a car?"

"Yes."

"And you have been tracking them on foot?"

"No. On my bicycle."

"Come with me. We'll follow them in the car."

"What about my bicycle?"

"We'll throw it in the trunk. Hurry."

The two of them, and the bike, hustled to the car. Fanny had just started their way and was elated to see one of the boys with Andrew.

"Are you Aleefa?"

"I am pleased to meet you. Are you helping us rescue Rapha?"

"You better believe it. Do you know where he is?"

"I am tracking the kidnapper's phone."

"Awesome! Let's go!"

The odd trio hopped in the car and sped toward the blinking dot on the screen.

"Aleefa, do you know what the car looks like?"

"Yes, it is a black car very low to the ground. The lights on the back are circles."

"Might be a Corvette." Andrew cringed.

As they crested the hill, the dot had moved. It was now on the highway and moving fast.

"Come on, Fanny! You gotta step on it."

"Let's see what this thing'll do." She pushed her foot all the way to the carpet and pinned the three of them to their seats.

"Aleefa, how did you keep up with the car on your bike?"

"They were not going fast until now. I'm glad you came Mr. Andrew."

"Me too, Aleefa. What happened? How did she take Rapha?"

"I do not know. I only saw them leaving. I was walking back to the dorm from class and she was taking him toward her car. He saw me and I could tell he was very scared. Instead of attacking her, I decided to follow them hoping to find their hiding place."

"You did well, Aleefa."

"There." Fanny pointed to a car up ahead. It fit Aleefa's description and was speeding in and out of traffic.

"Yes, it looks like her car." Aleefa agreed.

"Try to stay with them, Fanny."

"I'm trying! This car has like a one-cylinder engine in it! You need to call the cops! If we lose them, Rapha may be gone forever."

"You're right." Andrew dialed the detectives.

"Detective Oliver! This is Andrew Isaacson. I need your help. One of my boys has been kidnapped."

"Kidnapped? By who?"

"Someone connected to the mob maybe."

"Where are you? It sounds like you are in a car."

"I am. We are driving north on Highway 14, chasing a car we think has Rapha in it."

"With the kidnapper!?"

"Yes, but they're getting away. We need you to stop them."

"Where on Highway 14?"

"We just passed exit 58."

"What kind of car are they driving?"

"It's a black Corvette, about 2008 or so. I think it's a woman driving."

"We'll be out there as fast as we can. Do not, I repeat, do not engage the car under any circumstances."

"Understood."

No sooner had he closed the phone, the Corvette exited to Racine Road.

"Let's follow them, but keep your distance."

"Don't worry. I've seen enough cop shows to know what to do." Fanny took the exit on two wheels, nearly hitting a motorcycle and a pickup truck in the process. Andrew and Aleefa crouched down in the seats hoping the brakes were new.

"Are we Starsky and Hutch or the Dukes of Hazzard?"

"Shut up and hang on!"

She wasn't done. Fanny raced through the intersection on an orange light, but the black Corvette had disappeared.

"Where'd it go?"

"I'm not sure yet. Aleefa, do you see them on your phone?"

"No, the dot is no longer there. I am afraid she's turned off her phone."

"Fanny, you might as well pull over. We've lost them."

"Don't give up so easy. I can go up and down some of these streets. Maybe we'll stumble on to them."

Andrew's phone rang. It was Detective Oliver.

"Andrew, I think we've located the car."

"Where are you?"

"Fifth and Wheeling."

"We're pretty close."

"Go to Fourth Street and park by the Century Insurance sign. I'll be waiting for you."

"Got it."

Andrew guided Fanny to the meeting point which was less than a mile away.

"Follow me. We have a surveillance post on the third floor." Clarence led the trio into a dilapidated building and up two flights of stairs.

"Have they condemned this building?"

"Not yet. Actually, the police department owns it. The Karmazin Family has offices just across Fifth Street so we've used the space for a couple of years to keep an eye on them." Clarence opened an aged wooden door and the group entered a spacious room with windows overlooking Fifth Street. Three other officers were in the room actively monitoring their listening and viewing equipment. Tunney looked up and nodded at Andrew.

"Clarence, we noted the Corvette going in the garage, but no activity since."

"Hear anything inside yet?"

"Nothing worth talking about."

Clarence turned to Andrew.

"You'll probably get another phone call from them soon."

"What do I say?"

"You won't have to say much. I assume they'll tell you what to do to get your boy back."

"Should I agree to it?"

"I doubt they want money. My guess is they want to trade the boy for you."

"What do you suggest?"

"They are going to choose a place to meet that will allow them to lock us out. It'll probably be a blindfold in the trunk type deal. Maybe we can put a locator on you."

Andrew's phone rang, and he looked at the number.

"It's her. Hello."

"Mr. Isaacson? This is quite a surprise. We thought you were deceased, yet you have miraculously come back to life. Congratulations! We have many things to talk about." It was a man's voice. Evidently the female was just the catcher.

"I'm listening."

"First things first. As you know, your young charge, Rapha, has joined us for the evening. We are more than happy to take him back to campus and drop him off at his dormitory. But before we do, we would like to meet you."

"You've kidnapped an innocent boy to get to me."

"No no, Mr. Isaacson. We are simply entertaining Rapha. When we connect with you, he is free to go."

"And if I refuse to meet with you?"

"Now Mr. Isaacson, let's be reasonable. As you say, Rapha is an innocent boy. He shouldn't be involved in this at all. We would love for him to resume his activities at school. If the truth be known, I think you want to get to us as much as we would like to see you. So what do you say? Tonight, tomorrow? What works best for you?"

Andrew looked at Clarence and Bryce who were listening in. They gave him the green light to make a plan.

"The sooner the better. This morning. Where?"

"How about the MARTA Five Points Station at seven a.m.? You could wear a red t-shirt, then you will be easy to locate."

"Sure, and while I'm at it, I'll put a sign on my back that says 'Shoot Me'."

Detective Oliver looked at Andrew.

"Mr. Isaacson, please don't be curt. I simply want to facilitate an effective meeting. The bustle of the metro station will allow everyone to move about freely."

"Are you bringing Rapha?"

"As I indicated earlier, we will drop him off at the college campus after you join us."

"Not good enough. If I am going to give myself up for Rapha, I need to know he's safe."

"Give yourself up?! Mr. Isaacson, we simply want to talk with you. We are business partners now. I think we can forge an effective alliance and enjoy a successful endeavor."

Andrew was stunned. This had to be a charade for the police listening in.

"You send your goon to kill me in Africa, torture my best friend, and hire a whole team of killers to gun down Stella. And you have the nerve to tell me you are looking forward to working together?"

"Those are such unkind accusations. I'm sure it's been a horrible misunderstanding. So are we on for seven a.m.? We can drop Rapha off together."

"I'll see you at the station."

The line went dead.

"Well? I guess we're set. What time is it?"

"Almost two. That doesn't give us much time to get ready."

"What's to get ready? I'll go and give myself up for Rapha."

"Plenty. We have them red handed on kidnapping charges, and we need to organize the personnel in the station."

"Just wait outside and locate Rapha."

"You don't seem to get it. This is a police matter now. We know what we're doing. It's not just about you anymore. There's a teenage boy involved who doesn't have a death wish like you."

"I do get it, and so do the bad guys. Why else would they demand to meet at a metro station? They know you'll be there. This gives them the best chance to usher me to who knows where without getting caught."

"There has to be a way to recover Rapha without losing you." Fanny couldn't stay quiet any longer.

"It isn't the original plan. Taking Rapha turned everything upside down."

"I don't want to know what the original plan was." Clarence quipped as he and Tunney prepared to leave. He handed Andrew an electronic tracker to wrap around his ankle and a tiny communication ear bud. "Donny? Check this out and make sure we have a good link."

Donny did the electronic diagnostics on the tracker and the ear piece. "They're good."

Tunney then walked around behind Andrew.

"Hold still." He pulled up the hair on the back of his head and clipped a tiny something or other on to the hairs near his neck.

"What are you doing?"

"A secondary tracking beacon in case they find the ankle tracker. We won't turn this one on just yet."

"Andrew, we'll see you over there." Clarence called out as he walked out the door.

"Where will you be?"

"Don't worry. We'll be all over the station. I'll call you on the ear piece."
"Okay." Andrew looked at Fanny. "You ready?"

After a run to Fanny's house, she drove Andrew to his car. As Fanny
pulled up to the entry of the bar, she put the car in park.
"I guess it's too late to ask you to be careful."
"The world will be a much better place with a healthy Rapha rather than a
broken down artist."
"My vote is for the world to endure the both of you a little while longer."
"Thanks, Fanny. You've become as good a friend as anyone could hope
for."
Fanny leaned over and hugged Andrew long and hard. She nearly squeezed
the breath out of him.
"Don't let Mitch sell those paintings to just anyone."
"I'm keepin 'em." she said with a smile.
Andrew turned to Aleefa.
"I'm going to rescue Rapha."
"I know Mr. Andrew." He grabbed Andrew from behind and hugged him.
"You all act like I'm not coming back. This is just another day at the
office. I'll see you after."
Fanny simply nodded. The hint of a tear forming in her eye.

# Chapter 111

MARTA Dunwoody Station, Atlanta

Andrew parked his car at the station and rode the North line to Five Points. It was ten to seven. On his way there, he removed the ankle tracker and the beacon in his hair. He would take the ear piece out at an opportune time. His phone rang, and Sammy was on the line.

"Thad! Where are you? You are not going to believe what I just heard. Andrew Isaacson. Dude is alive!"

"What?"

"I know it sounds crazy, but it's legit. He's going to meet up with the boss this morning. I'm not sure how this affects what we are doing with his accounts, but it's got to be good. Listen, I'm going to be at the meeting so I can see him in person. Why don't you come?"

"The boss invited you?"

"Not really, but it's going to be at the Five Points Station at seven. They won't know we're there. Too many people."

Andrew couldn't believe it. Could this get anymore messed up? He had to think fast.

"Uh, yeah I can be there. In fact, I'm headed to the station right now. I'm going to meet with Karmazin for Isaacson."

"Wait, what? You know he's alive? Hey, why are you talking in an Australian accent?"

"That's my native accent. It's kinda complicated. I'll explain later."

"Well Karmazin isn't going to be at the station."

"What do you mean?"

"My buddy said the girl is going to take Isaac… I mean you to see him."

"Who's the girl?"

"She's the one who fingered Isaacson."

"Oh her. How can I recognize her?"

"Meet me at the station and I'll take you to her."

"Okay, I'll see you there."

The train reached the station and Andrew got off careful to not look at anyone. He made his way near the "Welcome to Atlanta" sign as working stiffs scurried to the exits or to the next train. Although Andrew easily spotted them in his peripheral vision, the police were doing their best to look anonymous. Maybe the criminals wouldn't notice. As Andrew moved further away, he saw Sammy coming down the stairs.

"Thad! Did you find her?" Sammy was sweating.

"No, I was looking for you."

"I'm sure she's close. Are you going to tell them about the bank accounts?"

"Probably not."

Sammy thought about it for a second. "You're right, better to wait. So where is this guy? How did you become his rep to the organization?"

"It would take too long to tell the story right now. Are you going to come with us?"

"I'm not sure what Mr. Karmazin will let me do. I'll hang back at first."

"Good plan. I'll contact you after."

"Let's go find the girl."

"What's her name?"

"She doesn't really have a name. They just call her 'the girl'."

They walked back toward the 'Welcome' sign and worked their way toward the turnstiles by the west entrance. As people pressed against them from all directions, Andrew slipped the beacon, tracker and ear piece into Sammy's jacket pocket. He was certain the mob boys would find them and use the gadgets against him if he didn't unload all of it. Maybe Sammy could be help him without knowing it.

"Sammy, what are you doing here?" Sammy turned around to see 'the girl'. She had snaked through the sea of people undetected.

"Hey, I'm glad I found you." Sammy cocked his head toward Andrew. "This is the guy you are looking for."

"You're Isaacson?"

"I'm Thad Carpenter. I'm going to take you and your boss to Andrew." The accent was passable. It better be good if he was playing a home-grown Australian.

"The boss isn't going to like this. Go back to Isaacson, wherever he is, and tell him he needs to be here."

"He will reveal himself when Rapha is safe. Where's your boss?"

"Close." Girl thought for a minute and decided to go with it. "Come on."

Andrew looked at Sammy. "I'll catch up to you later. Thanks."

"I'll call you."

"Keep up, we have to move fast." She began to cut through the mass of people like a ghost. She was only five feet tall which made her disappear like a kid through the corn stalks. Andrew put his head down and bulled through humans. She came to a stop on the northbound red line train platform.

"Where are we going?"

"Just stay with me." Girl wasn't interested in small talk and wasn't going to give Andrew any more information than was necessary.

The police were monitoring the ankle tracker and earpiece.

"Oliver, it looks like Isaacson is moving. The monitor shows he has exited the east doors and is moving northwest on Peachtree Street."

"What?! Chase Three is following Isaacson on the red line platform. How could he be outside?"

"Not sure Detective. That's just what the monitor is showing."

"Chase Three, do you have Isaacson in sight?"

"Roger that. Looking at him now waiting on the red line north."

"Chase Two, you're going to have to check out who is wearing the tracker."

"Copy, Team Leader."

"Here's our train. Get on." Girl stepped close to the edge of the platform. Andrew was happy to comply. He intended to follow willingly until they reached the boss.

Andrew's phone buzzed. Detective Oliver was texting him.

[Isaacson, are you still in the Metro station?]

Andrew texted back.

[Follow the tracker]

The girl saw Andrew pull out his phone and send the text. She lunged for it and yanked it out of his hand before he could react.

"Hey, what are you...?" In one swift motion she threw the phone in between the platform and the train to the tracks below.

"What else you got on you?"

"I'm clean now," Andrew said shrugging his shoulders.

As they got on the waiting train, the undercover officer copied their move two cars down. Andrew saw the police officer and assumed the girl did too, but she didn't seem to care. They sat in silence for three stops and the girl showed no signs of moving. As the red train rolled into the Midtown station, she stirred just a bit. The doors opened and people filed out, yet she stayed put. As if she were timing the stop, she grabbed Andrew's arm and prepared to pounce.

"We're getting off." Just as the doors were activated, she dragged Andrew through the opening and leaped to the platform. The officer had been watching them, but didn't react quickly enough and got stuck on the train. He frantically called the Detectives.

"Team Leader, the subject has exited the train and I am unable to follow."

Oliver wanted to throw his radio.

"Chase Three, copy. What's your location?"

"I'm on the red line going to 'Arts Center'. Subject is still at the Midtown station."

Oliver looked at the MARTA map. "Chase Three, get off the train at Arts Center and monitor the next train coming your way. Chase Four, stay in the Five Points station and wait on further instructions. Chase Five, drive to the midtown station and monitor the streets for the subject."

"Come on." The girl was off and running. They went upstairs and ran to the yellow line platform just as a train was coming to a stop. This one was going south. Once on the train, the girl took her phone out and texted an update to her handler.

"Put this on." She handed Andrew an old hat and some tinted glasses.

"Wow, you thought of everything."

"Sit here." She took a seat with her back to the platform close to an elderly Asian lady and waved Andrew toward the seat between them. The girl didn't say another word for the next twenty minutes, and three different people sat next to Andrew on their journey. The train ultimately came to the end of the line at the airport.

"We're getting off." The girl walked/ran to the escalator and climbed them two at a time to the street. She hailed a cab and told the driver to take them to an industrial facility west of the airport.

The cab pulled up to a metal building amidst hundreds of other metal industrial buildings. Andrew followed the girl into the structure which was nearly empty save for two cars and five men.

"Mr. Isaacson! It's a pleasure." The older man in a sport coat and trousers extended his hand to Andrew.

"Actually, my name is Thad Carpenter. I was sent to take you to Andrew. Are you Mr. Karmazin?"

The mob boss was clearly unhappy and just stared at Andrew for a minute. He looked up to question the girl, but she was no longer in the building. Andrew had not heard her leave.

"This is very irregular, Mr. Carpenter."

"I agree, but since your assistant was able to shake free of our police escort, we aren't being followed. It should be easy to contact Andrew now."

"Check him for electronics." Two of the goons present worked Andrew over physically and with an electronic wand.

"He's clean."

"What are we to do with you Mr. Carpenter?"

"The only thing to do now is go to where Andrew is."

"Where is he?"

"At his studio."

"Call Denzel at Isaacson's house and have him check the studio."
One of the goons made the call and a search was conducted. To no
surprise, Andrew was not on the premises.
"He does not appear to be at his studio. This is very inconvenient Mr.
Carpenter. Bobby is going to spend some time with you to clarify your
memory." He nodded to Bobby who seemed to know exactly what to do.
Bobby beat Andrew while two others held his arms. He seemed to enjoy
the backhand to the face the best. After several minutes, Bobby rested.
"Well, Mr. Carpenter?"
"I promise you, Mr. Karmazin," 'Thad' said between gasps. "Andrew said
if you will take me, he'll be there. As I told you, no police have followed
us. No one knows where we are going."
"Are you willing to bet your life on it?"
"I am."
"Who are you, Thad Carpenter? Why are you doing this for Mr. Isaacson?"
"Let's just say I owe him my life."
Mr. Karmazin gave the nod and everyone went to their vehicles. Andrew
was put in the back seat of the Suburban, and as he got in he noticed a
young person with a black hood sitting in the back seat of the other car.

"Somebody tell me something." Clarence was getting testy.
"Team Leader, we are in sight of the person with the tracker. It appears to
be Sammy Gallardo. Do you want us to arrest him?" Detective Oliver sat
back and pondered this as well as the text Andrew sent. What is Isaacson
up to? He gave all his surveillance gear to Gallardo and probably snuck it
into his pocket. Sammy probably doesn't even know he has it. No way he
would keep it on his person if he took it from Isaacson purposely.
"Chase Two, do not engage. Follow Gallardo at a distance for the time
being."
"Copy, Team Leader."
"Tunney, this is Oliver. Can you turn on Isaacson's earpiece and patch the
feed to me?"
"Of course. Stand by." Tunney flipped three switches and turned two
knobs.
"… yeah, the car is pretty clean, but the turbocharger wasn't working last
time I drove it… No, I'm not with the Boss… Carpenter is supposed to call
me later… What did he tell you?... You mean today?... Tell me the
address… I don't think the boss will care… I'll stay out of sight until I can
figure out what's going on… Yeah, I'll talk to you later." Sammy
quickened his pace, double timing it to get to his car.
"Team Leader, looks like Gallardo is going to drive somewhere."
"Copy. Chase Five, are you close?"
"One block away."
"Be ready to tail the car. Stand by for the make and model."

Sammy got in his Jaguar and motored north. The police listened for chatter on the earpiece and tracked him on their monitors. It was obvious after Sammy left downtown where he was going.

"Oliver, looks like he's going to Isaacson's house."

"Roger that. I'll call in the SWAT team."

The Karmazin convoy pulled into the driveway of Andrew's house and the lead car's driver entered the code. As the gate rolled out of the way, the cars drove around the house and parked in front of the studio.

I've got to change that code, Andrew thought to himself, everyone and their grandmother knows it now.

The goons assisted Andrew and Rapha into the studio, but left Rapha's hood on his head. The main room was relatively dim even though there was plenty of natural light. The mural created in a single strange night towered over the assembled crowd, but none of the mafia types seemed to notice.

"Well, Mr. Carpenter, where is he?"

"Let Rapha go."

"Go where?"

"Walk him out to the street. I'll call someone to come get him."

"No."

"I'll call his brother and have him come alone."

The group leader went over to Rapha, grabbed his arm and held a gun out for Andrew to see.

"The boss says you need to get Isaacson or I am going to put a bullet in the kid's head."

The status quo had changed. It was time to act.

"Okay. Will you give me a couple of minutes? Andrew will be here."

"The clock is ticking."

Andrew walked/half ran down the hall to the bathroom pulling his clothes off as he went. He locked himself in the bathroom and pulled out a razor. There was no time for a haircut, but with his hair slicked back, a clean shave and new clothes, the change would be believable. He went over his face twice and recombed his hair. Andrew studied his face in the mirror and for the first time in an age, the dead man looking back at him had come back to life. One of the goons pounded on the door.

"Carpenter. Hurry up. It's time."

Andrew met him at the door and startled the mafia man. Andrew just walked by him without saying anything.

He stepped into the open area of the studio and waited. Mr. Karmazin was conferring with his workers and had not noticed Andrew.

"Mr. Karmazin." Gone was the Australian accent. The mafia boss looked over at Andrew. The others fingered their weapons with the arrival of a stranger to the studio. Slowly, the realization of who he was crept over the attendees as some marveled under their breath how Isaacson had pulled one over on them.

"Mr. Isaacson. So nice to finally meet you. Apparently, you had some of my men fooled into thinking you were Thad Carpenter. Are you ready to visit?"

"Let Rapha go."

"Of course. My men will drive him back to the campus and let him off at his dormitory."

Andrew didn't like it, but at this point he had no more ideas.

"Give him his phone back so he can call me when he's there."

Mr. Karmazin nodded to the men and they escorted Rapha out.

"You see, Mr. Isaacson, I had no intention of harming young Rapha. I just needed to talk with you."

"So, what do you want to talk about? I'm not interested in selling you control of my company."

"Mr. Isaacson, I'm a businessman. I've been very successful conducting business in this area of the country, and I enjoy being in the art industry. You had an effective arrangement with Stella Manchester. I think we could do even greater things together."

"I didn't like the 'arrangement' I had with Stella, and I doubt it would be any better with your organization."

"I would take care of every business issue which would leave you to do what you love – produce art."

"Sounds familiar. Stella said the same thing. Except when the money starts flowing, the artist has trouble keeping the business partner out of the creative process. Mr. Karmazin, you're used to being in charge. I respect that. The other side of the coin is, if we were in business together, I would be nothing more than an employee. I'm just not interested in being an employee in my own business."

"Forgive me if I put too fine a point on it, but if the principles of the business are deceased, ownership and control goes into a trust. There are some prickly legal issues to work through, but in the end I will gain control over the trust. It's not my first choice, Mr. Isaacson."

Andrew already knew where this was heading.

"If I agree, and live, you have control. And if I refuse, I die, and you have control."

"You are an astute man, Mr. Isaacson. You have distilled the situation down to the core issues. What do you say? Shall we enjoy success together or will the Karmazin family continue Stella's work to capitalize financially on the assets remaining in AD Isaacson?"

"I won't live as a slave again, Mr. Karmazin. If there is no other alternative, then you might as well shoot me now. Most people think I'm dead anyway except for some friends, and the police."

"We know who your friends are, Mr. Isaacson, and the police are bound by law to act a certain way. We have a record of success in court proceedings; therefore I'm confident of our situation."

Mr. Karmazin motioned to one of his workers. "Mr. Isaacson, I have the necessary documents here for you to sign which will memorialize what we have discussed today. Have you made a decision?"

"The answer is 'No'. Unfortunately for you, whether you pull the trigger or not, a story is going to run in the newspaper telling of how Stella and I ran our art business unethically. There is a good chance the business will have no value after the word gets out, and you might have so many lawsuits filed against AD Isaacson, your organization will be decimated."

"You're bluffing. Why would you do such a thing to yourself?"

"Like I said. I'm already dead. Besides, the story needed to be told."

The door to the studio popped open and a small canister rolled into the room. Some of the mafia help who had military experience realized what was happening.

"Grenade!!"

Some dove for cover while others stood frozen, unsure what to do. The flash grenade went off and for a precious few seconds, no one could see, hear or move. The police special forces team breached and trained their weapons on all the attendees.

"POLICE!! Put your hands out and get down on the ground!"

One mafia man pulled his weapon – out of duty one would guess – scarcely able to see the police and it was his last earthly move. The officer with him in the sights gunned the criminal down with two quick shots.

"Get down on the ground! Get down on the ground!"

Police rescued Rapha and began to secure the goons who obeyed, cuffing and removing weapons.

As the smoke cleared, two men stood toward the back of the room. Mr. Karmazin had his arm around Andrew's neck and in the other hand was a .357 revolver pointed at his head.

Two police had their assault rifles aimed at Levente Karmazin's forehead.

"You police officers need to back out of here or Mr. Isaacson is going to get shot."

"Mr. Karmazin, there is no way out of here. All of your men outside are in custody. Even if you get out of this studio, there is nowhere to go and no one to get you there." Clarence Oliver was leading the police team.

"There is always a way. Now back off!" For the first time the mafia boss was showing signs of stress.

Andrew looked at the point man closest to him.

"Take the shot! It's okay. You'll hit him." Andrew said.

The point man looked at Clarence. Detective Oliver gave him the go ahead. "If you think you have a clean shot, do it."

Andrew held three fingers to his chest and made sure the officer saw it. Then he began to count to three with his fingers. One, two, three!

On the count of three, Andrew let his legs go limp causing the mob boss to have to hold up Andrew's full weight with his one arm. He bent down trying to maintain a hold on Andrew, and as he went down, the officer saw an opening. He put two rounds into Mr. Karmazin's right shoulder which caused his hand to flinch. The gun fell from his hand, and Andrew went to the ground. The revolver hit the concrete floor and discharged putting a .357 slug into the outer half of Andrew's right lung. Levente Karmazin stumbled backward creating a wide target for two officers. One centered two rounds in his chest and the other put two in his forehead. Mr. Karmazin slid to the floor directly below the mural and was dead before his body hit the floor.

A wave of relief washed over Andrew. In fact, he felt a little lightheaded. He put his head down to gather himself, but Andrew couldn't shake the cobwebs.

"I think I'm going to pass out," Andrew said to no one. One of the officers knelt by him and checked him out.

"You need to lie down."

Andrew wasn't sure why, but he liked the idea.

"You've been hit. Looks like one round went into your chest."

Blood was covering his white dress shirt and seeping into his trousers. The officer clicked his radio.

"We have an injured male approximately forty-five years old. He has one bullet wound in the chest. Request immediate EMT to 1421 Highland Circle."

The dispatcher responded "Roger that, 9184 officer. A fire unit with EMT is being sent to your location. If more units are required, please advise."

The officer turned Andrew on his side and tore open the shirt. He had a small first aid kit and pulled a bandage out and pushed it against the bullet hole.

"Mr. Isaacson, can you breathe okay?"

"Yes, I think so." Andrew was subconsciously taking shallow breaths to minimize the pain.

"Help is on the way. Try to stay awake for me."

As he talked to Andrew, the other officers were searching the building for any bogies hiding and verifying the deceased status of Mr. Karmazin. A moderate commotion was happening outside due to the number of gang members who were under arrest and being processed. Although there were two dead criminals, Andrew was the only living casualty. Officer Bryce Tunney came over to Andrew.

"Hey Andrew." He looked at the wound. "You took one for the team this time. Wish you would have had a vest on."

"I agree." Andrew was fading, but worked up a smile. "I'm just glad no police took a bullet tonight. How'd you guys know to come here?"

"You told us to follow the tracker. Gallardo did exactly what you thought he would. He wanted to attend your meeting and we followed him here."

"Good ole Sammy." Andrew was wincing with every word.

Tunney looked at the wall. "Did you do the mural? It looks a lot like you and Mr. Karmazin. The bullet holes are pretty accurate too."

"Weeks... ago."

"That is crazy! How'd you know Karmazin was going to get shot in that exact spot? That's you! Right there! Who's the other guy, Rapha?"

Thankfully for Andrew, the fire unit arrived and surrounded him. In seconds, they had him on the gurney with an IV and some kind of fluid going in him. Andrew was ready to crash. The EMT's wasted no time. As soon as they could, they were wheeling him out.

Tunney offered encouragement. "Hey, Buddy. We'll see you at the hospital."

Clarence walked up to Tunney as the gurney sped off. "How's he doing?"

"Not great. I've seen people die from less."

"Hope it didn't hit anything important."

"He was bleeding pretty good. Thankfully, Mr. Karmazin wasn't using hollow point bullets. Just have to see if they can stitch him up."

The EMT's lined up the stretcher and slid Andrew into the ambulance. One worker got into the back with him and continued to take his vitals as he attempted to slow the bleeding. Andrew looked up at him through sloshing eyes.

"Thanks."

"Try to stay quiet, sir. We'll be at the hospital in just a few minutes." The young technician busied himself with the monitoring equipment and recorded the readings. Andrew kept staring at him. Off and on, the tech would look and Andrew would catch his eye.

"You look familiar." The drugs were loosening Andrew's tongue even though is speech was halting. "I know you?"

"I doubt it. I'm new to Atlanta."

"From?"

"All around. I was in the Navy for three years. Just started as an EMT."

"So familiar...." Andrew faded out and didn't come back.

The rescue team pulled under the EMERGENCY sign and hustled Andrew out of the ambulance. The doctors were already notified and a team was waiting. Instead of detouring to the triage area, they took Andrew straight to surgery. For the next three hours, the doctors would fight for his life.

# Chapter 112

Grady Memorial Hospital

The drugs were beginning to wear off. Andrew turned his head and saw the light from his window through squinted, swollen eyes. Next to the window, slouching uncomfortably in a vinyl easy chair was Mitch, napping with his metal legs resting on the corner of Andrew's bed. He laid his head back and tried to get his wits about him. Well, I guess I'm not dead, he thought to himself. Mitch made a quiet snoring sound. Andrew thought about his friend. They had been through a lot together. Not intentionally, and not really together, but they were fighting the same foe with similar results. As with a number of other people, he didn't realize how close a friend he was until this conflict occurred and danger was upon them. Maybe they could get out of the foxhole now and go on to a different phase of life. Mitch stirred. He opened his eyes to find that Andrew was looking at him.
"Hey, you're back."
"Back? From where?"
"Death's door, brother. I didn't think you were ever going to get out of the operating room."
"Couldn't find the bullet?"
"No, the bullet went clean through. Through your lung actually. I guess it was a challenge to get everything patched up."
"My lung? Sounds bad."
"It is bad. You're going to be here a while." Mitch laughed. "We're quite a pair. You'd think we were soldiers or something. All these injuries from combat. At least they finally proved you're human."
"I was tired of you getting all the glory." Andrew smiled as he closed his eyes. Talking exhausted him.
"My vote is for someone else to get all the attention from here on out."
"Amen to that."

There was a knock on the door. The nurse came in to check vitals and check Andrew.

"You're awake. Good to see you, Mr. Isaacson. I'll let the doctor know." As she turned to leave, two men filled the doorway. The nurse pushed through and they stepped into the room.

Detectives Oliver and Tunney seemed to be in good spirits.

"Isaacson, how are you feeling?" Clarence asked.

"Aerated. But alive."

"Alive is good. I would have bet he was going to put one right in your melon."

"I'll forever be in your debt. Thank you. You guys remember Mitch?"

"Of course we do. Good to see you." Both men shook Mitch's hand.

"How are you getting around on the pegs?"

"Not bad. Sometimes I forget they're even there."

"Good to hear."

"How many gangsters did you haul in?" Andrew asked.

"Enough the Karmazin family may not survive. I tell you what, Isaacson. You're like a weapon of mass destruction. We need to throw you into some of our other cases."

"I'm with Mitch. We'd like the limelight to shine on someone else for a while. Hey, do you guys know the EMT's who came to the house?"

"Just seen them around here and there."

"Do you know their names?"

"The older guy was, uh, Miller I think."

"The young guy?"

"Mmm, I don't know, but I can find out."

"Thanks."

Fanny knocked on the door and stuck her head in the room.

"Hey, I heard you were awake."

"Hi, Fanny."

Clarence and Tunney rose to leave. "We'll get out of here. Hope you heal up fast. We'll call you later."

"See you. Thanks for coming." Andrew turned to Fanny. "How'd you find out I was in the hospital?"

"No thanks to you, gunslinger. I called every hospital in town hoping you were still with us."

"Sorry, I would have called, but I was in a coma."

"How many times have I heard that line? So, what happened? You saw some blood and passed out?"

"Yes. My own. Can't stand it. Got a hole in my chest too."

"Really!? You're not bulletproof. Who'd a guessed it?"

"Went right through me. Don't even get a souvenir to put on a chain. Have you talked to Aleefa or Rapha?"

"Yes. They are going to stay with me for a day or two. Both of them are a little shook up."

"Thank you, Fanny, you're the greatest. I wouldn't know what to do without you."

"You speak the truth."

"Did they say much?"

"Not yet, but I know a gal who's a good listener. She'll get 'em to talk."

"Don't take them to the bar."

"I guess I'll have to go to Plan B then." Fanny just grinned. "How long are you going to be laid up?"

"Not sure. I haven't talked to the doctor yet. I feel pretty good, but the painkillers are starting to wear off."

"Did you hear about Sammy?"

"No."

"A couple of his 'associates' came into the bar last night. I heard them say Sammy posted bail and skipped town, and no one has seen him since."

"Anyone associated with the Karmazin family may be running right now."

"Very true. Listen, I know you're worn out and need to rest. I just wanted to come by and say hi and let you know the boys are all right."

"I appreciate you, Fanny. Would you be able to bring the boys up here in the next few days? They might be happy to see I'm doing better."

"Oh, yeah. Sure, I can."

"See you later."

"Ciao."

"I'll go too." Mitch reached for his cane. "You wake up and the whole world is at your door. I'm sure you would like to rest."

"Thanks for being here. It was nice to have you here looking out for me."

"No problem. I've got to race over to the television stations to pimp your story. This might offset the interview if and when it comes out, and salvage your prices."

"Sweet. Shameless but sweet."

"I'm kidding. What am I, Stella? Do you need anything before I leave?"

"I think I'm good buddy. I'll let you know what I find out from the doctor."

"Okay, good."

Mitch received a text from Detective Oliver.

> [ Hey Mitch, are you still with Isaacson? Tell him the EMT's name was Hansen. Leo Hansen. ]

Mitch showed it to Andrew. He laid his head back against his pillow as the blood drained from his face.

"Andrew. You okay? You look like you just saw a ghost."

Andrew had to work a minute to collect himself.

"Uh, yeah, I'm fine. Just tired I guess."

"Rest up, I'll see you soon."

"All right. Have a good one."

He spent the better part of an hour wrestling with what to do. The chances were slim the EMT had any idea who Andrew was. He hit the morphine pump, and drifted off to sleep.

The nurse shook Andrew's arm.

"Mr. Isaacson? Are you awake? The doctor is here to see you."

Andrew roused, but was groggy from well, everything. He rubbed is eyes and scanned the room. Beside the nurse was a man in scrubs with a bag on his head. It looked like he came directly from surgery.

"Hello, Andrew. How are you feeling?"

"Not bad, considering."

"Good, you are going to feel waves of pain for the next several days. Just keep hitting the morphine button. We'll monitor your signs and check your blood for any infection, but if all goes well, you will be mending from here on out. We just want to control the pain along the way."

"How long do you think I'll be in here?"

"I've instructed the nurse to get you out of bed tomorrow to walk around as much as you can tolerate. Thankfully, the bullet that found your left lung went right through and the hole in your back is not much bigger than the one in front. It didn't hit any bones which is a minor miracle, and the EMT's got you here very quickly. All told, it was as favorable of a gunshot wound as you could hope for."

"Thank you, Doctor. It is good to know. Will there be anything I should avoid in the coming days?"

"As far as things to avoid, just don't take up smoking any time soon. And don't hang out with people who want to shoot you." The doctor smiled. "I'll be checking with the nurse regularly. If there's anything I can help you with while you're here, have them get in touch with me."

"Thanks, Doctor."

The nurse turned back at the door. "I just about forgot. Detective Oliver called earlier. He talked to Leo Hansen. He's going to come by the hospital tomorrow after his shift which will be about eight a.m."

"What time is it?"

"Three-thirty p.m."

"Thank you."

Evidently, the doctor was making his rounds after a full day of surgery. Andrew had all evening to think of what to say when Leo came by. Trouble was, he had no idea where to begin.

Although the nighttime hours at the hospital were bustling with activity and regular nurse visits to his room, Andrew slept relatively well – with narcotics – and awoke as the nurse on the morning shift reset the vital sign computer. Andrew tried to focus, and after he blinked several times, his eyes straightened up.

"Good morning, Mr. Isaacson. How are you feeling? We're going to get you up today."

"I feel like I've been shot."

"Great!" The nurse acted like she didn't understand what Andrew said. "After you and your guest are done visiting, I'll come back and we'll walk."

"Guest? I didn't know I had a guest."

Andrew scanned the room and noticed him in the corner sitting down. When he was acknowledged, he stood up.

"Mr. Isaacson. I'm Leo Hansen." He leaned over to shake Andrew's hand. He was in his EMT uniform and looked worn out.

"Hey, good to see you. Thanks for stopping by. I know you are probably tired after a long shift."

"It's not a problem. Brought a heart attack victim in and dropped him off downstairs a little while ago."

"Hopefully you didn't have to sit and wait on me too long."

"No, just got here. If I had been waiting very long, I would have been asleep too."

"I want to thank you for your efforts the other night. I might not have made it otherwise."

"You're welcome. Just doing my job. I'm glad we were close by when the call came in. Was that your house?"

"Yeah. Haven't been there much lately."

"It's pretty awesome. You been on vacation?"

"Sort of. I've been in Africa for nearly a year working at an orphanage in the Congo. I came back to get a couple of guys started in college, and to irritate one of the crime families here in town."

"Sounds like you were successful. It's all over the news."

Andrew was going to laugh, but he was afraid it would hurt too much. "Where'd you grow up, Leo?"

"Here and there. Graduated from high school in Savannah. It was just me and Mom. She didn't like living in the same place more than a few years at a time until I got older. After high school, I went into the Navy and have been doing this since then."

"Is Perry Hansen your uncle?" Andrew knew it was.

"Yes! You know him?"

"He and I go way back."

"Uncle Perry. I like him a lot. He's the one who steered me to the Navy."

"How's he doing?"

"Good, good. He's retired from active duty in the Navy and now he's teaching at the Academy." Leo paused. "So you must know my mother."

"Yes." Andrew pondered his response. "Yes I did."

"You'll have to forgive me for saying, but I don't remember either one talking about you before."

"Does your mother ever talk about your dad?"

"No, not much. He died not long after I was born. For whatever reason, I don't think they were close. Come to think of it, she doesn't even keep pictures of him around. Did you know my dad also?"

"Yes." Andrew couldn't even look at Leo.

"Tell me about him. What did he do? How did he die?"

"Your dad was a well-meaning guy who had a few issues. He was an artist actually, and a pretty good one."

"Really? Is there a way I can see some of his work?"

"Oh sure. I can show you quite a few pieces after I get up and around."

"Thanks. I'm blown away. I never would have thought I would be connecting with my dad in some way today. You know, it's one of those things you kind of put in the back of your mind and only think about on rare occasion. But, still I would like to know more about him. See if I'm like him or not."

"What would you say if I told you your dad is still alive?"

Leo took a step back. The smile faded from his face.

"It can't be. My mother would have told me."

"All I can do is try to prove it to you. I want you to know, I'm not calling your mom a liar. As far as she was concerned, your dad *was* dead. He was not in a good place, and she surely wanted to keep you safe."

"Just for conversation, let's assume I believe you. So where is he? Is he close?"

"Yes."

"What can you tell me to convince me he's alive?"

"Your dad left you and your mom when you were a little less than two years old. You were in Augusta at the time. I think you left Georgia and went west to Oklahoma for a while. Your dad stayed here in Atlanta and made a name for himself as an artist."

"What do you know about my mom?"

"Your mom's full name is Rachelle Marie Hansen. Only Hansen is her maiden name, she dropped her married name after the divorce. Her birthday is November 9th and she loves hot tea with orange slices. Her favorite movie is – or was – "The Long Hot Summer" with Paul Newman and Joanne Woodward. Her parents' names are Sandra and Neill. Did you call your granddad 'Poppy' growing up? And your full name is Leonardo Vincenzo Hansen."

Leo sat down and tried to catch his breath. He stared at Andrew for a period and gathered himself.

"You're either legit or you are a stalker. How could you know so much stuff about us? I've never heard of you before."

"There's one more thing I need to tell you. Your mom's married name was… Isaacson."

"What are you saying? You're *related* to my mom?"

"Sort of."

Leo's head was spinning.

"It can't be. What are you, a long lost uncle? A foster brother?"

"I was actually married to your mother."

"When?"

"1992 to 1994."

Leo's wheels were turning furiously. Then he looked at Andrew almost in horror.

"You're my…"

Andrew nodded.

"Dad?!"


The End

# ACKNOWLEDGEMENTS

Thank you, Kim
Thank you Meredith, Abigail, Caleb, Veronica, and Shea

Many thanks to all the family and friends who inspired me to keep working and finish this project.

There were many persons who read early manuscripts and provided valuable insight and editing labor along the way. For this, I am eternally grateful. Mom, you made it all possible through encouraging feedback and grammar expertise from the very beginning. Mary, I appreciate your input as the story took shape, and am in your debt.

I would love to hear from you, so drop me a line sometime.
Also, if you would like, I will let you know when the next book is ready for release.

The story continues for Andrew, Lala, Leo, Theresa, Mitch, and everyone at the orphanage. The work has just begun in the DRC, and strong forces have gathered to oppose this unlikely team of ministers. Without their united efforts, the country could be dominated by a wicked power even worse than the chaos that has continually plagued their African homeland. With God's help, they will risk it all and make their stand.

**jeffbagby63@yahoo.com**